# Rubicon

Barry Childs

ALGEN,
I HOPE YOU ENJOY, RUBICON.
I AM HONORED TO KNOW YOU.
THANK YOU FOR YOUR SERVICE TO
DHS AND OUR NATION.
BEST,
Barry Childs
9 SEPT 2022

Published by Barry Childs, 2022.

*Cover design by Ryan Schwarz.*

ISBN 978-0-578-39580-7 (paperback)

ISBN 978-0-578-84678-1 (eBook)

# DEDICATION

*The love of writing began in a small Virginia bedroom. I often misperceived the writing assignments as a punishment. Reflection illuminated the truth. The challenge to write about youthful beliefs, feelings, and pains of growth was the greatest parental gift. A gift set aside —awakened forty-five years later. The truth —the solace that I sought was within all along. Thank you, Mom and Dad.*

*For Pauline: A favorite author, Ernest Hemingway, once said, "There is nothing noble to being superior to your fellow man; true nobility is being superior to your former self." Each day of our marriage, I have tried to live the ethos. There was much to fix over the years. You patiently chipped away at the edges, smoothed the lines, and polished the final grade – until each piece fell in place. You mended each broken piece – even when I broke, once more.*

*With you, we found that love is a verb that needs two. You are the mystical force commanding the heart into the rhythm of life and the breath that draws into a gasp at first sight. I remain in awe. I remain in eternal gratitude that you said yes and still do. I still do.*

*For the children: Emma, Josh, Jacob, Paityn, Daniel, Samuel, and Elsie each inspired, encouraged, and endured the prolonged process of research, mapping, development, and writing. Each is a blessing and a joy. Thank you.*

*For friends and mentors: A few words for friends and mentors who made the finer details possible. I will keep your names secure. But I could not have completed this without B, B, M, T, D, S, M, S, and S. Thank you for your service and dedication to the security of the United States and your respective decades of service, putting it on the line so that others may live and sleep-in-peace. Thank you for your many contributions to my peers in the industry, and still in the fight. You helped me with the details to make it real and helped keep the secrets secret.*

*Finally: Wise words from a wise man; you cannot spell family – without ILY. Extended family and friends, thank you for the encouragement, coaching, and endurance of the long hours with understanding and grace.*

*THANK YOU.*

# FOREWORD

The next wars will be fought globally, on fronts traditional and novel. It will affect soldiers on the field and the civilians unfortunate enough to be in the area, and those "safely" back home. And while the concept of war continues to evolve, so too does the technology driving it. And, as usual, we find writers predicting how that might all play out.

By the mid-1960s, humans had developed, manufactured, and planned for the use of weapons that could physically rip world civilizations apart. The phrase "bomb them back into the Stone Age" was coined to describe just what nations could do to one another perfectly, should the mood strike the wrong person at the wrong time. The arms race this engendered ran for nearly 50 years and financially ruined one of its major players, the USSR.

As a species, we have largely learned to live with nuclear weapons over the last 75+ years, at least in the First World. It remains to be seen if those with less of a voice on the world stage will be able to resist the draw of such massive weaponry as it slowly seeps out of the exclusive control of the more extensive powers. Happily, none have been used in malice since that devastating week in August of 1945.

But as is typical for human societies, we have continued to evolve, both in technology and societal complexity. In the First World, we now live in cities and nations that are incredibly complex and interconnected system of systems. These systems are a baffling and marvelously complicated array of interconnected labor, production, mechanical support, and end-user consumption. Food delivery, water supplies, building materials, electrical grids, to name a few, are all critical to supporting not just our accustomed standard of living but for the maintenance of life itself. All of it, and more, are only possible because of computers.

As our societies have become more and more complex, computers have as well. They have infused themselves into every aspect of our society in doing so. And as fast as they have found their way into our society, they have gone from convenience to requirement just as quickly. We are now far beyond the point at which our way of life is "merely" dependent on computers and what they can do. We are dependent. We are addicted.

This addiction goes far beyond writing a book on a laptop or playing the newest first-person shooter on your console gaming system. Our cars, our stoves, our watches, our phones, they all depend on computers now. It isn't easy to imagine an area of our lives that does not lean heavily, if not wholly, on computerization.

More importantly, from a strategic perspective, the widespread use of SCADA systems is widespread. SCADA, an acronym for "Supervisory control and data acquisition," is everywhere, yet they are primarily unheard-of and unknown to most people. SCADA is a control system architecture composed of computers, interconnected data communication, and graphical user interfaces. It allows for high-level supervision of all kinds of machines and the tasks they perform. It is a remote access way to control all manufacturing and other processes. It is one of the most commonly used kinds of industrial control systems. And all these computers are incredibly vulnerable to cyber-attack.

Being able to physically devastate your enemy is an option members of the "Nuclear Club" have, but it is only one option. Such capability is politically advantageous, but it is limited in practical utility. Playing that card is full of downsides, some of which are potentially as destructive to the nuke-er as the nuke-ee. It's all well and good to win the nuclear battle, but if that opens the door to you losing (or even securing a "tie") the nuclear war that would very likely follow, you should think long and hard to find other options. Because crossing the nuclear Rubicon offers precious few ways back, the way forward is even more dangerous.

Let's say you only want to keep your opponent busy with other matters while you do what you wish unmolested, but you are not willing to bathe his entire population in a nuclear fire to do it. Nor are you ready to endure the predictable, inevitable retaliation. Then your biggest weapons "merely" allow you to influence events, not to control them. Your great big club may buy you a ticket to the grown-up's table at the international Thanksgiving Dinner, but that may be just about all it does in real terms.

There is also the fact that if you win a war fought with nuclear weapons, there is very little you can expect to take from your opponent and incorporate into your new world order. Such weaponry tends to be very hard on the other guy's stuff, including his land, material wealth, and people.

All these facts are what make the cyber-attack so very attractive. It is a much more flexible and exacting way of making war, yet far less evident and detectable than any conventional or nuclear attack. You can still functionally destroy your opponent, but you can do so with much more control and precision. If you can take over your enemy's computer networks, you have him by the throat in our modern societies. If you have the capacity and the skills to successfully attack and control their computer networks, your operational horizon, and therefore your strategic options, are open wide.

Here in America, where we have not had a war fought on our territory since 1865, the impact of a general, widespread conflict would be all the more devastating. We have no experience fighting a war at home, at least not for the last 150 years. We are, in many ways, a society of pampered folks at this point.

As a nation, we go to great lengths to ensure that we do not see a conventional war fought on our soil. With a defense budget beyond $700 billion, we spend three times more on our military than China, which is firmly in second place and ten times more than India, which is in third. Our nuclear capability is also beyond compare. Of the nations that make up the top fifteen defense expenditures globally, 12 are allies of the U.S.A. Fighting a war against the United States, with or without our allies' participation, is a losing proposition, and the entire world knows it.

Yet while our national defense budget is massive, only about $10 billion of that goes towards cyber defense. This still dwarfs other nations' expenditures (for example, China spends only about $2 billion a year on their cyber security, as far as we can tell, and they are number two in this arena). Still, it is a mere drop in the bucket when you consider just how much that is expected to defend. And our society is far more computer-dependent than China's, at least at this point. So, if you are going to try to attack the United States, doing so via computer may be difficult, but it gives you much better odds than any other method. It is our weakest point, and a successful attack against it would be potentially devastating.

It does not take any great sense of prescience to see that the cyber warfare battlefield is the future of war. And the future is now.

This is where this book comes in. How does the cyber battlefield intersect with current clandestine methods and abilities? What are the impacts of not just today's technology but the near-future tech that will be here sooner than we will be ready for it?

What about the players in such a world? We can be confident that, while the traditional big names will certainly be present, others will be vying to get in on the game, for their own geopolitical purposes. No longer is not having a massive standing army backed by a nuclear arsenal a bar to entry. In true modern style, everybody gets to play.

This book gives us a look at what just this kind of 21st century take on warfare may well look like. The nation-state actors are already on the field now. The technology described here is out there, either fully operational or on the near horizon of possibility. The fieldcraft and actions of the various actors described all ring true for anyone who is following world events.

Mr. Childs has done the research and crafted it into what you have here, a modern-day spy thriller that could literally be taken from the evening news. What you are about to read will take you on a fast-paced jaunt through a world lurking just beyond the headlines, a future reality that could be next year. Or next week.

Maybe even later today.

T.C. Fuller, Ed.D. FBI (Ret.)

# RUBICON Principal Characters

**Ridge family**

Xander Owen Ridge, Chief Executive Officer Shepherd Defense Systems

Gabriella Anne Ridge

**Ridge children**

Emily Taylor (25) – senior cybersecurity engineer SDS

Jonathan Owen (23) – 1st LT USMC

Fiancé: Lyn Templar
Father of Fiancé: Matt Templar

Sophia Anne (21) – graduate student College of Charleston
Charles Xander (19) – West Point

Amelia Grace (13) – 7th Grader

Dr. Katy Stone (Amelia's Doctor)

**Parents of Gabriella Anne Ridge**

Dr. Samuel Jonathan Cohen
Gabby Amelia Brown-Cohen

**Ross family**

Paul Frances Ross, Senior Vice President Shepherd Defense Systems Commercial Division

Isabella Marie Coutre-Ross

Henrique Coutre - father

**Ross children**
Marie Sara Ross
Olivia Anne Ross

**Rasulov family**
Farid Mahoumed Rasulov – Azerbaijani Tea Shop Owner
Sara Abbas Rasulov (spouse)
Lanie Rasulov (granddaughter)
**United States of America – Government Officials**
**President of the United States (POTUS)**
President Leonard Andrew Hammond

Naval Academy – the United States Navy Intelligence Officer, CIA Case Officer, CIA Director, Director of National Intelligence, Chief of Staff for the Vice President of the United States)

**First Lady of the United States (FLOTUS)**
Debbie Hammond
**President's Executive Secretary**
Ms. Patricia Bell

**Cabinet of the United States and critical supporting staff**

**Vice President of the United States**
Vice President Laura Kent
**White House Chief of Staff**
Dr. Betty "Tess" Mercier, Whitehouse Chief of Staff
CIA Case Officer (retired)
**Secretary of Defense**
Michael Cooke
**Secretary of State**
Rebecca Porter

**Attorney General**
Martin Bell
**Secretary of Homeland Security**
Dr. Bluma Freeman
**Director of National Intelligence**
General Michael Roberts
**National Security Agency**
General Shawn Wright
**Central Intelligence Agency**
**CIA Director**
Christian Frost
**CIA Presidential Daily Brief**
Dr. Malik Greene
**Federal Bureau of Investigation (FBI)**
**FBI Director**
Henry Mills

Special Agent Patrick Kelly (FBI – Counterintelligence)
Special Agent Mark Reyes "Marky Two-Guns" (FBI Cyber Squad)
Undercover name: Rick Jordan
Special Agent Ashley Brown
Undercover name: Amanda Post

**White House Communications Office**
**White House Communications Director**
Toby Isaac
**White House Press Secretary**
Jessica Wilson
**Congressional Gang of Eight**
**United States House Permanent Select Committee on Intelligence[1]:**
Anthony Silva (D-CA-28), Chair

Delbert[2] Nesbitt (R-CA-22), Ranking Member

**United States Senate Select Committee on Intelligence[3]:**

Monroe Ramirez (R-FL), Acting Chair

Matthew Webb (D-VA), Vice-Chair

**Leadership in the United States House of Representatives[4]:**

Nettie[5] Parks (D-CA-12), Speaker of the House

Kevin Moore (R-CA-23), Minority Leader

**Leadership in the United States Senate[6]:**

Malcolm[7] McLeod (R-KY), Majority Leader

Colter Stinton (D-NY), Minority Leader

**United States Military**

**Chairwoman of the Joint Chiefs**

General Lori Robinson

**Navy**

**USS Greenville SSN**

Captain R. Guy

**USS Lincoln**

Captain Amy Bauernschmidt

**Air Force**

**Combat Air Traffic Controller**

MSG S. Danforth

**United Kingdom of Great Britain and Northern Ireland**

---

1. **https://en.wikipedia.org/wiki/United_States_House_Permanent_Select_Committee_on_Intelligence**
2. https://en.wikipedia.org/wiki/Devin_Nunes
3. **https://en.wikipedia.org/wiki/United_States_Senate_Select_Committee_on_Intelligence**
4. **https://en.wikipedia.org/wiki/United_States_House_of_Representatives**
5. https://en.wikipedia.org/wiki/Nancy_Pelosi
6. **https://en.wikipedia.org/wiki/United_States_Senate**
7. https://en.wikipedia.org/wiki/Mitch_McConnell

**British Prime Minister**
Allister Adams Poole
**Chief of Secret Intelligence Service (SIS MI6)**
Sir Jonathan Hawkins,

Jack Webb, MI6
TC Morris, MI6

**China**
**Ministry of State Security (MSS)**
Li Chang –Case Officer

**Iran**
**Iranian Case Officer**
Daniyah Nour Rahman (30), Ross' mistress
**Ministry of Intelligence of the Islamic Republic of Iran**
Mahmoud Ashkan Abbas

GOI Saudi Aramco asset - Ismail Hussain
GOI Sanmen Nuclear Power Station asset - Le Ling

**GOI Case Officer – Non-Official Cover (NOC)**
Yuriko Ahmed (25) –
**MOIS Minister SIGINT**
Amir Begum (51)
**Qud Force**
Brigadier General Karim Abdi

Adel Begum, Qud Force Cyber

**North Korea**
**Permanent Representative of the Democratic People's Republic of Korea (DPRK) to the United Nations**
Kim Song

**Pakistan**
Ambassador of Pakistan to the United States
Mehdi Hamid Khan

**India**
**Ambassador of India to the United States**
Ranj[8] Rameshwar[9]

8. https://www.behindthename.com/name/ranj

9. https://www.behindthename.com/name/rameshwar

**Russia**
**SVR Case Officer**
Marina Kovalenko (manages JUDAS ISCARIOT)
**Operatives**
Miikka Koval
Roman Marchenko
Sacha Petrenko

**SHEPHERD DEFENSE SYSTEM (SDS)**
**Chief Security Officer (CSO)**
Daniel Bell "Danny"
Spouse: Anne Bell
**Chief Information Security Officer (CISO)**
Amira Said
**Chief Operating Officer**
Jacob Silva
**Chief Financial Officer**
Dr. Kelly Stewart
**Executive Protection Director**
Kenneth Cain
**Executive Protection Manager**
Kyla Rashid

Agent Sara Deagen
Ricko DeSante
Henry Rodriquez
Jack Bass

**Vice President Insider Threat**
Scout Moreau
**Vice President Intelligence**

Julius Lyons

**Vice President Digital Forensics**

Dr. Samantha Williams

**Vice President Cyberweapon Development**

Dr. Trinity Williams

**Vice President Malware Forensics**

Dr. Jennifer Garcia "Jenn"

**Vice President Aeronautical Research and Development**

Rachel Wilson

**Chief Medical Entanglement Researcher**

Ashlyn Chase

SDS Q4 Lauren Holmes, Surgeon friend of Katy Stone

**Executive Assistant**

Mia Richards

**Chief Pilot**

Dave Rogers

**Co-Pilot**

Aaron Bell

**OPERATION CODEWORDS:**

STURGEON – codeword for Farid Mahoumed Rasulov

HERON– investigation of 1st GOI cyberattack

PEACOCK – FBI Operation to arrest Paul Ross

Olympic Games – Stuxnet

Eagle Talon – drone strike on Qasem Soleimani

RUBICON – Ridge's advanced cyberweapon – quantum entanglement

CHAOS – 2nd GOI cyberattack

RAVEN – 3rd GOI cyberattacks zero-day exploits designed by Paul Ross

Angel Wings – Ridge's countermeasure to the RAVEN aviation threat

IRENE – go order for the missile strike on Iran IRGC HQ

RETRIBUTION – operation to degrade Iranian naval, air force, and air defenses

KATY- Phase II strike on Iran

TAURUS – CIA Operation to find high-level Russian Illegal within the U.S. Government

ISCARIOT – codeword for high-level Russian Illegal within the U.S. Government

# PROLOGUE

# A WISTFUL BREEZE SHEPHERDS A TEMPEST

*We are all doomed to die; from the beginning, there is an inevitable and inescapable end. We are bound to the ceaseless motion of a clock ticking off the moments to the point that you must decide your fate. My dear daughter —you must choose in this moment, will you serve the will of Allah in the service of Iran, or will you surrender? I pray for the former.* Daniyah smiled as her father's words touched her memories and awakened her soul. Daniyah steeled herself for the looming mission. This was not an easy target. Both are fully capable of killing Daniyah and the team. *Would this be her end?* thought Daniyah. *If yes,* she thought, *the why was revenge and the cause just. It will be a good death.*

*How long can you dance with the Devil before he consumes your soul? We must succeed —lest Iran will fall, and we die,* thought Daniyah gripping the radio tighter as her tension escalated. To calm herself, she looked west and waited for the sun to dip below the horizon, glowing orange against the deepening blue to black skies across the Caspian Sea. She just wanted to complete this mission alive. Rasulov was not an easy target. Daniyah and her Iranian hit team waited to strike back for the death of a beloved Iranian leader and mentor. The sea's ebbing tides pulled on her thoughts. A slim chance for Iran to regain world prominence. Each step carefully orchestrated —or Iran falls, *once Rasulov is dead —the thirteen-day clock to Armageddon starts ticking. If we cannot complete the attacks within the window, the Americans will figure out there is a traitor and strike back. The American counterintelligence capabilities are just too good. Especially Xander Ridge of Shepherd Defense Systems. We must succeed tonight and move quickly. Tonight, we kill Rasulov; then we can begin retribution —nine attacks against the Brits and the Americans. When the dust settles, Allah willing —America will burn —Iran emerges a superpower.*

As the sun slipped beneath the horizon, Daniyah ran through the mission in her thoughts. Daniyah, using the moment for reflection, checked each step that brought her and the team to the traitor's doorstep. *I am grateful for the tools to uncover Rasulov. He is a traitorous bastard and must die! —a deep-cover M16 and an American intelligence source —in our backyard. Rasulov is the first link in the Soleimani kill-chain. Killing an intelligence source is one matter. Killing an MI6, a Five-Eye, intelligence source is dangerous —the Americans and the Brits will strike back if they uncover the security breach and link Ross to Iran. To get to the traitor Rasulov —to avenge Soleimani, we made a deal with the Devil, known only as ISCARIOT. The Devil gave us Paul Ross, an American, a distasteful element of the deal. But Ross's cyberweapons were good —beyond the current capabilities of Iran. And you don't walk away from the Devil. ISCARIOT wants Xander Ridge's RUBICON, a new cyberweapon with unfathomable power. And no is not an option —the Devil will have his due. Who is this Devil? Why does he help Iran from the shadows? What does he want from us?*

A dog barking a few blocks away jolted Daniyah from her thoughts —quickening her pulse, shallowing her breathing, moving her hand from the radio to her sidearm. Surveying the area with careful scanning and observation revealed nothing to threaten the mission. She released the tension with a slow exhale. She thought, *now it was time to move on to Rasulov.*

Daniyah and Yuriko lurked in the falling darkness enveloping the small Azerbaijani town of Lankaran. Retribution was at hand, and Farid would soon be dead, along with his entire traitorous family. Daniyah ordered Yuriko and the Assault Team into final positions to wait for Rasulov's guest to arrive. Tonight, Daniyah would spill the blood of Infidels. Vengeance was the first order of the night —vengeance for the murder of General Soleimani.

FARID AND SARA LIVED forty years in the upper level of the Rasulov Tea Café in Lankaran, Azerbaijan. Together, they raised a family supported by the ceaseless tea trade across the Caucasus region and faithful caffeine habits. The Café sees an ebb and flow of locals and a rich diversity of travelers each day. Farid frequents the trade routes crossing Iran, Azerbaijan, Armenia, Georgia, Turkey, and Russia. A century of family business has enriched Farid with relationships that are the envy of the world's intelligence communities.

Recent tensions between Iran and the United States have increased Farid's communications with lifelong friend Jack Webb, Senior MI6 Intelligence Case Officer. Jack's tall and stout frame blends nicely into the region. Farid often jokes that he and Jack are cousins. Indeed, the Rasulov and Webb families have grown close over the decades. The Café has offered a welcomed shelter and means to pass the context of regional events to MI6. Farid and Sara have sheltered hundreds fleeing the Iranian regime, including dozens of Americans caught in Iran during the Islamic Revolution.

The people of the region know Farid Mahoumed Rasulov's family after a century of traversing the region. The smell of a century of tea greets you upon crossing the threshold of the Café. The tea shop holds a standing equally as strong and long ago settled into the character of Lankaran. The Rasulov Tea Cafe rests at the doorsteps of

Asia, Europe, and the Middle East. The Café presents a backdrop for debate at the continents' crossroads. Atop the rooftop patio, a view of the Talysh Mountains and the Caspian Sea has lured more than one guest into the relaxed setting of a warm meal, family matters, deep conversations, and secrets.

However, this evening held a new level of tension and fear. Farid returned home after brokering tea and coffee with news and the Iranian perspective of tensions with the United States. Farid dutifully completed an encrypted communique. Today's methods comfort Farid and lower the risk of discovery. All but vanished are the tradecraft skills of hiding in plain sight and using packages of teas to ship coded messages to faraway allies. Email, encryption technology, and burst transmission enable metadata to pass undetected, buried within the noise of streaming video and music loved by the grandchildren and guests alike.

Deeply fearing an escalation by Iran, today's message Farid composed and sent to MI6 troubled him. The United States, just last year, assassinated Iranian Major General Qasem Soleimani, the feared leader of the Iranian Revolutionary Guard Corps (IRGC). The assassination of Soleimani set the IRGC on a path of revenge and direct engagement with the United States. U.S. President Hammond, newly elected, is cleaning up the previous Administration's diplomatic tactic of using drone strikes to write national policy in blood.

A hint of awareness is growing of Iranian capabilities. Iran redoubled their cybersecurity defenses and cyberweapons capability in the years since suffering the embarrassment of the Stuxnet attack at the hands of the United States and Israel. Farid sees the leap in capability; this quickly, as alarming.

Weary and cold, Farid gazed upward to the warm glow of Sara's fire, noticing for the first time the whistle of the teapot and the aroma of baking bread. Sara always knew how to warm his soul. Farid sighed, heaved a leg to the first step, and slowly repeated. Sara waited at the top of the stairs with a broad smile framed with graying black hair pulled back into a shoulder-length ponytail. Farid's eyes met Sara's, melting the strain and tension of the day. A feeling of warmth washed over Farid as Sara pulled him into a tight embrace. Sara's left hand instinctively stroked the back of his head, as only a tenured wife knows to do. He breathed her into the depths of his soul and whispered, "I love you so very much." With a calming exhale, he felt Sara's breath chased with the hint of mint from her tea feather through his bushy greying beard. Absent a word, his soul heard Sara's return, my Love, I love you, deeply. Forty years of marriage guide Sara's hands across the familiar topography of her lover's shoulders and chest, aged but experienced and capable, still. Farid ached with arthritis pain set-in from years of abuse, torture really, first at the hand of the Savak and now the Vekak. The Revolution of '79 was to overthrow the Shah and end the brutality, but the new master is the same as the old. Sara caressed and soothed both organizations' work in the landscape of scars across her lover's body, broken and beaten across the decades. She loved the man deeply before her as he surrendered to her touch.

Farid slipped passed the sentries of stress and worry. He fell into the warmth of Sara, the glow of the fire gifting whisps of smoke and baking bread, dinner, and steeping tea with a lingering hint of Sara's beloved mint. Sneaking through the smoke and scents of wood, tea, and coffee was a familiar smell that pressed a slight smile through Farid's beard. He knew that Sara was grilling his favorite meal, grilled sturgeon, and a rainbow of grilled vegetables. Though he teased her often about the meals of 40-years past, he knew Sara was pièce de résistance in the kitchen. Still, he never missed the opportunity to kindle the memory of the post-nuptials first-year meals of burned offerings. Sara hated the teasing but knew Farid adored the first-year memories like a worn blanket, held tightly. Memories of Sara, their children, and the Café quieted the demons haunting Farid's past and brutal torture. Iranians seemed forsaken to dogmatic tormentors.

Farid pulled Sara close and squeezed just a little more than usual and releasing a long sigh as the remnants of stress scurried to the shadows of the firelight.

"Who is gracing us for this feast tonight?" queried Farid.

"Lanie is here, off singing that...that American, noise, country twang, and that soda, I mean pop... and Sharia and Mohammed should be here soon," smiled Sara.

"Ah, Lanie, I love to hear the singing. It reminds me of seeing you for the first time all over again. My mother hated your singing and cooking; where is Lanie? Could use a good granddaughter hug," mused Farid.

Farid ambled off, feeling lighter in step, better having seen and held Sara. Lanie was on the back deck, clad as usual in yoga pants, loose top, tennis shoes, and her long black hair pulled back into a ponytail. Farid had long since let go of his wish for traditional attire. He would settle for a good soul above packaging. Lanie was a good soul, helping those in need, including obsessing over her Pop Pop's travels. Lanie was fiery in her condemnations of the Vekak and the religious zealots within her faith. Farid stole a peek to see Lanie sitting on the deck lounge chair. Lanie with legs tucked under her core, singing her heart and soul into an older American melody, something about love. It did not matter; he loved her youthful voice. In Lanie, Farid saw the hope of peace, love, and enduring happiness for coming generations. He toiled to rid the world of the fanaticism, violence, and enslavement of life and thought. Freedom and faith sustain.

JUST BEYOND THE THRESHOLD of the Rasulov Tea Café sat a shadowy figure in a dark Land Rover with blackened windows.

*Retribution is moments away,* Yuriko thought to himself.

Yuriko's fingers continuously inventoried his weapons: a suppressed Sig Sauer P226 9mm pistol, a suppressed Heckler and Koch (HK33) short barrel rifle, his weapon of choice for silent "wet-work," and a Spetsnaz Kizlyar Bophoh fighting knife. Yuriko stroked the Bophoh's slender unbreakable black handle. He kept his hand at the ready as he practiced the mission, going over each step in his mind, silent and quick, four targets.

JACK WEBB PARKED HIS ragged car around the corner two blocks away from Farid and Sara's home. From a distance, the aroma of tea, coffee, pastries, baking bread, and even the hint of grilling fish – even if he had to strain to discern from the lofty mist emanating from the Café. Only Sara knew Jack was coming to dinner as a surprise to Farid.

Jack's thoughts and observations snapped back to scanning the surroundings. He would invest several moments reviewing the small town to ensure an eventless evening. Jack worried about Farid considering the series of deaths of deep-cover non-official cover case agents, assets, and sources worldwide.

*Someone was murdering assets and sources. Murder is too gentle a term,* Jack reflected.

*Slaughter! That is the word! Someone is hunting and slaughtering assets and case officers, and the Intelligence Community just doesn't freaking get it!* Jack screamed to his conscience.

YURIKO, WITHOUT MOVING a hair, relayed to the team, "The Brit arrived —be ready."

"He is parked two blocks down on the opposite side of the street of my position. He parked in the shadows, and I can barely make him out. Suspect he is looking around," said Yuriko.

"Overwatch: I have him, wait one," replied the Overwatch team member.

"Take HIM," Yuriko said coldly.

Pffffttt... Webb crumbled to the ground in a thud, falling straight down into himself. The overwatch sniper placed the shot right at the base of the skull, shutting Webb down instantaneously.

"Overwatch: target down – wait one," relayed the Overwatch team member. "He is down, no movement."

Yuriko opened the door of the Land Rover. He disabled the brake and interior lights. Yuriko carefully closed the door without a detectable sound. He slipped into the darkness with steeled readiness bound with a feeling of righteousness. Retribution was at hand; three more to go.

"Team Two, GO," Yuriko coldly ordered.

SARA THOUGHT TO HERSELF, *how wonderful we will surprise Farid*, and she smiled. Farid was not easy to surprise. Years of experience in surveilling and countersurveillance, interrogation, recruiting, lying, and hiding from Iranian intelligence services and the Zealots. Sara smiled a little; *I am pretty good too*, she thought. Sara focused on finishing the final meal preparations and leaned over to pull the bread from the oven. *Oh, don't forget the creaking step; avoid that, or Farid will turn too soon. I must remind Lanie and Jack! Don't step on the third step from the top; the creak always turns Farid's head on a swivel*, Sara told her memory.

YURIKO CLEARED THE front door swift and silent. He studied the layout, assessing the attack order and methods, scanning for threats, and counter probabilities. Sara returned to standing and entirely focused on the bread. Yuriko did not feel or notice a single step as he glided to the killing position behind Sara. He grabbed Sara across the mouth with his left arm, pulling her head leftward and down, and in the same move thrust the blade deep into Sara's kidney, reaching deep, severing the renal artery, and puncturing the abdominal artery. Yuriko turned Sara to enjoy the life draining from her body. He could feel her fear and agony. The satisfaction warmed him a bit, and he smiled slightly. Sara was gasping for a breath; she would never draw and struggled to meet the agony consuming her body. "Soleimani...," he whispered as Sara slipped away, her vision narrowed into darkness and her soul into silence.

Yuriko guided Sara's lifeless body to the floor and moved swiftly to reassess the area. *Next,* he thought and focused on the young teenager, still lightly singing on the screen porch beyond the kitchen.

Lanie, intently engrossed in an Instagram post, focused on breaking down the voice inflection in Pink's voice. Lanie dreamed of becoming an American Popstar and traveling the world. Yuriko slid behind Lanie and grabbed and looped her long hair in one vicious move, pulling with the left violently backward and thrusting forward with the right. The knife found the sweet spot. The thrust continued to the front of her throat, severing the spinal cord at the base of the skull, and worked like a switch. *Two,* he thought as he tossed the lifeless Lanie to the floor.

FARID, NOW RELAXED, enjoyed nightfall and the aromas of the coming meal drifting by on the breeze, driven toward the mountains from the sea. The near-constant breeze was comforting. However, when a tempest from a storm came, it was frightening. Tonight, would be joyous. The promise of a cool breeze for the duration of the evening, a crackling fire, family, and good company would soothe the soul. *Hmmm, Lanie has stopped singing,* Farid pondered to himself. *What was keeping Jack? He should have been here, likely checking and rechecking, as was his nature. Oh, I must act surprised.* Farid smiled, *Sara worked so hard to surprise me, so I will play my role this evening.* Farid settled down in his chair, positioned to see the sea and the mountains from the rooftop venue.

YURIKO APPROACHED THE steps with care —taking each wooden step with care to dampen groans and creaks from the old staircase. Though old, Farid was too dangerous to challenge with just a blade, despite Yuriko's skill, aptly proved moments ago downstairs. Yuriko made his way nearly to the top and could see Farid resting just where Overwatch described —a few more steps. The third step from the top was like an alarm bell for Farid. The Rasulovs knew to avoid the third step down when approaching Farid.

Yuriko cringed and looked down at his feet only for a second as the creak and groan of the third step screeched into the night —before the screech had faded, Farid rolled to cover —pulling a Glock 9mm pistol from under the chair. Advantage lost. Farid could barely see Yuriko in the poor lighting. But he knew the shapes, sounds, and presence of his family and Webb —the dark figure about to die was an intruder. Yuriko stepped as predicated to the right of the plank that complained so loudly —Farid snapped fired three rounds, striking Yuriko perfectly. Yuriko, stunned, fell backward down the stairs to the bottom in a thunderous crash.

"Sara! Lanie! Run!" screamed Farid, "Jack, help!"

Pfft—Pfft: Overwatch fired two rounds, dropping Farid to the rooftop floor. One of the rounds severed his spine just below the base of the neck stealing Farid's ability to move. Yuriko grabbed at the bulletproof vest, sucked in a volume of air, and thundered back up the steps while struggling to replace his earpiece.

"Ahmed, Overwatch – over...," called Overwatch.

"Overwatch, Ahmed. I am back up. Is he down?" asked Yuriko.

"Yes, target down, let's go," replied Overwatch.

Yuriko stepped back onto the rooftop patio. His eyes caught Farid, prone; the moonlight glistened off Farid's shirt, soaked with blood, chest heaving to suck in and push out the night air bursting from the wounds. Yuriko stopped at Farid's side and sat down.

"Your Sara is dead. I cut her open in her kitchen and cut off your Lanie's head. Your daughter and family are dead. Your Brit is dead. You, you... are dying," Yuriko whispered to Farid. "You have betrayed Allah and sold your soul to the Infidels," continued Yuriko. "We are hunting the traitors the world over and will strike a blow at the very heart of the Great Satan," boasted Yuriko.

Farid stared into the night's starscape shutting out Yuriko's taunts. He pulled in the final smells of the night, a slight hint of mint, Sara....

Yuriko slowly rose from the floor, swelling with pride and a sense of vengeance.

"Overwatch, Ahmed," Yuriko called into the night.

"Ahmed, Overwatch – you are clear to the South, exfil now...," returned Overwatch.

DANIYAH PAUSED TO KNOW with certainty that her team cleared Lankaran —in the boats and headed back to Iran. Daniyah's exfil was a three-hour coastal drive to Baku, Azerbaijan, the capital city. Daniyah had to call ISCARIOT to learn her destination from Baku Heydar Aliyev International Airport.

THE VIBRATING RHYTHM of the cell phone awakened ISCARIOT from his afternoon nap. The view from the sprawling Maryland Estate offered a relaxed setting and views of the countryside —positioned perfectly atop the highest elevation to offer a distant hint of the Washington D.C. skyline.

"Go," snapped ISCARIOT.

"I finished the chapter," reported Daniyah in code.

"It is an enjoyable book," smiled ISCARIOT, "Are you planning still planning for your vacation? I would like to treat if I may?"

"Thank you, I would love to start the next chapter as soon as possible," replied Daniyah.

"Great, you will have the link to your travel documents in the text that I will send," reported ISCARIOT, "Have a fun trip and enjoy the next chapter."

Daniyah's cellphone beeped when the call ended, noting the arrival of the expected text.

*Baku-Istanbul-Gibraltar —lunch meeting at Olas Café in Algeciras*

*Hmm, meeting Paul again,* Daniyah thought, *we can launch CHAOS with the last piece of the code.*

"MR. PRESIDENT, MR. President —ANDY!" pressed Tess. Waking the President, the President of the United States of America, despite a 35-year-old friendship, is a nervy act. POTUS's day is long and stressful, and a goodnight's sleep restores more than just the body. POTUS needs a clear mind and sharp focus, and Tess disrupted the symbiosis of deep sleep and sound reasoning. President L. Andrew Hammond, former Director of the Central Intelligence Agency, appointed Tess Mercier, former Director of the CIA National Clandestine Service. Nerves of steel —tested by years of CIA service in the darkest of the world's corners.

"Tess, why are you waking me up? I just went to sleep. And where is Deb," grunted President Hammond, "Don't you think Deb will find it awkward if she strolls out of the bathroom naked?"

"Well, Sir, that would be awkward... so it is a good thing Deb is in the gym and said it was okay to enter and wake you," replied Tess, "besides, you need to hear what I have to tell you."

"Another murder?" asked POTUS.

"Yes," answered Tess weightily.

"Get Xander Ridge and SDS on this right now and advise the NSC. You are on point. I want a full rundown in the PDB this morning, so read in Dr. Greene. Ridge can move faster than the NSC and IC, and he is smarter than all of them —and loyal," ordered President Hammond.

"Yes, Sir," replied Tess, "right away."

# CHAPTER ONE — PRESIDENTIAL DAILY BRIEF

N*ineteen dead,* thought Malik, the CIA Presidential Daily Briefer; *this is scaring me. Breaches such as this mean a betrayal; do we have another spy in our midst?* The thoughts added to Malik's stress. *And now the President was running late, never for the PDB; what could be happening?*

Malik straightened her dark blue with light pink pinstripe suit outside the Oval Office. Malik always fought back the pit of her stomach and the awkward proverbial lump in the throat. "Malik, I love the way you approach the Oval Office with such reverence and preparedness," smiled President Hammond's Executive Personal Secretary, Patricia Bell. However, everyone around The White House called her Ms. Pat, with respectful care. Only a careless fool would get on Ms. Pat's bad side. Even the Secret Service revered Ms. Pat.

Ms. Pat, tall with a dark complexion framed with long brown hair always sharply pulled into a low ponytail, was the epitome of the mind's eye of a Presidential Executive Secretary, sharp, loyal, focused, effective, and efficient. Ms. Pat, a fierce patriot, and long-time executive assistant to President Hammond, harkening to the President's academic, business ventures, and government service. Ms. Pat was well known for her studious nature, oft referred to as a Ms. Google, though never to her face.

"Thank you, Ms. Bell. I do appreciate your kindness," smiled Malik.

"Malik, you always do a fantastic job breaking down the President's Daily Brief (PDB). He really admires and respects you. You always give him a clear picture, and I know that he appreciates your work," Ms. Pat affirmed. The lump in Malik's throat weakened, and the accompanying pit relaxed.

"Thank you," Malik smiled again.

"I will go see what is keeping the President and let him know you are here for the PDB," said Ms. Pat with the classic sense of efficiency, pivot direction in a snap in a manner befitting a Marine Corps drill maneuver flawless execution. Keeping the Executive Branch on time was daunting. The look on Malik's face told Ms. Pat that today's challenge just got more complicated.

MS. PAT ENTERED THE Oval and found an already tense conversation. President Hammond sat in his favorite chair, a wooden rocking chair with leather coverings in just the correct spots for extra comfort during extended meetings. President Hammond likes the *Kennedy esque* look and feel of the chair and the Resolute Desk. Most would miss the subtle signs of the President's tension. But Ms. Pat missed nothing as she noted the President's grip on his fountain pen and the lack of rocking as his right foot —planted firmly pressed further into the floor. The room layout positioned the flat screens in the background to allow the President to monitor the major news networks. He liked to hear and see the news during briefings. Today he kept engagement in the conversation and on the news feeds —intently. The President was tense.

Seated on the couch to his left were Chief of Staff Dr. Betty Mercier, Michael Cooke, Secretary of Defense; FBI Director, Henry Mills; and CIA Director, Christian Frost. Directly across on the second couch were the Directors of the National Security Agency

(NSA) and National Intelligence, General Shawn Wright, and General Michael Roberts.

"Mr. President, Dr. Greene is waiting to deliver the PDB. Shall I show her into the Oval?" queried but with a firm look, conveying, we are behind schedule, Sir.

President Hammond polled the room with just a glance. He returned an approving look to his longtime aide and confidant, "Ms. Pat, please, ask Malik to join our discussion."

"Yes, Mr. President," responded Ms. Pat, retreating to the outer offices.

"MALIK! GET IN HERE," bellowed a smiling President Hammond as he stood to greet Malik. "Dr. Greene, how are you this fine morning?" opened Hammond, "I do miss pre-COVID days of shaking hands, but please come in and join us," finishing the welcome.

"Good Morning, Mr. President; I am well, thank you, Sir," Malik reported, "I do hope you are doing well this morning, as well?"

"Yes, Yes, please, take your seat here. Malik, I need your perspectives on these recent murders of sources," requested the President, bringing Dr. Greene into the fold.

"Mr. President, Mr. Secretary, Director Mills, General Wright, General Roberts, Director Frost, Dr. Mercier, Good Morning. I want to call your attention to an emerging trend of covert operations from the Iranian Ministry of Intelligence and Security (MOIS). Mr. President, murder is a polite term. Gentleman, nineteen deep cover Iranian sources have died, brutally, over the past three months. Killing suspected informants is not new for MOIS. What is new is the degree of accuracy. Each of the nineteen was directly involved in the intelligence collection needed to kill Major General Qasem Soleimani. Last night, a Government of Iran (GOI) Wet-Team, murdered the 20th member and most vital link in the Soleimani kill-chain, including the MI6 Case Officer. The GOI Wet-Team slaughtered the entire family of this source. The victim, codeword STURGEON, was a 40-year source in Lankaran, Azerbaijani, and supported the Five-Eyes, faithfully. Sir, I trained him at the Farm," stressed Malik to the room. The President caught the distressful tone and politely said, "I am sorry for your loss, Malik."

"Sir, thank you. Sir, my point is STURGEON was a deep-cover source, well trained and experienced, and capable, as was the MI6 Case Officer," continued Malik, artfully recovering from the fleeting importance of the moment. "Gentleman, the GOI is decades behind the Five-Eyes in encryption and decryption capability. Iranian capabilities have increased on a predictable path since Olympic Games, the cyberattack on the Natanz Nuclear Enrichment Facility in 2006. But Iran has never had a dramatic leap in capability and never in cryptography. Sir, the Iranians have a new cryptography capability, and we do not know the extent. The murder of STURGEON and the M16 Case Officer is a critical concern," warned Malik.

"Thank you, Dr. Greene; stay on this. Frost stay on this; I know you will give Dr. Greene all that she needs to run this down. Team, initial reactions?" said the President, studiously.

Director Frost spoke first, "Sir, I agree with Dr. Greene's analysis. Malik, thank you. This case is code-word clearance, HERON, is the reference from this point."

"Team, I want to bring in, with your concurrence, Henry, of course, Special Agent Mark Reyes. Reyes is a bit of a wild card. The smart ones are, it seems. Reyes is the best cryptologist that I know and is currently on loan to the NSA from the FBI Cyber Squad," offered General Shawn Wright, Director of the NSA.

"Yes, Shawn, I agree SA Reyes is top-notch. Dr. Greene, your analysis is sobering. Do you see any evidence Iran has compromised our secure communications or networks?" quizzed FBI Director Henry Mills.

"Sir, I do not know. A leap in capability such as I am seeing, needed help," said Malik candidly.

"I want to bring Ridge and SDS into HERON. There is no one better to pair with Reyes to support Dr. Greene. Concerns?" offered General Michael Roberts, Director of National Intelligence. "Sir, we need to include Secretary Porter," added Roberts.

"Yes, Ms. Pat!" summoned the President.

"Sir," reported Ms. Pat, "How can I help you, Sir?"

"Ms. Pat, please have Secretary Porter join us here in the Oval?" requested Hammond.

"Right away, Sir, I anticipated such, and Secretary Porter is in OEOB with Vice President Kent," emphasized Ms. Pat.

"Great work, Ms. Pat. Thank you. Please, ask both Laura and Becky to join us as soon as possible," finished the President, smiling at Ms. Pat, releasing just for a moment his grip on the floor, rocking the chair once.

"Yes, Sir," closing the door replied Ms. Pat, noting the effort helped ease the President.

"Cooke thoughts? You have been quiet, too quiet," tempted the President.

"Sir, Dr. Greene's assessment is humbling. Do you have an early assessment of who may be helping Iran?" quizzed Secretary of Defense Michael Cooke.

"Mr. Secretary, no, I do not. However, when I worked at SDS for Ridge, he often worried about such leaps in capability. Solutions to the impossible are not impossible, just challenging. Once a person thinks a solution through, it is infectious and can spread quickly. We have seen such with nuclear proliferation. The spread took longer because of the resources needed. However, with cryptography, one only needs a computer, a powerful one, but just a computer," Malik academically reported.

Ms. Pat knocked on the door, "Mr. President, the Vice President, and Secretary Porter are here. May I show them into the Oval?"

"Please," prompted the President.

"Laura, Becky, thank you for coming. I am grateful you are here. We need to get you plugged into HERON. Dr. Greene, please, cover the material again for the Vice President and the Secretary State," requested President Hammond.

"Of course, Mr. President. Madam Vice President and Madam Secretary," Malik began to brief out the HERON report from the Presidential Daily Brief.

# CHAPTER TWO — A SHOT ACROSS THE BOW

Paul seething with rage, slammed the wine down his gullet. He aggressively motioned for the waiter and switched to bourbon. Paul pressed his feet into the floor and pushed back on his chair. The chair moaned and creaked in protest. Paul glared at Daniyah —studying her face, and pulled a long draw on the cigar. The late lunch scheduled by ISCARIOT meant a successful Lankaran Operation.

Paul Ross was the quintessential good-looking man, tall-athletically fit-dark complexion-five o'clock shadow. Paul's stature topped six feet six inches, towering over most, with a chiseled from stone chest. He commanded the attention of the room when he entered. His native-American features complimented the chiseled athletic build with neatly cut onyx hair and equally dark eyes. Paul is an executive for Shepherd Defense Systems (SDS), a South Carolina-based defense contractor owned by Xander Ridge. As a premiant cyberweapon expert, he leads the Commercial Services Division for SDS. His career netted him a small fortune with a net worth exceeding $45 million. Paul is married to Isabella Coutre-Ross, whose grace and beauty rivaled if not surpassed that of his lover seated across the table. Paul cheats on Isabella without cause —absent care. Isabella is a loving and adoring wife and mother to Maria Sara and Olivia Anne, 17 and 15.

Daniyah's appearance turns heads —men and women stop and turn to check out Daniyah as she enters a room, jogs down the sidewalk, or simply sitting sipping tea at a café. Daniyah does not suffer —no. Daniyah is stunning at five feet nine inches with an athletic build, olive skin tone, bright green eyes, smooth, flowing, and mahogany hair. Daniyah's dainty model, like appearance, is deceptive. Nature is a cunning temptress. Daniyah is a counterintelligence agent's nightmare, as she could tempt sources into a betrayal with the slightest stroke of her hand or seductive glance. At 30, Daniyah is an accomplished assassin for the Islamic Republic of Iran. She feigned love with cunning guile to lure the likes of Paul, men, and a few women who seek power, riches, or just obsessed with their personas. She expertly exploited the human character flaws bending to her will with a DaVinci esque precision. Paul was a formidable adversary, she had learned. He would not hesitate. But he coveted what he could not or did not have, and his arrogance gave her the advantage. She sipped her wine and, with a simple tempting look, conveyed it was time to retire from the seaside las Olas Café. The view is stunning, and the food is light and enticing. Across the Bay of Algeciras, directly across from their table, the Rock of Gibraltar rose sharply from the sea into the sparsely clouded sky.

Paul caught Daniyah's temptresses' glance. He folded his napkin and laid the cloth across his plate, "The decryption software worked well for you. It seems the score is balancing. You should be careful not to hit so often and so boldly. Was killing the entire family and the British Agent really necessary? You can sit on the source and collect intelligence – an eye for an eye strategy will get you bombed back to the stone age."

"General Soleimani's death was not to go un-answered...," Daniyah gritted, biting her thin ruby lips. She took in a deep breath of the warm Mediterranean afternoon, soaking in the essence of a by-gone age of care-free living along the sea.

"Killing the Brit was a step too far; the family, I don't care, fine," returned Paul. "Selling you the advanced tech is dangerous. You need to wield carefully and not advertise that you have broken a code... it is simply —basic, tradecraft...," chastised Paul "you have started a clock —you have less than two weeks to pull this off —or we are all dead or in prison!"

"I see your point. The murder of Soleimani, perhaps —blinded us a bit. But what is done is done. Iran just put a shot across the bow that we shall not be trifled," retorted Daniyah. She reached across the table to gently stroke his hand with her fingers, playfully drawing suggestive shapes on the back of his hand.

"We paid the account, like always, but we expect more and soon," teased Daniyah. "Now, let's retire from this place and enjoy a few hours. I have missed you," she tempted.

"Fine, I didn't come this far to leave without shoving your head down," Paul shot across the table.

"You fear, Ridge, why?" checked Daniyah as they reached the sidewalk taking in the Rock of Gibraltar.

"No, not fear; he has a dangerous mind.... Xander is the most capable man even under the worst of conditions; he finds a way to win," reflected Ross.

"Fear," taunted Daniyah.

"No, in the end, the most committed wins, even over oneself; he is a warrior and committed. I hate him but do respect him. You and your government should, as well; only a fool wouldn't," retorted Paul.

"Kidnap Gabriella to pressure Xander?" Daniyah pressed, "to move this along."

"Not yet," Paul uttered as he opened the door to the suite, "I have set a plan in motion to strike at the heart of Xander's family —his youngest, Amelia. Grabbing Daniyah by the back of the head and pulling her violently into the room, "now, get to it..." he hissed.

PAUL NURSED A BOURBON and finished a cigar on the balcony with a helpful breeze offering a cooling sensation and swirling the thick cigar smoke up and towards the Rock of Gibraltar across the bay. Paul watched Daniyah stroll to her Uber and started to think about the day and life.

> *Damn, she is something. Daniyah releases me —to be me. I love sex —hot-rough-sex. Isabella is a dead fish -no action. At some point, I will need to leave Isabella and the girls without losing the house, yacht, cars, and money. She is not getting a dime! She wanted the girls —I never did. She can have the girls-clothes jewelry —just get out. Henrique is a DICK! He will make my life HELL if he can. He can take his daughter back to France. Where could Daniyah and I go? Where can we go? I like the Mediterranean Spain-Morocco-Algeria-Italy. If Isabella moves to France —that is too close..., Am I evil —if I end her? What about the girls? Henrique —no qualms, there... I could kill him with no hesitation. I need to work this out soon. Daniyah —when she returns to Tehran, the MOIS will move on the nine attacks —will mess them up, without a doubt. Her cyberpunks will screw up my masterpieces... Maybe, I should sell to the Chinese, the Russians. I am sure the DNI is considering a leak —with Daniyah is running around settling scores like the Cowboys and the Earp's —one-upping each kill on the way to the inevitable collision course at the OK Corral. I need to start locking down my security. I don't need a dumbass tradecraft error to give the FBI or DNI an edge. I don't need them thinking that I am ISCARIOT. No, the FBI is not my worry —it is Xander-Danny-SDS. SDS's inner circle on the government side is a tight team. It pisses me off —Xander and Danny never allow the commercial*

*team to collaborate with the government side of SDS. Xander is good. But he is an arrogant prick, and Danny is his hit man, knocking down every good idea from my side of SDS. We could make twice as much —if we just create bugs in the systems —and increased the frequency of upgrades, constantly chasing fixes with new capability. But NO! Xander insists that each product work, and he fixes —EVERYTHING at no cost! He gives the store away —he even supports our competition by sharing Zero Days and intelligence. The Zero Day hunting capabilities of SDS are worth millions! BILLIONS! If Xander would just exploit —the opportunity. Enough! I need to get some sleep. Xander will soon have enough to worry about with Amelia —with Xander distracted. I can get at this alleged RUBICON.*

# CHAPTER THREE — SO, IT BEGINS

Gabby's thoughts flickered on with the light slipping past the bathroom doors slightly ajar. *Thank you, God. Another night that Amelia survived. Please, God, let her wake up today*. The British Broadcasting Company (BBC) Global News Podcast played loudly on Xander's iPhone in the bathroom, stirring Gabby from a particularly but much-needed restful sleep. Amelia, finally, had a restful night's sleep. Amelia is the youngest of Xander's and Gabby's five children ranging in age from Emily, 25; Jonathan, 23; Sophia, 21; Charles,19; and Amelia, 13. Gabby turned over in the king-sized bed, snuggled the plush comforter, and settled in for a view of Xander. Xander stood six feet two inches of his GQ-ish body, toned abs, broad chest, stout legs, and football esque biceps. *He is still mine, my night and shining armor, God, I do love him*, gushed Gabby to herself. *Twenty-seven years of marriage, West Point and college years, the Teams, the deployments, the wars, and now Shepherd Defense Systems,* she thought, *reminiscing. Xander was a good man, my man, she thought. Like clockwork, he was up early, already worked out, completed the first run, checked in with each of the children, and stood over our sleeping, Amelia. He worried so much about her, as did I,* she reflected in her thoughts. The freshly cut rose caught Gabby's eye; every morning, a freshly cut rose, the first cup of coffee, and my iPad at the ready. She smiled, thinking *Xander was a can-do kind-of-man. Once he set his mind, Xander always found a way. Love, to Xander, is a verb. Every morning, a rose, coffee, and a fully charged iPad are ready for the day.*

"Good morning, My Love! How are you this morning?" teased Gabby.

Xander turned toward the sound of his angel and swept her into his arms in a tight embrace, "Now, it is a Good Morning, until this moment, just a morning. I do love you, Ms. Gabby."

"Oh, your Southern Twang isn't going to get you anywhere, and you know it," teased Gabby.

"Really, I do believe my dear sweetness, it has and shall again," breathed Xander across Gabby's neck. Xander had already swept Gabby's long, light brown hair to the side, allowing the hair to flow downward, with the appearance of water cascading over a fall.

"Okay, maybe it gets you a kiss, maybe a hug too," smiled Gabby, then bursting into a laugh as Xander tickled her a bit.

"Okay, Okay," Gabby pulled away while pulling her hair back to a ponytail in a sweeping motion, "How was Amelia? Did you check on her and Doctor Stone?"

"I did, Amelia was sleeping, thankfully, and I do like the new Doctor, Doctor Stone. She prefers Katy. The new room setup here at home is better for Amelia. Katy was very appreciative of the arrangements and the guest house. We made the right call to bring Amelia home. I did sneak a kiss on Amelia's forehead. She smiled a bit," quaked Xander, just a bit on the last portion.

"She loves her, Daddy. I am sure Amelia smiled at you," Gabby gently replied, with a reassuring stroke of her hand along the back of Xander's head, now resting forehead to forehead.

"What is the news of the day," queried Gabby as she walked over to her area of the bathroom suite.

"I need to get to the office. I expect a decent briefing today from Julius and our Intel team. BBC is reporting continued disruption of the power grid, ATMs, and sporadic disruptions at hospitals. I suspect a malware attack, but I am not sure yet. I am concerned about blowback from Iran or North Korea. I see odd behavior in

Asia," reported Xander in his flat, calm briefing posture, which was a clue for Gabby that Xander was concerned.

XANDER BUILT SHEPHERD Defense Systems (SDS) into a privately held defense contractor with annual revenue topping $100 billion. SDS designed advanced cryptography and encryption algorithms and software, quantum computing, and advanced drone technology. SDS engineered advanced air, land, and sea warfighting platforms and advanced intelligence collection technologies. Xander insisted on service to the country more than anything else. The SDS culture centered on an ethos, of *absolute equality to the founding principles that freedom, opportunity, and justice are open to all.* Xander was unique in his transparency. Xander insisted that Government oversight have full access to the company. The access included office space, free of SDS employees. Xander insisted that all bids for government contracts reflect an ethical margin of profit. Xander and SDS are apolitical, serving the American people, not a party, and thus did not contribute to political campaigns. Xander's vote was a private affair.

Xander was SDS, and SDS was Xander. SDS managed a healthy commercial business anti-malware software, cyber defense hardware, and intellectual property defense consulting, including cybersecurity and investigative and forensics services. SDS maintained strict intellectual property and insider controls. To SDS and Xander, trust is the core competency. Xander balanced the pyramid of ethos, logos, and pathos to personify his favorite principle, immortalized by Ernest Hemmingway, "There is nothing noble to being superior to your fellow man; true nobility is being superior to your former self." Friends and family know Xander for his tongue-in-cheek phrases around colleagues, friends, and family: *I believe in you, now go get your dreams; Good Enough is not a phrase we use; and his favorite*

– *chase your dreams, but don't be an asshole.* Xander held strong patriotic views and felt a fellowship with those that have sworn an oath of service.

SDS OFFICES RESTED in a large pine tree forested compound near Fort Mill, South Carolina. Xander designed the property to allow employees to live nearby on or off SDS property. Most of SDS headquarters were underground. The exact depth was a closely held secret. Still, local media speculated at deep caverns well under the Catawba River and extending several miles. The above-ground three stories of a domed structure covered in glass panels, mostly transparent solar panels serving as both a power source and window blended well into the natural topography and pine tree forest. SDS property as all SDS locations powered the buildings, factories, and laboratories with a closely held power source. Again, many local media suggest advanced fuel cell or battery storage to a secret nuclear laboratory. SDS Security was intense, professional, and capable to a nation-state level of defense, known for aiding local law enforcement agencies near the SDS location. SDS Security offered free next-level equipment to area law enforcement agencies. The perimeter and layered security of the SDS properties blended well into the landscape.

Xander's drive within the property required 15 minutes of his day, allowing time to listen to a few Podcasts or a partial Audible book. Xander arrived at the SDS surface parking lot, where parking was first come – first serve, unless one needed help, TLC, or completed a task. Xander rewarded success and encouraged employees to fail, first attempt-in-learning. Xander parked his F150 in the employee lot and walked hastily to the SDS Sensitive Compartmented Information Facility (SCIF), designed for U.S.

Government classified meetings Top Secret and above, and the SDS morning intelligence briefing.

"GOOD MORNING, XANDER. How are you and yours this morning, especially Amelia?" inquired Danny. Daniel Bell was the SDS Chief Security Officer and a former Teams member who served with Xander.

"Good morning, Danny, thank you," Xander paused from his aggressive stride.

"Amelia seems happier, still in a coma. She smiled at me when I kissed her forehead, poor kid. She is a fighter. I am well, kids are well, and Gabby is HOTT as always," teased Xander.

"HA! Great news on Amelia, small victories! You kill me if Gabby asks; you know I am ratting you out! But glad to learn, Gabby and Amelia are well this morning," snickered Danny.

"Good morning, Team," bellowed Xander as he and Danny bounded into the SCIF to meet the assembled SDS team. "How are y'all this morning? Does anyone need anything, and I do mean anything – there is nothing we cannot solve as a team, as a family?" checked Xander. The room responded that all were well, and all was good. Xander meant it. If an SDS employee needed help above the generous compensation and benefits, Xander and SDS were there. Money was never a barrier to success, life, liberty, or happiness. At day's end, how much does one really need? As they walked to the meeting, Xander's thoughts centered back on Amelia. The Q4 Quantum Medical logo caught his eye; *I am glad that we purchased Q4 to research cancer treatments. What good is it to have money if you don't serve humanity? And we can do this. I hope to get a cure or sustainable treatment before losing Amelia and the countless others suffering similar fates. We can do this for Amelia and the world. I promised Amelia —and vowed to Gabby, over objections —we will find a way. Q4 needed sustainable funding, rigor, and SDS resources to make this work. So far, it is looking good, and that is good for now.*

Today FBI Counterintelligence Special Agent Patrick Kelley attended the 0700 Daily SDS Intelligence Briefing. SDS leadership and cleared U.S. Government Agency on-site attended the Daily Briefing. The regular SDS Staff or designee attendees are Chief Security Officer, Daniel Bell; Chief Information Security Officer, Amira Said; Chief Operating Officer, Jacob Silva; Chief Executive Protection Officer and Chief Deputy, Kenneth Cain; Kyla Rashid; Chief Insider Threat Officer, Scout Moreau; and chaired by Chief Intelligence Officer Julius Lyons.

"Julius, what do you have for us this morning?" said Danny flatly.

"Good morning, Patrick. Thank you for being here," welcomed Xander.

> "As a reminder, this meeting is held in a Department of Defense approved Security Compartmented Information Facility requirement under DOD Directives. This morning, and with the aid of FBI Counterintelligence Special Agent Patrick Kelly confirmed the Top-Secret Clearance sponsored by the Department of Defense and or by the Department of Justice for each member in the room. Room, as I take attendance, please acknowledge for the record your presence with a clear 'Present' and compliance with DODD 5203.7 with a clear 'Aye,'" stated Julius in an academic tone.

The room quickly followed the *Present* and *Aye* directive, each sensing a concern in Julius.

> "Team, FIREEYE, SYMANTEC Security Response, Control Systems, and even Kaspersky confirm DHS NICC assessments that malware attacks have targeted

several Critical Infrastructure Sectors. The attacks appear like DDOS, but our analysis leans to malware right on the edge of an early generation cyberweapon, just restrained.

This morning, assessments note attacks on the following sectors: Communications, Energy, Emergency Services, Financial Services, and Healthcare.

Each attack is short in duration. There are no signs of attempts to exfiltrate data, user account information, or supporting malware to support an ongoing attack. Our assessment that I shared this morning with the IC is the malware is an early generation cyberweapon, circa 2003," reporting Julius, pausing for effect and comment.

Xander pondered the news and offered, "Correlation to Olympic Games or Eagle Talon?"

"Good question; we have not confirmed a threat actor or motivation. However, your questions align with my assessment, especially given the recent murder of deep-cover NOCs, Case Officers, and assets. Paranoid regimes often hazardously murder suspected spies or collaborators. However, in recent months, the accuracy of such is, well, spot-on. This shows a breach of data, a classified network, or both. Or simply good HUMINT. However, leaps in Iranian capability absent help are atypical," concluded Julius.

"Keep on this, Olympic Games – the attack on the Natanz nuclear site and Eagle Talon – the drone strike on Qasem Soleimani. These attacks energized Iranian capability in cyberweapons and drone/missile technology," Xander reported academically.

"Julius, what is wrong?" checked Xander, sensing more was coming from Julius, who seemed strained.

"Sir, Jack Webb was killed last night, sniper, headshot, in Lankaran, Azerbaijan," Julius paused. Lifelong friends, the friendship, brotherhood really, began in primary school in Winchester, Hampshire, in Southern England.

Xander tightened his grip on the leather conference room chair and tactically leaned forward, "Dear, God, Julius, I am so sorry; what do you need? What does Jack's family need? Really, anything you want to do, done. Our planes are at your disposal. Jacob, please see to it, as I know you will." Xander took a breath, "Jack and I worked coalition HUMINT for General McChrystal and General Hayden when he led the NSA."

"Thank you, Sir, Jack's boys, the twins, are at the University, second year," paused Julius, trying to compose himself.

"Jacob, please, work it out with Kelly, cover the full cost of tuition, food, housing, and offer SDS internships. Jacob quietly pay off any debt for the family and set up a trust for Jack's wife," Xander paused, "Jack's widow. Danny, assess the security of the Webb family, let M16 and 5 know, but get this done."

Two quick, "Yes, Sir," snapped from Jacob and Danny, crisply. When Xander focused and issued a directive, he intended to see the directive conducted and smartly.

> "Sir, Jack was killed, blocks away from his deep cover NOC, STURGEON. Sir, evidence suggests that three teams hit STURGEON and Jack. Two ground teams and an Overwatch team. The hit team executed flawlessly, well trained, and well planned. STURGEON and Jack were not easy targets; both worked in the area for decades. STURGEON and Jack were deep cover. Sir, I suspect a nation-state hit team. I suspect a GOI Wet-Team. MI6

agrees. What we do not know is how or who blew the covers," reported Julius. "Sir, *STURGEON's* entire family, is dead, all in a brutal fashion. This was 'wet,' bloody, DAMN BLOODY. This was personal, VENGEFUL," asserted Julius.

Stunned at the news, Xander stood and characteristically paced the room —the vertical briefing, Danny noted. "Thank you, Julius. I want you to take time off. Jacob will set you up with one of the planes. Ken, please, put an Executive Protection Team with Julius. Ken, do we have assets in London, armored cars, armed agents, secure hanger, and safe houses?" pulsed checked Xander. SDS has executive protection and security assets worldwide to support traveling employees and SDS's and Xander's and Gabby's philanthropic works. Xander's unique skillsets, experience, and capabilities required such efforts. However, Xander's commitment to family, friends, and SDS was limitless.

"Yes, Sir. I will see to it, no harm to Julius or the Webb family, understood, Sir," Ken smartly confirmed. Ken was a former Captain with the U.S. Army Rangers. Ken later joined the United States Secret Service. Ken looked distinguished with short, cropped black hair with distinguished grey notes with a masterful Eastwood-esque glare.

"Sir, I would like to review the security logs and malware activity. We should include the past few weeks," recommended Amira Said, SDS Chief Information Security Officer, diplomatically. Amira was a former Israeli Army Officer and team leader of the exclusive IDF Military Unit 8200, the Israeli equivalent of the U.S. National Security Agency and United States Cyber Command, in one unit. Amira was stunningly beautiful, with flowing long dark hair so dark that one could detect a hint of a demur blue sheen. Amira dressed professionally every day in a crisp business suit, perfect heels, and stunning blouses. She is a top-tier cybersecurity and cyberweapons expert. She was the tip of the spear and suspected of having supported Olympic Games at NSA's elite Tailor Access Unit at Fort Meade, Maryland. Amira's petit frame belied her athleticism. She runs an eight-minute mile, which she can sustain for a humbling distance. She is lovely in appearance and to her soul. She loved SDS and the 'there is nothing, we don't do for each other' esprit de corps. Though equally capable in the lethality of her male teammates, Amira was exceptionally giving of herself. SDS was Amira's home. Amira's teammates became family. Her heart ached for Julius and Xander, and Gabby. Amira visited daily with Amelia. Gabby adored Amira and cherished the friendship.

"Sir, the code, targeting U.S. Critical Infrastructure, is not malware —it is a cyberweapon. This is an old signature, pre-dating Olympic Games, simple and effective," Amira chronicled methodically. "Sir, there are hints of old but Nation-State capabilities. I don't have the malware captured yet. But when I do, I will be able to nail this down. Still, we need to encourage DHS to release a TLP Red through the ISACs, and I mean now," encouraged Amira, absent hesitation. TLP Red was the highest classification of information shared with the private sector. DHS shared the data through an Information Sharing and Analysis Center, one for each of the DHS Critical Infrastructure Sectors. Xander's pacing subsided, returning to his leather chair.

"Patrick, how about it. Can you get this to DHS Secretary ·eman?" Xander pressed.

"Yes, Sir. I will pass through the IC, but I will press to get the Red SDS analysis out. We need to get these attacks stopped. n't have medical devices failing, and bank accounts show $0 for g and savings accounts across the country," pledged Special Kelly. Patrick's comment tightened Xander's grip on the hair, as his thoughts ran the distance to Amelia's home hospital room. *No, we got this. No one's child or loved one, not on our watch*, thought Xander quietly. However, his face belied his thought to the room.

THE PRESIDENT WAS PACING behind the Resolute Desk. Ms. Pat checked on President Hammond and Chief of Staff Dr. Betty Mercier, ensuring the coffee flowed to expectations. President Hammond and Tess, as Hammond referred to the Chief of Staff, were longtime friends serving 20 years together of Tess's 40 years of service in the Central Intelligence Agency. Tess held the respect of President Hammond and his Administration, The White House Staff, and Congressional Members and Staff. Tess is a no-nonsense, tough-as-nails advisor and gave concise counsel to the President and anyone, asked or not. Tess did not have time for *Bullshit*, as she commonly retorted if you did not heed her warning and did not stop politics and the water's edge.

"You serve the American People or yourself. You cannot serve both," Tess often barked in a gruff voice from a retreating politico, having failed to challenge Tess's conclusion or directive.

"Tess, thoughts on Ridge and HERON?" queried Hammond.

"Andy, I think the world of Ridge and SDS. Ridge has proven himself and is a trusted patriot. He serves the United States and the American People unequivocally, often to his detriment. I trust, Ridge," flatly stated Tess, "I am Amelia Ridge's Godmother, for Pete's sake. Of course, I trust her father."

"I agree. Thank you. I need you to set up a call with Prime Minister Poole," requested Hammond. Hammond returned to hi: chair.

"Mr. President, please, include Hawkins. I would like to hear h assessment. We collaborated with him on nuclear proliferation

Pakistan, Asia, and North Africa. He is hardcore and true," advised Tess.

"Agreed. Tess, I am concerned. What is your assessment of the events leading to HERON?" pressed the President.

> "Well, I don't like the sequence of the events: the disappearances, the killings, and the cyber-malware activity. I do not like the accuracy of the disappearances and the killings. Capability absent rigorous discipline, research, and investment does not happen overnight. China and Russia are capable but adversaries such as Iran, North Korea, Syria, Somalia, Iraq, Nicaragua, Venezuela, Bolivia, and Lebanon are not capable, with little in the pipeline. The latter purchases capabilities from former KGB or Ukrainian and Russian Mafia. However, this capability is different. This capability feels like a nation-station. The motivation feels personal, retribution. Killing, umm, murdering Webb was personal. The manner of death for STURGEON was unnecessary. Farid and Sara, I can understand, but the child and his family. That was personal. I suspect blowback from Olympic Games and Eagle Talon," Tess reported factually.

"Please, keep the National Security Council and the Intelligence
munity aligned and focused. If you even get a whisp of a silo
or hoarding, deal with it, and keep me informed. I will not
politics with the security of the United States," ordered
t Hammond.

ourse, Mr. President," dutifully replied Dr. Mercier.

do you trust Wright?" pressed Hammond into dangerous
Wright and Tess's was conversational, thin ice.

ss returned flatly, "But, less over our failed marriage
t, loyalty. I don't trust his soul."

"Understood," reflected the President. A nagging theory tugged at Hammond's thoughts —but held in theory, longing for evidence.

A SHARP RAP OF THE door broke the intense discussion between President Hammond and Chief of Staff Mercier. "Yes, Ms. Pat, please, come in," responded President Hammond.

"Mr. President, Dr. Mercier, Chairwoman of the Joint Chiefs Robinson, needs you both in the Situation Room as soon as possible," shuddered Ms. Pat.

"Thank you, Ms. Pat. Ms. Pat, it is going to be okay. We will be okay," reassured President Hammond.

"Thank you, Mr. President," quaked Ms. Pat as she retreated from the oval.

"Let's go," said the President concisely.

THE WHITE HOUSE SITUATION Room, smaller than one imagines, commands reverence and attention, second only to the Oval Office. The Situation Room, well-equipped and capable of managing a global crisis, is the base of operations for Dr. Malik Greene. A summons to the Situation Room was serious, and President Hammond expected sinister news.

As President Hammond and Dr. Mercier, Chief of Staff, entered, the room's occupants snapped to attention with the sound of rustling chairs and straightening uniforms. President Hammond slipped past the table's end to his black leather chair with the Seal of the President awaited, at attention as well. The room held its breath. Hammond breathed in the scene of Military Officers and Aides, members of the National Security Council, and added today the Directors of the FBI and CIA, and Dr. Greene.

"Please, be seated," President Hammond ordered as he settled into command. "Let me begin. I am accustomed to the other end of this table and preparing the news – never good, not this end. I ask this, please be kind in the delivery," joked Hammond relieving the room's tensions, "and if you cannot be kind, just speak slowly with small words," he completed his joke. The room burst into calming laughter and resumed breathing as the final person found their seat and settled down.

> "Good morning, Mr. President," welcomed Chairwoman of the Joint Chiefs Lori Robinson, "Sir, we have detected a sustained disruption of Internet-based services. The disruption affects the Financial Sector, industrial control systems in the Energy Sector, and sporadic communication disruption. Government networks are still secure and unaffected," reported Chairwoman Robinson, taking a concerned deep breath. The General continued, "Sir, there have been sporadic reports of interference with 911 systems and medical devices. Sir, one person has died, Daniel De Luca, an elderly patient in Maryland who was on life support. The Internet-connected device adjusted the intravenous chemo-medicine flow. The monitors continued to display a normal heart, breathing, pulse ox, and blood pressure. The patient went into an undetected cardiac arrest," reported Chairwoman Robinson. "U.S. Government systems are unaffected, as are systems in Russia, China, and the Five Eyes. However, we detected disruptions in China and Russia's civilian networks and confirmed such in the Five Eyes. This is a Global Cyberattack," finished General Robinson.

Five Eyes (FVEY) is an intelligence-sharing collaboration amongst the top echelon allies of the United States. FVEY includes Australia, New Zealand, Canada, the United Kingdom, and the United States. The group expanded to Nine and Fourteen Eyes, including most NATO nations in a tightly managed intelligence flow to combat China, Russia, Iran, and North Korea.

"Who is not affected?" cutting straight to the edge, questioned President Hammond.

"Sir, we do not detect adverse cyber activity in North Korea, Iran, Syria, Iraq, or Venezuela," said General Roberts, Director of National Intelligence.

President Hammond glanced at Tess with concern. Then, the President paused as he turned in his chair toward Dr. Bluma Freeman, the Department of Homeland Security Secretary, "What is DHS doing to secure the Healthcare Sector and Energy Sector? Bluma, what is DHS doing to alert the private sector and critical infrastructure," pressed President Hammond.

> "Sir, DHS has engaged our digital forensics team to retrieve the medical equipment associated with the death of Mr. Daniel De Luca as well as several of our key Electric Sector Coordinating Council partners, that we trust," paused Dr. Freeman, as she collected a thought, "Sir, we have observed successful blocks with the commercial anti-virus products and of course the U.S. Government networks, protected by Shepherd Defense Systems and SDS Antivirus."

"Mr. President, per our discussion this morning, I spoke with FBI Special Agent Patrick Kelly, the SDS Liaison. SDS is in session in a secured room. Sir, I would..." started Dr. Greene.

"Mr. President. Excuse me, Dr. Greene, but I have concerns about going outside the U.S. Government. DHS can manage," interrupted Secretary Freeman, noting with a sideways glance at the Chief of Staff, Dr. Mercier, who few dared to cross. President Hammond noticed Tess's engaging forward lean.

"Thank you, Dr. Freeman; you and DHS have my full confidence," paused the President, noting Secretary Freeman's slight smile at the prospect of winning against Tess and Malik. The President continued, "However, SDS is a longstanding and proven partner to the United States, and as you stated, SDS systems commercial and government are unaffected."

"I do appreciate your engagement and ownership, and I have made a note of your commitment, Madam Secretary," finished President Hammond.

"Thank you, Sir. Of course, SDS is quite capable. Dr. Greene, again, my apology for the interruption," retreated Secretary Freeman.

"Malik, please read the room into HERON while the staff arranges the secure connection to SDS in South Carolina," ordered the President, still looking at Secretary Freeman, searching for a hint of discontent. President Hammond encouraged vigorous debate but did not appreciate the interruption. Tess caught President Hammond's displeasure and would follow up at the meeting's end with the Secretary. In this administration, everyone rowed in the same direction and on cadence or dealt with Tess.

AS DR. GREENE CONTINUED with the briefing, the President scanned the room's monitors —checking the news, to see the worlds outside of the Situation Room, The White House, and Washington D.C. Experience drove the President to keep the 24/7 news cycle continuously running.

CNN: the anchors were sharing the news of a patient's death and discussing with a subject matter expert on cybersecurity. Field reporters were out in several cities —tempting fears with a connected world —like medical devices.

FOX News: the anchors were not happy with The White House. DHS is not sharing fast enough with the private sector and the media.

NPR: Is linking the internet disruptions and the death of the medical patient —hinting at a deepening cyberattack and foreshadowing a link with the disruption of 911 across the United States.

"XANDER, THE RED LIGHT is on. Do you mind if I step out and receive the message?" asked Danny.

"Of course, Danny, I am terribly sorry; I missed the light, please," responded Xander, still concerned about the briefing. Danny excused himself and exited the SDS SCIF to retrieve the message. The SCIF's physical and cybersecurity measures prohibit the use of unauthorized equipment in the room. SDS used the old school red, yellow, green, and white protocol for simple messages. A red light meant for the meeting to stop for an emergent event or added news. Danny quickly returned and requested FBI Special Agent Kelly.

"Patrick, can I see you a moment?" requested Danny.

"Of course," quickly jumping to his feet and halfway to the door exclaimed Xander before his feet appeared to have hit the ground.

Within moments, Danny and Patrick returned to the SDS SCIF. "Xander, Patrick is arranging a connection to The White House Situation Room. The President would like SDS to join an ongoing discussion. Xander, additional cyber activity is occurring, Sir, it is bad," reported Danny.

"Very well," affirmed Xander, "seal the room," steeled Xander straightening his already perfect posture.

"GOOD MORNING, XANDER. I trust you and Gabby are well?" solicited President Hammond.

"Good morning, Mr. President. Thank you, Sir. Gabby and I are well. Of course, Gabby sends her love to you and the First Lady," Xander replied graciously.

"Xander, how is Amelia? Of course, Deb and I pray for her speedy and full recovery?" offered the President.

"Thank you, Sir. The cancer is taking a toll, Sir. Amelia is strong and a fighter. Gabby and I moved her home to her room, with all the hospital stuff. Thank you for the recommendation. Dr. Stone is a blessing, and Amelia adores her. Gabby and I are grateful to you and the First Lady," accepted Xander, with a tad quiver discussing 13-year-old Amelia's health.

"You are welcome, old friend. Xander, there is trouble, and I need your help," rounded the President.

"Yes, Sir. SDS Intelligence and Special Agent Kelly brought me up to speed on the events last night and the cyberattacks. Sir, I am concerned about the escalation in symmetrical and asymmetrical events. The killing and cyber activity do not seem to link. However, the events do link. Someone has a new capability and is acting," summarized Xander.

"HERON is the codeword for the agent activity, Xander. Dr. Malik Greene has HERON for the Government," offered President Hammond.

"Yes, Sir. Julius Lyons is the SDS Point of Contact for Dr. Greene," paused Xander, "Good Morning, Dr. Greene."

"Good morning, Dr. Ridge. It is an honor to meet you," politely offered Malik.

"Secretary Freeman, I passed to CISA the SDS intelligence for Critical Infrastructure and early analysis of the malware," reported FBI Special Agent Kelly.

"Yes, Thank you, Patrick. We have the malware signatures, and CISA is preparing the industry Red Alert for each of the Coordinating Councils. I expect the release to the private sector in hours," responded Secretary Freeman.

"Xander, what is SDS assessment of the malware," queried Secretary Freeman in a conciliatory tone.

"The malware is a code structure that we have not seen since 2004. The malware is a first-generation, cyberweapon," summarized Xander.

"Xander, are the U.S. Government networks secure?" queried Christian Frost, CIA Director.

> "Yes, Sir. Director Frost, the current malware that SDS is monitoring is not capable of breaking U.S. encryption. I do not suspect a breach of the Five Eyes, China, or Russia. However, the malware can decrypt coded messages passing to the U.S. or a Five Eye. However, the 'To' is still secure, based on current analysis. This is likely how STURGEON and his MI6 handler were un-masked," offered Xander. Xander paused and resumed the briefing, "Cyberweapons have a payload that does something. The attack on the hospital is an example. The payload targeted the Internet-connected devices checking life functions and the pumps delivering intravenous medicines. However, the attacks on the energy and financial sectors elude us for the moment. I am concerned that the attacks are not just a distributed denial of service. I am concerned

that the attacks left behind a piece of code. I designed the cyberweapon to attack multiple vectors when attacking a protected target. I leave pieces of the payload or allow the adversary a few wins to bolster confidence, then I wait. I continue with smaller subtle attacks hidden in the noise of the daily attacks. Until I have a full payload." Xander paused, "In 2016, a similar attack played out against the Nuclear Energy sector, the primary cyber defenses held. However, the APT shifted the threat vector to the supply chain and third-party vendors with lesser defenses and was successful. DHS and SDS did catch the attack in time. However, I recommend that DHS add to the TLP Red Alert for the Critical Infrastructure Sectors. Advise CI to harden down on third-party connections and supply chain security, especially in medical," finished Xander.

"You really scare me, you know that?" joked the President. "You make me want to drown my cellphone, crush my laptop, and stuff my mattress with my money," teased the President.

"Well, this is my business, Sir. SDS builds government and civilian defenses against such attacks," shared Xander.

"You do more than that, my friend," said the President leaning forward in his chair and toward the camera.

"Yes, we do. We build weapons for you and prepare for the next generation attack. Sir, this is an attack. The attackers claimed one life already. This attack is just beginning, a prelude, a taste. The assassinations of intelligence case officers and assets the World over and these attacks are an awakening. The dawn of a new global player emerging. I just don't know who, yet," finished Xander.

The room fell silent as each member in the Situation Room and in the SCIF at SDS contemplated Xander's summation.

The President rose to his feet to recognize the importance of Xander's reflection. The room snapped to customary but respectful attention. As did the SDS team and Xander alike. When the President stood —no one remained seated.

"Xander, get on it," ordered the President, "Tess?"

"Xander, I will coordinate any U.S. Government resources that you need. Each member of the NSC will fully support this partnership, and...." Tess paused, "Mr. President, please excuse me, General Roberts," requested Tess as she and the Director of National Intelligence stepped out of the room. President Hammond returned to his seat at the head of the table in the Situation Room —the rest of the room did as the President motioned —at ease.

"Mr. President, I will pause for Tess and General Roberts to return. However, I suspect they are learning of the explosions in Galveston, Texas City, Baton Rouge, and Belle Chase," reported Xander.

Tess and General Roberts returned to the room with stern looks and slightly ashen, "Mr. President, the major oil refineries in Texas and Louisiana have exploded. The pipelines ruptured at the same time. FEMA estimates the death toll to be in the hundreds and possibly as high as a thousand." Tess found her seat on autopilot, thinking, *My God, is this our 9-11, not again.*

A Naval Lieutenant fumbled with a remote for the President. President Hammond preferred to monitor the cable news and major newspaper websites during most briefings. It is best to see what the world sees beyond the presumptive context of classified briefings —sometimes secrets are not secret —the who, the how, the where —the exactness remained hidden, but the core secret was rarely as secret as reported —or hoped.

CNN, MSNBC, and FOX News reported the devastation with aerial footage streaming live —faster than the NSC could muster a satellite —though once the NSC resources locked on, the government resources were unmatched. The local commentary and interviews brought home the severity in human terms as families mourned —the stunned faces —black soot painted everyone and everything —today; everyone was black —Americans killed, dying, and suffering.

"Xander, you have your orders and our support; find these sons of bitches," ordered the President.

"Yes, Sir, SDS out," replied Xander ending the call. Xander thought for a moment and then looked at his team, his family, "So, it begins. Get to work."

# CHAPTER FOUR — AMELIA

"XANDER, didn't you see the Red-light flashing?" exclaimed Mia, the SDS Executive Assistant.

"No, I am sorry, we were all focused on the meeting. What happened?" pulsed Xander, in a tone suggesting he knew that Amelia had taken a turn.

"Come on, Xander, I will drive you," exclaimed Danny, as he grabbed Xander by the arm, "Let's go. We get up to the house in just a few."

"No, not the house!" breathlessly shrieked Mia, "Katy, I mean, Dr. Stone called 911, Amelia, Ms. Ridge, and Dr. Stone are with Amelia in the ambulance."

XANDER'S EYES STRAINED to see through the walls of the Emergency Room, desperately searching for Gabby and Amelia. Amelia suffered from primitive neuroectodermal tumors (PNETs). The cancer squeezes Amelia's brain stem, and all efforts to reverse it have failed. Xander, who commanded hundreds of special forces in battle —became the SDS CEO and the premier cyberweapon expert, physicist, and multi-billionaire —could not heal his baby girl.

Xander purchased Q4, a leading quantum physics research company. Quantum physics and computing aligned with SDS's mission as a defense contractor for the United States. Xander learned healthcare applications, purchased Q4, and funded the research with their work in the defense industry. Amelia was the motivation. But if quantum physics offered hope to humanity, Xander was all-in.

Gabby was gently stroking with a mother's love the bangs of Amelia's hair. At the same time, she fielded calls and text messages from the children. Each was calling on learning the news of the emergency. Gabby anxiously looked around the emergency care area until her eyes rested on Xander. Gabby smiled a bit and thought, *Xander, I Love you! Get in here, please.* As if he had read her mind, Xander shifted his search to find Gabby's eyes. Xander and Gabby have a strong connection, as if the very word love's definition emanated from their bond.

"Xander, oh, thank God you are here. Katy says we almost lost Amelia. Her medicines are not working," shared Gabby as she pulled Xander into her for an intense embrace. Xander held Gabby tightly for a moment and shifted his eyes from Gabby's to Amelia. Xander's breath stopped for an instant, and Gabby pressed her palm flat against Xander's chest. Gabby's touch always brought Xander back down. He and Gabby walked over to Amelia as Danny walked in to check on his friend's family in truth.

"Xander, I am sending a sample of Amelia's meds to SDS for analysis. I want to ensure the medicines, IV fluid, and everything is real. If we see an attack like you saw, I want to know," said Danny carefully.

"Thank you, Danny," Xander choked, "Please, brief Dr. Stone. Danny, only on the medical elements, nothing else," responded Xander.

"Yes, Sir," replied Danny as he pivoted to clear the room to find Dr. Stone.

"Xander, what is going on? Did someone target Amelia?" quivered Gabby.

"No, I don't think so, but I do suspect a broader attack on the United States. Kyla is on it. She will keep the family safe," reassured Xander.

PAUL RETURNED TO HIS wife, Isabella Marie, in Paris by early evening. Isabella often traveled with Paul, especially when he traveled to Europe. Isabella spoke French poetically, as one would expect of her. Her father and mother were French. Her father was a retired DGSE Case Officer, and her mother sadly passed during the COVID-19 Pandemic. Isabella was stunning, toned to perfection, with a deep olive-brownish complexion that displayed no hint of imperfection. Isabella desperately wanted Paul to love her, and in a way, Paul did. However, Isabella knew but buried the thoughts deep within her heart that Paul was not a faithful soul. Paul was not loyal to his friends, his company, and certainly not to his family. Isabella felt like an adornment, brought out for display and performance when Paul needed accompaniment. Paul's gentleness and grace faded over the years to the point, that Isabella feared sharing her body with Paul. Paul was rough and, at times, cruel. Gone was the man she fell in love with so long ago. Isabella held her two daughters close, Marie and Olivia, hoping one day Paul would leave.

Paul entered the room and glided over to Isabella, aggressively pulling her close. "Isabella, I have wanted you all day, and now I just can't hold back," smiled Paul.

"Well, I have missed you too, but shouldn't we get ready for dinner?" deflected Isabella.

"No, we have time, I have time," demanded Paul as he undressed Isabella, letting her dress fall to the floor. Isabella stood before Paul as if in a market for sale. Paul inspected her from toe to her long dark hair as if about to feast. Paul thought to himself, *I will pound her like I did, Daniyah, and then I will shower*. Paul grappled with Isabella and pulled her to the bed, ripping her panties off in one move. Paul was powerful, and Isabella surrendered.

Isabella was crying softly as Paul showered. She turned down the offer to shower with Paul, which meant the conquest for the day was not over. Instead, Isabella remained in the bed tangled in sheets, feeling a little less than before and empty. Isabella longed for a connection, but Paul was not interested in anything except himself. Isabella rose from the tangled sheets and made her way to the shower dutifully to prepare for her role as dinner companion and adornment to Paul's vision of a successful businessman. Paul wanted his own company and wanted the power of Ridge and SDS. Paul often lamented the wasted influence that Xander refused to wield. Isabella quickly showered and dressed for the evening, ignoring Paul's glares for not pleasuring him in the shower. Paul, she was sure, was unfaithful. Isabella's beauty was unparalleled and a sleek dress, a pearl necklace, diamond tennis bracelet, and deep lipstick though unnecessary, adorned a beautiful woman. Paul was sure to ignore.

THE BAR HEMINGWAY WAS a favorite haunt for Paul. Xander loved the Ritz Paris. Xander loved the Hemingway legend, Ernst Hemingway bursting into the bar with a gun in hand and ordering a drink, liberating the bar from the Germans. The regal nature appealed to Paul, so much so that his Maryland home entrance replicated the Ritz Paris grand lobby, as did his home bar. The Bar Hemingway is an elegant rustic feel adorned with hand-carved high gloss walls with touches of Hemingway himself. You can almost hear the brash tones of Hemingway's voice regaling the room of his exploits around the world, classic Martini in hand.

Paul and Isabella settled at their table and awaited the guests to arrive. Daniyah and Yuriko tucked away at the opposite end to survey the room before approaching their dinner guests. After a few moments and confirmation from Overwatch and peer agents nestled in to watch the Hotel Ritz Paris, the GOI countersurveillance team gave Daniyah an "all clear."

"Good evening, Ms. Coutre-Ross. You are stunningly beautiful. Mr. Ross does his best, but his words, I am afraid, fall short," flirted Yuriko, introducing himself to Isabella.

"Thank you," returned Isabella with a slight smile.

"Isabella, these are my friends Daniyah and Yuriko, my Turkish customers, who are helping me sell SDS to new markets. Daniyah, Yuriko, may I present my wife, Isabella Coutre-Ross," smirked Paul. Daniyah's and Yuriko's cover story was simple but effective, a Turkish Anti-Malware startup that Paul helped grow with SDS products.

"Isabella, I have heard so much about you. Paul talks about you and the girls all the time. I feel as if I have known you my whole life," offered Daniyah, calculatingly.

"Thank you; I appreciate the kind words. Paul really enjoys working with you, and I do hope your new business is an enormous success," offered Isabella politely while raising her glass. Clinks around the table as each person lifted the glass in response to Isabella's well wishes. Isabella tried to quickly bury the thought that she feared her face might belie, "Paul sleeps with this woman, and then she dares to mention my children." Daniyah caught the slight flash of tension across Isabella's face and thought, *she suspects I am sleeping with Paul. Well, I am and am prepared to kill him, you, and your children for Iran*. Daniyah smiled at Isabella with no hint of her thoughts.

"Paul, our first installment of malware protection is a momentous success. Sales are beyond our projections. We are ready for phase two, ahead of schedule," offered Yuriko, jubilantly.

"Growing too quickly can inhibit your overall strategy, such as growing beyond your current capabilities and unable or strained to support your customers under duress. You don't want your competitors noting your market share before you can defend against a counter-marketing campaign," reproached Paul.

"Ah, you may be correct," conceded Yuriko, "but we have a strong and experienced team, ready to act, and now is our time." Yuriko paused, and then laughed, taking a deep sip of his Mojito cocktail, a favorite of Hemingway. "Just like your American Hemingway, sometimes it is best to charge ahead and take life and opportunity as it comes, and so we shall," taunted Yuriko. "Same price, same account," gritted Yuriko. Paul slipped his hands into the breast pocket of his suit, slowly. His hand returned with two USB drives.

"Very well, I continue to offer my counsel in your best interests and future success. You are a paying customer. This defensive tool will help you against the narrower threat actors that may have an interest in disrupting your services. I wrote this myself," boasted Paul, with a slight hint of a smile.

"Thank you, Paul. We value your commitment to our success," smiled Yuriko leaning forward to take the USB drives. "I will forward the payment to your account when we verify the contents, as agreed. But now, I must have Isabella," paused Yuriko, with a smile, "Please, join me, my dear, for a celebratory dance to your husband's success as a cunning salesman and expert."

"Of course, Yuriko. Paul, do you mind," quaked Isabella, not expecting the offer.

"Please, Isabella. Enjoy yourself; we just made a great sale amongst friends. Yuriko is right. We should celebrate," boasted Paul cagily. Yuriko took Isabella by the hand and led her to a distant corner of the bar area, where enough space afforded an impromptu dancefloor. The Bar Hemingway was mostly empty and would be empty save for their party and the GOI minders, keeping watch.

"This version on the USB drives will allow us to attack deeper and into protected systems?" challenge Daniyah.

"Yes, but not Five Eyes, China, Russia, or any system protected with high-level SDS. Even lower-level SDS may evolve quickly to stop an attack," rigidly protested Paul. "You have not paid me enough to take the risk of treason, but I have given you enough so that your MOIS programmers can evolve this to the next level and hit broader sectors, aviation, financial, energy, medical, and most governments. MOIS should be satisfied," said Paul firmly.

"Isabella. She is a beautiful woman. Yuriko finds her to his liking, at least for a night. Perhaps. Isabella could join us," taunted Daniyah.

"Umph, you are getting what you asked and paid for with the malware. Years ahead of your capabilities. Though, I am not opposed to Yuriko getting her drunk. Maybe, drugged a bit, I could use the leverage at some point," paused Paul with a hint of a devilish grin, "One never knows how far a person will go." Paul reached under the tablecloth and between Daniyah's legs, driving her hands to grip the chair tightly. *Damn*, she thought, *He is good. It will be a shame to kill him too soon. I like how he drives me crazy right here in the Bar and in front of Isabella.*

"XANDER, GABBY, I AM so sorry," quavered Dr. Stone, "I am so sorry; Amelia is stable now. But I almost lost her. Her body seemed to reject or not absorb the IVs and her blood chemistry, already fragile, became dangerously imbalanced. She nearly went into cardiac arrest. Had it not been for the setup at home, she would have passed before we made it here."

Gabby reached out with both hands to Katy's trembling hands. Katy loved Amelia, which was clear. Katy was a competent Doctor and renowned researcher of primitive neuroectodermal tumors. Katy lost her family three years ago. Xander hired her as one of the SDS researchers and requested her transfer to Amelia's physician. The time with the Ridge family and SDS was a blessing. SDS had paid her student loans and her private debt without condition. Katy's bills piled up from her family's sudden loss and prolonged illness that finally consumed her mother just last year. Like many,

Katy found herself lost in grief and found new purpose and hope with SDS.

"Katy," still holding both of Katy's hands, Gabby offered, "Katy, Xander, and I love you and trust you. Amelia's illness is the cause, not you."

"Gabby, this happened too fast and does not make sense," said Katy, still looking at the floor, seeking an answer to the medical enigma.

"Katy, Gabby is right. You are a blessing to our family and SDS," consoled Xander, "tell me more about your suspicions with the IV fluid. Did you say it lost efficacy?"

"Yes, the IVs here worked. The IV was the only parameter we changed, nothing else. Xander, I am a researcher. I brought the IV chemo meds with me since I feared that the Hospital Pharmacy would not have them when needed," recounted Katy, knowledgeably.

"Do you still have an IV from home or any at home?" asked Xander while texting Danny the news.

"Yes, at home in the medical room at home and SDS. It is the same batch," accounted Katy.

"Thank you, please excuse me," purposefully replied Xander. "Danny, thank you. I need SDS Medica to evaluate the IV bags at SDS Medical and in Amelia's medical room at the house. Amelia's blood work was 'shot all to hell.' I suspect bad IVs. Danny, get Jacob. I want to ensure the SDS supply chain on every item, every item," ordered Xander.

"Yes, Sir," responded Danny, jumping into action. The results on Amelia's meds were almost ready, but Danny knew in his gut, that the Nation was under attack. Amelia nearly died.

# CHAPTER FIVE — CHAOS

The assassination of the Rasulov family and the MI6 agent —started the clock —ticking faster with each escalation —with the current package, the world would now know that a new world power is appearing from the shadows. It was ever more important that Daniyah deliver the current cyberweapons to MOIS specialists. The clock pounds in Daniyah's heart —Daniyah was good at her craft and escaping the clutches of the demons —But the Americans and Brits had counterintelligence agents and sources the world over —American capability was—deadly effective. Traversing across Europe and Asia with stolen cyberweapons took a risk with a heavy price —for failure.

Daniyah and Yuriko showed their mastery of spy tradecraft, weaving their way across Europe to catch a flight to Tehran from Istanbul. To disguise their travel Daniyah and Yuriko posed as investors in a social media platform for followers of Islam. Daniyah hid the USB drives in a fake tampon to discourage close inspection. MOIS eagerly awaited Version 2 of Paul's cyberweapon. Version 2 would go with the earlier released Version 1, which had placed substantial portions of the payload throughout the world's industrial control systems, just waiting for the final element of Version 2. Ross stole base versions from SDS and other malware companies. However, Ross was capable of independent design of cyberweapons. MOIS suspected Ross was holding out on capabilities for his gain. For now, MOIS needed Ross to expand Iranian capabilities, so he and his family remained untouchable, but many in MOIS wanted to kill him, including Yuriko.

The flight to Tehran was ahead of schedule due to a strong tailwind. Daniyah was sleeping a few rows up from Yuriko. He and Daniyah slept together, which troubled his Islamic beliefs because Daniyah used sex as an espionage tool. However, Supreme Leader Ali Khamenei excused GOI Case Officers from strict Shia Islamic law. Defense of Iran was a priority. But still, it seemed wrong not to be faithful to tradition. Yuriko gazed down at the terrain flowing by below the plane. The final approach would skirt Azerbaijan and Yuriko reflected on the week's extended mission. Yuriko felt pride in the assassination of Rasulov and his family. He tinged a bit at the brutality of the killing of the teen girl, Lanie. But she was a spawn of Satan. Rasulov had supplied the final piece needed by the Americans and the former American President to murder General Soleimani. Yuriko has spent months in the United States, helping MOIS disrupt the Presidential Election. Yuriko has spent weeks on end in the American Northwest, training ANTIFA and other like groups that he hoped would evolve into lone-wolf threats. Equally, he had trained white supremacist groups as well. Some had skills; Americans were strange, Yuriko pondered. Americans would join their armed forces, law enforcement, and intelligence services and turn on each other in select groups. They held no true beliefs or loyalty as he held.

Yuriko loved his homeland and the rich Persian history of conquest and glory. Yuriko thought of himself in the ole Persian ways. His spirits lifted when he glanced upon the mountain ranges on the horizon. Mount Damavand, the highest peak in Iran and a short distance from Tehran, announced that the flight was nearing the end. He was anxious to get the USB drives to the MOIS cyber weapons team.

Daniyah stirred awake with the slight turbulence and increasing chill of the airplane cabin. Daniyah wrapped herself up tightly in a long sleeve below the knee-length sweater to ward off the chill of the airplane cabin. Whether commercial or a military plane, it was always cold, but not as cold as parachuting into the MOIS training grounds, winter weather survival, or ocean survival training, but cold, nonetheless. To the untrained observer, Daniyah was a petite blond-haired person in her mid-twenties young woman traveling the world on business and enjoying life. She is equally capable of discussing complex business, finance, and cybersecurity issues that she posed as a cover. Indeed, she was adept in business and cybersecurity. Daniyah was a lethal GOI Case Officer and held in high regard by MOIS leadership. Daniyah found solutions to the impossible. Killing never bothered Daniyah, not since childhood. The Rahman family legacy dates to the انقلاب ایران, Iranian Revolution, of 1979. Daniyah's father, then an 18-year-old revolutionary, was a student protest leader and one of the first to breach the United States Embassy. Daniyah's father, Morteza Rahman, earned his bona fides in counterintelligence during the Embassy Siege. The senior Rahman interviewed hostages and sorted through the chaos of captured documents. In the following decades, Morteza honed his tradecraft working intelligence and counterintelligence. Morteza worked to build the Iranian Nuclear Program, countless operations during the eight-year conflict with Iraq, and operations against Israel and the United States. Morteza's most significant contribution to MOIS was, without challenge, Daniyah. Daniyah, trained from birth, was the most cunning and effective intelligence case officer in Iran's service.

The pilot chimed the *Fasten Seat Belt* sign signaling the descent into Tehran. Daniyah shifted in her seat, tensing her spine, as she felt the slightly oversized tampon move. The body cavity held the USB drives with hundreds of landscape pictures. Ross smuggles SDS base cyberweapons in compressed packets of information hidden within his landscape photographs' pixels, a basic steganography technique. Ross disperses the compressed packets across hundreds of pictures in a precise sequence to lower the risk of detection. An encryption algorithm conceals the compressed packets and the sequence to return the code to a program. The scheme was a new twist on old-school espionage tradecraft, hiding in plain sight. The dates of the photographs hid the decryption sequence. The decryption key Ross sends in an innocuous email. Ross and Daniyah correspond via draft messages, never sending a message. Nothing to trace. The more prominent elements, including the weaponized payload written by Ross, use a steganography technique in a sales presentation. The weapon's payload is hidden in plain sight in the slide presentation within the sales pitch's images, graphs, and videos. GOI agents and the Revolutionary Guard would have little trouble assembling the cyberweapon and the payload within hours.

XANDER ARRIVED AT THE SDS SCIF earlier than usual. Danny discerned the absence of the F150, "Boss, did you run to the office this morning?"

"Yeah, I got up early, read the briefing materials, worked out, read to Amelia, checked on the kids, and then decided to run down and get another work out in here in the office," Xander replied analytically.

"A Team's Schedule, tomorrow I will join you, where you go, I go, Boss," dutifully attested Danny.

"That would be nice, Danny. Hit the range later," pulsed Xander.

"Hell, yes!" returned Danny.

The SDS team loves their workout and training regimens. The gyms and firing ranges were full of resources for healthy living, healthcare, exercise, and tactical training. SDS employees often held meetings and design brainstorming sessions on the courts, weight rooms, tracks, and ranges. It was common to see an employee in workout clothes sitting cross-legged, fixated on a laptop, tablet, or notepad. Xander often bellowed in the office, "SDS must remain at the tip of the spear, and so we must train better, longer, and harder than our adversary. 'Good Enough is not a phrase we use. Pursue excellence in all you do.'"

"Good morning, Patrick, team. Please, call the meeting to order Danny and Patrick, please, give the SCIF briefing moment," stated Xander, studiously.

The meeting began, and the SDS team set about reviewing the situational intelligence around the World. Including emerging indicators of a broader cyberattack disrupting medical devices, pharmaceutical supply chains, emergency services, and financial markets. Today was looking dark. Chaos lurked in the shadows.

THE *Daily Intelligence Briefing* moved to the Situation Room, given the rapidly developing threat. The room was smaller than most imagine but capable. With the added attendance, space was a premium. DHS CISA Central, National Counterterrorism Center (NCTC), NSA Cybersecurity Threat Intelligence and Assessment, and U.S. Cyber Command joined by secure video conference. The scene foretold a pivotal moment for President Hammond, as he entered the room and steeled himself for what was coming.

CODY LOOKED AROUND the kitchen, mentally checking off the list: *keys, wallet, phone, and coffee.* Ah, and the backpack already slung over one shoulder. *Cody is a mess, and I swear he would lose his head if God had not attached it so firmly. How will I trust him with this baby when she arrives*? thought Anna, smiling behind her coffee cup, watching Cody dance around, checking off his list. Cody and Anna expected their first child, a baby girl, due in a few weeks. Prospective names clung to a paper on the fridge held by a flat magnet advertising some farm implement. The Hall Farm supplied several nearby Augusta, Savanah, and Charleston restaurants. Cody and Anna raised chickens for farm-to-fork restaurants for roasting and frying chickens and organic eggs. A small pasture enabled them to raise goats and lambs. Anna crafted the best goat cheeses in the Southeast. The eggs and cheeses from Hall Farm were valuable commodities in the coastal farm-to-fork white-table-cloth eateries.

"Anna, I need to run into town before hitting the fields to transfer the money for the Doctor's appointment," reported Cody. Cody needed the final payment for the OB appointment later that afternoon. He and Anna were living their dream and owned a small farm but with a high-deductible insurance plan.

"Great, Baby, I Love You; please text, so I know you are safe, BUT NOT WHILE YOU ARE DRIVING, CODY!" replied Anna with an elevated spousal tone.

The drive into town took a little more than 20 minutes, less if Cody knew where the Sheriff was sitting. However, as predicted, today, the Sheriff was at the Wagon Wheel, eating breakfast and flirting with the staff as if they all did not know he was married. Cody sped up a bit on the final trot to town and beat the time clock running in his head. Cody felt excited, especially after the first bolt of coffee made its way through his system. He bounded into the bank, "Good Morning, Janie; how are you?"

"I am well, Cody Hall. How are Ms. Anna, this morning, and that baby girl," quipped Janie. Hancock Landing, Georgia, was a small southern town just across the Georgia – South Carolina line. Small towns were a curse and a blessing. Your neighbor knew your business often before you did, it seemed. But Cody and Anna loved the feel of small-town Southern life and wanted to raise their children here.

"Janie, Anna is doing great, and the baby is right, where she needs to be, so says the Doc," Cody replied jubilantly, "I just need to withdraw the last $700, and I am finished with the baby's payment plan."

"Son, you have another thing coming if you think that is the last bill, especially if you said baby girl," quipped an elderly customer.

"Cody, did you overdraw your account?" said Janie worriedly.

"Of course not; Anna would have my butt. Why?" replied Cody.

"Well, your account looks wrong. Something is wrong here. Bess, can you come here and look?" summoned Janie. However, Janie's and all three tellers all had the same concern. Each customer's account reported a zero balance, as each protested. Frank, an elderly customer, clutched his chest and leaned into the counter, suddenly struggling to breathe. Bess grabbed a phone and called 911, but the call did not ring through. Cody leapt over to keep old-man Frank's head from crashing into the counter and floor. Cody at once checked Frank over and started CPR. Cody's Army Medic skills flowed through his muscles on autopilot, keeping Frank alive. A small town's virtue is the proximity of services in town. After Janie ran to sound the alarm, most of the fire department and medical staff ran from across the street to the bank. The medics quickly stabilized Frank and loaded him into the ambulance. Bess was still talking to 911 in Oregon, of all places. Despite calling 911 from the bank's phone or her cell phone, the call routed to a different city each time, just not Augusta.

"Cody, grab a cup of coffee and give us a minute to look at these accounts. I am sure it is a computer glitch," requested Bess, clearly addled.

"No problem," replied Cody.

Cody texted Anna to share what had happened at the bank with Frank. Cody held back the concern that their accounts showed zero. He was sure it was a computer glitch. But there was no reason to alarm Anna, so he shared that Frank had just had a heart attack and that the bank was having trouble getting the computers to work.

*Computer glitch, I am sure*, Anna thought to herself and replied to Cody's message with a simple, "ILY."

Cody walked over to the diner, *ARNOLD'S DINER*. *ARNOLD'S DINER* was an old train car resting on tracks long enough to hold the train and create the rustic old-time feel. The train car was an old *Chicago West Pullman* dining car with the original short-order kitchen. Palmetto trees adorned each end of the train car. Arnold had added a wooden deck so patrons could picnic and enjoy the Savanah River and wetlands' view. The mix of Palmetto trees, Saw Palmetto Palm ground cover, and the deciduous trees blended a unique Southern backdrop for small-town southern life. Arnold, the owner, was a crusty retired sailor, who claims to have served in WWII and might have, but no one really knew how old he was. Stooped over and wrinkled, Arnold could tussle eggs, bacon, hash browns, coffee, and peach pie all day and most of the night, without a hint of stress or tiredness. He loved his customer and the town-folk, even those that crossed over from South Cackalacky, as he called South Carolina.

"Cody, if you ain't got cash, I can't help, ya," bellowed Arnold, "the dern credit machine ain't working, and I can't raise any help on the phone!"

"No problem, I have cash. Can I have the breakfast special?" requested Cody.

"Yap," bellowed Arnold.

Cody looked down at his phone and saw a text from Anna, "Please, CALL." Cody quickly called Anna. Cody's mind was racing, "is she okay? The baby, what!"

> "CODY, the electric company is here! John says that we did not pay our bill for two months, and he has an order to shut us off. He is on the phone right now with the office. I have the canceled checks but online, no

payments! I checked our bank accounts, checking, savings, and our 401K. CODY! It is all gone! Argggh, oh, Cody, no," exclaimed Anna.

Cody was frantic. He ran out of the ARNOLD'S DINER right as Arnold brought his plate of eggs, bacon, hash browns, and coffee to the counter. Cody ran across the street, found Rob, a Paramedic, and asked for an ambulance. Rob grabbed his bag, jumped in a City Emergency Truck used for off-road emergencies, and chased Cody's truck. Cody was an Army Medic, currently in the Reserves, fully capable and equal in skill to a paramedic, but this was Anna. Rob graduated from Augusta High School with Anna. Rob's mind was racing with what he might face and the Hall Farm. Cody passed John's utility truck with flashing lights, speeding towards town. After several failed 911 calls to Seattle, Los Angeles, and Topeka, John had scooped up Anna. Anna had passed out, and when John saw blood on Anna's clothes, he jumped into action, scooping her in his arms and loading Anna into his truck. Cody saw Anna slumped over and jammed on the brakes into reverse, and in a perfect *James Bond esque, J-turn* was right on John's tail. Rob saw the move and turned around and pursued Cody, yet again racing towards town. Rob managed to pass Cody and John and escorted the trio to the County Hospital. Rob radioed the Emergency Room, advising of an incoming priority.

THE COUNTY EMERGENCY Room was an apocalyptic scene from a horror movie. All the medical devices malfunctioned, giving false readings. The hospital power, including the generator, kept fluctuating. The phones are ringing off-the-hook with 911 requests for people on the other side of the United States. The only medical devices still functioning are old-school devices with no Internet connectivity. Dr. Parker had a flashlight, blood pressure cuff, and stethoscope and was in the mix treating patience. He almost lost Frank, who suffered a heart attack in the bank. The news of losing his money, and his life savings was too much for Frank's heart. The defibrillator overcharged and almost killed Frank, but Dr. Parker caught the setting. After a few failed attempts, he grabbed a wall unit with success. Frank was resting on IV fluids and awaiting surgery.

ROB PULLED THROUGH the Emergency Room awning with lights and sirens to get the Nurses attention, allowing John to pull under the canopy for Anna. Cody parked and jumped out of the truck, almost floating before he felt his feet underneath him, running towards Anna. Cody, Rob, and the ER staff reached Anna simultaneously. Anna was still loopy but awake. Cody scooped up Anna, gently placed her on the gurney, and helped Rob wheel her into an awaiting bay. Cody searched Dr. Parker's face for a sign that Anna and the baby were okay. Cody dropped to his knees, begging God to take him instead.

"TESS, PLEASE GET US started," requested the President.

"Dr. Greene, please, give the briefing and include supporting elements as needed. Dr. Freeman, General Wright, remained focused on breaking news. Dr. Greene, if you please," Tess said sharply. Everyone in the room straightened and leaned in as if strapping into a rocket about the thrust from the surface of the Earth.

> "Mr. President, at zero four hundred Eastern Standard, DHS CISA Central and NSA detected a cyberattack targeting the Financial, Energy, Emergency Services, Healthcare, and Communication Sectors. The payload targets each differently. Connected medical devices and

devices needing limited connectivity for upgrades, maintenance, or checking vital signs, controlling IV fluids and IV medicines disparately failed across the United States. Sir, early estimates note dozens of deaths. Early estimates note a hundred deaths from heart attacks, car crashes, and other injuries. The attack routed calls to 911 to the wrong centers all over the country. EMS was unable to respond in time. Sir, we estimate that 30 percent, 40 million, of American Households across the country woke up to empty checking, savings, and investment accounts. Sir, 64 million more woke up to limited electrical power or billing errors threatening shutoff for non-payment on otherwise current accounts. Some of the larger energy companies with smart meters turned off at zero six hundred. Sir, one MI6 assessment notes a disruption weeks ago in the pharmaceutical supply chain, altering formulas of hundreds of maintenance medicines sourced from India and other Asian suppliers, representing over 20 percent of the global supply chain of generic medicine. Sir, we estimate the loss of life from altered pharmaceuticals to be over 1,000. Sir, several states report widespread chaos in cities," reported Malik.

"Is this attack limited to the United States? What is happening to our allies, our adversaries?" queried President Hammond.

"Sir, General Wright can expand. However, the IC detects attack patterns across the World. We do not see such in Iran, Russia, China, or North Korea," reported Malik.

"Sir, Dr. Greene is correct. I will add that the NSA has learned during our briefing that air defense networks in China, Russia, and on the Korean peninsula have intermittent contacts with inbound aircraft on trajectories to strike military targets," pledged General Wright.

"Are these real attacks," questioned the President.

> "No, our sensors and intelligence do not indicate a real attack. Further, we assess that Russia and China have only dispatched interceptor planes and have raised defensive postures. China severed its connection to the Internet. North Korea is the worry. Kim Jung-un surged offensive capability to the MDL and activated air defenses. Secretary Freeman, the NSA is sending an IC alert to DHS to warn civilian aviation. Secretary Porter, the NSA is sending the same to State," added General Wright.

The President stood and strolled to the working end of the Situation Rooms, home to the monitors and computers processing the incoming data —Hammond's familiar intelligence legacy —pressing his thoughts to analysis. The room snapped up —but seated with Hammond's hand gestures, never taking his gaze off the monitors and news feeds rolling story after story of the effects on American lives. The room fell silent for a moment contemplating the risk of North Korea, launching an offensive into South Korea. Or worse, launching against Japan or the United States.

> "My God, this is the new 9-11. Asymmetrical warfare is a nightmare scenario. Michael, prepare the Defense Department for counterstrikes and coordinate with General Wright. General Robinson ready Cybercommand, set the DEFENSE CONDITION TO 3, and move to THREAT LEVEL CHARLIE to all U.S. Commands. Tess, Malik, and Bluma work with Ridge to figure out how to stop this attack. Rebecca, return to State and coordinate with Five Eyes, China, and Russia. I

want to simmer offensive postures down before this gets out of hand. General Roberts and Dr. Greene coordinate with CIA and Frost to coalesce the IC. This is all-hands-on-deck! I expect you to remember the lessons of 9-11 and share intelligence and resources. One Nation One Response. Henry, keep Special Agent Kelly with Ridge and hunt these BASTARDS down. Get the FBI focused on counterintelligence within the United States. They must have assets here! Find them! Team, this is our moment, and we will not falter. We are under attack. Get us out of this CHAOS, DISMISSED," ordered a resolute President.

# CHAPTER SIX — SHEPHERD DEFENSE SYSTEMS

The SDS Daily Intelligence Briefing concluded with the collaboration calls with DHS Secretary Bluma Freeman, Whitehouse Chief of Staff Dr. Betty "Tess" Mercier, and Dr. Malik Greene, CIA Presidential Daily Briefer. This was an extraordinary group of patriots. Though Secretary Freeman held reservations, the private-public collaboration rose to the 9-11 esque challenge to stop this attack, find and neutralize the adversary, and reverse the Financial Sector's effects.

Paul Ross, Vice President of SDS Commercial Services Division (CSD), arrived at SDS Fort Mill in response to the recent breaking Global cyberattacks. Paul led the development and sales meeting in the CSD wing of the SDS Headquarters Compound. Paul led the commercial development of cybersecurity, including advanced firewalls, encryption, intrusion detection, and denial of service defenses. Additionally, CSD created products for personal use for mobile devices and home networks. Paul worked from the Washington D.C. office and monthly traveled to the Fort Mill Headquarters.

Founder and Chief Executive Officer Xander Ridge led the SDS Government and Military Division (GMD). SDS GMD developed next-generation cybersecurity defenses, encryption, and cyberweapons for the U.S. Government. Though new to SDS, Paul wanted to replace Xander as Division leader of the Government and Military Division. Paul was frustrated with Xander and the tightness and secrecy of the Government and Military Division. Xander and

Danny did not allow Paul or his division's employees near the Government and Military areas. Paul wanted to separate his division from Xander and his company. But this would never happen with Xander at the helm and with the closeness of Xander's team. Xander and his team behaved as though they were still active U.S. Military and Intelligence Community members. Xander and the Government and Military Division team were reservists. They held active Top-Secret Security Compartmentalized Information security clearances and Codeword clearances. Paul's division had to break all ties with the U.S. Government and agree not to interact with any Government Official, federal-state-local. The SDS Ethics Office was strict and relentless on such policies. The SDS Insider Threat Team enforced all ethics and oversight policies. SDS Chief Security Officer Danny Bell ensured no one left SDS with intellectual property and kept a vice-like grip on all cyberweapons, including ones to assess the effectiveness of Paul's division.

"Xander, Paul asked if you would like to join the CSD meeting after the Briefing and make a few remarks," shared Mia, the Government and Military Division Executive Assistant. Paul wanted Xander to stop by the Commercial Services Division (CSD) meeting and see the sales volume of CSD products since the cybersecurity crisis appeared a few weeks ago. The last 24 hours' events would drive sales beyond current expectations, especially with the proposed price increases for commercial and residential clients.

"Sure, I can go down. Danny, would you like to come with me," responded Xander.

"Yeah, let me grab another refill on the coffee, and I will join you. What do you think Paul has cooking?" asked Danny.

"I am not sure, but I have my concerns," pined Xander.

"Yeah, so does Scout. I told her to review Paul's travel and scan his devices. I want a full review," informed Danny.

Xander was not sure a full insider threat investigation was proper. However, he trusted Danny since the Teams and trusted Scout Moreau, SDS Insider Threat Vice President. Scout was a capable counterintelligence agent. She was equally prepared for the next black-tie event or HALO jump into combat. Scout was hardcore. If Scout is concerned, Xander is concerned.

"TEAM, I AM HONORED to share that SDS Founder and CEO Xander Ridge and CSO Daniel Bell will join our CSD meeting in a few minutes," postured Paul. Paul shared the recent increases in sales under his leadership with the team. He was thrilled to report a ten-fold increase in revenue between recent fiscal quarters.

"Xander, Danny, welcome to CSD. Can you give us some insight into current events?" postured Paul. The room could see the concern and strain on Xander's face. SDS employees loved Xander and Gabby. Xander dedicated himself to the development, safety, and security of every member of the SDS family. SDS benefits were the envy of the corporate world. Salaries hit 150 percent of market value when most board rooms targeted 85 percent. SDS employees enjoyed cost-free health and fitness care free tuition for employees and family members. SDS leadership focused on each employee and ensured each knew their value and purpose. SDS turnover was near zero, and those seeking fortunes in other areas had SDS's full support. However, SDS was not immune to rotten apples. The Government and Military Division Insider Threat Team ensured that SDS employees and families remained faithful to SDS's ethics and moral principles.

"Good morning, CSD. I am proud of your recent achievements and arduous work. The customer satisfaction metrics are top tier, the best in the industry. John, thank you for traveling to Texas to help the city of Odessa deal with the ransomware attack. You saved the city a ton by eradicating the ransomware and got the city behind SDS CSD firewalls, intrusion detection, and anti-malware. Ann, your work in Topeka was outstanding. Thank you. You helped protect the City Hospital from a DDOS attack and helped avoid paying a ransom. That is excellent work," beamed Xander.

"Xander, how is Amelia? I heard she was rushed to the hospital?" asked Becky.

"Thank you, Becky. Yes, Amelia gave us a scare, and she is tough and fighting. Her medicines and IVs were bad, and the recent attack on the pharmaceutical supply chain corrupted the IV fluids and the integrated chemotherapy. Katy and Gabby brought her home early this morning. Thank God for Katy. Thank you for asking. That means a lot to Gabby and me," replied Xander with a smile to the room.

"Xander, are we under attack?" asked John.

"Yes," replied Xander. "We do not know by whom or why or the objective. I apologize, but I cannot share working theories, and I cannot share the extent or vector of attack. Government and Military Division is collaborating with the U.S. Government, and it will work day-and-night to stop the attack, seek justice, and set the chaos straight."

"Xander, this is a great segue into sales projections and the perfect time to discuss the sliding scale increase in the prices of products and services. As you can see here..." started Paul but halted when Xander raised his hand to stop and stood up.

"Paul, let me make this clear. SDS will not profit from an attack on the United States and the American People. This is a time to increase our philanthropy and civic duty. This is the time to rally around the Stars and Stripes and act as one Nation..." retorted Xander, before Paul cut him off.

"Xander, I appreciate the tagline of duty and service. I served my Country, as well. I wrote code and the early days of cybersecurity and cyberweapons when we crossed the threshold of just moving or manipulating data into affecting real-world control systems. My point is that this is the time to use the SDS Commercial Services Division's quality to drive our competitors out of the game. SDS can own the market share. We can all be multi-millionaires," retorted Paul.

"Paul, I respect your point. If SDS was a traditional company with a profit-centered purpose, Paul, you would be 100 percent correct. A traditional company would lower your base pay and reward commission sales. But you know what that gets you, Paul?" quipped Xander.

"Rich," replied Paul in a cavalier tone.

"Paul, you are rich. SDS employees are all wealthy. SDS pays employees well above the market value and bonuses based on metrics of performance, not sales. Paul, the mission is to protect the United States. We are a defense contractor with a Commercial Service Division. Our mission is to protect the confidentiality of our customers' networks and data, protect the integrity of their networks and data, and ensure the availability and capability of their networks. Our mission is one of TRUST. We earn trust with every action. We base the Commercial Services Division metrics on our customer's mission's success – if they succeed, we succeed. If a customer's network or data goes down or is lost to a cyberattack, that is on us, and we own it. That requires a relationship beyond a Rolodex of contacts to sell products," coached Xander. SDS was unique. SDS paid all medical expenses for employees and extended family and other benefits directly from the Company, not docked from a paycheck. The concept was expensive. But Xander and the key leaders in the Government and Military Division owned SDS. Xander and the SDS Leadership lead with a '*begin with the end in mind precept*' and led personally and professionally principle-centered lives. The compensation and benefit construct produced incredible performance and an effective organization, even under duress.

"Xander, you are wrong," rejected Paul, "when the rest of the world is going one-way, it is foolish to think you can outsmart the world and go the opposite direction!" Danny bristled at the challenge from Paul. Paul was a veteran, but he never put himself in harm's way or led others. Paul graduated from the Naval Academy and rose to Commander. Paul never served in a forward command or in the Fleet. Danny respected Paul's capabilities but could never trust anyone who could not act to better others. Danny served with Xander in the Special Operations Teams. Danny was a retired SEAL Commander. Xander was a capable leader and battled-tested and battled-hardened. Danny did not appreciate Paul's challenge to Xander. But Danny was a professional and restrained himself from knocking Paul's pearly white teeth back into his throat.

"Paul, I appreciate your perspective. You are not wrong. This is SDS, and this is how we do what we do. It is a free country. You are free to make your choices, and I will fully support and respect you. However, I do not want to own and lead a profit-centered company," attested Xander with the command and composure of an experienced leader of warriors.

"Well, I appreciate the debate, Xander. I do. I appreciate you coming down to CSD for the pep-talk," closed Paul. Paul was seething mad inside. But he was a retired Naval Officer and knew it was time to retreat from his point for the moment. Paul needed to remain at SDS for a few more months to steal the advanced cyberweapon, Version 3 (V3). V3 was an early development of quantum computing capable of rapid decryption and delivering a payload before even the best firewall or intrusion detection can deny or detect. In a security schema designed to deter, detect, delay, and deny, V3 moved faster than current defenses allowing the threat actor to disrupt operations, deny access, degrade operations, or even destroy. V3 is a threat to China, Russia, and likely the United States Government and Department of Defense systems.

"XANDER, WHAT HAPPENED with Paul? Is he NUTS?" cried Mia.

"Well. Paul values glory, pride, and personal reward and lives a vibrant life. Paul has a vision of a traditional commercial company, driven and motivated by profit. SDS is not. SDS is principle-centered and strives to build trust and of service to others. But Paul and Danny had a vigorous debate and settled the matter," reported Xander.

"Well, I have always wondered. Why did you hire a person like Paul?" blurted Mia.

"He just doesn't fit the values. Xander, if this is how he treats you and how he treats his employees, how do you think he treats our customers!" exclaimed Mia.

"Mia, you are wise beyond your years and ears. A trait I dearly love about you," exhaled Xander.

"I hired him as a diamond in the rough. I thought that Danny, Jacob, Amira, Kelly, and I could smooth out the edges. I fear I underestimated the challenge," reflected Xander.

"Paul's older brother was his father's pride and joy —Paul was a mother's project. Paul resented his brother's relationship with his father, a New England English professor and world-renowned author. Paul's father invested in his eldest son —local hero-football star-collegiate athlete-stellar law student-FBI Agent-then an Assistant Director," shared Xander.

"I never knew," replied Mia.

"Yes, Paul is an elitist and a chauvinist —but he is just trying too hard —chasing a father's approval he will never gain —so Paul overdoes it everywhere," reported Xander, "For my part, I have tried to be a good friend —a good coach —and note successes. But I see that I cannot provide what Paul needs —perhaps doing more harm."

"Mia, have we heard from Gabby or Katy?" primed Xander.

"I will check on Amelia, Xander. Don't worry," replied Mia, calming down, "Amira and Scout are waiting for you in the Executive Conference Room. I will send in lunch as soon as the kitchen sends the meals up."

JULIUS LYONS, SDS VICE President of Intelligence, was in London to settle the Webb family's affairs. Julius attended the funeral the day before with Jack's Widow, twin university-aged boys, and former MI6 colleagues and teammates. SDS lawyers settled the Webb Estate, funded the Government Service Pension gaps, and covered the boys' university expenses. With the help of Ken, Julius developed a security plan and system for the Webb family. As Julius prepared to return to the States, Chief of Secret Intelligence Service, MI6, Sir Jonathan Hawkins, summoned Julius to MI6 for a briefing and to call his friend, Xander, for a secured video conference. MI6 uncovered a link to the death of STURGEON and the recent cyberattacks and needed Xander to fill in the blanks of the mystery. How did MOIS advance its capabilities so quickly?

THE MI6 BUILDING, SIS Building, at Vauxhall Cross is an impressive structure resting on the banks of the River Thames in Central London. The building is vulnerable to attack to the untrained eye and is merely another unique architectural design in London. To the trained eye, the Babylon-on-Thames is a fortress holding the State Secrets of the United Kingdom. The MI6 Building had the stately look of a castle with multiple roof lines and round rook-like structures set like bookends with twin towers in the center.

The spans of glass sparkled like diamonds on sunny days. They flooded the interior of the 130,000 square feet of offices, laboratories, server rooms, and secret meeting rooms with natural light. To Julius, it was home.

The Chief of Secret Intelligence Services' office suite rested in the center, enabling a complete view of the Thames River. The office suite was an architecture of classic wood and the British brass look, and modern open glass. The glass held a secret. During a secured conversation or video call, a press of a button turned the glass opaque instantly. The escaping air pressed from the room harkened a sense of dread as the room sealed.

"Good morning, Julius! Welcome Home, Ole Boy," bellowed Chief Hawkins. Standing in the office, Julius never shook the classic James Bond feeling but resisted calling Sir Jonathan Hawkins, M.

"I am well, Sir," replied Julius with a warm smile and handshake.

"Julius, TO Jack!" championed Hawkins, as he hoisted a stout cocktail glass with a liberal portion of an Old Fashioned into Julius' hand. The visit was not just about saluting a downed colleague, and Julius knew Hawkins wanted to share and learn information directly from Xander and SDS. Hawkins should share and request such directly with his counterpart, Director of the Central Intelligence Agency Christian Frost.

SDS HIRES FOR PASSION, talent, and commitment, not just for credentials and academic accolades. Xander learned early in Joint Special Operations Command that passion, skill, and commitment were the attributes needed to survive the horrors of the battlefield. Those are the people that just do not quit.

Dr. Jennifer Garcia leads the SDS Malware Forensics Team. Jenn is tenacious, constantly finding and delivering the impossible. Her parents immigrated to the United States from Bogota, Columbia, to escape the violence and retribution against Columbian Military Intelligence Officers. Jenn learned the art of intelligence tradecraft from her father, but her passion for life from her mother, whom she lost, last year in the COVID-19 Pandemic. She leads a team of 20 talented specialists with a variety of skills, talents, and accolades in the field of cybersecurity. Dr. Garcia's peers joined the effort to analyze the current malware ravaging the United States and most of the World.

Dr. Samantha Williams leads the SDS Digital Forensics team. Sam is renowned in the Digital Forensics space and oft counseled the NSA, CIA, FBI, and the private sector. Along with her peers, recruitment offers arrive weekly, daily. But SDS was an incredible culture. Sam was married to SDS Vice President of Cyberweapons Development, Trinity Williams. Trinity's mother was a devout Catholic and named him after the Father, the Son, and the Holy Spirit. Trinity, though religious, loved life and libation and was committed to Sam and his work. Sam and Trinity hoped to follow the Ridge Family and add several children to their family. However, Sam had lost a baby last Spring upon the emergence of COVID-19. Trinity has been there for Sam at every turn, but his heart ached.

The team unpacked the malware and readied the presentation for Xander and the leadership team. The malware was familiar to Xander, and he was correct.

THE SDS GOVERNMENT and Military Division development area and laboratories had the appearance of the set of Star Trek Command Deck. The lab area was a circular room with twenty-foot ceilings and walls coated with customized fiber optic cables creating a dense pixelization. The effect created a floor-to-ceiling monitor. The video sphere could complete 360-degrees of a massive screen or endless combinations of segmented displays with the specialized software. The cool element was the ability to toss an image from a tablet, laptop, or phone onto the wall.

You can write, draw, and manipulate with your hands with the virtual glasses. Each lab position allowed you to sit-stand. The standing circle desk enabled the user to twist and turn to any desired position. And if the user needed to have a secured call or privacy, a few sections and a dome extended from the floor, enclosing the entirety of the contraption. The inside view was like the main room with a complete video sphere. If the user wanted to drift in the deep ocean or float into space, the choice was at hand. The lab floor and every corner and edge held hidden micro-LEDs allowing for a wholly customized lighting pattern. The specialized floor also functioned as a monitor, as did the domed ceiling. If selected, the room could appear as though one stood inside a perfect sphere. The look was, in a word, cool.

Xander loved the lab area, especially when the team had the Milky Way Galaxy in sphere-mode. Xander entered the space quietly and began absorbing the data displayed throughout. Jenn always showed analytics from left-to-right and top-to-bottom. Xander's ability to quickly absorb enormous amounts of data and get to the bottom was impressive, even amongst the talented elite.

"Jenn, I see a common thread in the malware's construction. What did Y'all, name the malware?" asked Xander.

"CHAOS is the codeword for this version of the cyberattack. We confirmed with CISA Central, CHAOS," confirmed Jenn.

"Hmm, it is appropriate," accepted Xander.

"Jenn, this is an early cyberweapon issued to Cyber Command in 2006, if memory serves. However, the payload is a newer code. The structure is such that, well, rushed, but effective, cold. It is familiar," proffered Xander.

"It should," announced Jenn flatly.

THE SDS SCIF MIRRORED The White House Situation Room. Xander loved the Situation Room, and given the opportunity with SDS, Xander emulated the Situation Room, just improved. Improvements led to a larger room, comfortable chairs, faster technology, and positional line-of-sight to the video feed allowing each person to keep eye contact with each presenter and speaker. Though enticing to civilians, Military Grade was not always the best choice.

"Jenn is this an early SDS cyberweapon developed for Cyber Command, circa 2006?" opened Xander. Jenn was not one to mince words. CHAOS was an SDS design.

"Yes," confirmed Jenn, "However, the code has been modified recently at the same time as the payload. The structure and technique of the improvements and payload is recent technology but immature tradecraft."

"Jesus, this is an SDS product?" exclaimed Jacob, "We need to advise Counsel."

"It is, but we released this before some of us finished dissertations. This is old technology, just SDS good. However, the good news is that we can stop this and undo the damage in a few weeks. We do need Justice. The money from the financial transactions is bouncing around the Globe. Still, I suspect will coalesce to banks friendly with Iran and North Korea," reported Jenn.

"This is amazing work. Thank You!" applauded Xander, "Patrick, can you get Justice moving and the IC?"

"Yes, Sir, this is great news. Considering I am one of the millions that are sitting on empty accounts," grimaced Special Agent Patrick Kelly.

"Xander? Julius and I are following leads that lead to Paul Ross," Scout reported flatly. The structure of SDS empowered Scout Moreau to investigate without approval from SDS Leadership, including Xander. Transparency and accountability were vital SDS principles. Scout's parents were older and retired "employees" of the French Government. Rumor held that her parents were French Intelligence officers assigned to the United Nations in New York City during the peak of the Cold War. Scout was their only child and learned the intelligence tradecraft early. Scout was stunningly intelligent, and though she tried to disguise it, gorgeous.

> "Julius, Danny, and I opened a case to review Paul's entire history," opened Scout, "Paul travels to Europe, often. Sales in Europe support his work. However, the metrics for service do not. There are no requests for service, none. Paul is a good programmer and a retired Naval Officer, but he is not a case officer or an analyst. I found mistakes in the travel and usage history on the first hotel room's power, data usage, and call history," Scout recounted factually.

"First Room?" asked Jacob, SDS Chief Financial Officer, "What do you mean First Room?"

"Books a hotel room, check-in, and then slips out the back and travels to the real destination. I suspect he is not aware of using the room and consuming consumables, so it looks like he is there when he is not. He blew his cover," explained Kyla, former Mossad, and SDS Executive Protection.

"Precisely," affirmed Scout, "Patrick. It is time for the FBI to take this case. But I am going to keep investigating. Paul Ross is selling us out. I just cannot prove it. YET."

"As part of the Insider Threat re-assessment process, he answered, Caligula as the person most admired. Who the Hell admires a self-absorbed tyrant?" protested Scout.

"Paul's investments are risky and questionable. He has several foreign investments with European competitors and third-tier vendors. Though we prohibit investment in primary and secondary tier vendors, the aggregate of his investments is a concern. His net worth aligns with the position, as does his home, cars, loans, and other credit. He spends more of our money than his own. In the context of CARLA F BAD and MINCES, he is vulnerable to exploitation by money, alcohol, playing his ego, and sex," reported Scout.

SDS Government and Military Division must follow U.S. Government laws and regulations for staff working on Government contracts, including staffing an Insider Threat Program led by Scout. CARLA F. BAD and MINCES are mnemonic devices to remember the key elements of a background investigation. Both maps guide a case officer to exploit, turn, and manage a source. CARLA F. BAD stands for character, associates, reputation, loyalty, ability, finances, bias, alcohol, and drugs. MINCES, another mnemonic, stands for money, ideology, nationalism, compromise, ego, and sex.

JULIUS TURNED TO GAZE upon The SIS Building once more, one moment to reflect on a life's investment in the security of Her Majesty's Service. He reflected on tours hunting terrorists from the Irish Republican Army to ISIS. Julius realized a lack of peace in his life. Had he failed, he asked quietly of himself? Julius placed his hand on the roof of the SDS black armored sedan and motioned to the driver that it was time to return to the airport. An SDS plane was waiting for his return to the States. He would call Xander from the plane. Hawkins shared the concerns of MI6 of a suspected American that met with a high-ranking GOI Case Officer in Algeciras, Spain.

Julius did not believe in coincidences. Julius and Scout discussed Insider Threat Risk daily. Paul F. Ross was on Julius' list. Paul was a threat. If Paul is the mystery American cavorting in the South of Spain with a GOI Case Officer, Julius needed to move fast.

"GOOD MORNING, TESS. Dr. Garcia 'Jenn' and the team have completed the first assessment of CHAOS," opened Xander.

"Good morning, Xander and SDS! I hear you may have good news, well, some good news. Xander, how is Amelia, if I may, while we are still gathering here in the Situation Room?" greeted Tess.

"We do have news. Good is still under assessment. Tess, thank you for asking. Amelia is still in a coma. But she is home and well cared for by Dr. Stone," reported Xander.

Expected in the Situation Room for the CHAOS update were DHS Secretary Dr. Bluma Freeman, CIA Presidential Daily Briefer Dr. Malik Greene, NSA Director General Shawn Wright, and chaired by White House Chief of Staff Dr. Betty "Tess" Mercier.

"Xander, I understand that CHAOS is an older version of an SDS design developed for Olympic Games?" began Tess.

"Yes, it is. However, an unknown person has updated the base CHAOS structure's code and customized the payload to attack current Zero-Day vulnerabilities. If a company does not manage its network and patch devices, then the vulnerability to CHAOS increases. Therefore, CHAOS was not as bad as intended. But still bad," reported Xander. Tess queried the room for concurrence. SDS embedded members of the IC on the Malware Investigation Team.

"What about HERON? Dr. Greene. Are U.S. networks secure?" tested Tess.

"Yes, Ma'am. HERON and CHAOS did not affect U.S. networks," attested Malik, factually.

"Tess, someone captured this code at the target, on the way to the target, or stole from either you or me," Xander stated flatly.

"Any leads, Xander?" checked Tess.

"Yes, Ma'am. We are coordinating with the FBI and have kept constant access for oversight at SDS and will," accounted Xander, as he settled the record of transparency. Xander insisted on embedded oversight of SDS.

"Special Agent Kelly requested an undercover cyber agent from Headquarters. Special Agent Reyes is on his way here, as we speak," reported Xander, "Tess, the suspect worked for both of us during the period of the development of what is now CHAOS."

"Xander, Thank You. DHS is passing your findings to the Critical Infrastructure Information Sharing Coordinating Councils. This research will help each stop CHAOS. I understand SDS developed an anti-malware to eradicate the payload?" checked Secretary Freeman.

"Correct, Secretary Freeman. SDS is supplying the code to the Government for disbursement. SDS is supplying the code at no costs to our customers, well, anyone who needs help recovering from CHAOS," insisted Xander.

"Free," challenged General Wright.

"Sir, Yes, Sir. If you are my neighbor and your house is on fire, I do not charge you to use my garden hose or phone to call the Fire Department. We put the fire out," piped Xander.

"You are a rare breed, young man. But I should expect no less from a JSOC Army Ranger. Son, you get these BASTARDS," proclaimed General Wright.

"Yes, Sir," snapped Xander, "We will."

# CHAPTER SEVEN — A PROMISE

IPhones began buzzing and ringing at zero one hundred in the Ridge owner's suite. With the honed instincts of a mom, Gabby was on the phone and processing the news before Xander stirred enough to process the buzzing. Katy was calling and texting in an excited flurry. Amelia was awake and sipping water on her own. Still too weak to speak, she looked around the room and showed awareness of her room, at home. Maddie, Amelia's Golden Labrador, was by her side, wagging. Maddie wagged so hard in the excitement that her backend slid side to side on the hardwood floor like a broom. Katy brushed Amelia's hair and gently touched her face. For the moment, Amelia's vitals looked good.

"Amelia, Mom, and Dad are on the way over from their room," assured Katy. Gabby's feet did not touch the floor as she floated to Amelia. Gabby had just laid down for a few hours' sleep and had thought of sleeping again in Amelia's room. But Xander was home with the first good news in weeks.

Xander spotted Gabby's quick pace across the Ridge Mansion and smiled. With the grace of royalty, Gabby weaved the obstacle course and maze of rooms from the Owner's Suite to Amelia's room. The kid's end of the Ridge Mansion was the fun, happy place with the movie theatre, game room, pool hall, and one of the many causeways to the pools, tennis, and basketball courts. Xander and Gabby enjoyed equal access from the other end of the mansion. In total, the home was ten thousand square feet boasting ten bedrooms, 15 bathrooms, two gyms, a spa, two outdoor kitchens, a Hemingway-esque bar with connecting library, a vice both he and

Paul shared and the first bonding point for the two, and in the basement a full shooting range with lanes to one hundred and fifty meters. The house connects via a tunnel system and an above-ground roadway to the SDS Headquarters condition-dependent 15 minutes away, faster by the tunnel system. The home was a fortress. The security system included bulletproof windows and batter-proof doors. Several wings of the mansion cordoned off into safe rooms, especially the kids' area. With a JSOC background, Xander kept access to tactical kits: body armor, helmet, combat, knife, med-kit, sidearm, night vision, and short-barrel-rifle in hidden safes throughout. SDS Executive Protection kept a small team at the mansion with a larger contingent patrolling the massive five thousand SDS property acres.

Xander stood in the doorway, just awe-struck. Amelia was finally awake. A battle-hardened warrior stood weeping at the entrance of his daughter's bedroom door. Joy and relief flooded through Xander, overwhelming his abilities in every way possible. The sight of his love holding and talking to Amelia was simply too much. Amelia looks so frail and so small. Katy, Dr. Stone, was a godsend. With all the Ridge Family resources, Xander could not do more for Amelia and may not save her. But he would give all for one pain-free moment for Amelia. Xander agonized over finding the altar to sacrifice his life to ease Amelia's suffering. But no such alter existed for parents to visit, only the unrequited offer, one life for another.

Gabby has already marshaled the Ridge children on a video chat. Emily was chatting and coming through the mansion. Emily's EP Team brought her to the mansion. Emily lives on the opposite end of the property in a home Xander had constructed like the main home, just much smaller and to Emily's liking. Jonathan was on a PT run at Cherry Point with his unit. Sophia seemed to be at a party. A point Xander was sure Gabby would address. Nothing slipped passed Gabby, nothing. Still, Sophia was a lady through and through. Charles accepted the call under a little duress from West Point. However, his Cadre knew of Amelia's condition and would look the other way. Besides, Dad was a decorated West Point Graduate. But Xander would never make that call or request. The children insisted. Xander and Gabby resisted the temptation to smooth out life's wrinkles and let the children lead their lives. However, all would move Heaven and Earth for Amelia. Amelia's soul held a uniqueness. Fate records the ability to offer love and compassion in the annuals of remarkable souls but once a century.

"Daddy, please," Amelia took notice of her father shaking in the doorway.

"Oh, Xander," exclaimed Gabby, "I am so sorry. Please, join us. Kids, Dad is a little overwhelmed. Emily saw Amelia's glance and followed the request without delay. Emily glided to her father, "Daddy, she is okay. She wants to see you." Xander could not find his feet or the command to marshal the movement, so Emily prodded just a gentle nudge.

"Daddy, I have missed you," nearly inaudible, said Amelia. "Daddy?"

"Baby, I Love You," Xander managed through his tears; each breath was a struggle, "Baby, what do you need?"

"Can I kiss her on the forehead? Is that okay?" choked Xander. Gabby touched Xander's chest and leaned her forehead to his.

"Xander, it is okay. It is going to be okay," calmed Gabby. Xander was now bedside holding Amelia's hand. The family all struggled and grieved for Amelia as she fought for life. But none had really understood the depth of Xander's pain and love for each family member. Lost in the ethos and mission statements and principled-centered lifestyle, each had not seen the vulnerability of Xander's love. Unconditional love is given to and felt by all.

"Daddy, can we go see the Ocean?" asked Amelia.

"Which one," Xander pushed out through the tears with as big a smile as an overwhelmed father could muster.

"I would like to see Charleston again," requested Amelia in a fading voice, "I need to sleep for a little while. Daddy, I Love You. Mom, I Love You. I Love You, Family! Maddie, come here, girl; I Love You." Amelia closed her eyes and drifted back to sleep.

"I promise, Amelia, we will go to Charleston. Amelia?" quivered Xander.

"She is sleeping and not in a coma. For now, the swelling around the brain stem is down. The real medicines are helping. Y'all go on back to bed. I will keep watch and call you if she awakens. I expect her to sleep for a few hours," assured Katy.

Xander and Gabby made their way to the kitchen. Now aware that Amelia had awakened from the coma, the staff bustled about in excitement and love for the Ridge Family. Coffee, poached eggs, Lox, and fresh fruit greeted the Ridges. The Chef had the flatscreen tuned to the BBC World News for Xander.

"Good morning, Xander and Gabby. I have the BBC for you, Sir, and for you, Ms. Gabby. I asked Jill to come over a little early, so the Yoga studio is gearing up for a morning workout. I believe the class will be full. Everyone seems to be in a bustle today. Something about a plane out West, or someplace," reported the Chef.

> "This is the BBC World News. I am Anna Ford, and these are the top stories to top your morning. An American Passenger Airliner crashed in the early hours this morning, killing all on board. The Airliner went down in calm weather over Kansas cornfields one hundred miles northwest of Wichita in the Quivira National Wildlife Refuge. The Refuge's terrain and marsh conditions impede first responders' search for survivors. But overhead view shows a devasting crash site, and local

> officials suspect all 215 passengers and four crew members perished in the crash."

Xander dropped his coffee and ran to dress for the office. This was not an accident.

# CHAPTER EIGHT — RAVEN

Paul kept deep the secrets of his childhood —a smothering mother, a governess hovering over every aspect of Paul's life —a father enamored with his firstborn, Paul's brother, ignoring his second. Blamed for his brother's death on 11 September, Paul's father never forgave Paul. As the Federal Bureau Deputy Director of the Cyber Division, Patrick was in the Pentagon in the kill zone of American Airlines Flight 77 to see Paul's promotion to Commander of the Department of Defense Cybersecurity. Patrick stopped to see a colleague —and died in the ensuing explosions and fires.

The death of Patrick Ross and the sorted rumors drove Paul's father to disdain him —a childhood neighbor under suspicious means —fell from a cliff. Rumors in the Binghamton community suspected Paul —and that the fall was not accidental. Paul and the young girl were close —Paul's first love. But the young girl gave her friendship to Paul but her heart to the Upstate New York football hero, Patrick, Paul's brother. Rumors persisted that the girl did not slip on the rocks and fall to her death —rumors suggested —that Paul pushed her in a jealous rage. Neighbors saw Paul running toward the walking path —to follow, pursue, some say, the young girl. Patrick was in love with the young girl —her death was a blow, and he never dated another —dying unmarried on 11 September. Paul's father blamed Paul —the Ross name would fade from history.

Born 7 February 1979, Paul Frances Ross describes himself as bold, resolute, and the preeminent cyberweapons expert. Paul lived with a sense that if it feels good, roll with the moment, and he amassed extra-marital affairs. Paul strayed outside the lines in life and his career. To Paul, boldness equates to pushing the limits and then one more step. Paul's ethos is summed into a quote often shared, "It is okay if they hate you. As long as they fear you – Caligula."

Paul married Isabella Marie Coutre-Ross of Louisiana. Isabella was a descendent of Southern Aristocracy and heir to a sizeable estate upon her parents' passing. Neither were well these days. Both continue to suffer the effects of COVID-19. Isabella is stunningly beautiful. Her French and Choctaw Native American Heritage complemented her five-foot-eight-inch frame. Upon the first gaze, one noticed the long midnight-black hair. The seductive emerald eyes and diminutive lips adorned a glossy red that welcomed a firm look or inviting smile, all resting in a petite-toned frame. Marriage blessed Paul and Isabella with two capable and beautiful young daughters, Maria Sara and Olivia Anne. This entitled Paul to years of sorted tawdry affairs with Nanny after Nanny.

Isabella was at the end of the line with Paul and searching for a safe exit for herself and the girls. But escaping a powerful, accomplished, and resourceful man such as Paul —needed a careful plan.

SDS ALLOWED PAUL TO travel and work-from-home or the Washington D.C. offices at will. Paul increasingly chose to work-from-home, especially since he began working with Daniyah. Paul worked all night on the latest payload for the Transportation Sector. Attacking aviation and passenger and freight rail systems would drive his new company beyond SDS's financial successes. Paul loathed SDS and Xander Ridge. Xander was a boy scout – G.I. Joe – Ward Cleaver incarnate. However, part of Paul feared Xander. Xander was a capable man, led JSOC, and was one of Cyber Command's founders. If Xander abandoned the chains of his principle-centered life, he was lethal. But would he? How far could

Paul press into Xander? Enough to steal market share on defense systems and propel Paul to the ranks of the elite wealthy.

Paul marveled at the success of the newly drafted and executed payload. Paul toiled for days on the RAVEN payload, using a modified version of CHAOS to slip past the defenses proffered by SDS for free. The point infuriated Paul to no end. He was almost complete with the download of Version 3. He was unsure since SDS secured access to Government and Military Division. However, Paul's position enabled him to see some projects in development. Paul often lamented his wasted talent to Danny Bell, SDS Chief Security Officer, and Jacob Silva, SDS Chief Operating Officer, to no avail. Danny and Jacob were SDS sycophants owning zero courage to seize the moment to become great. RAVEN was pièce de résistance. Paul was expanding beyond Daniyah. MOIS paid too little and threatened too often.

"This is World News Today. I am Chelsea Kelley with your morning headlines...," assertively announced the newscaster. The following report detailed the horrific plane crash earlier in the day, RAVEN's handy work. Paul had not noticed the creaking of the door and the light footsteps approaching.

"Dad? Dad?" checked Olivia, "Dad?" Paul jumped when he noticed Olivia's presence.

"DAMN IT, OLIVIA, KNOCK BEFORE ENTERING!" bellowed Paul, "WHAT COULD YOU POSSIBLY WANT!" Forcing a tearful retreat from Olivia.

Olivia quivered, "Dad, I did knock several times and called out to you from the doorway. You were not responding or moving, so I was scared. I am sorry, Dad. I will leave."

"No, No, please come here. Focused, just focused on work," adjusted Paul, "I am sorry, Sweetheart. Please, come here." Olivia discreetly wiped her teary eyes to disguise the hint of weakness from her father. Olivia shifted her focus to the news story of the day, the downed passenger plane.

"Daddy, this is so sad. All those people... just dead. Do they know what happened?" asked Olivia compassionately.

"No. Human error is my guess: pilot, ground crew, loading crew, maintenance. Take your pick," Paul answered dryly.

"But Dad – they all died. Do you think it was painful?" pulsed Olivia, "Mom, Marie, and I are flying to San Diego soon. Do you think they will know by then?" Paul did not really feel the sense of the question. He never did have such feelings. But smart enough or a learned response told him to pass off a compassionate response, though he felt nothing, "Yes, Dear, I am sure they will know. Your flight will be safe. You will have lots of fun in San Diego. Now I have work to do, and I am sure you have homework to do." He paused for a moment and looked deeply at Olivia. *Gone was the gangly childlike frame. A woman appeared from the child he once knew* and watched Olivia with a tempting thought. "Now run along," prompted Paul. Olivia stretched to tiptoes and softly kissed her father, saying nothing, turned, and left the room. Paul's gaze followed Olivia to the door. Paul focused on RAVEN and readied for his meeting in a few days in the Bar Hemingway.

MOIS MINISTER MAHMOUD Ashkan Abbas summoned Daniyah Nour Rahman to his office to discuss the Paul Ross casework. Minister Abbas adored Daniyah not only for her unparalleled beauty but success as an MOIS Case Officer. Daniyah was effective and lethal. Her work with the American Naval Officer, Paul Ross, was superb and enabled Iran to strike at the heart of Israel, the Saudis, and the Americans. Minister Abbas served with Daniyah's father, Morteza Rahman, in the '79 Iranian Revolution. He looked upon Daniyah as a daughter.

Daniyah arrived at the Minister's outer office and dutifully waited until the Minister requested her presence. She bristled at the uncomfortable Hijab, and Manto needed when in-country. Within Iran or when attending Iranian State events, all Iranian women must wear a Hijab and Manto and longer clothes. She much preferred the western clothes worn abroad and the liberal freedoms of the West.

"Daniyah, please, please, come into the office. SabaaH al-khayr (Good Morning) As-Salam-u-Alaikum (Peace Be unto You), you need not wait in the Outer Office. Daniyah, how is Morteza?" boomed Minister Abbas.

"As-Salam-u-Alaikum (Peace Be Unto You), Minister, it is good to see you," dutifully replied Daniyah, "Alhamdulillah (Praise Be to Allah), Father is well. Aging slowly, he says. But well."

"Allahu Akbar (God is Great), I am pleased to hear that Morteza is well," bellowed the Minister, "Daniyah, this is Amir Begum, Minister of Signals Intelligence," introduced Minister Abbas.

"As-Salam-u-Alaikum (Peace Be unto You), Minister," greeted Daniyah, growing concerned with the meeting.

"Daniyah, let me get to the point. You are to meet your American asset in Paris at the Ritz to barter for cyber capabilities in a few days. Yes?" questioned Minister Begum.

"Yes," replied Daniyah.

"Good, MOIS Signals Intelligence intercepted an email from Ross to a Syrian Case Officer, dissident members of the Saudi Royal Family, and a Ukrainian, former KGB. I wanted you to know, that Ross is likely expanding his customer base," reported Minister Begum.

"Daniyah, MOIS is growing uncomfortable with Ross. The Supreme Leader will soon announce the emergence of Iran as a Superpower to the world. Still, we worry that Ross is living too large," proffered Abbas, "It is time for you to end, Ross. After the next delivery, plan his untimely heart attack or clever death, and it should not look like an assassination."

Daniyah left the Ministers to speak together and started processing her orders. She was sleeping with Paul and indeed found him revolting. She hated serving his oral fetish. But still, he was a valuable asset.

# CHAPTER NINE – HEMINGWAY'S BAR

Special Agent Mark Reyes arrived at SDS Headquarters. Reyes was awestruck in the SDS lobby, feeling he was inside the movie set of a Star Trek or science fiction set. Models of missiles and drones adorned the lobby as a small museum honoring each military service branch, the clandestine services, and other cool weapon tech displays. Headquarters assigned Reyes to set up an undercover meet with Paul Ross to assess the abnormalities in Paul's travel, finances, and odd work behavior. Reyes worked as an undercover Special Agent specializing in DOD contractors, especially cybersecurity and malware. DOD required all defense contractors to have an insider threat program to detect intellectual property theft and, in a word, treason. The SDS Ross case piqued his interest. He was anxious to get moving. Intelligence documented that Paul planned to meet a contact in Paris in the coming days, the Bar Hemingway of the Ritz.

"Reyes! How are you? It is so good to see ya, Brother!" shouted Special Agent Patrick Kelly.

"Patrick, I am great. Better now that I get to work with you. Slum with you! Wow, this place is cool. Security is better here than at Headquarters or Quantico. You got a good gig, My Brother," hooted Reyes.

> "Yeah, SDS is very cool. The people are righteous, well, most of them. The guy you are hunting is a dirtbag. Ridge should fire him, but Ridge is a solid Dude," shared Patrick, "Listen, the SDS team upstairs is top shelf. Most are

TS-SCI with serious history and credentials. The senior leaders, Xander's direct reports, and the weapons team are Special Access, obviously due to the weapons development, hypersonic inertia weapons, and cyber offense and defense. Xander is Yankee White due to engagements with USCYBERCOM, requiring alone time with the President. SDS is the real deal. Kyla will not be in the room. She is Executive Protection, but she is smoking-hot. Israeli, former Mossad, so don't mess with her. She can take you out, even Marky Two-Guns," quipped Patrick first in a serious context and sliding to collegial teasing.

"I get it. I am not comfortable meeting here where the target works. How do we know that we know that the target does not have access to the visitor logs, an officer on his payroll, or even the cameras watching us?" challenged Reyes.

"You entered through Government and Military Division, not Commercial Services Division," explained Patrick, "SDS is bifurcated between a government-military division and the commercial services. CSD does not have access at all, no visitor, no tours, nada, zip. However, if you are not comfortable, we can leave right now."

"You trust Xander and his team?" pulsed Reyes.

"With my life, yes. Xander is a former JSOC Officer and is transparent with his company and life, without exception. SDS is open to all oversight and audit. GSA, DOD, DOJ, Treasury, and even the IRS have private office space access. SDS detected the Ross Case and escalated it to the FBI. I or a member of my team office here, at will. I attend most of the Daily Intelligence Briefings. Xander often attends briefings via secure video conference directly to The White House. But, Reyes, this is your call. MI6 is already at the table, and I want the Bureau leading this case."

Collaborating with a private company on industrial espionage is normal, but collaboration involving nation-state espionage and an insider is unusual.

"Okay, I am good," decided Reyes as he exhaled a long sigh. Patrick's assessment matched Director Mills' and Attorney General Bell, both Reyes respected. Reyes served in the U.S. Army Rangers and was familiar with the legend of Ridge. Reyes had only met a few Medal of Honor Recipients, and Ridge was exceptionally humble.

Ridge earned the Medal of Honor during an intense firefight in the Battle of Ramadi in An Bar Province, Iraq. Armed with an M9 bayonet and a Colt 1911 45ACP, Xander charged into a building used by insurgents to behead Shia Muslims. Any person captured is different from the tightly held militant worldview and murdered. Ridge fought hand-to-hand, freeing prisoners from a horrendous fate and rescuing three wounded soldiers.

The U.S. Navy awarded Danny the Navy Cross for leading the supporting elements in the face of an overwhelming enemy counterassault. Neither man spoke about the decorations but often spoke of Iraq's people and fellow service personnel that fought and died alongside them.

Mark Reyes was no stranger to heroism or courage. Before joining the ranks of the World's elite law enforcement agency, the Federal Bureau of Investigation, Mark served as a First Sergeant in the United States Army Rangers. Reyes earned the moniker "Marky Two-Guns" serving in the FBI. Reyes was a new Undercover Agent assigned to work with a former U.S. Army Military Intelligence Officer involved in selling classified information. Reyes was well-versed in the investigation's subject matter and played the role of a disenfranchised NCO burnt on multiple deployments. The case went well. Reyes orchestrated the selling of classified information between a peer undercover and the suspect in the final meeting. But at this meeting, the suspect brought along a trigger-happy suspicious friend. Just as the deal brokered and information and money traded hands, both subjects pulled guns, first striking Reyes' partner agent, knocking him unconscious. Reyes faced 'two-guns' and the prospect of early and violent death. Reyes, without hesitation, swept the first and then the second off their feet, grabbing both guns in a series of lightning-fast moves. As the covering FBI SWAT members entered the room, they found one unconscious Agent, two dazed dirtbags, and one extremely excited Agent Reyes with a gun in each hand, outstretched, and covering the threats. Reyes was barking out commands to the dirtbags and checking on his partner. Reyes proved he was a capable and cool customer under duress. A senior FBI Undercover Agent entered the room, taking in the scene, and walked up to and gave Reyes his FBI moniker, "Marky Two-Guns!" as he surveilled the scene to ensure agents cuffed the subjects and treated the down agent, "Well Done, Son, well-done."

PAUL ARRIVED AT CHARLES de Gaulle Airport from Dulles in time for lunch with Daniyah at Restaurant le Meurice Alain Ducasse. MOIS ordered Daniyah to kill Paul soon after receipt of the next delivery. Paul's expansion beyond service to Iran angered the Supreme Leader and MOIS. Iran did not want blowback on Iranian infrastructure. Under the earlier U.S. Administration, the sanctions devasted the Iranian economy plunging millions of devout Muslims into abject poverty. Daniyah intended to set the World right and restore the once-mighty Persian Empire.

"What do you have for me," asked a tense Daniyah.

"What is your problem?" fired-back Paul.

"I have been traveling. The trip had complications, and I am tired," lied Daniyah covering for her frustrations and anger with Paul for being greedy. Iran paid Paul well for the cyberweapons.

"What is the recent version?" pressed Daniyah.

"Did you see the news of the crash in the States?" teased Paul with a slightly devilish grin.

"Yes, you can do this?" asked Daniyah as she straightened in her chair. Even Yuriko listening a room away, sat up in his chair. "You brought down the plane in mid-flight?"

"Yes," paused Paul, "How is your jetlag, now?"

"I need to send a message to home," stammered Daniyah, "this is a game-changer."

"I bet it is," said Paul dryly, "interested in RAVEN?"

"Yes, RAVEN. Interesting Edgar Allen Poe reference and poetic. I will call Tehran. We can discuss a new price for your challenging work," marveled Daniyah.

FBI SPECIAL AGENTS Patrick Kelly and Mark Reyes enter the SDS SCIF to assess Paul Ross and the plan to approach. The Department of Justice espionage case against Paul centered on stealing intellectual property and aiding a foreign government. Paul violated dozens of Federal Laws selling weapons to a foreign state, especially an enemy of the United States. However, the center of the case played to Paul's vanity. Paul was capable of stealing SDS's intellectual property without detection.

SDS Vice President of Insider Threat Scout Moreau prepared a full briefing on Paul Ross from family, education, Naval Academy, Naval career, finances, emails, texts, travel, and intelligence collected by Julius Lyons, SDS Vice President of Intelligence, including the shared intelligence from MI6. Of crucial importance is Ross's character makeup. SDS required each employee to complete a personality assessment and supply in-depth background information. Only Government and Military Division staff working on U.S. Government contracts submitted to a polygraph examination. However, Scout and Julius did interview every SDS employee.

"Ross is an only child. His father died of cancer in '09. The elderly mother is retired and lives in Paul's childhood home in Binghamton, New York. He is an extravagant man's man: tailored suits, tailored shoes, Omega watch, fountain pen guy – Mont Blanc, sports cars, Yankee and Patriots fan, lives, travels, and dines top shelf," inventoried Reyes, summarizing the SDS briefing.

"Yes, he considers himself highly," concluded Scout.

> "He hates Xander and is envious of Government and Military Division. Paul is angry that Danny and Jacob denied his request to join the Government and Military Division. Despite earning $12 million a year with a net worth of $40 million, he hates commercial sales. Paul spends a ton of SDS money traveling the world in grand style. However, he grows the CSD market share and revenue higher and higher. Paul is a narcissistic prick," opined Julius.

"Paul's team does not respect him. The employee feedback paints a dark picture that he is resentful, angry, rude, and condescending," added Jacob, SDS Chief Operating Officer.

"He is a womanizer," blurted Scout.

"Good, tell me more," requested Reyes, sensing a path to connect to Ross, "Ross is in Paris, landed this morning. We need to get moving."

"MI6 reports the Government of Iran (GOI) Case Officer is with Paul, staying with him at the Ritz. Dissident Saudis are meeting Ross in two days. Ross is trying to move a new cyberweapon," reported Julius. A few weeks ago, MI6 observed an American in Algeciras, Spain, with the same GOI Case Officer known as Daniyah. The missing piece of the investigation was Paul. Paul is the American surveilled in Spain by MI6. Reyes and SDS were piecing together the timeline and understanding the Ross Case with each passing moment. Julius was boiling mad but kept his anger in check. He had lost friends in combat and in the Secret Service. But he was boiling mad that Paul Ross was looking to be a traitor and responsible for Jack Webb and SURGEON and his family's death. Ross was going to die either by Iranian, British, or American hands. Ross was going to die.

XANDER OPTED TO RETURN home for lunch to visit Amelia and Gabby. The SDS team and the FBI left for a rare lunch to treat Reyes to Carolina barbeque at the Blue Smokehouse & Bar. Blue was close to SDS offices and a favorite local location, along with the Springs Greenway, the Grapevine Wine Bar, Local Dish, Improper Pig, and the Flipside Café.

Amelia was awake. A blessing that Xander would not squander. After three months of silence with just the sounds of medical instruments and a maze of cables, Xander and Gabby could hear their baby girl once more. Gabby was a warrior. Her strength and endurance in holding the family together, stretched by age and distance, would impress any and all military planners. Xander worked out the details to fly Amelia, Katy, and Kyla to Charleston and Kiawah Island to fulfill his promise. Xander would try to make the flight. He was not able to join the Paris operation. A person of his stature could not easily slip into Paris unnoticed, especially with the World's Intelligence Community playing cat-n-mouse hunting for the source of the cyberattacks and the "who" behind the murder, assassination, of case officers, assets, and sources.

The tipping point was the death of MI6 Case Officer Jack Webb, STURGEON, Farid, and Sara. The losses were tragic and threw the IC into a tailspin. A war that begins asymmetrically will end with bullets, bombs, and, if not stopped, ICBMs. If Ross were the American in Spain, confirmation would not take long. An FBI "bump" at the Bar Hemingway in the Paris Ritz plays Ross's vanity. The bump would break this case wide open. They were increasing the possibility that Ross would flip on his partners. Reyes hoped this would bring Ross to justice and end the craziness before Armageddon. This would give Xander and Sam time to dig into the plane crash. They needed the black box to start the investigation. Still, SDS Forensic, led by Sam, had already started scanning for anomalies with the Airline. Secretary Freeman had DHS searching as well but suspected another cause. Dropping a plane mid-flight was a step too far for the best of cyberweapons. However, Tess learned long ago never to underestimate the tenacity or capability to assess the risk of Xander Ridge. Xander often reminded peers in the JSCO and CIA Operations that a failure of imagination that closes the mind to the possibility of the impossible gets the innocent killed.

REYES ARRIVED IN BRUSSELS under a cover identity and then drove to Paris. The FBI Undercover team working the Ross Case took hard to trace routes into Paris, with only two at the Ritz. Reyes selected the FBI Agent to "bump" Ross in the Bar Hemingway to appeal to Ross's vanity. Special Agent Ashley Brown was to play a young cybersecurity professional, with a love for all things Hemingway and the more refined elements of a gentleman. Brown was sure to play to Ross' vanity and love for a Kentucky Knob Creek Single Barrel Old Fashioned. Commonly made in France with a whisky, so the rarity of Bourbon would appeal to Ross. Brown graduated from MIT with a master's degree in Cybersecurity. Her cover identity worked for a French Defense Contractor. Agent Brown stood five feet ten inches on a small athletic frame with long blonde hair and a caramel complexion. Ross would notice. He could not help himself. Surveillance teams from the FBI and MI6 would keep the GOI case officers and countersurveillance teams under watch. It was a spy thriller in the making, hunting killers, cyberweapons, and traitors, except real people were dying.

DANIYAH RECEIVED NEW orders from Tehran. Keep Ross alive and allow the sale of the payload to the American and Israeli enemies, but not to anyone who would use the payload against Iran. Second, obtain the weapon, and pay Ross's price to secure RAVEN.

Daniyah was sitting in thin silk panties and bra at the antique vanity. She needed no makeup. However, she employed the use to accent her Persian features. If born to another culture, Daniyah would grace the silver screen or Parisian catwalks of fashion models. Paul stopped in the doorframe of the bathroom, observing Daniyah. Though cold at heart, he followed the lines of her body, enjoying her. Paul struggled with the comprehension of loving another that others displayed. He never quite got there. Paul felt numb. With Daniyah, he warmed. Even Daniyah thought Paul was less aggressive and gratuitous in his self-pleasure.

Daniyah returned to Tehran in the afternoon with RAVEN and Yuriko for security. Only a small GOI surveillance team would remain in Paris to watch Paul. Daniyah knew she owned Paul. Paul walked to Daniyah and presented her with a Tiffany's Turquoise Blue jewelry box. Daniyah locked her eyes into Paul's as he slipped a gold Victoria Tennis Bracelet onto her wrist. The diamonds complimented her Persian complex. Paul caressed her shoulders and gently kissed the top of her head, wishing her safe travels.

Paul was falling. Daniyah was gaining control.

ISABELLA AND THE GIRLS, Marie and Olivia, finished packing and collected the final necessities for the cross-country flight to San Diego. Isabella held the tension deep within her and hid the fear of Paul from the girls. Isabella's father arranged a meeting with an attorney. Isabella's father secured the support of the French Government and the General Directorate for External Security (DGSE) to help the family disappear. Isabella needed to sit for questioning. Father said it was a debriefing on Paul and his work. Isabella used the smuggled device to connect to Paul's home computer. DGSE had a strong interest in Paul, especially something about STURGEON and a RAVEN. Then the plan was to escape to New Zealand and start anew.

The car parked across the street worried Isabelle. Fear restrained the impulse to call the police. Two men sat in the dark sedan, both with dark hair and beards wearing dark hoodies. Neighbors were never home, or the pretentiousness would have already called the police and the armed neighborhood security. If these were Paul's men, she would pay the price for calling the police. She waited and would follow the plan Paul arranged to avoid detection.

Freedom was an hour's drive to Dulles and then a few hours on a plane. San Diego meant a chance to escape. Isabella regretted not telling Gabby. But Isabella would have to walk away from her life and family entirely to escape Paul. The way Paul looked at the girls terrified her soul. Paul was a monster. Isabella could take tortuous behavior and pain. Not the girls.

FBI AGENTS, DGSE, GOI, and MI6, gathered in and around the Paris Ritz. Each was investigating an aspect of the recent event. All were trying to piece the mystery together: the assassination of case officers, assets, sources, failed encryption, loss of state secrets, and cyberattacks. The pathways of investigation intersect at one place and time, the Bar Hemingway, an American, and GOI Case Officer.

Special Agent Ashley Brown arrived early in Paris and settled into an expected routine of an early weekender. The in-the-know teams knew Agent Brown. GOI had no idea and observed Agent Brown as an attractive young woman, waiting on a partner. Ross kept to a pattern, which is odd for someone proffering cyberweapons and trade secrets. Ross could program, but intelligence tradecraft was a developing skill, if at all. Agent Brown would stand at the end of the bar facing Hemingway's typewriter and bust. With the selected dress and seductive position, Ross should take the bait.

ROSS DAWNED A TUXEDO for the evening with a white jacket, a black vest and pants, and custom black shoes. He strapped on the Omega watch and pocketed the Ernest Hemingway Montegrappa Traveler fountain pen. Xander waited too long to buy one, leaving Paul occasionally flaunting the acquisition. It was one of only a few items to get Xander's attention, a sign of trust in Paul's abilities to lead the Commercial Services Division or negligence. Xander wasted opportunities to expand market share, especially with the current crisis. SDS CSD could save the world and repeat the cycle, driving revenue through the roof. Create a crisis and save the world, repeat.

Paul checked his image in the vintage floor-length mirror. Tuxedo, Omega watch, Montegrappa for the Bar Hemingway, and just the right five o'clock shadow. Paul made his way down to Bar Hemingway and scanned the area. He found nothing circumspect, just a few business people and a couple sharing a drink before dinner at Salon Proust. Paul's eye took note of a beautiful young woman at the end of the bar. Paul noticed a beautiful specimen in a short-cropped red silk dress that accented her perfect skin complexion and toned frame from her arms all the way to her legs. Paul sauntered over, waving to the Head Barman as he closed in on Agent Brown.

"Good evening, you know he once said, 'When I dream of afterlife in heaven, the action always takes place in the Paris Ritz,' and if he had seen you standing here, he would not have it, if I did not offer you a drink," opened Paul.

"I am sorry, who," teased Ashley.

"Ernest Hemingway, the namesake of Bar Hemingway, loved the Ritz. He felt it was Heaven. And with you here, my dear, you must be an Angel," continued Paul.

"Thank you, you must enjoy Hemingway," stated Ashley, "I love the Hemingway collection. My boyfriend just missed snagging one."

"My Boss did, as well. I like to tease him with it, sort of a cat and mouse," shared Paul.

"The cat always wins in the end," quipped Ashley turning slightly to her drink.

"May I offer you a drink? The Head Barman can make you anything you care to have," offered Paul.

"Bourbon Old Fashioned would be wonderful to start the evening. My boyfriend should be down soon. He is finishing a call trying to convince his office of an opportunity. Still, his boss is not having it, but he is trying. He is too smart for that company," shared Ashley.

"If he asked you, here, I agree," teased Paul.

"Bourbon," paused Paul. "Few Bourbon connoisseurs in Paris," quipped Paul, testing Ashley.

"Well, we have two, and three would be a waste of good Bourbon," teased Ashley.

"Touché," smiled Paul, relaxing into the evening's pursuit. A boyfriend would be a challenge, but Paul was working on getting Ashley in his room by one am.

"What brings you to Paris, my dear? Oh my, my manners. Forgive me. I am Paul, Paul Ross," opened Paul.

"Amanda, Amanda Post," teased Ashley.

"What brings you to Paris, Amanda," continued Paul.

"An interview," offered Ashley, "I am trying to move here to be with my boyfriend. He is a cybersecurity professional."

"Interesting. If I may, what is your interview?" continued Paul.

"Cybersecurity Analyst, I completed forensics certifications but can't seem to get a start," shared Ashley, "and Rick, my boyfriend, will help me. I am sure, but his boss does not want to capitalize on the current attacks. I cannot imagine a better time to push new products and services, especially forensics. I am sorry I am rambling about my problems."

"Not at all, my dear. Everyone needs a little help. I am starting a cybersecurity firm in France, and I am recruiting young talent. I am the President of the Shepherd Defense System Commercial Services Division. I would be interested in your talents," smiled Paul.

"Oh, my, that would be wonderful. SDS is amazing. I have tried to get into SDS, and I cannot progress past human resources. President, congratulations. I am honored to meet such a pioneer in the cybersecurity sector. You are famous! Wow," teased Ashley, "I could chat you up all night."

"We have all night, my dear," offered Paul, "perhaps you and Rick can join me for dinner here at the Ritz, my treat, of course. But forget about SDS. You want to work for me, right here in Paris."

"We would love to join you. Thank You. I will text him right now," quipped Ashley, leaning forward just enough to lower the edge of her dress to allow Paul a glimpse.

Ashley hooked Paul for the evening. Reyes listened upstairs and readied himself to join Ashley "Amanda" in Bar Hemingway shortly after the text and finished pulling Paul into the ruse. Ashley would not have to spend the night with Paul, despite Paul's best efforts.

Ashley was good for a young agent. A top student, Ashley excelled in the FBI Academy and in the arduous FBI Undercover Training. The course is demanding physically and mentally. Ashley excelled and continued to prove her value this evening.

Once Reyes entered Bar Hemingway, DGSE would enter Paul's room to copy his laptop. DGSE had yet to share the operation in the States to rescue Paul's wife, Isabella. The Coutre family, well connected in France, implored the DGSE Director to play a close hold with the Americans. The Director would share only relevant findings from the American operation, but not yet. France needed to advance its cyber offensive capabilities to keep pace with the Americans, Russians, and Chinese.

REYES MADE HIS WAY down to the lobby and steeled himself for Rick Jordan's play. Reyes turned the corner and at once caught sight of Agent Brown. Wow, he thought, no wonder she hooked Ross.

"Amanda, I am sorry, Sweetheart. The call had me trapped trying to convince the Boss to investigate the plane crash and the recent malware case. They are good people, smart. But a lack of imagination and seeing beyond today's impossibility as tomorrow's reality," opened Reyes as he leaned in, to kiss Ashley.

"'But man is not made for defeat. A man can be destroyed but not defeated.' – Hemingway is a fitting quote given our current locale, Bar Hemingway," opened Reyes extending his hand toward Paul, "Rick, Rick Jordan, an honor to meet you, Sir.

"Honor is all mine, Rick," said Paul, standing to greet Rick, "nice Hemingway quote for the evening."

"Wow, forgive me. But is that a Hemingway Traveler, Montegrappa?" exclaimed Reyes, "Wow, congratulations, only the elite were able to snag one."

"It is Rick, here please, take a closer look," offered Paul.

DGSE entered Paul's room and investigated Paul's disappearance, and downloaded Paul's hard drive. DGSE needed to move quickly and leave the room precisely has found. Paul was an excellent weapons designer but a newcomer to spy tradecraft. DGSE quickly found the laptop. DGSE found no evidence of tamper markers, such as infrared ink markers, small pieces of tape, or cleverly placed string to note a tamper if found missing. But DGSE found nothing physical and no evidence of electronic surveillance, except their own. DGSE intended to hold back intelligence. Anticipating the lack of team play, Reyes requested support from HQ. FBI Director Mill and Attorney General Bell enlisted the help of General Wright and the NSA to watch DGSE and remotely copy the laptop and the evidence collected in the DGSE American operation. Spies spy. Sharing is a commodity even among allies.

"This is really nice. I chased on for two years before giving up," admired Reyes.

> "Rick, that is the difference, and let that be a lesson. Do not give up, never quit," taunted Paul in front of Agent Brown, "Like you, my Boss, considered to be the pinnacle of success, does not want to use the current crisis to increase sales and market share. To most, this is a defeat. But like you said, '...man is not made for defeat...' So, I am starting my own defense contract company for cybersecurity and cyberweapon development. Why should only the United States receive help from SDS? In fact, I was just discussing our dear Amanda's future? I understand you have a like view of the current crisis."

"I believe we do," reflected Reyes looking over the Montegrappa, "this is a good lesson to seize the moment and grab what you want when it is in front of you. I won't make that mistake again."

"Keep the Montegrappa has my gift. A night to remember with bountiful food, nascent friendship, and —a beautiful woman," offered Paul.

"Sir," started Reyes.

"No, you learned a lesson. Did you not?" continued Paul, "acceptance is a virtue."

"Sir, Thank you. I am honored. Let's drink to celebrate a new friendship and for possibilities of the unbridled," bellowed Reyes as he motioned for the Head Barkeeper to stop over.

"Sir, please, a bottle of Pappy Van Winkle Bourbon," requested Reyes.

"Oh, you have my heart, Rick! An American Bourbon connoisseur here in Paris," exclaimed Paul, who was starting to feel the effect of several straight Bourbons.

DGSE offered the Head Barkeeper a significant sum of money to sleight of hand the bourbons to the table, straight for Paul and diluted for Reyes and Brown. Reyes and Brown slipped altered drinking glasses that looked just like Paul's but with much less content. Paul was easy to hook. Vanity and indulgence were powerful weapons.

Reyes and Amanda bantered with Paul to the end of the bottle of Pappy Van Winkle, or the second. The Pappy Van Winkle left Paul —drunk and hammered, and he lost control of his tongue. "Amanda" increased her flirtations and pulled her hemline to tease Paul distracting his thoughts as "Rick" continued to build rapport. The GOI Counterintelligence grew tenser by the hour as Paul began to brag about Daniyah and building his new company. Paul tore into SDS for being too big to be nimble and drive market share dominance. Paul lamented about Xander and wanting to destroy SDS and emerge as the new broker of cybersecurity defense and cyberweapons from the chaos. In short order, Paul hired both Reyes and Brown.

"We should meet for an early run in the morning, Amanda," bellowed Paul. Brown looked to Reyes for consent as her undercover boyfriend.

"Don't look at me, Sweetheart. The Boss wants to go for a run. Seize the moment!" proclaimed Reyes raising his new $10,000 Montegrappa.

"A run it is, 5 am?" offered Paul raising another glass to Reyes.

"I would love to. I will be out front at 4:45 am," offered Brown.

"Friends, I am off to retire for the evening," reported Paul as he staggered to his feet.

---

DANIYAH'S COUNTERINTELLIGENCE team passed the news to Tehran. Americans contacted Ross in the Bar Hemingway and scheduled a morning run. The GOI CI team suspected the run was a ruse to kidnap or arrest Paul. This would cut MOIS off from the cyberweapons before the Supreme Leader was ready.

The deep of night in the Pasdaran District of Tehran seemed incredibly dark on this rainy morning. Ministers Abbas and Begum awaited in the darken Minister's suite with new orders for Daniyah. Daniyah, a steeled and experienced Case Officer, increased her situational awareness and readied herself for an attack. The MOIS hallways were dark, and each step awarded any attacker with a thunderous clap and echo. Daniyah slipped off her shoes to finish the journey barefoot. If the Minister had ordered her death, it would be glorious. She reached the carpeted outer office and slipped her shoes back on her feet, regaining a little height. The night blackened the office save for the blinking lights of desktops, monitors, laptops, printers, and the occasional forgotten desk lamp. The rain puttering against the fifth-floor office windows signaled a deary day, come sunrise.

"SabaaH al-khayr (Good Morning) As-Salam-u-Alaikum (Peace Be unto You), Daniyah. We have little time. You need to return to Paris this very morning. You can just make it. We have a government plane standing by. Daniyah, time is of the essence. You will need to HALO jump into Paris and rescue Ross from an imminent arrest by the Americans. We must not allow Ross to fall into the enemy's hands. You may kill the young female American agent if you must buy time for you and Yuriko to get Ross out of France. Once complete, you need to contact us. We need Ross to continue his efforts to sell RAVEN to a mutual enemy of the Americans and the British. We need a separate attack for our advantage. A divided union amongst the Five Eyes is critical to press our goals," opened Minister Abbas.

"Inshallah (if Allah wills), Ministers. Thank you, I must leave. I have a plane to catch," replied Daniyah with excitement. *A HALO jump, a potential murder, and a kidnapping are fun ways to start a day in the business of spying*, she thought.

"Fi Amanillah (May Allah Protect You)," offered Minister Begum, in a rare display of pride in a woman's work. However, Daniyah proved her loyalty and willingness to die for Allah, the Supreme Leader, and Iran.

Daniyah dressed on the flight to Paris. She wore a jogging suit for the final leg of the mission and prepared the equipment for a HALO jump. A HALO jump was dangerous. But over a foreign city is an act of war and would stress the limits of Diplomatic relations if Daniyah failed.

# CHAPTER TEN — HALO

The Iranian flight en route to London passes directly over Paris. The diplomatic plane flew a commercial route and appeared to European Air Traffic Control as a routine flight. Daniyah would jump from 37,000 feet and free-fall to 2,500 feet, pull the parachute, and glide into a dark field. She began GOI agents on the ground would dispose of the HALO equipment and parachute. If all goes well, Daniyah is jogging the streets of Paris to the Ritz in five minutes.

REYES COORDINATED A snatch team three miles from the Ritz in a Parisian park area at the far-end of Avenue des Champs-Élysées. The park offered limited seclusion. Reyes found one area secluded enough in the early morning to bump Ross with a sedative and scoop him up in a waiting emergency vehicle. It would look as if a person had become ill to the untrained eye. A staged medical team is prepared to respond and complete the pickup, snatch-n-grab.

The GOI snatch team closed in on the Ritz. The plan was a simple push into a moving non-descript white delivery van that would quickly pull into the back of a larger delivery vehicle typical in the morning to restock restaurants and hotels. The GOI team lined the van and truck with copper mesh and panels to prevent anyone from tracking Paul.

Daniyah fitted the mask over the face and began breathing the air mixture 30 minutes from the target area. The mixture would prevent hypoxia as she jumped and decompression sickness through the 200 mph seven-mile jump. Daniyah wore a jogging suit under the thin protective outer jumpsuit, which protected against the extreme cold of the high altitude. Daniyah jumped out of the plane at 165 mph and began the free-fall to 2,500 feet, just 1,500 feet taller than the Eiffel Tower a mile away. The view from seven miles above the Earth was breathtaking. She felt at one with Allah and at peace with defending the *mīhan* میهن (fatherland). The Eiffel Tower was the perfect target to adjust the freefall trajectory. At 420 am, the city took on the appearance of a bright night sky. Even the sun was not peeking over the horizon. The surrounding darkness soothed Daniyah's tension as she plummeted toward the Earth, which was growing larger and larger by the second. The air rushing passed —pummeled the ears with a deafening roar. The rushing air is soothing to Daniyah. For a few moments, the World was a peace. Daniyah could almost see an Iran full of food, happiness, warmth, and greatness on the World-Stage. The HALO was worth the risk to herself and her people. Daniyah moved her attention to the wrist altimeter. Timing was critical. She pulled the deployment cord handle and cringed. If the parachute does not open, Daniyah will hit the ground at 200mph. At least, it will be a quick death. Allah Akbar, Daniyah felt the violent impact of slowing from 200mph to 12mph instantly. She guided herself to a precision landing right on target to meet the GOI ground crew. Daniyah quickly dropped the HALO gear and removed the outer jumpsuit. Daniyah was safely on the streets of Paris and jogging towards the target area.

Paris in the morning and the Caribbean by dinner. FBI Special Agent Ashley Brown was on the Ritz Paris sidewalk as planned and ready to lead Paul to a headache and then Guantanamo Bay. Agent Brown loved the FBI.

Reyes was three miles away dressed as a Parisian EMT, ready to get Ross loaded on a medical gurney and out of Paris. The FBI planned to arrest Ross as soon as he regained consciousness and on a U.S. Military transport plane.

The GOI snatch team would close in on Ross, Agent Brown, and Daniyah within minutes of leaving the Paris-Ritz. At seven in the morning, the area near the hotel was quieter and darker under the tree line. The GOI team, earlier in the morning, disabled several streetlamps. Darkness was a force multiplier.

"Are you ready for a great run, Sir," opened Agent Brown.

"Yes, I finished my routine in my room this morning. I am ready to see what you have, Amanda," flirted Paul. He missed the self-imposed deadline, one am deadline to sleep with Amanda, but he might make 6 am after the run.

"Let's go," urged Agent Brown as she started to jog down the dark sidewalk and toward the awaiting FBI team and then back to Washington, or SDS, to learn more about the cyberattacks.

Agent Brown and Paul began the run down the darkened streets. Paris was only contemplating waking to meet the new day at five in the morning. Only a few delivery drivers were up and delivering to hotels, businesses, and restaurants. Agent Brown observed one such van with the doors opened in the next block. She thought for a moment to cross the road but remained on course when she saw one of the delivery men drop a carton of eggs and heard another bellow, "At Least! You saved the WINE, like a good Frenchman!" As Brown and Ross closed in on the delivery van, two delivery men graciously stepped aside. They motioned for the pair to continue their run with broad open smiles. Agent Brown felt a massive impact from her left side as they passed, knocking her into the van as she collided with the copper mesh. The impact dazed her as she struggled to regain her wits. The world spun as her ears recoiled from the thunderous roar of the sliding door slammed shut, sealing her into darkness. Someone flipped on red lights, and she could make out a motionless Paul. Someone was using zip ties to bind his hands and feet. Another slipped a black bag over Paul's head. Agent brown felt someone pressing a wet silky material against her mouth and nose. She was struggling to catch a breath. The addled vision from the impact grew worse, and darkness closed in until Agent Brown fell limp in Daniyah's arms. Daniyah quickly ripped off Agent Brown's clothes and pulled the kit from her jogging pack holding the evidence. Daniyah quickly covered Agent Brown with the evidence leaving the appearance that Ross had raped and murdered Agent Brown. Daniyah, in one smooth twisting motion, snapped Agent Brown's neck. The van pulled into a darkened alleyway and dumped Agent Brown's lifeless and beaten body near a dumpster. The van sped away, turned into the next alleyway, and up the ramps into an awaiting delivery truck. The GOI team would drive to a small town outside of Paris to an awaiting airplane to smuggle Ross out of the country.

REYES WAS ALARMED THAT the DGSE surveillance team had lost sight of Agent Brown and Ross. Over Reye's objections, the DGSE team was following in a town car, though not unusual for Paris, still hard to surveil targets running. Reyes had insisted Agent Brown wear a tracking device concealed in her sports bra. The tracking unit had been flashing in one location for too long. Reyes raced as fast as possible to the beacon location. He and the DGSE team arrived to find a crate of broken eggs and empty delivery boxes at the kidnap scene.

Reyes looked around on the ground for any signs and saw the tracking device. Ross and Brown were missing.

THE NSA SHARED THE collected data from the DGSE download of Paul's devices with the SDS Forensics team. The joint teams worked throughout the evening and night to unpack the data and defeat Paul's encryption. Paul was good and slowed the team down. But SDS was the preeminent expert in cybersecurity and encryption. Exhausted, Sam and the SDS Team were on the hunt and pulling together the extent of Paul's treachery. It was clear that Paul had stolen older versions of SDS cyberweapons used to assess the defenses of the United States. However, he designed his payloads and exploited a dozen or more Zero-Day vulnerabilities. A few of the vulnerabilities SDS was just discovering. But, Paul was weeks ahead of SDS on the exploitations. A troublesome payload, RAVEN, eluded the team and Dr. Williams. Sam would not stop but would need Xander's help. The briefing was a few hours yet, so she had time to unpack RAVEN.

HIDING UNDER COVER of a humanitarian aid flight to the Caucasus region with a full load of medicine, food and water, the small GOI team, Daniyah, and Paul Ross, slipped away unnoticed. The flight to Iran departed less than an hour from snatch to the team's arrival in the cargo hold. The team planned to make an emergency landing in Iran, address the non-existent repairs, deplane the GOI team, and continue to the Caucasus region. Paul was still unconscious.

THE PRÉFECTURE DE POLICE de Paris notified DGSE of a body, an American woman matching the description of the missing FBI Special Agent, in an alley. The investigators reported that an unknown person beat and sexually assaulted the American woman. DGSE phoned Reyes and asked that he come to the scene a few blocks from the Paris Ritz.

Reyes's heart sunk to his stomach. He summoned all his strength to overcome the sense of dread in each step. Ashley was missing. He held her tracking device in an evidence bag and shoved it into his FBI jacket. His instincts were screaming that the body he approached was Special Agent Ashley Brown. Labored breathing caused Reyes to feel dizzy and disoriented. He paused a few yards away from the body. Closing his eyes, Reyes regained control of his emotions and body. Agent Brown needed all his focus to bring her home and find the killer.

Reyes opened his eyes, completed the last few strides to the body, and gazed down. His eyes revealed the truth as he knelt to console Special Agent Ashley Brown lying naked, beaten, and assaulted in a dreary and damp Paris alleyway.

> "Hail Mary, full of grace. The Lord is with thee. Blessed art thou amongst women, and blessed is the fruit of thy womb, Jesus. Holy Mary, Mother of God, pray for us sinners, now and at the hour of our death. Amen," prayed Reyes over Special Agent Brown's body.

"Can we get her out of this alley, please?" asked Reyes.

"Yes, replied the Inspector. We need to hold the body for the investigation," returned the Inspector.

"No, Special Agent Ashley Brown is returning with me to Washington," said Reyes flatly. DGSE nodded to the Inspector to comply.

DANIYAH GAVE PAUL A shot to speed the recovery from the drugs used to knock him out. Daniyah had Paul sitting in a concrete-floored and walled room with a wooden timber ceiling. A single light hung from the ceiling and was swinging slightly. Paul was still bound by the zip ties at the wrists and ankles. Daniyah had further secured Paul to the folding chair with duct tape. An MOIS

Interrogation team stood observing in the shadows just behind the light.

"Wake up, Baby," taunted Daniyah, "Baby, come on, wake up." Paul was groggy but slowly waking up. Efforts to move his arms and legs failed. He felt the restraints biting into his now swelling hands and legs. The drugs' effects and the surprise hit into the van pounded in his brain, forcing his head to move with each drum roll of pain. His stomach threatened to heave the dinner and Bourbon from the night with Amanda and Rick. He felt cold. But a familiar voice called to him.

"Baby, are you awake? Come kiss me," laughed Daniyah. "Wake up," slapping Paul's face. The impact spun Paul's head around to meet the blaze of Daniyah's eyes. Her eyes glowed red with fire to a woozy Paul. For the first time, Daniyah saw fear in Paul's eyes.

"You have work to do with RAVEN," demanded Daniyah.

"No, I won't help you," refused Paul.

> "Sweetheart, everyone is chasing you: the Americans, the British, the French, and MOIS," reported Daniyah, "don't you remember. You raped and murdered FBI Special Agent Ashley Brown, your Amanda Post. You raped her and snapped her neck like a twig. You left her in the alleyway and fled Paris. NO ONE knows where you are, and the World is hunting you. Sweetheart, you have no choice. You work for us now," reported Daniyah in a chilling tone.

The reality was setting in on Paul, increasing the pressure in his head and chest as if he might explode, bursting from the chair. Paul felt anger pulsing through his veins —straining against the restraints —to no avail. *I will kill this Bitch*, thought Paul, pressing his fear to back-of-mind.

"You can rot in an American jail as a traitor. Or you can work for us and live out a life of captive luxury working for Iran," demanded Daniyah.

"Okay, Okay," surrendered Paul.

DR. MALIK GREENE FINISHED the Presidential Daily Brief and sent it to the limited review team. Parts of the PDB were *President's Eyes Only*, so the notations of the NSA hack of the DGSE, Malik, blacked out. The NSA had the data and engaged SDS to understand the extent of Paul Ross's treason. Malik's office was next to The White House Situation Room. Malik pulled analyst reports from across the Intelligence Community, including some reports from the Five Eyes. The World was under attack from an unknown enemy with an emerging capability of cyberweapons. Cities and towns across the United States continued the struggle to recover from the disastrous effects of 40 million American households losing all their money. However, SDS's efforts to reverse the payload were working. But recovery would take weeks. With rare collaboration with The White House, Congress passed unprecedented financial aid to affected Americans, exceeding by a factor of three the amount given during the earlier Administration during COVID-19 recovery.

Malik worried that such enormous government spending would strain the U.S. economy to the verge of collapse. However, the Department of Treasury Intelligence Analyst assured Malik that increasing debt is not good. The percentage against GDP is within an acceptable or manageable range. The U.S. Government borrowing has shown a negligible effect on private sector borrowing. Money flowed, even with the disruption to 30% of American households. Congress and the Administration acted quickly to freeze prices, and stopped the termination for nonpayment of essential services such as energy, healthcare, water, and lending. Banks cannot foreclose.

Renters cannot evict. Like measures have kept the United States going through a crisis and would so again.

Malik's office was exceedingly small and suited her to a T. A small ornate wooden desk accented with the carved lion's paws on each leg. The oversized black leather chair formed her body like a well-worn glove. The room did have overhead LED lighting that adjusted to bright and brighter. But Malik preferred the small brass lamp with a dark green glass shade. The look reminded her of her father's legal practice. She liked the quiet space next to the Situation Room and its proximity to The White House Mess. The Navy made the best coffee. Malik knew she would sleep once again in her office and gazed longingly at the photograph of her finance walking on the coastline of South Carolina. She hoped to marry her soon. But the demands of the CIA and The White House blocked the occasion. Malik was starting to understand that she must make room for her life, or it would slip away. She texted a quick, "I Love You."

THE MORNING BRIEFING with President Hammond would be a full house again and make use of secured video conferencing across several members of the U.S. Intelligence Community, The White House, and Shepherd Defense Systems. Malik opened the meeting, introduced the members in attendance, and gave a high-level briefing. Knowing the President would dive into the CHAOS, the recent cyberattack, HERON, the investigation into the potential break of U.S. encryption, PEACOCK, the FBI Operation to arrest Paul Ross, and RAVEN, the unknown payload that Ross wrote for nation-state threat actors.

> "Good morning, Mr. President. Malik, Thank You for the briefing. For those joining by video conference, I am Henry Mills, Director of the FBI. The FBI secured an

arrest warrant for Paul Frances Ross in the District Court of the United States for the District of Columbia for the murder and assault of Special Agent Ashley Brown and under Title 18 of the United States Code Section 793, engaging in acts of espionage against the defense of the United States. The FBI family and I are sad to report the murder of Special Agent Ashley Brown in Paris. The FBI assigned Agent Brown to contact Paul Ross at the Bar Hemingway in the Paris Ritz Hotel. This morning while on a run with Paul Ross and en route to the arrest location, we believe Paul Ross physically and sexually assaulted Agent Brown, broke her neck, and dumped in behind a dumpster in a Paris ally way just a few blocks into the run. We believe he discovered that she was an undercover FBI Special Agent. Investigating Agents found Agent Brown's tracking device near the scene of the murder. Paul Frances Ross is at large and is now at the number one position of the FBI's Most Wanted," reported Director Mills.

"Henry, I am deeply sorry. Please, accept my and Debbie's condolences. Tess, I would like to call Special Agent Brown's family and parents later this morning. Henry, I would like to go with you to Andrews when the FBI brings Special Agent Brown home," replied the President, still in disbelief of the loss of Agent Brown.

"Mr. President. Henry, my condolences, and the condolences of the entire NSA family. I am General Shawn Wright, Director of the National Security Agency for those on the video conference. Mr. President, the SDS, and the NSA team have unpacked how CHAOS unfolded. The SDS breach appears minimal. The real threat is Paul Ross. Ross can find and exploit Zero-Day vulnerabilities. Each of the CHAOS versions has attacked the United States and our allies over several weeks. The delivery vehicles are SDS products. SDS and NSA confirmed. However, the delivery vehicles date from 2005 to 2010. The original designs were used to assess the vulnerabilities of the United States and its Allies. The delivery vehicles are in the wild. Ross did steal the original SDS versions used in the Commercial Services Division. The assessment stands that CHAOS is not a threat to U.S. networks or encryption. However, the number of Zero-Days is a growing concern. The Joint Team uncovered a new Payload, RAVEN. The assessment continues, but RAVEN is the largest of the payloads to date. We are genuinely concerned that RAVEN represents a danger to the United States' critical infrastructure. Secretary Freeman, DHS has a full copy of the analysis to date," reported General Wright.

"Xander, thoughts?" check President Hammond.

"Ross is a unique talent in the cybersecurity space. He was a top-tier recruit from the Navy. The danger here is to underestimate the capability of Ross or fail to imagine what comes next. This is not over. Looking at the payloads of CHAOS and early reviews of RAVEN, I am concerned Ross will attack or do so through a proxy critical infrastructure. Ross needs only time and resources to build upon CHAOS. We need to focus on RAVEN and the discovered Zero-Days before the release of RAVEN. We need to know how Ross can uncover the volume of Zero-Days before the industry that hunts for them does," concluded Xander.

"Mr. President. For the call, I am Rebecca Porter, Secretary of State. We learned from DGSE that Paul Ross is no longer in France. Current intelligence suggests he fled shortly after returning to his hotel room. DGSE believes he fled the country with his Iranian Case Officer," reported Secretary Porter.

"My God is Ross working for the Iranians?" exclaimed the President.

"We do not know yet, Sir," replied General Roberts, Director of National Intelligence.

"Find OUT," the President said flatly.

# CHAPTER ELEVEN — FURY

"Glad you are finally awake. Do you remember where you are and the conditions that allowed you to wake up alive this morning?" pulsed Daniyah.

"Yeah, you are a real, Bitch," grumbled Paul, rubbing his head.

"You have no idea. Yet," taunted Daniyah, "There are coffee, breakfast, and pain killers by the bedside. Get up, eat, shower, and dress. We have a meeting in an hour. You have work to do with Raven. The Minister of MOIS wants a demonstration of your commitment to Iran and our arrangement."

Paul awoke with the Sun warming his face. His vision was blurry at the edges, and the sensation of a pounding headache echoed in his ears. Arms and legs held little strength and pain pulsed from each branch to the core. Paul slowly became aware he was not alone in the room. The smell of Persian coffee lofted on the air and carried to Paul with a gentle breeze. Waves lapped against a nearby shoreline. Paul pulled against the sheets to a sitting position.

"DAD, THANK YOU FOR helping us get away from Paul. I am scared," quivered Isabella.

"I Love You, forever and always. I love and cherish Maria and Olivia. We will get you away from this monster. He will never find you. DGSE will set up a new life and identity and launder the funds to hide the money trail. You will disappear from Paul's sight and beyond his reach," reassured Mr. Coutre. Henrique Coutre, a retired DGSE Agent, called in a lifetime of favors to rescue his daughter and granddaughters. However, DGSE refused to cash in Coutre's favors and wanted Paul Ross as an asset and the cyberweapons. DGSE created new identities for Isabella, Marie, Olivia, and Henrique. Henrique could not lose Isabella and the girls and would walk away from his life in the States. With DGSE's work nearly completed in San Diego, just one plane ride stood between Isabella, the girls, her father, and a new life of freedom.

"Dad, are you sure? Paul does not know we are here or where we are going?" quivered Isabella.

"Yes, Sweetheart. I am sure. DGSE is good. We just have one last plane trip. And you and the girls are safe, from Paul," reassured Henrique.

PAUL DRESSED, TAKING in the spectacular view of Daryacheh-ye Sadd-e Sefid Rud, a lake nestled in the mountains next to Manjil, Iran. This was Paul's new home, prison. He soon realized that his new home was on an island in the middle of the lake in a desolate area of Iran, which complicated escape. He hoped an escape opportunity would present itself on the trip to Tehran. However, Daniyah prepared the home for a visit, not a trip. Paul was not leaving this island anytime soon. Daniyah expected Minister Abbas within the hour.

Paul walked about the home, stretching each limb, working the motion and blood flow to fingers and toes. *Daniyah or someone really knew how to tie a person up*, thought Paul. Paul wandered into a room set up like his home office. The computer equipment, upon inspection, was top-notch and powerful. Off the office was an anteroom with a male Iranian soldier armed. Daniyah did not intend for Paul to try an escape. Paul noticed with a smile that Daniyah chose all male guards for this detail. Jealous was the fleeting thought. He sat down at the desk, exactly like his home office, including the style of laptop and his fountain pens, as well, down to the stationary. *How could they possibly know these details?* asked Paul to himself. The chair was a customed build, challenging even for an artisan in the States. But here it is. The differences in the room were slight. Paul turned on the new equipment and found the settings identical to his home office in Maryland. This is amazing. He thought to himself, "How did they know all this information about me?" Daniyah stood in the doorway to the office, scanning the room for details, checking each surveillance camera without allowing her eyes to betray the camera's presence.

"Good morning, Paul," opened Daniyah, "Do the house and appointments meet your requirements?"

"Amazing and unnerving," shared Paul.

"You are important to the Islamic Republic of Iran," beamed Daniyah, "You will have all the comforts of home, here in Iran, working for us."

"Am I a prisoner, or do I still get paid?" snapped Paul.

"You are a treasured asset. Yes, we will continue to pay you, provided you prove your loyalty," said Daniyah with a sense of coldness.

"But I can never leave this island?" snapped Paul again.

"In time, you can travel with an MOIS escort. With a new identity and a little surgery to change your looks, the Americans and Five Eyes won't find you," taunted Daniyah, "After all, you did rape and kill an American FBI Special Agent. And you are a traitor."

"I didn't kill her. And, I have not given you a weapon that can touch the Americans and nothing classified, so I am not a rapist, murderer, or traitor," barked Paul.

"True. But the Americans believe you did. Your prints were on Ashley's neck. Your semen on her body. And the FBI raided your home and found: your emails, USBs, and of course, money in your gym bag. So, you belong to us now," recounted Daniyah coldly.

"Who the Hell is Ashley?" snapped Paul.

"FBI Special Agent Ashley Brown is also Amanda Post," reported Daniyah.

"What!" exclaimed Paul.

"Yes, I am afraid so, Sweetheart," replied Daniyah, "You were going to cheat on me in the same room that you gave me this bracelet. It is lovely. Thank you."

"So, I supposed I don't get to sleep with you anymore?" taunted Paul.

The sound of an approaching helicopter interrupted Daniyah and Paul. Minister Abbas and his entourage were moments away.

PAUL REALIZED HE WAS a prisoner, paid or not, for his services. Paul's mind was racing about the FBI; *how had the FBI known about his work? It had to be Xander. Every time I get ahead of him, he slams me back down. That bastard was going to pay. Surrounded by water flowing with dangerous currents at a great distance to the shoreline,* Paul judged *a swim too risky. There were no fences as far as he could tell. But the surrounding area was mountainous and remote, increasing the challenge of a quick escape. If he did escape, how would he stay beyond the reach of the U.S. Intelligence Community, especially the FBI? His only hope was to get to one of the agencies and flip.* Paul knew he had value to the world's intelligence community. Everyone may want him. But everyone needed him, especially now. Paul settled himself to escape but would play along, for now, get Daniyah a few more times. Paul admired the ornate Persian teapot next to the desk. An antique tea ball box sat next to the teapot. Engraved, by hand, was the name of the tea company, RASULOV TEA TRADING. He scooped the tea leaves into the tea ball and dropped them into his cup with hot water.

"SABAAH AL-KHAYR (GOOD Morning) As-Salam-u-Alaikum (Peace Be unto You) Minister Abbas. Welcome to Artaxerxes," opened Daniyah.

"SUBHANALLAH (Glory to Allah)! Daniyah, you have honored the Prophet Muhammad with valor and success," praised Minister Abbas.

"Paul Ross," inspected Minister Abbas, "the Islamic Republic of Iran welcomes you to our country. I trust you find your accommodations befitting?"

"As such as they are, yes," quipped Paul, "I am a prisoner, framed for treason and murder. I am a businessman selling you what you needed."

"You are fortunate to be alive and in our charge. Daniyah saved your life and rescued you from your country's electric chair. Paul, you committed several immoral acts. However, if you serve the Republic, I will assure you of a full and happy life here in Iran. You can have a front-row seat to the emergence of a new World Power," offered Abbas, "Besides, you have no home to return to. No wife or daughters to cherish."

"What do you mean, NO WIFE OR DAUGHTERS!" demanded Paul, "Where is my family!"

"Paul, Paul, I would never harm your family. Islam does not allow such violence. Paul, I assure you. Your wife and daughters are quite safe. In fact, the French Intelligence Services, DGSE, is about to put your family on a plane and help them escape. You," lectured Abbas.

"Escape, I don't understand?" queried Paul, "What do you mean?"

"Paul, your father-in-law is retired DGSE, a foreign service officer for French Intelligence Services, is helping your wife, Isabella, and two daughters escape to a new life with new names and your money to New Zealand, in exchange for giving DGSE your recent work. Well, our work that we paid you to build. The French want to steal it. DGSE wants to steal your work, Paul. DGSE wants to steal your family, your money, your life," taunted the Minister.

"How do you know my family is leaving me?" challenged Paul.

> "The same way you marveled at the accuracy of this room, Paul. We know you. We are your new family now. I know you love Daniyah. You are not Muslim, not Shia. But we welcome exceptional people into our culture, our Country, and our family. Paul, you are exceptional and worthy. Don't you want revenge on Xander, Danny, and Reyes?" taunted Abbas, "Reyes played you in Bar Hemingway. Xander betrayed you. Danny denied you. Isabella abandoned you. Let us help you get your revenge."

"I am not a traitor to my Country," Paul hissed.

"You are not a traitor, Paul. You are not," reassured Abbas, "You are betrayed."

"Paul, your country has betrayed you. Denied your career track to Admiral in the U.S. Navy, denied you the Government and Military Division at SDS, and turned your wife and daughters, Olivia and Marie, against you," pressed Abbas.

"You, Paul are not a traitor," opined Abbas.

"You framed me for murder and treason!" snapped Paul.

"Paul, we must have assurances, Paul, that you are with us and not against us," assured Abbas, "In time, we will help reveal a new truth in the death of Special Agent Ashley Brown."

"To set you free of the American betrayals, we must know that we can trust you," continued Abbas.

"What assurance do I have that you will clear me of the murder and selling you cyberweapons? How can you clear me of selling you cyberweapons?" tested Paul.

"Paul, we are exceptionally good. Better than your CIA, NSA, and FBI credit us to be. We can leak evidence that you were in love with another woman, which is true. We can make it look like the DGSE stole the cyberweapons. The DGSE framed you to make it look like you had a connection to the Islamic Republic of Iran," offered Abbas, "To do this, Paul, we need more from you and a test of faith. A test to prove that you can do what we need at the moment without hesitation. Like our lovely, Daniyah."

Abbas opened a laptop and played a grainy surveillance video of the FBI raid on Paul's Maryland home. The video, a deep-fake, documented the raid and field interviews with Isabella, Henrique, and daughters, Olivia and Marie. Each, in turn, detailed a narcissistic, greedy, sex depraved husband and father. Olivia and Marie parroted how he abused them as little girls and continued until days ago with Olivia. The field interview includes SDS employees, Xander, Chief Security Officer – Danny Bell, Chief Information Security Officer – Amira, Senior Vice President Insider Threat – Scout Moreau, and others. Each, in turn, detailed that Paul lacked leadership and talent. Xander recalled failed attempts for promotion and that he lacked confidence in Paul's ability. Xander stated that he planted John Sellers in the Commercial Services Division to collect information on Paul's failed business dealings. Xander planned to replace Paul in early January, but the current crisis accelerated the need to do so. Gabby, Xander's wife, shared Paul's misogynist temperament and mistreatment of SDS women employees. The images, voices, and the very interviews were all deep fakes. Undoubtedly, Paul would verify video on CNN or other news sources for American news. However, MOIS redirected all of Paul's searches to deep fake news. Nothing Paul would find is or was real.

Minister Abbas was a proven counter-intelligence officer for MOIS and talented at working assets and sources. His efforts to turn Paul were easier than expected. Abbas offered to let Paul rest in his office. Abbas and his entourage would retire to another part of the large estate for a meal. This left Paul alone and unguarded for a few hours, or so it seemed.

PAUL SAT FOR SEVERAL moments, contemplating his conversation with Abbas. *Abbas had not tied Paul to a chair, nor did anyone drug, waterboard, or deprive Paul of his basic needs, dignity, or human rights. He and Abbas just talked. Abbas was open and honest.* Abbas, Daniyah, and the entire staff left Paul to his office and thoughts except for the kitchen staff, who catered to Paul's needs. He ordered lunch and received an exquisite meal replete with the proper wine paired with the rack of lamb, served at the perfect temperature. After the dinner, a Cuban cigar and a 1792 Kentucky Bourbon. Paul opened his new laptop and scanned American news sources. The American news did not have surveillance videos from Iranian Intelligence Services. But the basic storyline was true. SDS buried Paul in the news. The FBI painted Paul as a traitor, rapist, and murderer. The President had commented on Paul as a lackluster Naval Officer with a less than average career. Paul was fuming. Abbas was not lying. Isabella's words tore him up, especially the comments of his wanting prowess. Olivia and Marie buried him in the news with claims of abuse. Paul's anger grew to a state of rage.

"Excuse me, Mr. Ross," opened then respectfully paused a house attendant. Paul looked up and nodded.

"Mr. Ross. Sir, Minister Abbas requested your permission to rejoin you in the office, along with Ms. Rahman," finished the house attendant most respectfully.

"Yes," paused Paul, "Yes, thank you. Please, show the Minister and Daniyah to the office."

"PAUL, HOW WAS YOUR meal, my friend?" opened Minister Abbas.

"Fine, thank you. The bourbon was especially so. Thank you. Forgive me, but I thought alcohol is forbidden in Iran?" asked Paul.

"Paul, consider this small island and modest estate your country. You write your own Constitution and Bill of Rights," smiled Abbas.

"The News about me is bad," mused Paul.

"Yes," replied Abbas, "But in time, with trust, you and I can set the record straight with the Americans."

"Paul, I want you and Daniyah to come to Tehran and join my family for dinner in a few weeks. The grandchildren would love to meet an American. You and Daniyah warm my heart. I hope you two will continue your relationship but now on open trust," opined Abbas.

"Minister Abbas, I would love to attend dinner," replied Paul, feeling accepted.

"A State Dinner in your honor to meet the Supreme Leader of the Islamic Republic of Iran," beamed Minister Abbas.

"Daniyah, would you join me? Escort me and help me with the proper protocol?" asked Paul, forgetting his circumstances for the moment. Daniyah smiled warmly, wiping away recent transgressions.

"Yes, Paul. It would be my honor to escort you to meet the Supreme Leader and the Minister's family," replied Daniyah dutifully.

"Paul, I need to know that I can trust you," balanced Abbas, "I am continuing to pay you handsomely out of respect for your skill and talents, giving you your own island and estate, inviting you inside my home, and inviting you to meet my leaders."

"Yes, Minister?" questioned Paul.

"I need you to demonstrate your power to our Supreme Leader. There are many in MOIS and Qud Forces and others in the Iranian Revolutionary Guard Corps that doubt your skill and talent. And think me a fool, to trust you and to reward you," confided Abbas.

"I need you to help me, Paul. Will you help me?" queried Abbas.

"Yes, Minister, of course, anything," dutifully offered Paul.

"I need you to use RAVEN and bring down an airplane," said Abbas coldly.

"This airplane holds four people who have betrayed you and several who have betrayed Iran. I need you to bring this plane down in a fiery crash," continued Abbas. Paul opened his laptop and found all his software and settings, to be exact. If not for the new keyboard's stiffness, Paul could believe this was his laptop in his Maryland office. Paul only needed a few moments to open RAVEN and a Zero-Day vulnerability.

"Which airplane, Minister?" boastfully asked Paul.

"Skyway Airlines Flight 2846 departing San Diego, California, flying to Auckland, New Zealand. Flight 2846 should be an hour into the flight," offered Abbas. Paul's grew pale, and he shivered.

"Minister, who is on this flight?" quivered Paul.

"DGSE Special Agents that killed an MOIS Case Officer in cold blood and a few other enemies of Iran," offered Abbas.

"What other enemies, Minister?" continued Paul.

"Henrique Coutre, Isabella Coutre-Ross, Marie Sara Ross, and Olivia Anne Ross," replied Abbas, coldly, "Paul, you said anything. After what I have shown you, I appreciate how you might feel. But we must know, Paul. Can you do what is necessary at the moment? Are you worth the price, Paul? Prove me right to the Qud Force, the IRGC, and the Supreme Leader."

"Yes, Minister," replied Paul, remembering his rage at the betrayal of Isabella and the girls —still killing his children, gave him pause.

Paul's memories flew across time to a first betrayal —Paul's first love rejected his overture —she ran from Paul, fleeing to the hiking path to seek solace and think. Paul shadowed her path. Deep in the forest near the cliff and waterfalls, Paul pressed his case for love —again. The young girl did love Paul —But not in the way Paul desired. She recoiled —retreated. Paul felt rage for the first time —his memories clear, never fading with time. Paul pinned the girl to the ground and tried to kiss his love —met with a vicious slap, leaving deep cuts across Paul's neck. At blood's sight, Paul flew into a rage —finding himself ripping away her skirt and panties. He found his senses at the end and panicked. He repeatedly apologized —saying, *I Love You*. Once clothed, she started to run away from Paul —screaming. Paul panicked, giving chase. She fell —striking her head on a rock. Paul picked her moaning body up —kissing one last time —then simply tossed her to her death. He watched her fall —hair reaching out to him —arms grasping for a hold in midair —none came. He stared for a long time into her eyes wide open in horror —the eyes betrayed the soul, and she had betrayed his love. Isabella, Olivia, and Maria have betrayed him. He must summon the strength to act —now as then.

Paul worked on the keyboard for several moments and hit the enter key with a loud click. The flat screen blinked to life, already tuned to Tehran News Network. Paul turned around to search for a remote to control the flat screen.

"Minister, this should not take long. Flight 2846 will explode in midair in moments. The how is a trade secret, I am afraid," gritted Paul, with a chilling voice. Paul locked his gaze on Daniyah, who was smiling slightly. Daniyah and Abbas had turned Paul.

ISABELLA STARTED TO relax, looking around the cabin for Marie and Olivia. The girls seemed relaxed and happy on a journey to a new life, free of their Father. Paul was emotionally abusive and looked at the girls in a way that sent shivers of fear and hatred pulsing through Isabella. Paul was never going to fill the void in his soul. Isabella toiled to fill the chasm within Paul. Paul's dominance shrouded everyone in a nightfall of fear and control. Isabella had always tried to please Paul so that he would leave the girls alone. But it was never enough.

Isabella pulled a blanket over her father to keep him warm —Henrique had fallen asleep. He worked so hard the past few months to make the escape possible. The family had enough money to live comfortably and educate the girls absent of challenge or concern.

OLIVIA NOTICED HER mother starting to nod off. Isabella desperately needed to sleep. Olivia closed her eyes. The plane viciously shook, and fire rolled and licked through the cabin. Frozen in fear, Olivia watched the fire as if breathed by the Devil himself, consume her mother and grandfather. The front section of the plane vanished. The plane's nose and the front rows ripped away from the fuselage, rocketing down to the black Pacific Ocean. Olivia grabbed Maria and began to pray. The plane violently pitched upward as if seized by a demonic force and shoved higher, taunting God to stop the disaster. The violent ascent pressed Olivia and Maria back into their seats, thrashing back and forth like dying prey trapped in a predator's clenched teeth. Finally, the plane came to a gentle stop, and debris and bodies floated about Olivia and Marie. The screaming quieted. Olivia hoped that God had reached down to catch them. A loud creak beginning rearward and thrusting forward foretold the coming hell. Passengers started screaming in terror and pleading for God. The plane stalled and slowly rolled, pitched, and plummeted back toward the Earth with engines roaring. Olivia's eyes, wide with terror, could see her father's face in the lapping flames and debris of the falling plane. She and Marie held tightly. But Marie ripped away into the blackness of the night. Olivia knew this was her father's hand, the penalty for breaking the oath and veil of secrecy for wanting to live free. Olivia thought *Marie could sleep in peace now. Mother, I Love You. Marie, I Love You. Pappas, I Love You.* Then silence and darkness consumed.

PAUL SWITCHED THE NEWS to the BBC for breaking news. "This is the BBC World News Report...," in the trademark BBC announcer tone. The BBC reported that a passenger plane exploded and broke up in midair. The pundits and reports pressed theory after theory; the United States Navy accidentally fired a surface-to-air missile, and the airline was sloppy with maintenance and repeated a TWA 800. None offered a cyberattack on an industry exposed to Zero-Day vulnerabilities with its head in the proverbial sand defending its networks.

> "Incredible, we have much to discuss with you, Paul," marveled Minister Abbas, "the Prophet Muhammad has foretold with the breaking of the rock, 'by the name of God.' Muhammad hit it once, breaking a third of it. He said, 'God is greater; I was given the keys of Sham (present-day Syria, Jordan, Palestine, and Lebanon), by God; I see its red Palaces now.' Then Muhammad hit it again, breaking its other third, and said, 'God is greater, I was given the keys of Persia, by God, I see its white Madayen (capital of Persia) palace, then Muhammad said, 'by the name of God' then Muhammad hit it a third time

> cutting the rest of the rock, then said, 'God is greater, I was given the keys of Yemen, By God, I do see the doors of Sana'a (a major city in Yemen) from my place now.'"

Minister Abbas extended the meaning of the Prophecy of Muhammad to mean that the Islamic Republic of Iran intended to regain the Persian Empire, at least what are the lands of Iraq, Syria, Israel, Jordan, and Kuwait. The ambitious plan would need a degradation capability of the United States, China, and Russia. Daniyah worked Paul to this end to expand Iran's cyber weapons capability and level the battlefield with asymmetrical cyber warfare. Paul understood his role in the unfolding war, seeing opportunities for power and wealth beyond imagination. However, he knew the capabilities of the United States, China, and Russia, and a war that begins with bits and bytes will end in bullets and bombs.

"Daniyah will go over the order of events with you this evening," shared Abbas, "We begin our work tomorrow."

"Thank you, Minister. I look forward to working with Daniyah and dinner this evening," replied Paul, "But I do have a few targets of my own and scores to settle. I will ensure I shroud the attack and deflect. I trust you saved my briefcase from the Paris Ritz?"

"Daniyah?" queried the Minister.

"Yes, we left an exact copy in the room for the Americans, DGSE, and Brits," reported Daniyah.

"I will need that case, now," asserted Paul, "I have work to do."

"I have the case here," said Daniyah, with a smile, "Xander is flying this afternoon. Perhaps a short flight within South Carolina."

"Get me the case; this is my case, not a duplicate?" pressed Paul excitedly.

"It is yours, the original," shared Daniyah.

"Good, it is time," smiled Paul.

# CHAPTER TWELVE — HELL UNLEASHED

Danny was waiting for Xander in the lobby. Xander was running to and from the house and office these days. CHAOS, RAVEN, Ross, and Amelia weighed on his mind. Amelia's health distracted Xander, rightfully so. Amelia's health continued to decline, but Xander, Gabby, and the family could at least talk with Amelia now. Amelia was finally awake from her months-long coma. Xander's release was running, lifting, shooting, and the obstacle course. Xander could still outshoot the best SDS shooters and most anyone else. Xander rounded the corner and took in the view of the SDS offices. Xander could see Danny waiting through the glass lobby on the second floor.

DIGITAL FORENSICS WORKED around the clock to unpack the cyberattacks HERON and CHAOS. Sam and her team supplied the structure of CHAOS and sequencing, allowing the banks and investment community to unwind the devasting effects of zero-balanced accounts. Sam remained focused on RAVEN. RAVEN scared her. RAVEN was advanced and capable of erasing itself, making detection difficult. RAVEN delivers a payload and waits for another prompt to execute.

HERON, CHAOS, and RAVEN had ties to SDS but were standard cybersecurity testing programs. The National Laboratories in the United States developed RAVEN, and SDS was the only government vendor to defeat RAVEN. Based on her forensics investigation, Sam was confident that Paul had picked up RAVEN on the Dark Web. Paul's skill and talent impressed and frightened Sam. Sam was certain that Xander was better. Paul was good, damn good.

"GOOD MORNING, BOSS! How is the Ridge Crew?" opened a smiling Danny.

"Good, I got to talk with Amelia early this morning. She struggled to sleep, so we talked about sea turtles, sunsets, and Charleston. Oh, and crab legs. I will fly down with Gabby, Katy, Emily, and Amelia to Kiawah Island and take everyone to Hyman's in Charleston for dinner. Amelia loves the Hyman's and the salt soap stuff," smiled Xander, "Good Morning, Danny. How are you and Anne?"

"Anne is doing well. I am concerned about Paul. Sam has some good stuff for us to look at this morning," outlined Danny.

"Danny, why don't you and Anne join the Ridge crew and come with us to Kiawah and Charleston? I need you with me," asked Xander.

"No problem, Anne and I would love to join you," replied Danny.

"I am going to hit the showers and join you in the briefing room. Team ready?" checked Xander.

"Yes, ready to go," confirmed Danny.

THE SDS TEAM ASSEMBLED to brief Xander on the HERON, CHAOS, PEACOCK, and RAVEN. HERON and CHAOS were Paul's first attempts to sell cyberweapons. Paul was effective against sixty percent of the world's networks. Paul devasted economies, businesses, personal accounts, and cost hundreds of lives. Xander,

Sam, Amira, Trinity, Jennifer, and the entire SDS cybersecurity, forensics, and weapons design teams were on point to eradicate Paul's work.

"Good morning, team," opened Xander, "How is everyone?"

"Good, Sir. Xander, we are confident that we can give DHS and NSA the needed malware profiles to stop HERON and CHAOS. We are equally confident that Paul stole test malware from inventory, including an SDS version of RAVEN. The version he is selling to criminal elements and Nation-States is a Dark Web version. The Dark Web version, I am confident that by week's end, we can stop. I expect to have another packet for DHS and NSA by 1800 today," reported Sam, Digital Forensics.

"Sir, Sam and I are confident that Paul is more capable than we assessed," proposed Jennifer, SDS, Malware Forensics.

"He is," affirmed Xander, flatly, "Paul is a capable designer of cyberweapons, and with the SDS version of RAVEN, he has a workable weapons platform. The SDS RAVEN follows the precept of STUXNET or Olympic Games, exploiting Zero-Day vulnerabilities, and covers the infiltration. The payload can just sit there and watch, record, or attack."

Xander continued, "Still, SDS RAVEN is old, and we can deal with it if he does not expand an attack on a large scale."

"Are the U.S. networks secure?" checked Xander, "In my assessment, Yes. But I want you to confirm."

"Yes, on this, Sam, Trinity, and I are confident," replied Jennifer, "the U.S. networks are secure."

"Patrick, get that to your teams and to Malik and Secretary Porter, please," asked Xander.

"No problem, Xander," replied FBI Special Agent Patrick Kelly.

"Patrick, I am deeply sorry about the loss of Special Agent Ashley Brown. I have asked Jacob and Kelly to cover funeral expenses for the family, cover any costs needed for the family, and donate five million to the FBI Agents Association Memorial College Fund. Agent Brown's murder leaves me boiling. We will find Paul and bring him to justice. Patrick, I am deeply sorry," offered Xander.

"Sir," paused Patrick, "Xander, Thank you. This is a wonderful team, a charitable company, and a loving family. I don't have the words." Xander raised his hand, offering comfort to Patrick.

"Patrick, no words are needed. We are family, and we do what we can because we can," offered Xander.

"Thank you," accepted Patrick.

"Sir, I have a lead on Ross. MI6 confirms that Paul is collaborating with the Iranians. One analyst believes that Paul did not murder Agent Brown," opened Julius with the intelligence briefing.

"What!" exclaimed Patrick, "the forensics evidence confirmed by Quantico says, DIFFERENTLY!"

> "Yes, it does. I am deeply sorry about the loss of Agent Brown. A larger plot is unfolding than Paul stealing a dated SDS RAVEN version and selling malware to Iran. MI6 has tracked Daniyah Nour Rahman and her team leader, Yuriko Ahmed, since the Iranian attack on the British tanker ship, Heritage, in 2019. Rahman and Ahmed trained and equipped Hezbollah sleeper cells within the United Kingdom. At the end of 2019, Daniyah picked up on Paul Ross and shifted focused on expanding GOI cyber warfare capabilities," reported Julius.

"Retaliation?" pulsed Xander.

"Yes, and no," responded Julius, "Daniyah and Yuriko, favored operatives of Major General Qasem Soleimani, murdered STURGEON out of revenge. STURGEON, Rasulov, was a key link in the EAGLE TALON, Soleimani drone strike, operation."

"So, Paul Ross enabled the Iranians to decode Azerbaijani Intelligence for the minor elements to detect Farid Rasulov and MI6 Case Officer Jack Webb. Does MI6 suspect Ross was able to detect the Rasulov communique?" pulsed Xander.

> "No, Sir. MI6 confirms that Ross did not breach the US or UK encryption or the networks, same as SDS confirmed. However, Ross did enable the Iranians to decode intelligence communique from Turkey, Syria, Iraq, Yemen, Saudi Arabia, Oman, Pakistan, India, Indonesia, Venezuela, Cuba, Brazil, North Korea, Vietnam, and the Philippines. The breach is significant, given the breadth of the undetected compromise of Nation-State and intelligence communique. GOI agencies, MOIS, IRGC, and paramilitary unit IRGC, Qud. Rahman's team collected data and sorted the metadata to collect the names of assets. Then basic surveillance led them to case officers. The IC got complacent. Rahman exploited old-school tradecraft and burned us. Webb and a lot of good case officers and assets are dead, along with the innocent. Ross set the whole in motion. However, there is a broader plot," reported Julius, "This is why the Chief of Secret Intelligence Service, Hawkins, held my trip over after Webb's funeral. MI6 has been pulling this together and passing it to the CIA."

"Does Malik have this information?" pulsed Xander.

"Yes, everything, as of this morning," attested Julius.

"Agent Brown?" pressed a frustrated Patrick, "how does this clear Ross of her RAPE and MURDER?"

"That is just a theory of an MI6 analyst at this time," respectfully replied Julius.

"And?" pressed Patrick.

"MI6 passed the intelligence to MI5 this morning to pass to the FBI. But I will share with this team," elaborated Julius, "MI6 analyzed the evidence from the crime scene and picked up an anomaly, mixed DNA from the rape kit. The consensus is that Ross had sex with his case officer, Daniyah Rahman, before the rape of Agent Brown. Patrick, ask Quantico to go over the rape kit again and look at the DNA. MI6 found significant decay in the Ross DNA sample. The rate of decay does not match the timeline of rape and murder. MI6 theorizes that someone else murdered Agent Brown and planted the evidence. Reasoning suggests Rahman or someone on her team." Patrick leaped from his seat and headed toward the door with a nod to Julius and Xander.

"Thank you, Julius. That is damn fine work, Sir," complemented Xander.

"Sir, we are hunting the location of Ross with every available resource," relayed Amira, "what did you mean, '...RAVEN is old...'? Sir, RAVEN, is the latest malware delivery vehicle. Are you suggesting Paul evolved RAVEN?" queried Amira. Xander looked at Danny and Trinity, and both nodded.

"No, Paul has not evolved RAVEN. He is leveraging a function of RAVEN to hunt and find Zero-Day vulnerabilities and exploit," reported Xander.

> "Xander, and I, along with Trinity and the cyberweapons development team, suspect the two plane disasters are not accidents. The Midwest and Pacific crashes show a similar profile just before the attack. The flight recorder of the Midwest crash shows a sudden and catastrophic loss of flight controls. The Navy and Coast Guard are still searching the Pacific for the San Diego flight's flight recorder. But the final radio transmission points to fear

and chaos in the cockpit, and then all communications and tracking stop, except radar sweeps," reported Danny.

"RAVEN?" continued Amira.

"I have been working on a next-generation cyberweapon. Only Danny and Trinity are aware, currently. Quantum computing is an emerging threat to the United States and our allies. I developed RUBICON to assess the limits and have a new target to evaluate. I have developed, and Trinity is testing against current defenses a new cyberweapon, RUBICON. RUBICON is analogous to Pandora's box. I wish I could unthink and dis-invent," finished Xander.

Patrick returned to the SDS Briefing Room and shared that Quantico would explore the MI6 theory on the DNA evidence. The FBI focused on criminal investigations as the American Court Systems did not accept the science or theory of aging DNA. However, in the context of espionage and misdirection, FBI Director Mills would not leave a stone unturned. Mills committed the FBI to find Agent Brown's killer Paul Ross or others.

"RUBICON? Based on quantum computing?" pressed Amira.

"RUBICON?" pulsed Patrick.

"Yes. And based on quantum physics. RUBICON allows me to control entanglement. Entanglement is no longer a theory," stated Xander flatly, "It is frightening, the capabilities. RUBICON stays in the box, PEOPLE!"

"Julius?" pulsed Xander.

"Sir?" replied Julius.

"Find, Ross, as soon as possible," ordered Xander.

"Amira, Patrick, please stay in the room after the meeting, and Danny will read you in on RUBICON. I need a defensive strategy for RUBICON, and I need it now," ordered Xander.

"Yes, Sir," replied Amira.

"Sam, continue the breakdown of HERON, CHAOS, and RAVEN. I want all three off the table for Ross," ordered Xander, "I want you to focus on the plane crashes. We need to know as soon as possible if Ross found a Zero-Day in the Aviation Sector and is exploiting."

"Ken, Kyla, are you accompanying us to Charleston and Kiawah Island?" checked Xander.

"Yes, Sir. But I want Sam and Jenn to look over the SDS Aviation fleet to ensure we are secure. Sam, Jenn, if Paul uploaded something can you find it?" checked Ken, head of SDS Executive Protection. Sam and Jenn traded confirmation looks. Sam shook her head, yes.

"Sam, Jenn, upload a sniffer on the aviation network. If Ross makes an attack, we can capture the signature during an attack," ordered Amira. Sam and Jenn nodded their understanding.

"Team. Do not underestimate Paul Ross. The enemies of the United States and the Free World hold Paul Ross in great esteem. 'If the enemy sees value in a position, dig deep and plan carefully. For this, they will defend.' Xander's own words from the battlefield. This precept kept us alive and out of ambush after ambush. Iran sees immense value in Paul. Paul held talent and skill that we undervalued, though evil. With motivation even supplanted by GOI and the resources of a nation-state, Paul Ross is now lethal," surmised Danny. Xander looked at Danny with a long, thoughtful gaze. Danny knew that Xander was conflicted with Paul's betrayal, the deaths of so many, the murders of Ashley Brown, the Rasulovs, and Jack Webb, and the release of asymmetric warfare. And if the current situation was not enough, the looming loss of Amelia weighed heavy on Xander. Xander was a warrior, through and through. Like all warriors struggled to balance the deeds of the battlefield with humanity. Did the sins of war need repayment? Did this drive Xander to give so much of himself and punish himself for Amelia's cancer?

Danny and Xander knew that a war beginning with bits and bytes would end in bullets and bombs. Danny could see his words had an impact. Danny needed Xander to return to the mindset of a battlefield leader to defeat Paul. Xander was still a world away. Danny, the right-hand Executive Officer, excelled leading up. Danny and Xander held strong bonds of trust and friendship forged in sand, sweat, and blood.

"Get to it. Dismissed," ordered Xander.

Danny completed the RUBICON briefing for Amira and Patrick. Patrick left with the briefing materials to pass to Director Mills and the National Security Council through Malik Greene, CIA Presidential Daily Briefer. Xander and Danny lived core principles of trust with the United States Government. RUBICON was no longer experimental. The need to brief was relevant. With Paul Ross in the wild supported by Iran, the world could ill afford a failure to imagine what comes next. Every defense needed to be in service, even if Xander feared opening Pandora's Box.

GABBY AND KATY FINISHED packing for Amelia, helping her embrace the essence of a teenage girl. Amelia had pepped up, and her color returned with the thought of getting to leave the house and a hospital setting and wearing a swimsuit and setting toes in the warm salty surf.

Xander completed his daily run with the jaunt back to the residence. Xander focused on Paul's next move and was coming to terms with Paul's hatred of himself and Danny. Xander could never understand the context of Paul's jealousy and deep-driven greed for power and status. Paul was already successful and wealthy. Paul's narcissism turned most off, especially at SDS. However, the Commercial Services Division needed a driven salesperson, and Paul was good. His character was wanting. But Xander felt compelled to coach and mentor. Xander knew that Paul was now a lost cause. Xander turned his focus back to Paul, RAVEN, Iran, and what could come next. This was a deadly chess game.

SDS AVIATION STOPPED by the Ridge residence to pick up the luggage for the quick trip and set up Amelia's space. Chief Pilot Dave Rogers flew the Ridge family. He collaborated with Executive Protection Ken Cain and Kyla Rashid, often to ensure SDS employees' security. However, with current events, the planning was in-depth and detailed. Xander was a target, though he hated the need for security. Xander would not risk the family or his employees.

DANNY AND ANNE WAITED at the SDS Aviation Center. Anne was excited to visit Charleston and Kiawah Island. Anne and Gabby enjoyed spending time together, dating back to when Danny and Xander served together. Long deployments and longer nights forged a tough, unbreakable friendship. Anne was excited to see Amelia taking a trip. Danny enjoyed watching Anne pacing the hanger lobby in anticipation of the journey. Danny enjoyed seeing Anne happy. Danny thought about how much he loved her and missed Mya more each day. Danny and Anne lost Mya after three short years. Mya's heart just did not work as it should. One evening Mya went to sleep and never woke up. If not for the Ridges, Xander and Gabby, Danny and Anne might have divorced. Danny almost ate a bullet one evening. But it was Xander who stopped him and fought to bring Danny back from the depths of grief. Danny knew the pain that was coming for Xander. He would do anything to spare Xander. But it was out of Danny's hands. Danny enjoyed working at SDS, especially with his lifelong friend, Xander. But more so because SDS operates from principle-based leadership. SDS planes are available to every employee and are often used to support charities, veterans, and members of the military in times of need. SDS owned two ocean liners and supported members of the military, first responders, charity events, and SDS employees. SDS owned private yachts for the same purposes. SDS employees and family members, with their educations paid for by SDS, went on to work for competitors, start their own companies, or serve in the military. But each one takes the principle-centered leadership and life with them. Except one, it seems. Xander and Danny believed in doing the right-thing the right-way, every time. SDS charitable contributions and give-backs stayed in the background and did not seek recognition. The reward for such was a clean heart, Xander often said. This sense of servant leadership and life appealed to Danny and made him love Xander like a brother. Danny was less restrained and would snap Paul's neck in a moment, without hesitation. If pressed, Xander is lethal. But Danny knew that Xander would avoid such at all costs until no other option was available. Xander is a Warrior, cunning, deliberate, and precise. Xander was the scalpel to Danny's broad sword, Danny often joked. But it was true, and Paul knew this.

The Ridge entourage arrived at the hanger. Anne embraced Gabby and held hands to open the SUV's door to visit with Amelia.

"Look at you, sweet girl. I love you, Amelia. You are just gorgeous!" opened Anne. Amelia smiled broadly and beamed with pride.

"Thank you, Aunt Anne! I love you too, so much. Thank you for coming with me. Mom and Katy got me a new swimsuit!" beamed Amelia.

"I know! And I brought you new earrings, a necklace, an anklet, and new beach shoes! And if Dad is not looking, we may sneak a belly-button ring," beamed Anne.

"Oh, Thank you, Aunt Anne! I am so excited!" exclaimed Amelia. Gabby was beaming and tearing up seeing Amelia with family and dear friends. Gabby held Anne's hand tightly and hugged her again. Gabby's eyes fell upon Xander. Once again, standing in the doorway, not knowing what to do next. Xander did not even react to the belly button tease. He just stood at the door, drinking in the sight of Amelia enjoying herself. Danny walked up and hugged his teammate.

"Colonel, that is why we do what we do," proclaimed Danny.

"Yeah, Danny," paused Xander, "I don't have the words."

"I know," paused Danny, remembering Mya, "I miss Mya too, every damn day. But you need to stop focusing on an end until it is the end. You don't know how this will turn out. Amelia could survive."

"I pray," choked Xander. He turned to look at his old friend and take in the moment.

"Let's go and get some crab and those Hyman's boiled peanuts!" challenged Xander, "and a good single-barrel Knob Creek Bourbon."

"RIDGE IS DUE TO TAKE-off from SDS soon, Paul," reported Daniyah, "Based on the flight profile, we believe Ridge is using a Boeing 737."

"Surprised the arrogant prick isn't using his 747 to show off. Xander owns a fleet of planes, yachts, and two ships," lamented Paul, "he could make a fortune off the ocean liners. But he refuses the most basic of business common sense."

"Xander feels morally superior to everyone and holds back true talent," pressed Paul, "He is blinded by jealousy and the desire to be the smartest guy in the room. So, he can go home and bang his trophy wife and crank out ungrateful kids."

"SDS just purchased a healthcare research company, Q4. Q4 is pressing the concept of Quantum Physics in healthcare. Xander is pressing for medical and quantum physics advances to help Amelia.

But Xander is likely to cure cancer, only to turn around and give it away," complained Paul as he typed away on RAVEN, lining up the attack.

"We suspect SDS has an advanced cyberweapon based in quantum physics. Does SDS have such technology?" pulsed Daniyah.

"I believe Xander is working on quantum computing and physics," paused Paul, "Why do you ask?"

"Iran will never match the United States, Russia, or China in head-to-head warfare," confessed Daniyah, "But with asymmetrical cyberweapons, Iran could level the playing field by degrading the capabilities of the Superpowers."

"Iran will never defeat the United States," replied Paul coldly, "In the end, the American will to win and innovate is greater than anyone on the battlefield. China and Russia both steal from the United States. Allies steal from the United States. I mean, look at me. Iran had to kidnap and frame an American to help you innovate."

"Iran is making you rich. Don't forget that," fired-back Daniyah.

"True, enough," conceded Paul with a slight smile.

"Does SDS have a quantum capability?" pressed Daniyah.

> "I say Xander does. The answer lies with whom Xander recruits and the companies he pursues. Xander is chasing a treatment for Amelia. He is racing to defeat me and a rising Iran in the cyber warfare arena. Xander is pressing the quantum computing and physics space hard to advance. Why? So, he can ensure he protects the United States before Iran gets there. Thus, why Americans always win," lectured Paul, "If you want to know what SDS is doing, look at whom Xander is hiring and buying. Look at his supply chain. This is how I knew to get at him by attacking the pharmaceuticals supply chain. Xander

purchased the generic manufacturing capabilities. He used SDS Commercial Services to protect the supply chain. He missed the insider, me."

"How do we get to Xander?" queried Daniyah.

"You don't," replied Paul, flatly, "SDS security is bar none more capable than most nation-state capabilities. SDS manufactures weapons, not just cyberweapons. Xander, with just his research and development assets, can level the likes of Iran and give Russia and China a good reason to take-a-breath."

"How do we get to Xander?" pressed Daniyah, "Everyone has a price."

"Not Xander; you can't pay him enough to break him from his principles," avowed Paul, "But you can press a man hard enough to break him or get him to move off his principles, long enough for someone like me to exploit the window and steal what you are chasing."

"Of course, that will cost you a lot more than you are paying me now," teased Paul, "And there is no guarantee of success when going head-to-head with a focused Xander. Danny will never let you get that close."

"Look, I hate Xander. He is selfish and short-sighted and refuses to move off his principles even when it hurts our bottom line," lamented Paul, "But, Xander is dangerous. Your best bet is going after Danny, a member of SDS leadership, or get yourself a lever that will force Xander to play, like Gabby. We have talked about this before in Spain."

"There, we are ready to hit Xander's plane," proudly trumpeted Paul, "But, this is Xander, so this is a fifty-fifty shot at success. But it is worth to take that arrogant prick off the chessboard, once-and-for-all."

"Execute," ordered Daniyah.

"With pleasure," replied Paul.

---

THE SDS BOEING 737 was a breeze to fly for Chief Pilot Dave Rogers, a former Air Force Fighter Pilot, and Co-Pilot Aaron Bell, a former U.S. Army $160^{th}$ Special Operations Aviation Regiment, $160^{th}$ SOAR (A), Pilot. Aaron was an SDS Co-Pilot for fixed-wing and Chief Pilot for SDS rotary-wing aircraft. Both Rogers and Bell were cool-headed warriors. The flight time to Charleston from the Charlotte, North Carolina area is a short 30 minutes, but it would take just a little longer this evening to get around turbulence. Plus, Amelia loved to fly and look at the ocean, so Dave and Aaron took the flight plan on a little diversion to give Amelia the best ride possible.

Amelia was sitting up transfixed on the large window in the bedroom area of the plane. The plane had four bedrooms, including a medium-sized cabin for the pilots and crew. A prominent owner's suite under the cockpit was spacious and atypical for a 737 configuration. However, a converted 737 did not need the cargo area of a commercial version. The plane had several areas that took advantage of extra space allowances, including a larger kitchen and crew area below the main deck. The plane offered a conference room, scenic workstations, and quiet spaces. Several spacious entertainment areas and six full bathrooms ensured the comfort of the passengers. SDS spared no detail to allow SDS employees and guests the luxury flight experience. Xander loved the flights for members of the military transitioning from the battlefield to a rotation home or to civilian life. Xander felt blessed to enjoy philanthropic works during life than waiting until after death. "If it is worth doing. It is worth doing the right-way right-now," is a quote attributed to Xander and Danny, though it is unknown which one said it first. And neither would share.

Dave and Aaron settled in for a smooth ride down to Charleston with the planned extension to allow Amelia to enjoy the ocean from 25,000 to 30,000 feet, a little lower if conditions allowed over the Atlantic. Xander, Gabby, Danny, Anne, and Katy rested outside Amelia's bedroom to enjoy their friendship, and Amelia enjoying the flight.

"Xander, there is a call for you on secure comms from SDS," reported Aaron from the cockpit.

"Thank you, Aaron," replied Xander. Xander and Danny decided to take the call from the conference room adorned with flatscreens, LED lighting, and micro-LED screens giving the appearance of a mini-SDS Research Lab back at the HQ. Amira and the SDS team detected an anomaly with the flight.

"Xander, the team detects an attempt to alter the flight controls of your flight. We have worked with Dave and Aaron to isolate their movements from the payload's attempts. Boss, someone is trying to crash your plane," Amira reported in a succinct tone.

"Is this RAVEN or a derivative?" checked Xander.

"Yes, we are limiting our transmission to the plane. I will send you the data when we finish collecting it. I don't want to alert the attacker," informed Amira.

Amira was a former senior commander in the Israeli Defence Forces Unit 8200. Unit 8200 was the NSA and U.S. Cyber Command of Israel, in one unit. Amira was a top-tier Chief Information Security Officer equally effective behind a keyboard, fighting Krav Maga hand-to-hand and the ubiquitous M4 carbine rifle. Xander and Danny had zero concern that the APT, Advanced Persistent Threat Actor, Paul, would be successful in attacking the plane.

"We are pushing the attack to the honeypot simulator to allow the APT to think the attack is moderately successful and capture as much of the payload as possible," described Amira behind a stern expression. But Xander and Danny knew Amira was smiling behind that stern expression. Amira loved the hunt as much as they did. If Amira could get her hands-on, Paul, Paul would not live long or long enough to get useful intelligence and then exit this world, painfully. Israelis played by different rules. Amira's perspective was simple on interrogations. "I grew up with every bordering nation wishing to annihilate my race from the face of the Earth, so I have fewer restrictions on tactics," quantified Amira when the topic of enhanced interrogations came up in the office.

"Is he going for the 'honeypot'?" checked Xander.

"Of course, he is," beamed Amira, "Paul is good, exceptionally good." Amira paused for a moment to check that RAVEN flowed right where she wanted. "But I am better and studied harder and longer. We have this setup to make it appear that RAVEN is working against the SDS planes. But he does know this is SDS and knows he will not be successful. We are letting him send his message. Dave and Aaron will decrease speed and altitude over the Atlantic out of commercial airspace. We get a twofer," bantered a now smiling Amira.

"A 'twofer'?" quipped Xander, as Danny laughed, "What the hell is a twofer?" Danny started to offer a smart-ass answer. But he held his tongue in check with a broad smile.

> "Xander, a twofer is a two-for-one," tutored Amira, "We trick Paul and give Amelia a better view of the Atlantic, which she loves. No one is none the wiser. Jacob and the SDS communication office will release a pre-scripted press release on your safe arrival to a secure location and hint that an SDS plane experienced a possible cyberattack

> that tried to control airspeed and altitude in an attack. But SDS detected and stopped the cyber-attack before anything serious occurred. Paul will think he was successful. And we will have captured his payload in full."

"This may stop him from attacking commercial planes if he thinks we can stop his attacks," offered Danny.

"Maybe, we need to unpack the payload quickly and determine how to detect and stop the delivery into the controls systems. The problem is the control systems and cybersecurity. The Aviation Sector is in poor shape," informed Xander.

"The Energy Sector heeded the warning but is still vulnerable with operational technology. All DHS Critical Infrastructures are behind the curve," continued Xander.

"Paul was pressing hard to leverage the current attack to press more anti-malware products and operational technology into the market, faster," recounted Xander, "I failed to imagine he was behind the attacks."

"He sold his soul to the Devil," contended Danny.

"No, he is the Devil," offered Amira, "He has a dark soul and had a choice to build his character toward the light or toward the darkness. He was free-to-chose."

"Paul Ross chose his path, with intent," concluded Amira, "He is no different than some in the West Bank. Some have legitimate sovereignty claims and a right to coexist with a Jewish state. Others just want a means to kill Jews. Paul Ross seeks power and dominance. Paul Ross just wants to wreak the world. Light a match and watch it burn the world."

"If we get a chance, kill him," said Amira coldly, "create an opportunity and kill him. But kill him."

"Xander, in the context of failure to imagine," opened Trinity, SDS Vice President of Cyberweapon Research and Development, "What is next?"

"Depends on what we unpack in this payload," offered Xander, "designers stick to a profile, personal, company, or Nation-State, but stick to a profile, adapting when they want to throw off the hunters."

"Is Paul at that level," asked Amira.

"Yes," offered Trinity.

"I agree," affirmed Xander.

"Xander, Paul is hooked into the honeypot, so you need to tell your passengers what is going on and to expect a few turns and altitude changes. Patrick is collaborating with his Intelligence Community peers and has informed the FAA of our plan," reported Amira, noting a change in Paul's attack. Danny left to inform the passengers, except for Amelia. Xander remained in the conference room to keep watch on the unfolding attack. If successful, SDS may save the lives of the next airplane targeted by RAVEN.

> "OMG!" exclaimed Rachel Wilson, SDS Aeronautical Research and Development, "RAVEN brought down the flight in the Pacific, based on effects of what the APT is attempting here. The attack is brutal. He is trying to slam one engine into reverse throttle, the other forward full throttle, and slam the flight controls opposite the spin. The torque will rip the nose of the plane right off. The plane would break up in midair and look like an explosion."

"Patrick, do you have the names of the passengers of Flight 2846?" queried Xander.

"Yes," replied Patrick, "What are you thinking?"

"Julius, can you run the names with MI6 against DGSE?" pressed Xander.

"Yeah, what am I looking for and why," replied a puzzled Julius.

"Isabella and girls have not been seen since the day before the crash of Flight 2846, and the last known location was a flight from D.C. to San Diego. Isabella's father is a former DGSE Case Officer. I met him once at Paul's home in Maryland. Great Guy, but an old school spy trade crafter," offered Xander, "I am betting Flight 2846 was an intended target. We need the flight recorder and need to know who was on the flight, really on the flight."

"Jenn, run the list and compare the age and gender. I suspect you will find a family traveling with an older gentleman, a woman, and two girls within the age ranges of Henrique, Isabella, Maria, and Olivia," requested Xander.

"Xander, Paul is attempting to attack the plane's connected devices. The signature of the attack aligns with CHAOS. It looks like he is attacking the connected devices to attack the IV pump. He is after Amelia!" exclaimed Amira.

"He already tried that with CHAOS and the earlier version HERON. He attacked the generic pharmaceuticals supply chain. Paul damn near killed, Amelia," confirmed Xander, "Capture the data, Amira, stay the course. We need as many of his payloads as possible. Can you edit the honeypot in real-time to give Paul a target?"

"Trinity and Jenn are already on it," Amira replied coolly, "We will give him a shot at the medical monitor, too."

> "Dave and Aaron are reporting an in-flight emergency to Charleston Air Traffic Control," reported Patrick, "So expect a bit of a welcome wagon upon arrival. I have two Special Agents from the Charlotte Field Officer and four Special Agents from the Columbia Field Office at the Fixed Based Operation to run interference for you. The

FAA inspector is one of ours. You might recognize him, so play dumb."

"Xander, we are leaking the in-flight emergency to the media in Charleston?" checked SDS Chief Operating Officer Jacob Silva.

"Got it, Jacob," confirmed Xander, "make it look real like we discussed. Paul and his Case Officer must think this attack was real and a near-fatal experience. Jacob, follow up personally with each family as soon as possible. I do not want to worry anyone's family."

"Got it, Xander," Jacob replied calmly, "We have the playbook, just like the old days."

"Amira, where are we?" pulsed Xander.

"We got it! Payload signatures for RAVEN and CHAOS and most of HERON. We have made it look like he altered the plane's altitude, speed, flight recorder, and controls. We allowed a successful attack on the plane's connected devices, altering Amelia's IV and monitors," reported Amira, "Paul thinks he hurt us."

"Xander, look disheveled getting off the plane," remarked Julius.

"Ken and Kyla have a larger EP team in Charleston and Kiawah Island to keep the media and threats away from you," verified Danny, "We have it covered."

"This is twice now that he has tried to kill my baby girl," asserted Xander in a cold manner that most on the call are unaccustomed from Xander. Danny knew the change in tone meant Xander was moving towards addressing Paul head-on. And Danny thought to himself, *Strap-in. When Xander engages, HELL follows with him, and Xander will UNLEASH HELL.*

# CHAPTER THIRTEEN — NINE MOVES

Paul leaned back in his chair with a sense of exhaustion and exhilaration. He was not able to take down Xander's plane. But Raven proved quite effective. Paul had expanded the payload to include the operating system of the plane. Paul added the capability to attack connected devices, communications, the flight recorder to cover RAVEN's footprint, and the medical equipment. The longer he could keep Xander distracted with Amelia, the more time Paul had to further RAVEN's development.

"I am impressed, Paul. We need to review the plan step by step. The execution needs to be flawless," sketched a smiling Daniyah.

"Just to be clear, I can use attack signatures within the code that points to the Israeli Defence Force 8200 Cyber Unit. But Nation-States and weapons designers do not sign their code. It does not work like that in real life. Even if it did, there is zero credibility in such. I can fake a signature in the code, and I can steal certificates," confirmed Paul.

"Don't worry, MOIS manages such through tradecraft. You don't need to know. It is better for you not to know," attested Daniyah, "Are you ready to launch the attack? I need to set the board Saudi Aramco."

"I am loading the attack sequence now," apprised Paul, "Did you share with the Minister the success with the SDS plane?"

"Yes, I included the mission in the evening update," reported Daniyah.

"Do we have clearance to start our run with Move One and attack Saudi Aramco?" pulsed Paul.

"Yes," affirmed Daniyah, "Go."

SECURITY AT THE SAUDI Aramco Ghawar Field is among the best in the Oil and Gas Industry. Ghawar Field extends 160 miles with a width of 16 miles and is among the largest in the industry. Terrorists allegedly linked to Iran used drones to attack Ghawar, located close to the oil fields, in September 2019. Saudi Aramco dramatically increased its physical, cybersecurity, and air defense capabilities post-attack. The failure of imagination left the adjacent areas vulnerable to attack. A mistake the state-owned Aramco would not make again.

Saudi Aramco often experiences cyber and physical attacks against networks and infrastructure. However, Aramco is state-owned and does not move with agility or speed. The lack of advanced measures, given the history, surprised Paul. RAVEN and the payload would decimate the facility. The Ismail, a GOI asset, slipped into place with a thumb drive holding a malware weapon like the 2012 cyberattack. Ismail carried hints of an Israeli connection. In his apartment, the Saudi Secret Service would find added clues of a link to Israel. Ismail waited for the precise moment on the clock and walked into the control room using a forged access control badge that set off an alarm. An Aramco security officer turned to see Ismail entering the room and running toward a computer. Ismail just made the distance to the computer inserting the thumb drive. Ismail saw his blood splatter in a fine pattern across the computer and the workstation as he slowly fell to the floor. Allahu Akbar, Ismail completed his mission.

ARAMCO SECURITY AWAITED the arrival of the Saudi Secret Service to initiate the investigation into Ismail Hussain. Aramco Cybersecurity jumped into action, isolating the affected machine from the network, even as Ismail's blood dripped to the floor, pooling next to his body. The Aramco Cybersecurity team began assessing the network for indicators of an attack.

Salah Ali stood in the main Aramco Ghawar Field control room, watching the security monitors for indicators of an added attack. Salah secured the main control room and adjacent server room, requesting additional armed security and only allowing entry with an identification challenge. Salah, positioned in the middle of the control room, could watch all the security monitors and the control systems of the world's largest oil production facility. Under Salah's watch, the Ghawar Field produced 3.6 million barrels of oil per day, sixty percent of Saudi Aramco's daily production. A blinking indicator caught Salah's attention on a far monitor. Salah calmly walked to the operator's position to assess and watch the operator managed the overpressure alarm. The operator's efforts increased to decrease the pressure. The adjacent operator position detected a dramatic increase in pressure on critical valves. If the operators could not vent the overpressure, dangerous gases would build up in the refinery. The center console controlling the fluid catalytic cracking process began to alarm with overpressure indicators. The alarms consumed the room and sounded in the facility, reaching a deafening crescendo. Salah kept calm, knowing he was moments from a catastrophic explosion. Salah opened the emergency shutdown button and slammed his palm down. Salah held his hand pressed on the button, expecting systems to shut down, oil to stop flowing, vent valves to open, fire suppression valves to open, and pressure to drop. Salah lifted his hand, resetting the button, and slammed his palm down again. Nothing.

Spilling vapor found the inevitable ignition source. The chain of explosions moved closer and closer to the main control room. Salah stood resolute in the center of the room. The progressive blast waves reached Salah, first slamming him into the wall at the back of the control room, then sending Salah flying into the monitors. With a broken body, Salah looked up to see the fireball engulfing the room and the searing heat boiling his skin. Silence.

"MOVE ONE, COMPLETE," reported Daniyah into a secure communique to MOIS in Tehran, "Permission to proceed to Move Two." Paul and Daniyah worked to ready Move Two. GOI assets were flooding social media news sources with linking Israel to the Saudi Aramco attack that leveled the Ghawar Field with a protruding black cloud twisting to the upper limits of Earth's atmosphere. Hezbollah signaled Move Two at the ready to Tehran.

"Green, GO," ordered MOIS.

"Paul, GO," ordered Daniyah. Daniyah heard the thundering clicks of the keyboard, still amazed that a keyboard could wreak such havoc.

TALIA MORAN, AN EXPERIENCED *Rav seren*, Major, commands the Israeli Air Defence Command on the evening shift. Intelligence suggested Hezbollah's movement to the east of Haifa in southern Syria and a risk that Hezbollah slipped into the North Sinai to target Jerusalem and Tel Aviv. The IDF Air Defence system ranked among the world's best. The IDF Air Force earned the reputation as lightning-fast and lethal. An undeclared nuclear power, Israel's regional enemies nicked at the defensive posture but held back out of fear of annihilation.

Talia ordered surveillance drones to the north to cover the Syrian border and the Golan Heights to the south to cover the Egyptian border and the North Sinai. Talia wasted no time ensuring all missile batteries and Patriot Systems, counter missile systems, were online and ready. Talia observed a control operator intensely focused on their station and repeatedly entering a command, leaning forward as if ready to pounce.

"Chief, status?" pulsed Talia.

"Major, I cannot connect to the Patriot Systems," reported the Chief, in a worried tone, "I have lost connection."

Another Air Defence Operator reported a loss of radar. Another Operator followed, reporting a loss of drone control and video surveillance. Talia grabbed an alert phone and reported the degradation in Defence capability. Only the satellite surveillance remained in a cruel quirk or planned action, allowing Talia and the operators to watch the dozens of rockets launched from the east, just east of the Jordanian border in the desert of Saudi Arabia. The attack did not originate from southern Lebanon, Golan Heights, or the south in the North Sinai.

Talia continued to report to IDF Strategic Command of the incoming attack. The incoming missiles targeted Jerusalem, Tel Aviv, and Haifa. Talia could hear the air-raid sirens from the control room and listened to the confused chatter as the air defense system failed progressively. The inbound missiles would strike, killing hundreds. Based on the satellite images, though conflicting with the intelligence, the attack came from the Kingdom of Saudi Arabia. A back-channel Saudi intelligence partnership was the source of Hezbollah intelligence.

Internet news sources exploded, pressing the narrative that the Saudi Defence Force struck the heart of Israel for the attack on Ghawar Field. This was moving too quickly for commanders in Saudi Arabia and Israel to process and understand, much less challenge the logic. Both now followed the defensive and retaliatory plans, setting the Middle East on a war footing.

NEWS REPORTS SHOWED a grisly scene through Israel. Hundred died from the surface-to-surface missiles that rained down in the early evening hours. Hundreds of structures collapsed, straining the emergency services. IDF moved to a war footing, but the damaged infrastructure complicated a reservist call-up. Then darkness.

Paul had the green light from Tehran on Move Three. Move Three plunged Israel into darkness. IDF used intelligence from the Americans to protect the Israeli power grid. But Paul moved to RAVEN and exploited new vulnerabilities to execute the same payload. Paul moved on to the emergency services and healthcare facilities, connected devices that would give incorrect readings on vital equipment checking patients. Paul moved on to cell phone communications. Finally, Paul used RAVEN to cripple the financial sector across Israel. Israel burned in the night, blind, and in CHAOS. The predators lurking at the gates stirred, sensing the moment to strike. The predators did not know who or why. But the predators smelled Israeli blood, Jewish blood.

AS ISRAEL BURNED AND the Ghawar Field in Saudi Arabia burned, Paul unleashed Move Four. Paul returned to the Kingdom and plunged Saudi Arabia into darkness. Under Paul's command, RAVEN again looked to destroy communications, healthcare facilities, emergency services, and cripple the financial markets. Paul hit two added Aramco oil fields, lighting up the night again with massive explosions, shaking the Kingdom to the core. Finally, Paul degraded the Royal Saudi Air Defense Forces' control of missile batteries and radar warning systems, leaving the Kingdom vulnerable. Paul hit the Royal Saudi Air Defense Forces fuel farms sending each exploding into the night sky. The dwindling jet fuel supply limited the Royal Air Force to short brief sorties. The Kingdom and Israel stepped closer to a shooting war, tipping the entire Middle East into a warzone.

INTENT TO SET THE WORLD on fire in one night, Paul and Daniyah continued. Paul and Daniyah walked out of the office for a moment on the deck. The moon was full, bright, and glistened off the lake, shimmering off Daniyah's skin, accenting her beautiful structure. Paul noticed Daniyah wore the tennis bracelet.

"You look gorgeous tonight, Daniyah," commented Paul, as he moved his hand to Daniyah's. Daniyah felt nothing towards Paul. She felt a little for Yuriko. But Daniyah thought she could not love in the sense of the Western culture. The Eastern notions of love and the woman's role differed from the West. Daniyah struggled to reconcile such norms and customs. Daniyah did enjoy sex. Sex with Paul was exhilarating and fun. But Paris demoted the passion. The essence of the passion was the thrill of secrecy and the fun of the adventurous games. Now out in the open, the passion faded. Daniyah turned inward into Paul's chest, running her hands up his chest outward to Paul's shoulders, following down his arms, and finally resting with his hands.

"Thank you, Paul. I do enjoy the bracelet," whispered Daniyah. Daniyah felt relieved when the phone dinged. Tehran decided on the most dangerous of the night's moves. Move Five opened the door to Armageddon.

THE CHINESE POWER GRID is simply an updated version of the aging American grid. The scale of the Chinese power grid dwarfs the American grid. This is the vulnerability Paul prepared to exploit with RAVEN. The American, Chinese, and Russian militaries were a step beyond RAVEN's capabilities. The essence of asymmetrical warfare is to avoid the adversary's strength and attack the weakness. Move Five centers on the Chinese power grid and the Sanmen Nuclear Power Station[1]. Melting down the core of a nuclear plant, especially a superpower, was a risky move. But Iran's plan to step onto the world's stage after tonight as a superpower called for bold action. Daniyah's and the MOIS plan of attack for the Sanmen Nuclear Power Station was the moment. And she held Paul to the commitment to attack.

LE LING IS A JUNIOR Control Operator at the Sanmen Nuclear Power Station in southeastern China outside Zhejiang and directly south of Shanghai. GOI Case Officers worked Le using his ailing parents as leverage. GOI Case Officers smuggled Ling's family out of China, moving to the United States, where American doctors could treat the elder Ling's lung cancer. Yuriko had murdered the Ling family weeks ago and showed Le a deep-fake video of the Ling family in a new home in the United States. Le committed to complete his end and insert the thumb drive at a precise moment on this day. Le smuggled the thumb drive in a rectal plug. Le just returned to the control room from the restroom, where he removed the rectal plug. Le placed the thumb drive in his front pocket and tossed the rectal plug in the toilet. Le watched the clock on the wall intently. The senior control operator spotted Le's fixation on the clock and the nervous twitching of his legs. Such indicators caught the attention of nuclear control room operators the world over. The senior control

1. https://en.wikipedia.org/wiki/Sanmen_Nuclear_Power_Station

operator, first concerned with Le's health, noticed Le's hand in his pocket holding an object. The senior control operator alerted an armed security officer just as Le pulled his hand out of his pocket and inserted the thumb drive on cue. Le felt himself falling backward, staring up at the overhead lighting in an endless fall. The blood splatter and spray caught Le's attention in the last moments of his life. Le collapsed to the floor.

Paul, at the appointed moment, unleashed Raven. The Chinese power grid reacted a little differently than the American power grid. Once the outages began, the cascading effect traveled rapidly across eighty percent of China. During the chaos of the Le shooting, the Senior Control Room Operator did not notice a loss of pressurized coolant water spilling out into the containment room. The room's operators fixated on their dead colleague lying on the floor were afraid to touch a control panel with the armed officers in the room. After several moments of diverted cooling water, several alarms whelping in the plant awakened the Control Room Operators from the fixation of the shooting. The Senior Control Room Operator quickly assessed the issue and tried to regain control of the plant. Each Control Room Operator attempted to solve the loss of pressurized water. The control room quickly realized the automated industrial control systems had failed. The Senior Control Room Operator promptly moved to manual processes to replace the pressurized water. The temperature in the containment soared to 900 degrees Fahrenheit, and the steam pressure was rising rapidly.

The Sanmen Nuclear Plant Emergency Response team drilled the scenario of losing control of the pressurized coolant to the plant's reactor core. The drills documented corrective actions for a cyberattack scenario and loss of industrial control systems. Plant Operators mobilized the moment that the Senior Control Room Operator signaled a loss of control. The design of the containment vessel allowed more reaction time to replenish coolant with a backup system. The Plant Operators shut off the failed pressurized water, and they switched over to the manual system powered by an isolated generator with no connectivity. The closed-loop system began cooling the reactor and allowed the operators to safely lower the control rods from the backup controls to shut down the reactor core. The core temperature began to drop, reducing the probability that the Plant Operators would need to vent radioactive steam into the atmosphere.

The Ministry of State Security (MSS) would find evidence that Le Ling was an asset for a militant Hong Kong activist group. MSS would find cash and three thumb drives with rectal covers in his small apartment, showing more planned attacks on the nuclear plant and other critical infrastructure. The Senior Control Operator's quick thinking and actions saved China from a core meltdown. But MSS would hunt for more insider threats, creating havoc for months.

"MOIS AGENTS CONFIRM a large blackout across China and an emergency at the Sanmen Nuclear Plant. But they do not detect an explosion at the plant," reported Daniyah, "Will the core meltdown?"

"Not at this point; I suspect the plant has a backup coolant system with an isolated or 'air-gapped' control system," replied Paul, "however, the plant is offline. I suspect the plant and the core sustained damage. There is no explosion. But we took the plant offline and damaged the core. The radioactive coolant water did leak. So, the plant is offline for months."

"MSS is following the lead back to Le Ling's apartment. We will watch for a retaliatory move against Hong Kong and Taiwan," shared Daniyah.

"Paul, you are delivering on your promise. The world is looking everywhere for the origin of the attacks except Iran," beamed Daniyah.

THE DEBATE IN TEHRAN reached a fevered pitch as conflict rose between the Ministry of Intelligence of the Islamic Republic of Iran (MOIS) and the more politically powerful Islamic Revolutionary Guard Corps (IRGC). Senior IRGC leaders expressed outrage that the Supreme Leader allowed MOIS to engage with offensive weapons. IRGC cyber units watch the MOIS Manjil Operation closely. IRGC narrowed down the location and prepared a strike team to hit the small island where Paul and Daniyah worked to burn the world in one night.

> Ali Khamenei, the Supreme Leader of Iran, held his hand to end the debate, "The years-long turf war between the intelligence services and the military ends tonight. Iran will rise tonight as a superpower on the world stage. The petty bickering ends now. MOIS will continue the operation under my direction. The Revolutionary Guard will continue preparations to seize the Persian Gulf and Northern Iraq to the Syrian borders. Go now and make your preparations. But go as one Iran, a rising Empire."

The ministers took note of the directives and left to fulfill their mission. But deep divides in the IRGC threatened the Supreme Leader's plans and risked the lives of Minister Mahmoud Ashkan Abbas and Minister Amir Begum, as well as Daniyah and Paul.

TEHRAN DEBATED MOVE Six with the Supreme Leader approving Minister Abbas to continue. The Manjil Operation was proving to be a successful night of attacks against the world. Daniyah received approval to press forward with Move Six and called Paul back to the office to begin.

Targeting Russia exposed Iran to discovery and retaliation or a Spetsnaz attack on Manjil. Russia was a formidable foe, like a caged animal. If one got too close to the bars, the predator would reach out and slice you open. Paul, from his days in US Naval Intelligence, knew Russia well and worked on cyberweapons targeting the natural gas pipelines in Russia. Disabling the pipeline network would cripple western Europe and aid a later move. The Russians though powerful, were lax with cybersecurity in the operational technology environment. Paul noted the irony of this fact. The United States records Russia as an Advanced Persistent Threat actor, attributing dozens of attacks against American operational technology. However, the Russian lax behavior and attitude with their operational technology was a threat vector for Paul in Move Six.

The weakness of Russian cybersecurity saved Daniyah and Yuriko the effort of turning a Russian asset to insert a thumb drive. Daniyah would release MOIS in a few moments to flood the Internet's new services with fake news and deep fake videos linking Ukraine and the Turkish National Intelligence Organization, known as MIT. Recent Russian aggression toward both was an easy target for Daniyah and Paul. Paul readied RAVEN for the sixth time this evening, targeting the Russian natural gas pipeline networks.

Paul readied RAVEN to give it right back in a gesture of poetic revenge. For added irony, Paul loaded RAVEN's payload with elements of Black Energy Malware, a cyberweapon suspected to be of Russian origin used to attack the Ukrainian power grid. Daniyah did not need to sacrifice a GOI asset for Russia to believe Ukraine sent RAVEN return-to-sender.

Paul planned a minor attack on the Foreign Intelligence Service of the Russian Federation, SVR. Paul intended to knock on the door with no expectation to gain entry. A Turkish breach of SVR would not have the desired effect. The Turks' cyber offensive capabilities were lacking. So, an attack with no payload was the signature Paul wanted to send.

Daniyah nodded to Paul, still listening to the debate in Tehran within MOIS on the evening's attacks. Paul turned to the keyboard and, for the sixth time, engaged, RAVEN.

MISHKA SOLOVYOV WAS on edge with news breaking every hour of more explosions and cyber events worldwide. Mishka is proud to be a third-generation employee of Gazprom, the largest corporation in Russia. Gazprom is a public company but Russian state-owned. Mishka studied hard for five years to earn the education and credentials for the Senior Control Room Operator position for Gazprom's natural gas pipelines. Mishka continued to pursue her education, working to earn a second degree from Saint Petersburg University in Cybersecurity. She knew that Russian operational technology and industrial controls needed to advance or suffer the same fate breaking in the news across the globe. The Gazprom Central Pipeline Control Room lagged the industry with lax physical security. Gazprom lagged the industry using late 2000s industrial control systems and supervisory control and data acquisition systems. Many of the pressure monitors were old and slow to react. This left much of the pipeline system vulnerable to attack. Paul exploited the vulnerability with ease.

Mishka observed progressive pressure alarms showing a dramatic increase in pressure. The increasing pressure would force natural gas to vent, which would vent into the atmosphere and dissipate. However, Gazprom engineering needed to move propane through the system for an eastern European order. Propane is heavier than air and would sink to the lowest point until hitting an ignition source. The Americans experienced a like event in California, leveling a residential neighborhood. Mishka and her operators tried to regain control of the systems to lower the pressure. But found their access revoked and the mouse icon moving about the screen over pressurizing the system absent an operator's control.

Mishka alerted the loss of system control to Gazprom Emergency Management. But the earth's rumbling informed Mishka that the escaping propane found an ignition source. Each explosion destroyed section after section of the above-ground pipeline loaded with propane gas. The explosions would continue until the first sectionalizing valve. Mishka desperately tried to close and dispatch a field operator to close to no avail. Two hundred miles of above-ground pipeline lay engulfed in flames, with hundreds of structures in the area destroyed. The death toll could exceed hundreds if not thousands by morning. The secondary fires threatened to consume added pipelines, compressor stations, and regulating stations. Billions of dollars worth of Gazprom assets burned in the night air.

It would not take SVR long to analyze the malware forensically. Within a few days, Russia would find the evidence Paul left in the Black Energy payload to point to Ukraine, and the SVR would need less time to figure out the failed attack pointed to Turkey.

DANIYAH PAUSED TO WATCH Paul working, sleeves of his dress shirt rolled, the old-man readers resting atop his forehead and leaning forward into his laptop and the array of computers and screens before his command. Daniyah worried about the divisions with IRGC and MOIS. Paul was gold. Everyone wanted him dead or working for them. Being with Paul was a death or life sentence.

Daniyah was a loyal and proud Iranian. But Daniyah, a pragmatist, calculated the danger of a divided Iran with scores settled with a bullet pressed against a cold, dark, and damp block wall. Iran would kill her and Paul, think nothing of it, and praise Allah for their deaths. Daniyah needed an exit plan.

Paul's focus impressed Daniyah. Right on cue, he turned and nodded that Move Seven was set. Paul limited the attack in London to the targeted threat actor's capabilities, Pakistan. The operational controls of London's Underground Transportation Network were an easy target for RAVEN. Lack of central cybersecurity governance offered an easy target and assured lack of network isolation, firewalls, and updated system patches. Paul could walk right in.

Pakistan was a rising threat in the context of cyber espionage. The favored target is India. Pakistan's and the United Kingdom's diplomatic relations are trending towards global partnership. However, the Pakistani Intelligence Services and Military have separatist beliefs harboring ill-will from British Colonialism, ending after World War II. The population shifted toward a Sunni-Islamic perspective, and elements of the Intelligence Service and Military have supported radical and militant Islamic extremists. The United States killed Osama bin Laden in Pakistan, just blocks from the Pakistan Military Academy. The UK's alliance with the United States and Israel divided Pakistani military leaders further. Within this context, Paul limited the UK attack, using a payload from Pakistan's cyber-espionage attack against India, Operation Arachnophobia.

LONDONERS WERE WAKING early to start the journeys to work. Two million would use the Tubes to traverse from home to office, factory, clinic, shop, or café. Londoners are a resolute population. Despite attacks on the undergrounds dating to 1883 and as recent as 2017, the Tubes are full and a constant means of transportation and as British as tea. Paul focused RAVEN on the operational controls, just a slight deviation from the aviation attacks.

Willie arrived to work at 4 am, shaken from the early morning BBC World News Podcast. The brief painted a world on the verge of Armageddon and aflame and burning. She shuddered at the description of the destruction in Israel. Like most hearing the podcast, she knew that Israel would defend against any invasion and further attack. The risk of expanding war, including the United States and Britain supporting Israel. Willie worried about her fiancé, who would deploy with the 1st UK Division 2nd Medical Brigade[2] as a medic. Willie loved her job as a London Tube Driver. The electric trains were fun to control, and the schedule allowed her to care for her aging father and three-year-old daughter, Liz. She and her fiancé, Tibbs, planned to marry last year, but COVID-19 delayed the plans to this year. Willie was worried that a British Army deployment would delay the plans again.

Willie pulled her electric train from the depot, moving toward her first station on the Central Line. Today, Willie's shift of Tube Drivers would shuttle a million passengers about London's Underground at a slow pace of twenty miles per hour. Willie's dream was to drive like electric units on the longer runs at speeds of 80 miles per hour and faster. However, the shortstops and curves within London limited the pace to 20 miles per hour. Willie made the first, second, and third stops right on time. Her train nearly loaded pulled out for the longest run. Willie kept a close watch on the electric train's displays, noting security cameras of the passenger areas, door sensors, brake temperature, electric motor revolution-per-minute, and speed. Willie left a small window in her cabin open for a gentle breeze and to hear the rails clacking. The quickened breeze alerted Willie to look at her gauges. Her train picked up speed from 20 to 30 to 40 to 50. Willie tried to lower the speed, apply the brakes, and

2. https://en.wikipedia.org/wiki/2nd_Medical_Brigade_(United_Kingdom)

press the emergency button. She was on the radio sharing the speed reports and the failing efforts to regain control. Central Dispatch raised alarms to other drivers. But reports flooded Central Dispatch with Tube drivers unable to stop their trains, move, or open doors once loaded.

Willie and 600 Londoners traveled in the tube at 70 miles per hour, approaching the next station. Willie prayed the outbound train had left the station and the safety measures stopped her train. Willie had no control. Central Dispatch had no control. Willie texted Tibbs, "I Love You; I am sorry. I don't have control of my train; I may die in a moment." Willie texted their daughter Liz, "Baby, Mommy Loves You and no matter what, always will. Be strong for Daddy and listen to Nana. I Lov..."

Willie's train slammed into a parked outbound train at the station, fully loaded, doors locked. Paul had reversed the airflow to keep the noxious roiling smoke, heat, and inferno in the tube and stations. Paul directed RAVEN to tax the emergency communication systems delaying first responders and increasing the confusion, panic, and chaos. Hundreds died in moments from speeding trains, searing heat, and asphyxiation, as flames consumed the last life-sustaining breathe.

---

"THREE MOVES TO GO, Paul," said Daniyah in a worried tone, "Paul after Move Ten. You and I are moving."

"Why," pulsed Paul.

"Trust me, Paul. We need to move. Move-to-Live," responded Daniyah.

Move Eight added pause to Tehran and the debate of each move amongst the Supreme Leader, the President, and the Guardian Council. The Supreme Leader carefully reviewed each move with the top levels of the Iranian government, less for the inclusion of thought, more for political calculus. The Supreme Leader was politically savvy and wanted necks to stretch before his own. Like Moves Five and Six, Move Eight carries a risk of an Armageddon response. The Democratic People's Republic of Korea (DPRK), North Korea, already on edge from the Moves One through Seven unfolding through the night and early morning hours, moved the national defenses to high alert status. The world's intelligence communities looked intently at North Korea as an instigator of tonight's attack. The world was on fire.

Paul focused Move Eight on the DPRK oil reserves and one refinery found in Rason. Rason, nestled in the northeastern region along the Chinese and Russian borders, is an industrial town responsible for oil refinement and rubber production. North Korea relied heavily on refining 11,000 barrels of oil a day in the region. North Korean cyberwarfare capabilities were a global threat responsible for global ransomware attacks, espionage, and sophisticated denial of services attacks. However, North Korea joined the international community, lagging in securing the industrial controls of operational technology. A mistake Paul exploited.

Chul Moo was on edge. The DPRK state news reported that the United States launched a global cyber-attack using Asian allies to attack. Chul is the Senior Shift Control Room Operator at the DPRK oil refinery Sŭngri Refinery. Sŭngri is a strategic DPRK asset protected by a small army detachment and a single anti-aircraft battery. Ranson is a remote town cold and bleak. The nearby political prison is a stark reminder of failure. So, Moo settled into his shift with an extra, on an attack. Chul kept watching the flow rates and pressures. Refineries are dangerous and susceptible to explosion. Pressure changes and flow rate deviations are indicators of a problem. A sense of urgency can save the day or lead to doom, destruction, and death.

Chul detected a pressure increase in the cat-cracker supply line. He quickly scribbled an instruction for an operator to open a valve and ordered the runner to hurry. Four of the product line valves slammed shut. Chul could not open the valves and ordered another runner to instruct Operators to open the product valves. Pressure and heat built up in the main column. The regenerator valve venting excess combustible gas to the atmosphere closed, forcing the feedback down the lines. Chul hit the plant evacuation alarm to no avail. The refinery would explode if the operators did not open the valves before the fumes hit the boiler.

Chul grabbed the public address phone and ordered the plant to evacuate. Chul repeated the alarm over and over. Chul saw peers and fellow employees running from the plant out his window. But Chul remained in the control room, working the systems to vent the building fumes. Chul thought of Soon, his wife of ten years. Chul pulled her picture from his pant pocket and held Soon close to his heart. Chul repeated the alarm on the public address.

Ranson shook in the early morning hours. The explosion mushroomed into the predawn sky from horizon to horizon. Underneath the roiling flames, thousands of structures collapsed, killing 576 sleeping souls.

PAUL STOOD FROM THE desk chair. Daniyah walked over and began to work the knots from Paul's back and shoulders. Custom or not, Paul's back ached from the night's work.

"I am impressed with your work tonight, two moves left before sunrise, and the stage is set for the Americans, Chinese, and Russians to fight it out together or through their proxies. Iran will appear as a new Superpower.

Qud commanders of the IRGC fumed at the MOIS Manjil Operation. Qud moved three teams around Manjil to surveil

Daniyah's team. Qud cyberweapon experts toiled through the night to capture RAVEN and the payloads. The aviation payload captured first was in Damascus. The Qud Force planned to use RAVEN and the aviation payload to attack American commercial aviation. Qud would strike at the heart of America. Qud would not allow the American asset to leave the island.

"Are you prepared for Move Nine?" pulsed Daniyah.

"Yes, Move Nine is easy," confirmed Paul.

"What is Ten?" inquired Daniyah, "MOIS, planned nine moves."

"Ten is personal," gritted Paul, "SDS stopped CHAOS before I was ready."

"I am stunned at our success," confessed Daniyah, "Not that I doubt you're talented. The devastation of one man and a laptop is impressive. In a physical attack, we lose lives getting this close and years to work and turn assets and sources."

"Well, it is more than just one man and a laptop," grumbled Paul, "Development of cyberweapons does take time and others, a team. But I cannot exploit a secured system. I must find a vulnerability. Humans are lazy and give me hundreds of vulnerabilities. Some of the payloads are six years old and known."

"You are impressive," teased Daniyah.

"Thank you," smiled a tired Paul, "I set up Move Nine, awaiting your go. You can watch Europe go dark using a six-year-old payload. CISOs should lose their jobs over the ineptness exploited tonight. I made millions closing these gaps and should have made hundreds of millions. But Xander just won't exploit a crisis."

Daniyah paused to read the message from Tehran, "Greenlight, Paul."

Once more, Paul turned to the keyboard to send RAVEN into another theater. Europe was wearily entering the daily routines of early morning. The unfolding global cyber-attack held Europe's breath in anticipation of disaster —with the hope that sunrise brought escape from the night's events. Dawn's promise shattered as the power grids progressively collapsed. Grid operators locked out of the control networks just sat and watched the cascading outage sweep across the network, blowing transformers and breakers as the surge swept Europe into darkness. The payload originated from a Russian source in 2014. But few had bothered to close the vulnerability that made the attack against Ukraine possible. A steep price to pay for ineptness and arrogance.

GABBY WAS HAPPY TO be back home. She loved to travel. But Paul's attempt to kill them really shook Gabby. Still, traveling increased Gabby's concern for Amelia's health. A simple illness, much less COVID-19, presents a life-threatening risk in her compromised condition. Gabby wanted to visit her father, Dr. Samuel J. Cohen, but feared making his condition worse or picking up a bug that would endanger Amelia. Xander designed several plans to get Gabby to her father, including a plan that made Gabby laugh —involving hazmat suits. Gabby laughed as Xander laid out the plan with Danny, affirming the plan would work. She felt terrible when she realized Xander was one-hundred percent serious. Gabby loved Xander to the ends of the infinite Universe. He tried so hard to set the world right for everyone. For now, the Jewish Hospital Intensive Care Unit gave great care to Dr. Cohen, managing the post-COVID-19 chronic obstructive pulmonary disease. Each day presented a struggle to breathe. But Dr. Cohen proved his stiffness, surviving a bout with cancer, COVID-19, and now COPD. Gabby settled in for her daily video chat with her father and mother. She is in the room with Amelia, and they are in the ICU room.

"DO YOU KNOW THE NAME and location of the hospital providing for Dr. Samuel J. Cohen?" pulsed Paul, "I am ready for Move Ten."

"Paul, we need to move now. I suspect the Qud Force is going to hit us. I have lost communication with Tehran and MOIS. IRGC may have taken out Minister Abbas. I can keep us alive, but we need to go NOW!" exclaimed Daniyah.

"The hospital!" asserted Paul.

"Yes, hit it, and then we need to move," returned Daniyah as she collected her exfil pack and weapons, "Yuriko will be here in five. Can you get this done and exfil?"

"Yes," confirmed Paul.

Paul moved to the keyboard one last time, targeting room 506, Dr. Samuel J. Cohen's suite. Paul disabled the room's alarms watching Dr. Cohen's vital signs. Paul altered the display to show expected returns on pulse and breathing rate, oxygenated blood, heart rhythms, and blood pressure. The new system checked and readied an attached defibrillator due to Dr. Cohen's history of heart attacks and fibrillation. Paul removed the safety limits set on the auto-defibrillator, increasing the output to dangerous levels. Paul watched the vitals and hit the enter key.

GABBY JUMPED AT THE expression on her father's face. Dr. Cohen grimaced, enduring a surge of pain in his chest. He began to gasp for air, fighting for life's breath. The defibrillator hit Dr. Cohen again, triggered by RAVEN. Gabby watched her father close his eyes and slowly fade. Released from the searing grip of pain, his body released the last break sinking into the mattress and death. At first, Gabby thought the incident had passed. But quickly realized her father had died before her, Katy, Amelia, and her mother. Ms. Cohen desperately pressed the nurse call button to no avail. Ms. Cohen, too feeble to walk unassisted, fell to the floor and crawled to the door, yelling for help. The Charge Nurse rushed to the room with a crash cart with peer nurses in tow. Dr. Cohen was dead. The display monitors all, noting a healthy heart, breathing, pulse ox, and heart rhythm. But Dr. Cohen was gone.

PAUL CLOSED HIS LAPTOP at the sound of the helicopter, "It is done. Let's go."

# CHAPTER FOURTEEN — DEFCON 3

President Hammond was still in the White House Situation Room. In the past twenty-four hours, the world was on the brink of Armageddon, World War III. The Situation Room watched nine sophisticated cyberattacks unfold, affecting Saudi Arabia, Israel, China, Russia, the United Kingdom, North Korea, and Europe. Fires raged in the Middle East and Asia. Thousands of lives were lost, burned, and crushed by falling debris.

The President ordered the United States Defense Condition (DEFCON) set to Three (3). DEFCON 3 readied all American forces to mobilize and harden positions against attack. DEFCON 3 prepared the Air Force for a 15-minute response, putting planes on the tarmac. The Air Force prepped nuclear bombers to take off on-demand. The U.S. Navy moved two battle groups to the Middle East into the Persian Gulf and two added battle groups into the Mediterranean. The U.S. Navy ordered the Doomsday Plane, an E-6B Mercury at the ready. The United States Secret Service prepared to move the President to the White House Presidential Bunker at any moment.

"Sir, DHS is reporting an attack on a hospital in Asheville, North Carolina. One patient has died, a 79-year-old male with respiratory disease and a heart condition. The attack disabled the ICU monitoring and used a defibrillator to increase the output to a lethal level twice. The patient died of heart failure," Dr. Malik Greene, the CIA Presidential Daily Briefer.

"My God, what a horrible tragedy," lamented the President, "Why are the safeguards not in place! Did SDS provide the data to protect the Critical Infrastructure Sectors?"

"Yes, Sir," asserted DHS Secretary Freeman, "Xander and SDS supplied all the current signatures used in the attacks, including last night. The industry is moving as fast as possible to close the gaps."

"How does he have last night's data so quickly?" pulsed the President.

"Sir, we can add SDS, Xander, to the call, if you like," pulsed Malik.

"Yes, please," barked an agitated President Hammond. This was the Hammond Administration's September 11th. This point was made clear by the breadth of the attacks and the inherent vulnerability of the sixteen Critical Infrastructure Sectors.

"Mr. President," opened Xander.

"Xander, how do you have the attack signatures from the attacks unfolding so quickly?" pulsed the President.

"Sir, everyone has them. There were nine attacks in total, but several were re-treads of using payloads dating to 2014. The threat actor used RAVEN and old and readily available payloads to set the world on fire," reported Xander.

"Are you saying we had six years to prevent this attack? SIX YEARS!" exclaimed the President.

"Yes, Sir. I am," briefed Xander, "Sir, most CISOs weigh the risk in the context of probability and consequence versus costs. Most are slow to react to DHS and industry warnings."

"Tess, prepare Jess and the Communications Team. I want Jess on the White House Podium driving home the need to act on these vulnerabilities. I have Xander and SDS running these threats down, DHS passing the findings, and Critical Infrastructure dragging their feet! This is unacceptable!" ordered the President.

"Yes, Sir," affirmed Tess as she left the Situation Room to brief Jessica Wilson, the White House Communication Director, Toby Isaac.

"Secretary Cooke?" pulsed Xander.

"Xander," returned Secretary of Defense Michael "Mike" Cooke.

"Mr. Secretary, SDS updated all Department of Defense firewalls, intrusion detection systems, and the artificial intelligence hunt capabilities. SDS worked through the night with our counterparts on the government side of the Intelligence Community," reported Xander.

"Bet that earned you a pretty penny," quipped General Wright.

"No, Sir," replied Xander, "SDS nor I make a penny on a crisis, General. The investigation, the upgrades, or the payload profiles do not cost the Government a penny —not one. Sir."

"General Wright, has NSA assessed the attack? Do you have attribution?" interjected the President, clearly agitated at General Wright's swipe.

"No, Sir," advised General Wright, "We are still running forensics on the SDS data and confirming the authenticity."

"Xander, attribution?" pulsed the President.

"Sir, SDS documented nine attacks in the past 24 hours. Each of the moves sequenced, one-two-three, repeating to nine," reported Xander, "each used the same threat vector codenamed RAVEN with dated payloads tied to vintage cyberattacks."

"Where are you going with this, Xander," piped General Wright.

> "Sir, each sequenced attack used tailored vulnerabilities to exploit each target," summarized Xander, "This is Paul Ross. Tucked away with Iran, Paul fired the nine attacks to misdirect us based on the threat's vulnerability, importance, and correlation to the signature of the payload. Paul tailored the Aramco attack to fit an Israeli

signature. Paul made the Israeli attack look like a Saudi retaliation. Paul designed the China attack signature to look like Taiwan and Hong Kong protestors. The Chinese seem to have already concluded this point. But will exploit the matter to move against Hong Kong and Taiwan. The Russian attack, Paul pointed to Turkey and Ukraine. Paul made the London Tube attack look like a rogue element of Pakistan's Intelligence Services (ISI). Paul customized the North Korean attack to look like Japan and South Korea. This is the powder keg moment. Kim Jong-un is a hothead and will not listen to evidence. Paul designed the final attack in Europe with a Russian signature. Each signature is designed for the target. The geo-political math works. State agrees. However, the IC and State concur with SDS. Logical math does not add up. These nine moves were choreographed to set the world on fire and tip the scales to a shooting war. But the coordination of disparate groups attacking the same day within hours. It does not hold. The nine moves were one attacker, Paul Ross, working with Iran."

"I understand you have an advanced cyberweapon in development at SDS. I understand that you can stop this attack at any moment. Why are you holding out?" pressed General Wright.

"I do have an advanced cyberweapon in development —RUBICON. General Wright, you and the entire IC have read the SDS RUBICON Brief. RUBICON is not ready. I named the concept RUBICON for a reason. Once we open the underlying technology, there is no going back," shot back Xander, "RUBICON is not your concern. Aviation vulnerability is. Secretary Porter, if I may transition, General, the focus needs to center on the threat to the Aviation Sector."

"Pretty thin, theory, Xander," quipped General Wright.

"The logic is sound, General," Tess remarked coldly.

"Thank you, Xander. I do want to elevate the risk to the Aviation Sector," confirmed

Secretary Porter, "Mr. President, I agree with you. The U.S. Government needs to press the Critical Infrastructure owners, the bulk of which is privately owned, to accelerate threat and vulnerability risks."

"Toby is working on a message theme for all departments and a speech for me in a few hours. Jess will pound from the Podium all day and on the talk shows," directed President Hammond.

"Xander, do you have the Aviation concept, ANGEL WINGS, completed?" pulsed Secretary Porter.

"Yes, Ma'am," reported Xander, "SDS is providing the tool as we speak to DOD, DHS, and the IC."

"ANGEL WINGS?" pulsed the President.

"Sir, SDS developed ANGEL WINGS after the capturing the payload during an in-flight attack on Xander's plane, carrying his family, including Amelia, to Charleston," reported Secretary Porter, "Xander used his flight as bait for Paul Ross. He took the bait."

"XANDER, YOU USED YOUR FLIGHT AS BAIT!" thundered President Hammond.

"Yes, Sir. I did," claimed Xander, "And, we now know how Paul brought down the planes. He never stood a chance to take my plane. The same way I know Paul cannot take down your Plane, Sir."

"I bet my plane is nicer," teased President Hammond calming down, with a sense of pride in Xander's sacrifice.

"I doubt that, Sir," quipped Tess, pressing the room to light laugh, "Your plane was built by the lowest bidder and not by Xander."

"What does 'ANGEL WINGS' do?" asked the President.

"Sir, AW allows DOD Combat Air Traffic Controllers deployed throughout the United States the capability to override RAVEN Aviation and safely land the plane," reported Xander as the room sucked in a collective gasp, "Risky, yes. But this is the best choice. We do not need to watch planes fall from the sky. After the Nine attacks last night, two planes, and attacks with HERON and CHAOS, I have had enough of Paul Ross."

"Nine?" pulsed the President, "Xander, this is splendid work. Thank you. But Nine?"

"Yes, Sir. Nine distinct cyberattacks last night," relayed Xander.

"Xander, DHS CISA received a report of a Tenth attack this morning. A hospital in Asheville, North Carolina, suffered a breach of a patient's..." started Secretary Porter.

"A heart attack," finished a shaken Xander.

"Yes, a 79-year-old male died after the malware shocked the patient with the defibrillator and altered the monitored vitals to show a healthy patient, disabling the alarms. The patient was in cardiac arrest resulting from a fatal shock," reported Secretary Porter.

"Mr. President, this confirms the "thin" theory," proclaimed Xander.

"How so?" pressed General Wright.

"Mr. President. The 79-year-old male was Dr. Samuel Jonathan Cohen of Asheville, North Carolina," shared Xander.

"Yes, that is correct," disclosed a stunned Secretary Porter.

"Mr. President. Dr. Samuel J. Cohen is my father-in-law. Gabby was in a video chat with her parents when Dr. Cohen passed away, in front of Katy and Amelia."

"Sir, this is Paul Ross. He is behind the Ten attacks, attack on generic pharmaceuticals, the two planes, HERON, and CHAOS," concluded Xander.

# CHAPTER FIFTEEN — ANGEL WINGS

Yuriko jumped from the helo running to cover Daniyah. Daniyah and Paul broke cover and ran with Yuriko. Once onboard, Yuriko slammed and secured the door and motioned for the pilots to dust-off in a combat maneuver, with a low profile to ground cover. IRGC's Qud Force was on the hunt and wanted Paul.

Minister Abbas narrowly avoided an assassination attempt. The Supreme Leader ignored such when not in his presence. IRGC, angered by the Manjil Operation, wanted Paul and the cyberweapon capabilities. And, IRGC wanted Abbas, Daniyah, Yuriko, and the MOIS team dead.

"AMIR, THIS IS YOUR, Son?" pulsed Brigadier General Karim Abdi, Commander of the IRGC's Qud Force, "Yes?"

"Yes, Karim," replied MOIS SIGINT Minister Amir Begum, "This is my son, Adel."

"Young Man!" boomed General Abdi, "Can you make this RAVEN Aviation work?"

"Yes," replied a nervous Adel Begum, "Yes, Sir. I monitored Manjil closely. The Americans built a straightforward package with a payload. If the Americans have not closed the vulnerabilities, RAVEN Aviation works. If the Americans have closed the vulnerability, we are at square one. We may need the American, alive."

"I want one of the flights approaching Ronald Reagan Washington National Airport[1]. I want you to divert the plane into the White House at the last moment. Can you do this?" pulsed General Abdi.

"Conditional to the vulnerabilities, mentioned," clarified Adel, "Yes."

"Understood. I understand the vulnerabilities and keeping the American alive. Do it," ordered General Abdi.

"Yes, Sir," dutifully replied Adel.

ADEL HAD A NARROW WINDOW to use RAVEN Aviation. The approach to Ronald Reagan Washington National Airport swings out to Middleburg, Virginia, following an easterly vector to Chantilly, Virginia, following I64 to Arlington, Virginia. Commercial airlines follow a strict flight path into Reagan National Airport (DCA). Commercial traffic passes over the Potomac crossing the southern tip of Theodore Roosevelt Island for a hard southerly turn directly over the Lincoln Memorial, then straight to DCA. The approach window is narrow and passes close to the State Department, the White House, Congress, and the Supreme Court.

PILOT SOPHIA CLARK and Co-Pilot Amy White commanded Reagent Airways Flight 4100 from Charlotte, North Carolina, to Washington D.C. Reagan Washington National. 4100 flew three daily routes between Charlotte and the Nation's Capital. 4100 was a popular flight with a near 100 percent on-time rate, excellent customer service ratings, and well-planned departure and arrival times. 4100 got you in and out, on time, with no hassles, perfect for the day-trippers. Clark and White led an all-female and diverse

1. https://www.flyreagan.com/dca/reagan-national-airport

crew, and the frequent 4100 passengers got to know their crew and built a loyal following. Clark and White served in the U.S. Military. Still an Air Force Reservist, Sophia Clark flew the F-16 Fighting Falcon with several combat missions to her credit. Amy White is a United States Marine flying a V-22 Osprey with dozens of combat missions in Iraq and Afghanistan and a cool hand under pressure. Clark and White read the FAA Brief this morning on the risk of RAVEN in the aviation sector DHS CISA alerted the FAA of a scenario that an APT could disable the cockpit from controlling the plane. The FAA continued to study the Midwest and Pacific crashes for a specific threat. One source unverified by the FAA provided the sector with threat indicators. A DOD and DHS Briefing followed, noting that pilots experiencing a loss of control need to inform air traffic controllers without delay using the CODEWORD ANGELWINGS (Alpha Whiskey).

"Almost there, Amy," shared Sophia, "The news of these attacks looks really bad. I suspect you, and I will need to plan for another deployment before this is over."

"I know. The devastation in Israel is heartbreaking. I have not heard from my Aunt in Tel Aviv. She moved there from Florida a few years ago. I will be glad when the FAA demands that Reagent upgrades and secures the company network," opined Amy, "this is scary. It Brings back memories of September 11th. Now terrorists don't need to take the plane. They can use a keyboard, stay offshore in a bunker, and kill us. They have turned commercial aviation into a drone program."

"Reagent 4100 maintain flight level 10, ten thousand and contact AML 113.5," directed ATC, Air Traffic Control.

"Reagent 4100 contact Washington Center 124.7," squawked DCA ATC.

"Washington Center, this is Reagent 4100," responded Amy.

"Here, we go," affirmed Sophia.

SIX THOUSAND MILES away in a remote area outside of Tehran, Adel squared up to the keyboard with a room full of IRGC, ready to see the strike at the heart of American Power. Adel reviewed the link with Reagent 4100, tested the connection, and pressed execute.

"SOPHIA, WE ARE PICKING up speed," reported Amy.

"Throttle back," ordered Sophia, "No effect. Disengage Auto-Pilot, no control," shared Sophia, looking at Amy with a look of grave concern.

"Washington Central, Reagent 4100 – we have no control of the airplane – Alpha Whiskey – I repeat – Alpha Whiskey," reported Amy.

"Reagent 4100, Washington Central, say again, are you declaring Alpha Whiskey?" pulsed Washington Central.

"Roger, Reagent 4100 is Alpha Whiskey, Alpha Whiskey, confirmed," replied Amy.

"Roger, Reagent 4100 Alpha Whiskey," confirmed Washington Central.

"ALL SET, DR. GREENE," quipped Ms. Pat, "The President is almost ready. Tess gave the look."

"The 'President is pontificating, again' Look," joked Malik.

"Yes, the President does ask a ton of questions. I guess I see why with all the activity. My Lord, the images from Israel break my heart. My head is spinning with the explosions, plane crashes, banks, and medical care. My Lord, you can't even trust the medicines you take," droned Ms. Pat.

"Malik, the President, is ready," interrupted Tess.

As Malik rose, the Secret Service burst into the Oval Office, rushing to cover the President!

"Mr. President, we are taking you to the Bunker, NOW!" informed the lead agent, almost scooping up the President in a dead run.

"Tess, Malik, with me," ordered the President.

"Sir, there is an Alpha Whiskey plane inbound," reported the lead agent. The Vice President detail swept the VP to a secure location as details in the White House, Capitol Hill, Supreme Court, the State Department, and dozens of agencies reacted to secure key staff, employees, and the public to safety. Within a few moments, President Hammond was in the secure elevator and on the way down to the Presidential Bunker.

"WASHINGTON CENTRAL, Reagent 4100 – we have control of the landing gear and fuel dump, minor systems," reported Sophia.

"Reagent 4100, Washington Central, Roger," replied Washington Central.

"Reagent 4100, squawk 233.2, immediately for USAF ATC," ordered Washington Central.

"Reagent 4100, 233.2, Roger," responded Amy.

"233 is a military freq.," explained Amy.

"Yeah, this could get interesting," replied a calm Sophia.

"R4100 AF ATC," pulsed the Air Force Combat Air Traffic Controller.

"AF ATC, Reagent, 4100," replied Sophia.

"R4100, we don't have time for formalities. I am Master Sergeant Danforth. I understand, Sophia; you are Air Force, and Amy, you are a Marine," checked MSG Danforth.

"Yes, Captains Clark and White, MSG Danforth," replied Amy.

"Okay, simple plain English, I don't have a lot of time. I did not have time to get all the instruments set up to fly you in. I am executing an experimental cyberweapon to regain control. If this works, I will follow your instructions on flying your plane. I will have control of the airplane —Sound Good," pulsed the MSG.

"Danforth, Clark, it is better than letting Haji, crash us into the White House expedite Danforth," agreed Sophia.

"Y'all good," pulsed MSG Danforth, "I am almost ready."

"We are good. So, death by an experimental tool designed by the lowest bidder or death by a terrorist. We are good," joked Amy.

"Nah, this is SDS gear, really high-end," assured MSG Danforth, "The government would never pay for this. Col. Ridge is a solid DUDE. If Col. Ridge says this works, it works. We were just not set up yet for full deployment. Y'all were about 45 minutes too quick on your Alpha Whiskey."

"Sorry to mess up your schedule, MSG," poked Sophia.

"That is okay, Captains. Officers have been messing up, my day good, since 1776," poked MSG Danforth, "Okay, I gotcha!"

"I am going to slow your speed. Give me the correct number," pulsed MSG Danforth, "I am here in Washington Central, so the airspace is clear. So, it is just us."

"We are pushing 500 knots; drop us to 200 and back to 9 thousand, please," ordered Amy.

"Confirm speed and altitude correction?" pulsed MSG Danforth.

"Roger, speed is dropping, and the glide slope is aligning for DCA approach," confirmed Amy.

"Okay, we gotcha. You will walk me through it, and ILF and Whiskey Charlie will help me on this end. Sophia, Amy. I am going to get you home," reported MSG Danforth.

"Does, Haji, know you ruined his plans?" checked Amy.

"Nope, Col. Ridge is a smart DUDE! He is sending false data back and doing some other crazy smart dude stuff. SDS can see your instruments now," reported MSG Danforth, "SDS is taking control of your airplane and are on the freq. now. An Air Force Pilot is commanding your airplane. You just need to provide visual confirmation of instruments."

"Roger, this is a first in Aviation," affirmed Sophia.

"Yes, it is Captain Clark. This is Colonel Andrews," opened Colonel Andrews.

"Sir, it is good to hear your voice, Sir," quipped an excited Sophia.

"Captain Clark and Captain White, we will get you down. I am diverting to Joint Base Andrews. We need to get the flight recorder to SDS and the NSA smart people to combat this attack. So, sit back, relax, and enjoy the ride. We have a drone over your airplane to help me with visual flight. But I still need your eyes."

Colonel Andrews guided Reagent 4100 and the 180 passengers to a smooth and safe landing at Joint Base Andrews. SDS captured added RAVEN Aviation data. Enough to give DHS a clear path to protect commercial aviation. The industry would need to move quickly. Xander tucked the geolocation of the signal away for POTUS. Xander slipped a note to Special Agents Patrick Kelly and Mark Reyes. Reyes rejoined the SDS team to hunt for Paul Ross. Agents Kelly and Reyes looked at Xander's note, "NOT Paul Ross. This attack was not the same. The attack came from IRAN —Urmia, Iran! This was IRGC, Qud Force."

Reyes looked at Xander with an are you sure look. Xander nodded. Reyes and Kelly at once left for the SDS SCIF.

# CHAPTER SIXTEEN — IRENE

President Hammond wasted no time pulling the National Security Council together in the White House Situation Room. He was furious that the industry was not moving fast enough to improve cybersecurity, with DHS and SDS pushing out the critical vulnerabilities, patches, and indicators.

"Let me be clear, the SIGINT from SDS is confirmed by the IC, except the NSA. I want this resolved, and I want to know if I can hit the IRGC HQ in Urima!" gritted an angry President Hammond. General Wright, NSA, held back on the SDS data despite having full access. General Wright was growing more suspicious of SDS and Xander. Several detected a sense of professional jealousy. Rumors circulated D.C. like flies on cow patties. And Rumors pondered a transition at NSA.

"General, what is your status on the SDS intelligence," pointed the President.

"Sir, the NSA analysts cannot confirm the SDS intelligence, specifically the source is IRGC in Urima," reported General Wright, "SDS uses an unknown tool and algorithm. To be sure, I need the SDS RUBICON."

"RUBICON is off the table, Shawn. SDS is using in experimental status only and under my authority," fired back the President.

"Sir, you are using an experimental tool to collect complicated SIGINT for attribution to launch a strike. You need me to have RUBICON to confirm," returned Wright.

"General Roberts, do you agree with the SDS intelligence, Henry, Christian, Becky, Malik!" exclaimed the President.

"Yes," affirmed a unified group.

"I respectfully disagree," argued a defiant General Wright.

"Duly Noted, Shawn," leered the President.

"Secretary Cooke, are you prepared to STRIKE," pulsed the President.

"Yes, Sir. USS Greenville is in position and locked on IRGC Qud Force HQ in Urmia. Captain Guy is locked and loaded," reported Secretary Cooke.

"Secretary Porter. Thoughts?" pulsed the President.

"Strike, Sir. We need to send a clear message. The United States will not tolerate an attack on our Homeland or Forces abroad. Or stand by while Iran attacks our friends and allies around the World. I appreciate General Wright's reservation. But strike Sir," said Secretary Porter in a firm tone. Secretary Porter held back her concern for General Wright's opposition. Wright seemed wound tight about RUBICON.

"Vice President Kent. Thoughts?" pulsed President Hammond.

"Strike," agreed the Vice President, "I agree with Madam Secretary."

"Move U.S. Forces to DEFCON 2," ordered the President.

"Secretary Cooke, IRENE," ordered the President. The Secretary of Defense rose and walked the Ensign standing by with the Pentagon on the phone. He spoked into the handset, "IRENE." IRENE. Captain Guy turned to the crew of the USS Greenville, "Battle Stations! Man, Battle Stations Missile, IRENE. I say again, IRENE." The USS Greenville hovered 150 feet below the surface of the Persian Gulf, opened two missile hatches, and fired.

ADEL BEGUM AND MINISTER Amir Begum enjoyed tea in an empty café area of the IRGC Qud Force Headquarters in Urmia, Iran. The IRGC managed Syrian and Iraq operations at this post. IRGC collected intelligence and did not share it with MOIS. The rivalry stunted the effectiveness of Iran. A weakness exploited by the United States, despite repeated warnings from Russian and Chinese Case Officers. The Americans stoked the fires of jealousy, as did Israel. Attributed assassinations to the Mossad were, in fact, Iranian against Iranian, borne of distrust and fed lies by the enemy. IRGC did not understand the nuances of tradecraft. The Manjil Operation, Daniyah, and Paul buried the SIGINT signatures of each attack. Young Adel is inexperienced.

"Begum! The plane! Your target did not crash! You failed to hit the White House!" exclaimed General Abdi.

"Sir, the Amer......"

The American missiles struck. The first missile penetrated through the thick concrete and rebar reinforced against a bombardment, ripping the building open. The second missile plunged deep into the soul of the IRGC and exploded with American rage. Iran had tugged on the tail of a sleeping giant one too many times. The sleeping giant was awake and hungry. A wisp of August 1945 breezed across Iran.

# CHAPTER SEVENTEEN – EXECUTIVE ORDERS

With a prideful stride, the President walked into the Oval to set the day and record straight. America had struck at the heart of Iran, bringing justice to evil men who plotted the deaths of so many of the World's peoples. President Hammed held DEFCON 2 and would announce such to the World in a few hours. The United States was on a war footing. Hammond took a deep breath before the portrait of John Fitzgerald Kenned, the 35th President. The 35th and 46th shared a bond in history —the only Presidents in history to order DEFCON 2. Hammond steeled himself for DEFCON 1. Praying to order a strategic series of moves on the global chessboard back to DEFCON 3. Timed with the afternoon press conference, the Pentagon would unleash RETRIBUTION. Hammond intends to knock Iran back to throwing rocks. The United States Airforce and a Naval armada planned to decimate Iran's ability to perpetrate terrorism and armed aggression.

"Malik, what news do you have for me this morning?" pulsed the President.

> "Sir, Good Morning. The battle damage assessment of the Urima strike shows a direct hit by two bunker-buster missiles. The IRGC Qud Force bunker is now a smoldering crater. Russia and China are holding DEFCON, not matching our current readiness. A clear sign that neither wants to escalate tensions with the United States. However, Russian and Chinese

intelligence operatives are active in the Mediterranean theater. Considerable activity in and around Casablanca. Sir, the movement suggests that Paul Ross or his Iranian Case Officer Daniyah Rahman may be running or dead. Intelligence suggests the IRGC failed to assassinate MOIS Minister Mahmoud Ashkan Abbas. The Urima Strike killed the man who wanted Abbas dead. SIGINT and HUMINT confirmed Brigadier General Karim Abdi is dead, and so is MOIS Minister of Signals Intelligence, Minister Amir Begum. Begum and Abdi in the same place is interesting, considering IRGC and MOIS despise the souls of one another," reported Malik Greene.

"Abdi and Begum in the same place, interesting. Where the hell is Ross? Did we get him in the strike?" pulsed Hammond.

"No, Sir, we do not have confirmation that Ross or Rahman were in Urmia. Sir, intelligence suggests Rahman and Ross are together. SIGINT and HUMINT suggest Rahman and Ross left soon after the Tenth attack on the Ridge family. They just missed an assassination attempt by IRGC Qud Force. Qud Force wanted Ross to build cyberweapons direct, cutting MOIS out of the loop. Daniyah was too fast for the hit. She and an MOIS team dusted off just seconds before the attack on their position," clarified Malik.

"Is Ross capable of follow-on attacks?" pressed Hammond.

"Yes, Sir. He is capable as long as he is alive," confirmed Malik.

"General Roberts, FROST, find PAUL ROSS AND DANIYAH RAHMAN, NOW!" exclaimed Hammond.

"Get Ross off the chessboard, NOW!" continued Hammond.

"Tess, get Xander up here. I want to discuss RUBICON. I am certain Xander can find Ross with RUBICON. I appreciate his concerns, but I want Ross off the board," ordered the President.

"DANNY, TESS PHONED this morning. She invited Xander to meet with President Hammond in the Oval Office," reported Mia, SDS Executive Assistant.

"Invited, Tess," quipped Danny with a gruff, "Mia, that was a summons to the principal's office."

"The President wants Xander to do something, and I suspect he wants RUBICON," theorized Danny, "I will inform Xander. Thank you, Mia.

Danny ran down to the SDS gym and changed into his old Navy PT gear. Chilly as it was, he balled it out in the Navy-blue shorts and classic golden yellow T. Danny took off at a brisk pace to beat Xander before leaving the residence. Today, the first meeting is a running meeting; Danny quipped to himself with a slight smile. He and Danny often worked out complex issues by running around the base, forward operating base, post, and now at SDS. Xander and Danny were lifelong friends, brothers. Danny knew Xander would need to think this through. Telling the President of the United States, no, was not easy. But true leaders did just that. Speaking truth to power is the ultimate test of command.

GENERAL SHAWN WRIGHT and a small security detail touched down at a small airfield outside Nice, France. Wright arranged to meet Paul Ross to discuss a covert arrangement with the NSA. Wright wanted, desperately, the technology of RUBICON. Xander was a long shot and too close with his old pals at the CIA, Tess, and the President. Wright needed RUBICON at this moment to keep America's edge post-Manjil. A deal with the Devil and his Mistress is not too high a price.

"General Wright," opened Paul, "This is an interesting turn of events. Not what I expected."

"Is this Daniyah?" taunted Wright.

"Yes, Sir," replied Paul, "This deal does not work without Daniyah."

"You killed a good agent in Paris. Most of this room wants to put two rounds in your chest and one in your head. I have not decided yet," opined Wright.

"I see it, like this. You are a warrior for your flag, your country," lectured Wright staring down Daniyah, "You did what needed doing. Now your country hunts you. They want what I want. But I offer you a new life. Work for me and live. Refuse, die here, right now."

"Do I stay with Paul?" clarified Daniyah.

"Yes, if he wants you," taunted Wright.

"Do I have to betray Iran?" pressed Daniyah.

"NO, I don't need anything from you about Iran. I need you to keep Paul alive. Kill only when I tell you," pushed Wright.

"What about it, Paul? I will set you up with a lab, a new name, and a place to hide. But you need to develop the RUBICON technology and off-the-books cyberweapons for the NSA," offered Wright.

"Where could I go? Where could we go?" tested Paul.

"I will arrange for a new location. I will tuck you away in the state of Washington or Idaho in a remote safe house in the mountains," continued Wright.

"So, I can run or be your prisoner," postured Paul.

"No, you can die right here. Or you can work for your Country and redeem your soul," countered Wright.

"Okay," replied Paul, "But I need more from Xander. I need more on RUBICON to get what you want. We need to put pressure on him to give it up or allow Daniyah an opportunity to slip in and steal it."

"I have a plan," teased Wright, "Xander's weakness is his family. I believe your Persian Lover had a plan to kidnap Gabriella Ridge. Did you not?" Daniyah's insides were wretched with fear and surprise. But a professional spy did not flinch a muscle, flick an eyelash, or twitch a pupil, just steadfast stone-cold expressionless.

"Hmmm, you are good, my dear. But like I said, I need nothing from you about Iran," pressed Wright with a devilish grin."

"A deal with the Devil is edgy," offered Daniyah, "The question is: who is the Devil and who is the Saint in our little arrangement. But I agree to my end. I will keep Paul alive and help obtain RUBICON. Grabbing Gabby is an effective way to pressure Xander."

"I like her, Paul," concluded Wright with eyes steadfastly locked on Daniyah, "Paul, I need an answer. Or my boys here will kill you and your team outside."

"Yes," answered Paul.

---

"XANDER, WELCOME TO the Oval Office," beamed President Hammond.

"Thank you, Mr. President. How can I help you?" opened Xander, wasting no time.

"Straight to the point, as usual, Xander. I have missed having you on the teams," confessed Tess.

"Xander, how vulnerable is the Critical Infrastructure in the United States to a RAVEN type attack?" positioned the President.

"Extremely, the recent event proved the exposure and the consequences," noted Xander, "CI in the US is privately owned and exposed. The priorities are balanced against consequence and probability versus cost."

"What could my administration do to drive the private sector to do more?" questioned the President.

"Sir, you can use the pulpit of the Presidency to set the priority. As one of the Government's top-tier cyberweapons designers and providers of cybersecurity defenses, I can tell you that human error is the root cause of a cybersecurity breach in 70% of the cases. A person opens a link, violates a rule, allows a threat actor unauthorized access, downloads a tool, or is the cybersecurity manager who manages costs versus consequence," reported Xander.

"Can you stand with me during a briefing?" asked the President, "Then I would like to have dinner with you and Tess in the Residence."

"Of course, Mr. President. But you want to discuss RUBICON?" proposed Xander.

"Yes, I do," quickly replied the President, "I am worried about what comes next. And your presentation earlier stuck in my head. Quantum Computing and entanglement scare the hell out of us."

"You should be. But I just made advances. I did not create a weapon to be used against the United States, Sir," delineated Xander.

"I am not worried about you," explained the President, "I am worried about our enemies getting the upper hand with Quantum Computing and entanglement. I am worried about what my predecessor would have done with this capability. I am worried about General Wright, a holdover from the predecessor."

"Sir. I appreciate your concern. I trust you. I don't trust the office to always do right based on the greater good and not the political good," tendered Xander.

"Xander. I am not going to ask you for RUBICON. I see your points. I need something else from you," reassured the President, "I am concerned about a traitor in my administration."

"Well, that is a problem," agreed Xander.

"XANDER, IT IS AN HONOR to meet you, Sir," opened Toby Isaac, White House Communications Director.

"Honor is mine, Toby. If you can make this man look Presidential, you are a talent without equal," quipped Xander with a smile.

"Easy, Colonel. I can draft you back into Military Service," joked the President.

"You two served together?" questioned Toby.

"Yes, Toby. Before he held such esteem, the Colonel worked for me through JSCO at the CIA. The Colonel is a cunning warrior and the bar none, the best battlefield strategist in the profession. He can find a path to victory in the direst of predicaments," praised President Hammond.

"Tess, you as well?" checked Toby.

"Oh, yes," confirmed Tess, "Xander, Danny, and the President wrought ruination of many an enemy with our schemes."

"It is an honor to work with each of you," Toby expressed respectfully.

"Toby, you served as well, in the Air Force, a Major, if memory serves. You flew Puff the Magic Dragon," credited Xander.

"Yes, I did," Toby claimed proudly.

"Then you are my savior. Puff the Magic Dragon saved Danny's and my asses dozens of times," cajoled Xander.

"Aside from this Post, the best job I ever did; it is an honor," finished Toby.

"Okay, Toby. Walk me through our message," aligned the President back to the purpose.

Toby presented the press briefing talking points for the President. The message centered on the missile strike on the Qud

Force Headquarters and the IRGC's role in the cyberattacks. Toby laid a timeline included in the press briefing packet and, on an easel, displayed in the room.

The President will point to Xander's role in defending the United States by designing the weapons used to strike Iran and the strike announced during the briefing. The United States planned a broader strike against Iran, degrading the Iranian Air Force, Navy, and ground forces. The attack would use, for the first time in the history of warfare, hypersonic weapons, designed by SDS and Xander, to surgically strike targets without the type of collateral damage from guided munitions and smart bombs.

The President would announce that he is awarding Col. Xander Ridge U.S.A (Ret.) The Presidential Medal of Freedom and the Congressional Gold Medal with the Speaker of the House and the Senate Majority Leader for the work saving Reagent 4100 from the Iranian Attack. The President would present Master Sergeant Danforth with the U.S. Air Force Cross for his heroic actions in saving Reagent 4100.

The wrap-up ends on a challenge to the Sixteen Department of Homeland Security Critical Infrastructure Sector to lock down cybersecurity. The President would jointly announce an emergency spending authorization to help Americans recover from the attack with Congress. The President would suggest the risk of Executive Action if the private sector did not quickly close cybersecurity gaps.

"SIR, I AM HONORED, doubly so," quivered Xander, "I do not deserve such." The President held up his hand to pause Xander respectfully.

"Xander. You and SDS gave the American people a chance to fight back and saved hundreds of American lives," recounted the

President, "Xander, I need you to investigate General Shawn Wright, Director of the NSA."

"We, including CIA Director Frost, believe that Wright is working his agenda," reported Tess, "We suspect he knew about Iran compromising Paul Ross and the exploitation of RAVEN."

"Xander. I am not asking for RUBICON. I am asking you if RUBICON can investigate Wright without tipping our hand. Can we spy on the Nation's top Spy?" queried the President.

"Sir. RUBICON is not an experiment. We have pushed beyond Quantum Computing and solved Quantum Entanglement. In short, we can blow past firewalls and encryption like a searing hot knife through warm butter," countered Xander, "RUBICON is technology three steps beyond our control. Entanglement theory is scary stuff, Mr. President. We can lock on to an inflight ICBM and precisely guide a hypersonic missile. We do not know what entanglement can do or quantify the risk."

"Understood. I appreciate your respect for such power, Xander," acknowledged the President, "This is why I trust you to wield this power. I am authorizing you to engage with RUBICON to defend the United States, if necessary. I authorize you to engage and investigate the National Security Agency Director to determine if General Wright is a traitor, misguided, or acting independently of my authority. All three possibilities are dangerous for the United States of America and are a Clear and Present Danger.

"Yes, Sir," responded Xander.

# CHAPTER EIGHTEEN – ABDUCTION

"Mom, did you sleep last night?" asked Amelia.

"Oh, Sweet Girl, you don't need to worry about me," quipped Gabby, "I am fine. I just don't sleep well if Daddy's out of town. Too many deployments over the years bring back bad dreams. But I slept enough. Thank you for letting me have a 'Girl's Night' in your room. Dr. Katy even had fun."

"Do we have to go to Charlotte today?" asked Amelia.

"Maybe. Dr. Katy will need to make the call if you need the added test," compassionately shared Gabby.

GENERAL WRIGHT SET up Daniyah with a new team of mercenaries to conduct the mission. Paul's twist on the mission was a step too far, even for an experienced operation like Daniyah. One needs to consider how far to push the Devil. *The Devil has a breaking point and is a formidable foe. He can strike back at your heart and soul. Qud Force learned this lesson and ate two missiles. How far can we push Xander Ridge before we get RUBICON, or does he consumes us? All of us,* thought Daniyah. *Or is Paul the Devil? Am I dancing with the Devil, sleeping with him, or falling in love with the Devil himself?* thought Daniyah as she waited outside the SDS compound for her target.

Daniyah expanded her deal with General Wright and secured an escape for Yuriko. Yuriko was loyal to Iran to a fault but still loved Daniyah and followed her. The Qud Force attack on Manjil and the attempted assassination of his father, Minister Ashkan Abbas, pulled on his soul. *What was the meaning of loyalty to a state, sworn by oath to give your life, will willingly take yours for no cause*? wrestled Yuriko's thoughts. Yuriko had no such conflict with killing for the state, the People of Iran, or Islam. But he struggled when a leader such as Abdi threw warriors for God to the wolves for political gain. He hated Americans but hated traitors of Islam more. Americans were like dogs. A dog is a dog and does what it does. But the Qud Force had a choice. And Abdi betrayed Iran. The dog consumed him. Yuriko was sure of only a few things. First, he loved Daniyah. Second, his devotion to his Islamic faith was just and true. And third, Paul was the Devil. With whom Daniyah danced too closely.

"KATY, CAN YOU DRAW my blood for the tests? The nurses are nice. But it hurts when they try to find my veins," asked a nervous Amelia. Amelia needed blood work and full-body scans periodically to watch for the spread of her cancer. Xander and Gabby planned to add the capability to the SDS medical facilities. But the construction crew needed more time to finish the project, so off to nearby Charlotte. Gabby hated the trips, despite the Charlotte medical team's excellent care, and much preferred to be at home in the capable care of Katy. Ken and Kyla, the SDS Executive Protection team leaders, were due back from Washington along with Xander. But a weather ground stop for fog delayed Xander and the team's departure. Xander preferred to have Kyla, a former Israeli Mossad Officer, travel with Amelia and Gabby. With the delay, Ken and Kyla phoned the SDS EP team in Fort Mill to detail the instructions on the visit to Charlotte.

Daniyah and Yuriko had concerns about the new team, men of divided loyalties and skill. General Wright praised the black operators as capable of a simple snatch and grab. But the men arrived, heavy. Heavy in the context of full battle rattle prepared for a full-on engagement, American style. A kidnapping was subtle work. Wright insisted on the SDS location rather than a quiet snatch-n-grab at the Charlotte hospital, Daniyah planned. Gabby and Amelia should be in the middle SUV. The lead SUV is the surveillance and blocking vehicle. The last SUV is the counter-assault team. The stolen garbage truck planned to ram the third SUV down the embankment, giving Daniyah's team the time to hit the middle SUV. Daniyah's team planned to hit the middle SUV, take out the lead EP agent, grab Amelia and Gabby, and exfil.

"DANNY, WOULD YOU LIKE to join us for a run?" teased Special Agent Kelly, "Reye, here says you are old and broken down. You couldn't catch him running downhill."

"Wait, Danny, he is messing with you!" protested Reyes. Reyes Danny was retired Navy but had only recently learned that Danny was a SEAL Commander.

"Ha, Marky-Two Guns want a shot at the title!" teased Danny, "I will run you two FBI girls into the ground if you get wet and sandy and meet me in the grappling pit down by the river, afterward!"

"Okay, now, you went too far with that one," teased Reyes, "I am a good grappler, so you are on!"

"Well, you may be good. And if you were Agent Love, well, maybe I would be concerned. But he says you suck," taunted Danny. Danny burst out, laughing at Reyes' ashen look. Agent Love was a badass and reputed in the FBI as an agent who loved to grapple and get it on with bad guys for fun. If Danny considered Love, a student, Reyes wrote a check that his skill could not cash.

"Come on, Boys, let's go for a run. We can take the long route by the residences by the main road. It will give me a chance to see Anne. Anne is going with Gabby, Katy, and Amelia to Charlotte," suggested

Danny. The threesome started the run with a rowdy chat of fitness routines and best practices. It was good for Reyes to get out. Danny was busting his chops for fun but knew that Reyes was hurting losing his partner in Paris. Danny worked to get Reyes back into a good headspace. Running, getting wet and sandy, grappling, and shooting were good activities to get him focused. Danny knew all too well the pain of losing a teammate in battle. And the importance of keeping the edge and focus. The fight was still out there. The enemy was lurking.

"GABBY!" EXCLAIMED ANNE as she walked up the Ridge driveway and under the covered area of the main entrance.

"Anne, I heard you might join us," exclaimed Gabby, "Xander, Ken, and Kyla are delayed getting out of D.C."

"I heard the President awarded Xander the Medal of Freedom! Congratulations!" declared Anne.

"Thank you. Xander will not admit it. But he was a bit surprised at the Medal of Freedom. I suspect he will look at it once and bury it with the rest of his awards and citations from his service," appreciated Gabby.

"Aunt Anne!" squealed Amelia, "Are you coming with us to Charlotte?"

"Yes, I am Sweet Girl!" beamed Anne, "And when the doctors finish with that Medical Stuff, I am taking my Girls out to lunch!"

"Yes!" squealed Amelia. She hated the immune system restrictions leaving her to the house, considerable as it was, and the SDS grounds. COVID-19 left her imprisoned at times, if not within a coma, within the secured lines of home and SDS. The risk presented too great a danger for Amelia's compromised immune system.

"Sara, are you ready?" quipped Anne, "To get this gorgeous young woman on the road to meet a handsome Doctor!"

"Anne!" squeaked Amelia.

"Oh, thou protest too much," beamed Anne, "Somebody likes her handsome Doctor!"

"Sara can Anne ride with us," pleaded Amelia.

"Sure, we can make that work. I will ride with John in the lead SUV," confirmed Sara. "DeSante, Rodriquez, Bass; I am in the lead vehicle with DeSante. Rodriquez, keep it tight. Let's roll."

The three black armored SUVs made their way through the wooded and winding roads within the SDS compound to the main gate. The advance team observed a crew repairing a flat tire on a local garbage truck and a work crew working on an adjacent property. But did not detect a threat. Anne pressed her face to the window as the convoy motored passed Danny, Patrick, Mark, and Julius, running the SDS outer loop. Danny whooped and hollered at Anne, Gabby, and Amelia. But the armored windows muted even his lion-like bellows. Anne quipped that it was coming from Danny and likely, not proper for Amelia's gentle ears. Amelia smiled and cackled. The teasing made her forget about cancer and the pain.

BAAAAAMMMMM!!!!!!! The thunderous crash shook the armored SUV carrying Gabby, Anne, and Amelia. A sinking feeling of fear and dread wiped away the joyous mood of the morning. Gabby turned to see the Third SUV smashed by the Garbage Truck rolling over and over down the hillside. The swoosh of the rocket-propelled grenade yanked Gabby's head to the lead SUV, now engulfed in flames. Another vehicle had rammed the middle SUV, but no one was sure what, where, or how during the commotion. But Gabby's ears were ringing. She could see Katy attending to an unconscious person, maybe, Amelia or Anne. Gabby's vision was going in and out. She felt something pulling at her arms and yanking her away from the vision of Katy pressing on someone's wound.

The guys heard the garbage truck crash and the whoosh of the RPG. It was a starting gun for the experienced team of runners. Each found themselves in a dead run with sidearms at the ready, sprinting towards the sound of RPGs, explosions, and gunfire.

Danny reached the scene first and saw a blonde woman yanking Gabby toward a black van. Three tangos were assaulting the Middle SUV with M4 rifles. Danny could see SDS EP Agent DeSante engaging the three tangos. Danny zeroed in on the blonde woman, hitting her center mass in the back. Body Armor! He moved up and hit her below the neckline, dropping her to the pavement. Reyes engaged next, taking two of the tangos direct with headshots at a dead run. Patrick engaged the van's driver hitting him in the upper body, following with a shot to the head. Julius engaged a dark-haired male shooting from the garbage truck, hitting him just above the armored vest line, felling him to the grass.

Four added tangos bolted from a fourth vehicle grabbing Gabby and firing into the middle SUV. Katy slumped over Amelia, shielding Amelia with her lifeless body. Anne grabbed the gun of a dead tango and opened up, striking the tango, shooting in the vehicle. Anne aimed at the tango pulling Gabby to the van, hitting him in the back and upper leg, noting his body armor. Danny trained Anne well. The tango spun and fired at Anne, striking her in the chest and felling her to Amelia's seat. Danny reached the area and engaged the two tangos finishing off DeSante, hitting both in the head. Danny spun to see a fallen Anne with a gun in her hand. He kept his focus and finished off the tango pulling at Gabby. Reyes joined him and continued the fire on the van. But a fifth tango pulled Gabby into the van and sped from the scene.

Danny rushed to the Middle SUV and found Anne bleeding and unconscious but alive. Katy was dead. DeSante was dead. Amelia was bleeding from a head wound but alive. Danny fought through the debris and called in the black van speeding away with Gabby.

Reyes looked down at the gurgling blonde woman, pulled back her hair to identify the shooter, and began giving aid.

"I know your face," paused Reyes, "You were in Paris with Ross?" Daniyah locked into Reyes' eyes, not showing fear or remorse. Reyes knew in an instant who was lying before him.

"I know your face," Reyes whispered, menacingly, "The last words you will hear, 'Special Agent Ashley Brown.'" Reyes stabbed Daniyah below her body armor and just below the ribcage with a piece of debris. He pressed the debris in slowly and twisted to open the wound cavity. Daniyah lurched forward, gasping for life's breath, drowning in her pooling blood. Reyes pulled Daniyah close to enjoy death's kiss and whispered, "I know your face. You killed my Partner. 'Special Agent Ashley Brown.'" Reyes dropped Daniyah's body to the pavement. Fully aware of her pain and the chill of death pulling at her soul, Daniyah let go and faded to darkness.

Julius swept the garbage truck for a tango. Special Agent Kelly ran to aid the Third SUV, finding injuries but nothing fatal or immediate. The SDS EP detail crawled out of the wreckage and joined the security perimeter the team set up around the ambush site. Julius found a dying Yuriko in the wreckage.

"You are a bloody mess, mate!" exclaimed Julius, "I don't think you are going to make it. So why don't you tell me what this is all about?"

"You are a Brit!" declared Yuriko.

"I am, mate," replied Julius.

"Yeah, I met a Brit," coughed Yuriko, "a few weeks ago."

"I figured you had," surmised Julius, "Now, I can rest easy. The last words you will hear are the King's English. For Jack Webb!" Julius fired two rounds into Yuriko's head and watched the brain matter splatter in the tangled debris and spilled trash.

# CHAPTER NINETEEN — ONE MINUTE TO MIDNIGHT

General Wright's phone alerted him to check a secure message from his team. GOI times two down, five sierra papa down, three sierra delta tangos down, one package secure on the way to Romeo-papa. The kidnapping was messier than General Wright wanted, especially within the United States. The mission to kill the GOI Agents was successful. Evidence left at the scene points to an attack by the IRGC on American Soil. The attack would motivate America to a war footing with Iran and the Iranian proxies, encourage Paul to press hard to develop an off-the-books RUBICON out of revenge, and press Xander into using RUBICON. General Wright needed Xander to engage with SDS so that Ross could steal RUBICON. The abduction was a risk worth taking, and the dead were collateral damage in the fight for freedom.

Xander stood resolute by Danny outside the surgical waiting room. Anne suffered two gunshot wounds, one in the chest area and a second in the abdominal area. Anne was tough and had dropped two tangos and saved Amelia's life. Danny turned and embraced his friend, quivering just a bit.

"Xander. I am sorry I was not faster," opened Danny.

"NO, NO, NO, Danny. You fought hard and saved several lives, including Amelia," consoled Xander.

"Anne got the bastard that killed Katy," paused Danny to choke back his emotions, "I smoked the two that got DeSante. Boss. He fought till he bled out. The first RPG messed him up bad. He was close to the lead SUV. But he pulled his rifle up, busted sights and all, and fought through the pain and blood loss. He held them off until I was able to engage."

"Julius is working with MI6 to figure out who these bastards are. But Reyes and Kelly are certain this was a hit by IRGC. The female GOI agent photographed by the FBI and DGSE was in Paris and likely is the one who killed Agent Brown. Boss. Reyes was good. He was right on my six and covered the flanks. He got a little dirty once he recognized the female GOI. She took shrapnel in the RPG strike. She is done," reported Danny.

"Took shrapnel?" pressed Xander.

"That is how I saw it, the fog of battle, you know," briefed Danny.

"The dark-haired GOI? Two rounds to the head?" pressed Xander.

"Guess he was rude to Julius," replied Danny, "That old SAS cranky bastard can shoot and move."

"Boss. The boys did this old school. I was there and did not stop it. Do we...," paused Danny, noticing Xander's hand.

"There is no issue. I needed clarity. I needed to hear it. Danny, they hit our families. They took my Gabby. Amelia is back in a coma. Katy is dead. Sara, DeSante, Rodriquez are dead. Anne is on the table," Xander paused and drew in a breath, "They crossed a line with me. Ross wants a war?" Xander paused to collect his thoughts.

"Boss?" pulsed Danny, "What do you want to do?"

"Get Gabby back," stated Xander as cold as ice, "Then kill them all."

PAUL EXPLODED WITH rage when informed of the disastrous mission to kidnap Gabby and Amelia. He wanted both to press on the jugular of Xander's soul, to break him down.

"With dead SDS EP Agents, Amelia's doctor dead, Danny's wife wounded, and many more wounded would only enrage Xander! I needed him in a state of fear and panic!" roared Paul at General Wright.

"You got Daniyah killed using your piss-ant mercs!" ranted Paul.

"Daniyah was a GOI Assassin! You killed her, NOT ME! The moment you slept with her and started selling MOIS, IRGC, and Iran weapons. You did this... She died a warrior's death!" fired back General Wright.

"WE HAVE XANDER OUT IN THE OPEN NOW. WE HAVE HIS WIFE! RELEASE A VIDEO! TAKE OUT YOUR RAGE ON HER; VIDEO IT! AND RELEASE IT! XANDER WILL USE RUBICON, AND YOU CAN STEAL IT!" screamed Wright.

"Earn your honor back and complete your mission," slowed Wright lowering his tone, "You can accomplish your mission, earn your millions, and I will set you up anywhere you want with a new life, as a rich and powerful man."

"Ok!" snorted Paul through his teeth, "But I want Gabby brought here to me!"

"Fine," directed Wright, "Get the world focused on an IRGC attack in America. Point the finger at Iran for this attack. Avenge Daniyah!"

TESS PULLED THE PRESIDENT to the Situation Room before exploding in a rage in front of the White House staff.

"Damn! Tess, get Malik in here!" demanded the President, "I want to know who conducted this attack! Does the FBI have a lead on Gabby Ridge?" Tess did her best to calm her old friend and Boss. But the brazen attack and murder of Americans on American soil targeting an American hero's family enraged the President. The President would move decisively to counterattack.

"Mr. President, NSA provided an intercept between the now identified GOI Agents and GOI Case Officer in Libya. The IC agrees that we have the evidence you need to tie this off and around the necks of the IRGC and the Supreme Leader of Iran," noted Malik, the CIA Presidential Daily Briefer.

"Sir, State received word from the Swiss Ambassador from sources close to the Supreme Leader. The President of Iran is publicly lauding the Iranian Agents' heroic attack working in the United States. However, back-channel sources close to the Supreme Leader report that the Supreme Leader disavows the attack on American soil and says that the Iranian Government did not authorize the attack," reported Secretary Rebecca Porter.

"Becky," squared up the President, "There are two dead Iranians in a South Carolina morgue!"

"NSA reports confusion all over Iran and a breakdown in their communications with operatives," briefed Malik, "Further, the NSA picked up an Al Jazeera news story with pictures of the scene outside SDS. The footage is from the body cameras worn by the unidentified agents believed to be Iranian mercenaries."

"The footage is bad, Sir," declared Tess, "It shows Amelia bleeding profusely from the head injury and her dead Doctor, Katy, lying over Amelia. The video shows Anne gurgling blood."

"It also shows a news banner in Persian claiming responsibility for the attack," detailed General Wright.

"Nice of you to join us, Shawn," barked an angry President.

"Yes, Sir. With SDS offline, NSA is running down leads all over the world, Sir," reported General Wright.

"Secretary Cooke! Are you in a position to carry out Phase III?" pulsed the President.

> "Yes, Sir. Phase II degraded the Iranian Air Force to only a few fighters and one base. The Navy pounded the IRIN.

> The Navy sunk or heavily damaged five frigates, three destroyers, and 21 fast attack patrol boats, two with torpedo capability. Navy Fighters struck and sank the one Coastal submarine. The USS Greenville hunted down the three attack submarines and sent them to the bottom of the gulf. In Phase III, we need to hunt down the fifteen smaller hybrid subs that could cause security concerns for the fleet closer to Iranian territorial waters. And I want to hunt down and destroy the remaining mobile missile launchers. At the end of Phase III, Khamenei will have horses, rocks, and spears." Reported and emboldened Secretary of Defense Cooke.

"Codeword to execute?" pulsed the President. Tess checked and passed the note to President Hammond. He looked up, smiled, and thought, "This is appropriate."

"Secretary Cooke. KATY," ordering the Phase III assault on Iran, "Hold American forces at DEFCON 2."

GABBY BLEEDING, BRUISED, battered, and groggy from the drugs, lay on the floor in front of Paul.

"Leave us!" Paul shouted at his security detail. Paul was not sure if the guards understood. But they followed the basic commands. However, if Paul tried an escape, he was confident the guards would not be supportive.

Gabby moaned as she tried to move to a position to breathe. Her hands were bound. Paul snatched Gabby up by her hair and then drug her to the bed using Gabby's bra strap as a handle. Paul tossed her on the bed and ripped her slacks, exposing Gabby's panties and battered legs. He assessed the injuries as serious but not life-threatening. Paul pulled on a mask to increase Gabby's fear. He could smell and taste her fear. He had been without the pleasure of a woman for several days since making his deal with Wright. Gabby would do.

"DANNY. HOW IS ANNE? I just learned she is out of surgery!" exclaimed Xander, praying for good news.

"Xander. The bullets missed the good stuff! She is going to pull through! Thank God," quivered Danny as he embraced his friend.

"Xander, Patrick, and Mark are running point on the abduction case and chasing every lead to find Gabby. Those boys will find her. The FBI pulled every agent to find Gabby and hunt down Paul. Paul Ross is now America's Most Wanted Top Ten Fugitive," Danny paused, reading Xander's face, "What? Amelia?"

"Yeah, it is not good," quaked Xander, "Amelia took a hard hit from the RPG blast. It looks like she smashed against the armored glass and cracked her skull. Her brain is swelling, and she is in a medically induced coma. It does not look good."

"Danny, we need to get back to SDS. For starters, I need you, Amira, Scout, Julius, Sam, and Jenn," requested Xander.

"Yeah, what is going on?" pulsed Danny.

"Not here; we need our SCIF," directed Xander, "Danny. Lock it down."

PAUL WORKED THROUGH the night but found his target. Not all IRGC committed to die for Iran in the outer regions; most were conscripted locals forced into service. During the shock and awe of the Phase II American Strikes, conscripts abandoned a Hormuz Mobile Missile Launch Vehicle in the desert. The conscripts fled, leaving the power to the systems enabled and ready. The IRGC dispersed the few tactical nuclear warheads throughout the country to hide them from American satellites, spy planes, and drones. The American Military destroyed most of the Iranian nuclear capability in the Phase II attack. But the Americans missed one. A mistake they would fix when the President launched Phase III.

RAVEN proved effective again. Paul set the trajectory working out the path to each target. Paul had three missiles to manage. Missile One set to strike the Knesset in West Jerusalem. Missile Two aimed at the heart of power in Israel, the Prime Minister's Office in the Kiryat Ben Gurion Building. Missile Three sought to strike the Western wall set to stab the Jewish people's hearts and spirits. Gabby groaned in pain and struggled against the restraints. Paul rose from his chair and walked to Gabby, donning his featureless black mask. Paul stood over Gabby. He walked back to the desk. Paul scanned the Hormuz systems, checked the status of the missiles, and the target trajectories, then pressed enter. One away, two away, three away... unknown to Paul, missile one was nuclear-tipped.

"TEAM, I HAVE IN FRONT of me a Presidential Authorization, with each of your names. Special Agents Kelly and Reyes, a second letter from the President and signed by the Attorney General, authorized your access and assignment to this detail. Tess confirmed each of your security clearances as TS-SCI," opened Xander, "I am reading you into a CODEWORD assignment. TAURUS."

"Team, Danny is going to walk you through the evidence momentarily. Our mission is to hunt down a traitor to the United States. Our mission is to determine if General Shawn Wright, Director of the National Security Agency, is colluding with the Iranian Republican Guard Corps and Paul Ross."

"Damn," said Reyes.

"Damn is right!" exclaimed Danny.

"I want to avoid using RUBICON, if possible. However, I will not risk American lives or the confidentiality, integrity, or availability of DOD or IC systems. If we need RUBICON, we will use it. President Hammond authorized us to use all means," shared Xander.

TESS ROUSED THE PRESIDENT from bed at zero two hundred, "Sir, you need to come to the Situation Room right now!"

"What has happened," asked a weary President Hammond, "News on Gabby, Amelia, or Anne?"

"Anne is out of surgery. The prognosis is good. Amelia is worse. The prognosis is bad. Nothing from the FBI on Gabby, Sir, please," pressed Tess, "There has been an incident in Israel, nuclear."

"Oh my God!" exclaimed the President, "On my way!" President Hammond leaped from the bed and dressed quickly. The United States Secret Service escorted the President to the Situation Room. The Director assessed the need to move the meeting to the Presidential Bunker.

"Mr. President. We are engaged with the remnants of the IRGC ground, air, and naval forces such as they are," opened Malik, "Sir, within moments of the assault, we detected three missiles launched from the western desert of Iran near Azaz. Sir, a mobile missile, a Hormuz Mobile Launcher, fired three missiles at Israel, targeting the Knesset, the Prime Minister's Office, and the Western Wall. U.S. Patriot Missile Systems took out two of the three and damaged the third. The third missile hit the Knesset, exploding but not detonating the nuclear tip. It did spread Uranium over a ten-block area."

"First, Secretary Cooke, launch the B-2s and B-21s planned for Phase IV," ordered President Hammond, "General Robinson, I want the IRGC air defenses reduced to dust by morning. Then I want you to pound the Iranian Nuclear Program to HELL."

"Yes, Sir," replied Chairwoman of the Joint Chiefs.

"Cooke, Porter, what assets are needed to help Israel clean up the radioactive material?" pulsed President Hammond.

"Sir, DOD, and DHS are coordinating support for Israel. DOD has the lead," reported Secretary Cooke.

"Sir, we need to move another Battle Group into the Mediterranean. We need further deterrence of aggression toward Israel," offered General Robinson.

"So ordered," directed President Hammond.

"Becky, how is State," pulsed President Hammond, "Reactions from Russia, China, and what is North Korean doing?"

"Sir, I have spoken with the Chinese and Russians. The Russians urged restraint. However, after the attack on the White House, the attack and kidnapping in South Carolina, and the missile attacks, one attempted nuclear. Their heart is not in the fight. Intelligence suggests the IRGC hit the gas pipelines. Russia is still in a state of readiness. Planes are on the deck, and the Fleets are in port.

China is the same," reported Secretary of State Porter, "Sir, everyone is hunting Paul Ross. We need to capture or kill Ross as soon as possible. He is still a clear and present danger."

"Frost, where is Ross?" pulsed President Hammond.

"I do not know," reported Director Frost, "But, I am HUNTING, SIR. If we must turn over every rock on Earth. We will."

"Wright, any insight or SIGINT on Ross," pulsed President Hammond.

"None, Sir," shared General Wright.

"Odd considering, he has to use SIGINT to conduct an attack, don't you think?" pressed President Hammond.

"Yes, Sir," noted General Wright, "I share Director Frost's passion for locating Ross."

"Becky?" pulsed President Hammond, "Where is the Israeli Prime Minister? Can we get the Israeli Ambassador here in the White House? I would like Malik to brief her on Phase III and IV."

"Yes, Sir," answered Secretary Porter.

> "Ladies and Gentlemen, the United States is still at DEFCON 2. We are one minute to midnight on the Doomsday Clock. I want a plan to dial this back and keep Russia, China, Israel, Pakistan, India, the United Kingdom, France, and North Korea off the Nuclear Button," ordered President Hammond, "Work the relationships, assure our allies, make clear to our enemies that we are resolute in finding the threat actors of the cyberattacks that we have all suffered. Keep the nuclear arsenals in check. We are reducing by one a member of the nuclear powers."

"Yes, Sir," affirmed the room.

"Tess, stay behind, please," requested the President. The room cleared out, and Malik's aides turned off the room's audio-visual equipment. President Hammond wrote on a notepad gently, "Get to South Carolina, support Ridge." Tess nodded, and Hammond burned the sheets of paper. Hammond is an old-school CIA Officer and an investigator at heart. He knew Wright was dirty. Hammond needed to get General Wright off the chessboard. Now.

# CHAPTER TWENTY — BEACON OF HOPE

"Tess, it is good to see you," expressed Xander with a deep exhale.

"How are you kids," hugged Tess, "I am praying for you. The President is praying for you. The whole country, really."

"I don't know how to tell her about any of this when she wakes up," choked Xander.

"She is going to wake up, Xander," affirmed Tess, "Amelia survived several attempts on her life. She is one tough kid!"

"Tess, the team is working on TAURUS," reported Xander, "But I am going to need RUBICON, especially after an attempted nuclear attack. Paul has lost his mind. And Wright is hyper-focused on getting the technology behind RUBICON. We cannot let this out. I will use RUBICON alone, find Ross, collect the evidence on Wright, find Gabby, and get my family and life back. I will destroy RAVEN," Xander paused and drew a deep breath, "And then destroy RUBICON."

"Xander," paused Tess, "You already are."

"YES," said Xander drawing a deep breath, "He has Gabby. I am the only one that knows how to use RUBICON. I designed and wrote the code. The team pushed the science. But I alone took the final steps. Tess, he has Gabby."

"Xander. I took a leave of absence from the White House," shared Tess.

"WHY?" exclaimed Xander.

"Amelia is my Goddaughter, Xander," stated Tess, "And you keep using a pronoun that perks my ears. And you don't bring up Gabby's abduction in conversation."

"What?" quipped Xander.

"Paul has Gabby. Paul killed Katy," paused Tess, "Xander, I have known you since West Point. You were the brightest, most gifted, principle-centered, focused, and detailed student to ever come through my course. You were the beacon of the CIA. You are the closest that I will ever come to knowing the honor, the pleasure of having a son. I know you, Son."

Tess continued, "You know who is behind these attacks. You know the who behind the who. You are trying to find Gabby first. Then you are going to do what you and Danny do best. You will do what ravages your soul and drove you from the CIA. You are going to hunt them down and kill them. I took a leave of absence to do that for you. I made peace with losing my soul long ago. Now, let's get the BASTARDS!"

"Thank you," noted Xander as he reached out to embrace Tess.

"Hammond knows that you know. He will move the heavens for you. You know Hammond will. He says that you, Danny, and I are the last of the Patriots," shared Tess.

> "No, Tess," said Xander aligning eyes with Tess, "No, there are many others. It is why I love this country. In times of need, Patriots step forward. They shake off the dust of the fields, the stresses of Wall Street, the grime of the factory, the blood of the emergency room, and from every corner, coast to coast, and border to border to step forward. Not for glory or riches but for a Nation of divided views, religions, and diversity of culture and races that often curses and spits on them. Paul is the antithesis of this spirit. General Shawn Wright betrayed his solemn duty.

> Patriots are a beacon of hope that freedom endures. Young men like Reyes and Kelly, who followed Danny into harm's way."

"I wish more talked like you do," noted Tess with teary eyes of respect.

# CHAPTER TWENTY-ONE – ENTANGLEMENT THEORY

Xander and Gabby purchased Q4 after researching innovative cures for Amelia. Sophia Ridge, a College of Charleston Biochemistry Graduate, shared the research with her parents, hoping to find a path for Amelia's care. Xander's SDS also pursued Quantum Physics in cybersecurity and advanced weapons design. The physics per se is the same. The application of such is the difference. So Xander and Gabby purchased Q4 and used the SDS advances to press forward innovative cures for obscure diseases.

Amelia's head injury in the attack complicated the care for her cancer. The injury's swelling and the tumor's growth forced the medical team to induce a controlled coma. Xander's heart ached, and he screamed in silent anguished desperation. All the money, all the power, all the resources, he failed to save family, friends, and cherished teammates. If not for Tess and Danny, the anguish would overrun his heart and rip a divide through his soul.

Xander mapped out the physics of entanglement and shared the SDS research with Q4's researchers. Ashlyn Chase, Chief Medical Entanglement Researcher, made significant progress with SDS research. SDS struggled to press entanglement beyond the particles of the atom to matter. SDS wanted to selectively disrupt, delay, or destroy the elements of an enemy's weapon system. Ashlyn and Q4 wanted to use entanglement to disrupt, delay, or destroy cancer cells. The pursued theory could allow researchers to develop a guided missile to target cancer cells and spare healthy cells.

Amelia's hope of surviving was approaching midnight and narrowing with the passing moments. The added stress of trauma hastens Death to collect her soul. Xander's gift was imagination. Failure of imagination was not an option for Xander, and he sought alternatives, where most found dead ends. This gift allowed him and Danny to escape certain death, hunting the World's worst for the CIA dozens of times. The purchase of Q4 and collaboration with Ashlyn was such an effort.

"Xander?" pulsed Mia, "Do you have a moment for Ashlyn?"

"Of course," confirmed Xander, "Where is she?"

"In the lobby downstairs," noted Mia, "She seems excited, looks exhausted, and a bit stressed if you ask me. What do you have that poor girl working on?"

"Life, just life," exclaimed Xander. Xander vaulted the handrail and bounded down the winding stairs. His heart leaped from his chest, hoping that Q4 found a path.

"Xander, Oh Wow!" paused Ashlyn to catch her breath, "Xander! The tumors in the test animals are shrinking faster than we hypothesized. Entanglement is disrupting the replication of cancer cells without damaging healthy cells. The Quantum Computing capability of SDS allowed Q4 to advance faster than I imagined in my lifetime. We have mapped out the ability to use quad dimensional imaging to affect the atoms of the cells. Like holding a magnet to a glass tube filled with ferrous shavings, like that game I had for car trips as a kid!"

"Show ME!" exclaimed Xander excitedly.

Q4 walked Xander through science. Xander requested Samantha, Trinity, Jenn, and Rachel over from SDS and Tess to review the Q4 briefing. Ashlyn included Lauren Holmes, the Q4's Chief Medical Officer. Trinity agreed to assess the Q4 solution with the advanced SDS Quantum Computing to model the effects on the human body.

"What is our codename for the technology," asked Trinity.

Ashlyn paused and looked at Xander, "TEMPLAR."

"TEMPLAR," noted Xander pausing to choke back emotion, "for Matt?"

"Yes, Sir," replied Ashlyn, "I could not get there in time for Matt. But I am working around the clock to get there for Amelia. He would want us to." Matt was the father of Jonathan Ridge's Fiancée, Lyn. Matt fought leukemia with every ounce of his soul for his family and endured in private. Xander had noted on several occasions the courage of the man. Battle is man's proving ground. The form and context of the battle are not relevant, armed conflict, overcoming self, or locked in a fatal fight with a disease. Matt proved a stoic hero, a father, husband, and friend.

"Thank you," quivered Xander, "Please, keep pressing."

Tess knew Xander would struggle with the decision, absent Gabby. He would shoulder the consequences of a life-and-death struggle with Amelia. Tess was a Godmother and would offer only an opinion for consideration if asked.

"MR. PRESIDENT," OPENED Malik, "NSA picked up on chatter in North Korea. Reconnaissance General Bureau (RGB) briefed Kim Jong-un that the United States plans a missile attack on North Korea after Phase IV in Iran."

"Sir, North Korean leader Kim Jong-un increased his country's defense condition, aligning with the United States at DEFCON 2," briefed Secretary of Defense Cooke.

"Becky, can you get in front of cameras and start dialing back our messaging? Michael, Lori, thoughts on sparring Iran from Phase IV and holding our readiness to press Iran?" pulsed President Hammond.

"Sir, I think lowering our DEFCON from 2 to 3 is a clear message," opened Secretary Cooke, "I reviewed the Iranian battle damage assessment. Iran's capabilities are severely degraded, and not quite to the days of horses and spears."

"I concur with Secretary Cooke," noted General Robison, Chairwoman of the Joint Chiefs of Staff, "Dialing back to DEFCON 3 and holding at Phase III."

"Okay, Mr. Secretary, Chairwoman Robinson, please proceed. Move to DEFCON 3. Madam Secretary, work the Press today, full-court, get this message out. Toby, coordinate with State and Secretary Porter. I want a clear and succinct message sent to North Korea. The United States does not intend to attack and never did. There is no evidence suggesting North Korean involvement in the recent cyberattacks or acts of terrorism," ordered the President.

"What is the source of the intelligence," pulsed the President betting in his head; the answer was the NSA, General Wright.

"Sir, the NSA intercepted a communique from Iran to North Korea," noted General Roberts, Director of National Intelligence.

"Thank you, General Roberts. Please, thank General Wright when you see him," quipped the President.

PAUL WAS RESTING FOR the night's work. RAVEN, to his surprise, stayed an effective threat vector to exploit Zero-Day vulnerabilities. The World was not moving fast enough to close the exploitable holes. It was like an open invitation for Paul to attack. RAVEN proved effective with a simple payload passing face intelligence reports between nation-states like Iran, North Korea, Syria, Iraq, Vietnam, the Philippines, Pakistan, Jordan, and Italy. Paul waited two months to evaluate RAVEN's capabilities beyond the known group. He did not want to exploit too many vulnerabilities at once. IRGC learned the lesson of rapid exploitation without isolation, the hard way, twice. Two precise missile strikes are a hard lesson to learn once. The current suite of compromised intelligence services was enough to proffer fake intelligence to confuse the World's intelligence community.

"Paul, clever work on the intelligence plant for North Korea," opened General Wright, "Good Work! The President and the NSC bought lock, stock, and barrel."

"Thank you, Sir," reported Paul, "I have the new base camp setup. Where is the satellite gear that I requested and the four servers? To avoid NSA and SDS detection, create deep fake videos, and pass fake intelligence, I need the gear to hide in the noise with burst uplinks. If you want Jong-un to bite on the intel to the tune of a missile launch, I need to keep pressing the noise floor up."

"The gear and a few other toys are due this morning," noted Wright, "I am adding to the protection detail. No one knows your real identity. No one will enter the house or the fenced-off area, so wear dark glasses and a ball cap if you go out. We cannot afford the security detail to figure out they are protecting the World's most wanted man. Once you get the gear, we need to fake your death. A dead man is hard to find. Is the woman still alive?"

"Yes, she is a useful toy," sneered Paul, "Once the setup is complete, I will send out a hostage deep fake pointing towards Iran. That will press Hammond into Phase IV and panic North Korea."

"XANDER, THE ANALYSIS shows successful manipulation of the cancer cells using the Q4 TEMPLAR solution. Using our best models, we simulated hundreds of human trials, showing positive results with negligible effects on healthy tissue. Xander. Understand that Quantum Computing, as good as it is, is an approximation. Nature and the human body can react independently and radically different than the best models can simulate," reported Trinity.

"Sir, I met with Amelia's Doctors. Amelia's organs are showing early signs of shutting down," reported Lauren, SDS Q4 Chief Surgeon.

"Xander," opened Tess, "I am here if you want to talk this through. Making this call without Gabby, I know, is doubly hard. I am here to listen."

"Boss, Anne is awake and briefed up," offered Danny.

"Oh, My God, that is great news, Danny!" exclaimed Xander, "How is she? What does she need?"

"She is heartbroken about Gabby, Katy, and Amelia. She wants to see Amelia as soon as possible. She needs us to find Ross and kill him," reported Danny.

"Yeah," affirmed Julius.

"Boss, do you want to go for a run and think?" offered Danny, "I can run my mouth the whole time like usual and annoy you, or just be with my brother while he works this out."

"Yeah," said Xander, "Docs, do I have 40 minutes?"

"Yes," reported Lauren, "The Hospital will not sign off on the experimental care. If this is a go, we need to move Amelia here. I have a mini-hospital set up at Q4 here at SDS. Ken and Kyla worked out the security for transit. Aaron and Dave will fly Amelia here."

"Xander, we have worked out all the details. Our legal team is working with the Hospital on the pending discharge to our care," reported Jacob, SDS Chief Operating Officer.

"Thank you," noted Xander, "Danny and I are going for a run. I will make the call when I return. Does anyone want to run with us?" Julius, Agents Kelly and Reyes, and Kyla jumped up, ready to go. Xander smiled, "Thank you."

PAUL ENJOYED THE WALK down to the basement of his new mountain refugee. He managed to score, really, nice prisons, he was thinking on his walk. The basement is large and open and home to a small theater, gym, bar, pool, and spa area. Paul had Gabby tucked away in the guest suite, chained to the bed. He kept her handcuffed and in leg irons for bathroom trips and showers. Paul wore the mask and kept Gabby drugged and in a mild state of unconsciousness. The drugs left Gabby's head spinning with blurred and swirling images matched with confused and garbling sounds as if straining to see and hear from the bottom of a dark pool.

"Amelia is dead," taunted Paul, as he pulled Gabby close to his mask with his hand on the back of Gabby's neck. Gabby began to sob. Through the garbling noise, she managed to piece together Amelia was dead.

"Katy is dead," pressed Paul. "Anne is dead," lied Paul. Anne survived. But Paul enjoyed the torture of Gabby immensely.

"Soon, your precious Xander's neck will be under my boot," tormented Paul as he pressed the syringe into Gabby's bruised arm. Paul tossed Gabby back to the tangle sheets and slithered into the bed once more.

"GOOD GOD, WHAT IS HE made of?" quipped Reyes, "Damn, Xander can run!"

Danny laughed out loud, "And you thought I ran you down! Army can outrun most SEALs half his age! And has outrun me since we met!"

"He made up his mind, so watch out. The pace is picking up," reported Danny.

"Picking up!" exclaimed Kelly and Reyes.

Xander double-timed the run back to SDS and the conference room. He sat down, scanning the faces in the room. Danny, Julius, Kelly and Reyes, and Kyla limped back into the room, sucking air.

"Save Amelia," ordered Xander getting up and heading back to his private lab with Tess and Danny in tow.

# CHAPTER TWENTY-TWO – JUDAS SPEAKS

"Ms. Pat, I am here to see the President," announced General Wright.

"Yes, Sir," noted Ms. Pat, "I will check with the President. Please, wait here."

"Mr. President, General Wright, is here to see you, Sir," reported Ms. Pat.

"Very well, show him in," quipped the President. Ms. Pat returned to the Executive Secretary's office to escort General Wright into the oval. Ms. Pat's bristled at his presence and much preferred to hit the Secret Service distress button and reign hellfire upon the arrogant bastard.

"Right this way, General," smiled Ms. Pat betraying her thoughts, "No, Thank you. Ms. Pat."

"Mr. President, Good News! Paul Ross is dead. His Iranian friends took him out in Casablanca last night. The NSA captured the assassination from nearby security camera coverage," reported General Wright. Wright opened the cover on his tablet and spun the screen for the President to see. The President watched grainy video of shadowy figures following a single featureless shadow to a cornered alley, ending with the flash of what could be gunfire and falling shadow. Wright taps the tablet and shows a photograph taken by local police of the shadow, Paul Ross.

"NSA intercepted the fingerprints locals sent to INTERPOL. NSA confirmed this is Paul Ross. The police report notes the 9 mm ammunition stamped with DIO, which is an Iranian Ammunition

Company. Here, this is the photo of the spent cartridges found next to the body," continued Wright.

"Interesting," heeded the President, glaring at Wright.

> "I don't believe that Paul Ross was behind the cyberattacks," postured Wright, "I offer that Paul was a convenient scapegoat. The press is sniffing around on a story that SDS leadership wanted sustainable and predictable profits. The network plans to run a piece in a few days, pending another source. But there is enough noise; the network is sure to find this bit of footage and other puzzle pieces. There are rumors that Gabriella Ridge is in Iran, a hostage, to force Xander to deliver RUBICON. He danced with the Devil and paid the price. It is why Iran risked an attack on American soil on Xander's doorstep."

"Interesting theory, Wright," leered the President.

> "Politically interesting to tie up the press and Congressional Hearings for months or years, right up to the Midterms," threatened Wright, "Your ties to SDS and the Ridge family date back for years. Ridge has Yankee White access, so it is not a leap for our enemies to tie the cyberattacks right back here. Of course, it is all speculation. It is time you wrap up your little exercise with SDS and get Tess back from vacation from visiting her God-Daughter."

"Thank you, General Wright," glared the President, "I will take your counsel under advisement."

"THE PRESIDENT HAD A tense visit with General Wright this morning," reported Tess.

"General Wright never lets a crisis go to waste by allowing ethics to impede his path to what he wants," noted Xander, "Though gutsy to challenge Hammond, arrogant. Wright and Paul share the same weakness. We can use that as a way. We can exploit arrogance; do you have the video?"

"How do you know about the video?" pulsed Tess, "I didn't share that yet."

> "I am learning how to use RUBICON; I found the video late last night looking for anomalies in the metadata. The video shows a man shot by two shadowy figures. The crime scene photo showed the face up close. It was not Paul, so I moved passed. If the videos are the same, I am betting Paul or Wright made a mistake. He cannot use NSA assets for his private spy game, except for a few loyalists. Wright's risky plan limits his choices, and, like the young IRGC Qud Force, arrogance allowed SDS to exploit his location. He ate two missiles from the USS Greenville," reported Xander.

"Always five moves ahead," noted Tess, "I have missed working with you."

"What are we looking for in the metadata," pulsed Special Agent Reyes.

> "A link between Wright and Ross, between Ross and any of the attacks, or a link between Wright, the NSA, or Ross and these deep fake videos are needles in the mountain of needles," shared Xander, "RUBICON aided with our Quantum Analysis will sort the data. Once we have the target systems, we can use RUBICON to blow past the

security and encryption to find Gabby. We can collect the intelligence needed to find, kill, or capture Ross. We can then take out the systems driving RAVEN and capture the vulnerabilities used in the payloads. And if we are lucky, capture Wright."

"Are we building a case against Ross and Wright for prosecution, or are we...," paused Special Agent Kelly at the raised hand of Xander.

"We are building a case," noted Xander, "BUT I am not risking American lives. We have lost too many in this battle with Ross and Wright. If this ends with you two on a 'Perp-Walk' with Ross and Wright in handcuffs, that is a win. If we must end this attack by killing them, that is a win. Clear?"

"Crystal, the latter is easier, which is why I was asking," quipped a smiling Kelly, "Reyes and I are here for a win."

"I am good with the latter," added Reyes, "These bastards killed my partner. Danny and I got one, but we have work to do."

"Roger that," noted Xander, "Gabby first, then Ross and Wright."

"Xander," opened Tess, "The President signed a revised authorization for this team, and he wants us to speed up. The President authorized RUBICON's use on any U.S. intelligence asset to find Paul Ross and collect the evidence that Wright has betrayed the United States. This is a close hold. DNI and NSC do not know. Kelly, Reyes, the FBI does not know."

"Team, Wright, and Ross are about to open up a war on us," prepped Xander, "They will smear us, mess with us, and try to hurt and kill us. Strap-in and stay-focused on the mission's priority."

"Welcome, back! Boss," exclaimed Danny. Xander smiled at Danny's prompt. Xander lived by a strong ethos framed with a principle-centered structure. A good man does not mean weakness. Paul and Wright have made a fatal mistake by assuming a good man will allow evil to prevail.

PAUL PICKED UP ANOTHER packet of the drugs to keep Gabby in a confused compliant state, well, more unable to resist. He dragged Gabby to a cold shower, allowing a few minutes for toiletries. He allowed only ten minutes a day for food and then shackled to the bed for twenty-three and a half hours. "Being dead is liberating," smirked Paul, "as he rolled out of bed."

Paul returned to his new office overlooking the evergreen forest in the foreground, accompanied by the background's snowcapped jagged mountains. An idyllic setting for a prison. However, with the deep-fake video of his death, Paul could regain his freedom. Paul had Gabby, and now it was time to extract more from Xander.

> "The smear campaign has begun, Xander," noted Julius in the SDS morning briefing, "Cable news is running the Paul Ross death story. The deep-fake video got an upgrade, showing some facial features of one of the shooters. There is a resemblance to Xander. The 24/7 talking heads are spinning a narrative of an American Hero exacting revenge for his wife's kidnapping, near-death of his child, and murder of his friends and employees. A few are taking the next step implicating SDS to Iranian weapons development and a deal gone wrong. This is the spin for the motivation of the SDS attack and Gabby's kidnapping."

"DO WE HAVE THE LATEST video?" pulsed Xander.

"We do, Boss," shared Julius, "Trinity is already running the analysis with Samantha."

"Boss," paused Julius, "MI6 collected autopsy photographs, DNA, and fingerprints from the morgue in Casablanca. I will have the packet by this afternoon."

"The President knows the score, but the circle of trust is tight on the Wright investigation, so expect the D.C. two-step," shared Tess.

"We need him to bring it and feed his arrogance," noted Xander, "Once I get a bead on Wright and Paul, I can lock it in with RUBICON."

"Xander, Mia, tripped the 'red-light,' she needs you to step out," noted Tess. Xander excused himself from the SDS briefing. Dr. Lauren Holmes, Q4 Chief Medical Officer, met Xander in the lobby to share an update on Amelia. Lauren assumed Dr. Katy Stone's role as the Chief Medical Doctor for Amelia's care.

"Sir, Amelia spiked a fever after the first TEMPLAR treatment. The tumor shrank by three percent, but the swelling from the impact is complicating a good lock. The next 72 hours are critical. We are working on treatments to bring the stem swelling down, which will allow us to attack the tumor. But we cannot get a good lock," reported Lauren.

"Thank you, Lauren," noted Xander, "Thank you."

"XANDER," OPENED JULIUS, "It is now a full-court press from the media. They have a new video of Gabby held captive in Iran. Iranian College students are holding Gabby in what looks like the basement of the abandoned U.S. Embassy with the IRGC negotiating her release, conditional on a cease-fire from the United States. An IRGC source released evidence linking SDS and Xander to an agreement to sell weapons for an exclusive contract to provide cybersecurity to Iran."

"The same unnamed IRGC source provided evidence that a rogue element within the IRGC attacked SDS killing several Americans and kidnapping Gabby to force Xander to comply with the agreement to sell the munitions and cybersecurity tools. The source alleges that Xander kept the payment, and the kidnapping was a message to deliver. An unnamed member of the Intelligence Community and ranking U.S. Government official confirms that the IRGC source's claims are under investigation by the U.S. Government. The sources link Xander directly to the cyberattacks casting a shadow on the recovery. The media is running the allegations," reported Tess.

"Ok, well, that sucks," exhaled Xander, "But, this emboldens Wright and Ross to take the high ground, get lazy and stupid, and make a mistake that we can exploit."

"Judas was a bitch, then and now," noted Danny with a snarky expression.

# CHAPTER TWENTY-THREE – NUCLEAR WILDCARDS

"Mr. President, I appreciate your loyalty to a perceived American Hero and to a colleague from your days at the Central Intelligence Agency," pressed General Wright, "But, the Chairpersons of the Senate Intelligence and the House Armed Services Committees are beginning an investigation to review the allegations of the Administration's ties to Shepherd Defense Systems and Xander Owen Ridge." General Wright paused to let his comments circulate around the room and sink into the moment.

> "General Roberts, I suggest that you suspend the security clearances for Ridge and all SDS staff. Secretary Cooke, I suggest you suspend SDS contracts and consider an alternate supplier of cybersecurity. Director Mills, I want you to open an investigation into SDS and Xander Owen Ridge and consider seizing RUBICON for NSA analysis and probable link to the cyberattacks and Intelligence Community breaches," pressed Wright.

"Shawn, when I need help running the Defense Department, I have a list. Sir, you are not on the list, so you can...," paused Secretary Cooke as the President raised his hand.

"Shawn, your concerns are noted for the record. I will consider your points. I just need some time, as this is moving all so quickly," offered the President.

"Michael," pressed Wright, "As DNI, are you suspending the security clearances?"

"No, Shawn," noted General Michael Roberts, "I am not. I do not react to investigations in the press. I react to facts. There are NONE HERE."

"NONE!" exclaimed General Wright, "HOW CAN YOU SAY THERE ARE NONE!"

"General Wright, none of the Five Eyes intelligence services corroborate the Iranian claims. Considering we are in a de facto state of war with the Islamic Republic of Iran, a disinformation and misdirection campaign is not out of the question. And your obsessive need to control RUBICON is, frankly, a concern for me. SO, IF I AM GOING TO REVOKE ANYONE'S CLEARANCE, IT WILL BE YOURS!" fired back General Roberts, "SO I SUGGEST YOU GET A TIGHTER GRIP ON YOUR HORSES AND FOCUS ON THE EVIDENCE."

"This is outrageous! I am the Director of the National Security Agency and a proven Patriot!" fired back General Wright.

"Okay, thank you for the debate," noted President Hammond, "Shawn, Thank you for your perspective. I promise you I am considering."

"General Roberts, stay and join me for lunch, would you please," requested President Hammond.

"Thank you, Mr. President," responded softly General Wright, "I appreciate your consideration and comments."

AFTER THE DAILY NSC in the Oval, General Wright rushed to get on his secured private line to press on Paul to release the planned false-flag to prompt Pakistan to escalate tensions with India. Wright wanted North Korea back on edge to counter President Hammond's efforts to de-escalate tensions with the United States. The only way was to get Xander out in the open, using RUBICON, so Wright and his select NSA analysts could capture the code. Wright met unexpected resistance from Hammond loyalists who were capable of punching holes in the false-flag intelligence just brokered by Wright, and that was circulating in the Press. Snagging the press with a false-flag was one thing. Snagging the US Intelligence Community was quite another. The clock was ticking. With Tess not in the Oval, Wright assumed Tess had joined forces with Xander and Danny. And this meant gave Wright cause to worry. He and Ross need to move faster to win and survive.

"You need to hurry up on the false-flag intelligence to Pakistan and North Korea. We need the nuclear wildcards on a war footing and disrupting the news cycles. If Xander thinks Pakistan and Jong-un are about to use nuclear weapons, he will use RUBICON to disrupt a launch," pressed Wright.

"I am close and will begin releasing the false-flags through India and Turkey. Both have zealous case officers willing to bite on a false-flag if the narrative aligned to an entrenched belief," offered Paul.

"What is the bait?" pulsed Wright.

"I have satellite images of India moving troops into Kashmir. After releasing the chatter of a pending assault and suicide terrorist attacks by Pakistani-backed militants, India will move troops. Once both are engaged, I will release false-flag movements of escalation and a false radar signature of a missile attack from India," paused Paul, catching his breath, "This will prompt Pakistan to a potential nuclear strike."

"Do it now," pressed Wright.

"Already have, General Wright," noted Paul, "the new gear is set up and working perfectly. I can move faster and stealthier."

"Excellent, we need to press on North Korea," pressed Wright, "We need both nuclear wildcards in play."

"What is your North Korea play?" pulsed Wright.

"False-flag leaks of South Korean movement to exploit the degraded response capability of the North. I know since I weakened KPAGF air defense capability and ground force communications, which sucked before I broke it. Jong-un knows that he is in trouble. I have noted increased chatter through Japan and Turkey of the leaked threats of the North to hit Seoul with an artillery bombardment and move tanks south to counter the perceived attacks from the South, Japan, and the United States. I am stoking the post-Iran phase IV," noted Paul.

"Both plausible, if leaked correctly. The equipment that I sent is enough to get this done. Yes?" pulsed Wright.

"Plenty," replied Paul.

"MS. PAT," OPENED MADAM Secretary Porter, "How are you this morning?"

"I am a mess. That is what I am!" exclaimed Ms. Pat.

"Tess is not here. General Wright creeps me out! And this smearing of the Ridge family, while Amelia is dying, Gabby is missing, and Xander is working so hard...," paused Ms. Pat to catch a breath and reposition her composure, resuming in a hushed tone, "It is just bullshit. That is what I think."

Secretary Porter laughed out loud and hugged Ms. Pat, "Don't you worry. I worked with President Hammond, Tess, Xander, and Danny at the CIA. I know that team better than my husband and children."

"Madam Secretary...," began Ms. Pat, as Ported leaned into Ms. Pat.

In a hushed tone, Porter offered, "Ms. Pat. Don't you worry about all of this? We will sort it all out in the end. If it is not sorted out yet, we are not at the end. You know the truth in your heart, so stay true to your heart's truth and ignore the 'bullshit' as you say."

"Ms. Pat, don't you think we should start the President's Daily Briefing?" pulsed Porter.

"Oh my, yes!" exclaimed Ms. Pat, "I told you. I am out of sorts."

THE PRESIDENT TRIMMED down the Daily Brief and NSC meeting to the DNI, CIA, DOJ, DHS, State, and SECDEF. The President pressed General Wright with a new goal of vetting the Iranian intelligence. At least that was the given reason. It is entirely plausible that the NSC needed a time-out. The President expanded the need-to-know circle on TAURUS, the covert investigation of General Wright. The downsized Daily Briefing played the scene out in the Oval Office and parted ways. The President slipped out and rejoined the team secretly in the Presidential Bunker with added Secret Service.

"Malik, thank you for the generic but plausible rundown this morning. I especially liked the confirmation of Ross's death and implications against Ridge. If Wright did bug the Oval, that fed his ego," noted President Hammond, "Well Done, Dr. Greene!"

"Tess and the SDS team unwound the deep-fake videos of Paul Ross's death. Ross did not die in that video sequence, and his status, alive or dead, and location are unknown. The leaked intelligence on the IRGC is a false-flag with an insignificant risk of escalating tensions. Though Phases I through III degraded the Iranian capabilities. The Iranian false-flag is not my concern," reported Malik, "Though it is important to note, the Iranian false-flag intelligence links directly to TAURUS. However, I am leaving that to Tess and the team."

"I agree," noted President Hammond, "I am concerned with the nuclear wildcards and hotheads in North Korea and Pakistan, who don't recognize bad intelligence and false-flags."

"Correct," noted Malik, smiling since her pupil got to the point of the class. However, her pupils were some of the brightest American minds, including the President of the United States, "Yes, the North Korean false-flag intelligence is the concern. The movement of North Korean forces and the mobile missile launchers shows that DPRK leadership, including Jong-un, believes the false-flag intelligence. North Korea believes Japan, South Korea, and the United States intend to attack."

"Well, that is bad, Secretary Porter," quipped President Hammond, "How are we planning to communicate to the Jong-un that we do not intend such."

"I am traveling to New York to meet with the North Korean diplomat at the United Nations. By going to him in New York, I am showing deference and hopefully earning a little credibility, and I am eating a little humility," noted Porter.

"A little humility to stave off a nuclear strike," noted President Hammond, "is worth the gesture. Good Plan. But what is the plan when that does not work if it does not."

"Invited the DPRK UN representative, along with the South Korean and Japanese Ambassador to the Oval Office," reported Secretary Porter.

"Okay, let me know what you need," requested the President.

"I need TAURUS gift wrapped for the world. You in front of the cameras at the UN General Assembly laying the case out that the bad guys, Iran, Wright, and Ross are wrapped up," noted Secretary Porter, "That is what I need to stop Armageddon."

"So, do I," noted the President, "So, do I."

"Pakistan," transitioned the President, "Assuming you are finished with North Korea?"

"Yes, Sir," replied Malik, "Pakistan is our other nuclear wildcard. The false-flag intelligence is pressing the Indians to move added troops to Kashmir, believing the bad intel that a terrorist attack by a Pakistani terrorist. Since India is moving troops for real, Pakistan believes the false-flag intel that India is using the chaos of the world to move on Kashmir, since the big three are a little busy and preoccupied."

"We need to add another Secretary of State," quipped the President, "You cannot be in two places defusing the same false-flag bomb."

"Correct," nodded Porter, "However, I suggest you, Mr. President, and General Roberts invite the Ambassadors of India and Pakistan to the Oval Office and review the false-flag intelligence."

"Okay," agreed the President, "Porter, set up the meetings. The team keeps all of this below the proverbial radar and out of Wright's ears. We need to buy Tess and Xander a little more time."

"MADAM SECRETARY, IT is an honor to host you in New York. The threats by your government have me pressed for time, as you are aware. American Special Cyberwarfare Forces attacked the Democratic People's Republic of Korea in recent days by Americans. The same American attackers launched missiles at their ally, Israel, and used the pretense of the attack to launch a military offensive against the Islamic Republic of Iran," noted Kim Song, the North Korean representative to the United Nations.

"Representative Song, the United States of America does not intend to take the Democratic People's Republic of Korea. I am here to provide this assurance to the Supreme Leader of North Korea, Kim Jong-un, from the President of the United States. The United States did not conduct global cyberattacks. The Government of Iran and a criminal who is an American, Paul Ross, did. The United States

Government is hunting Paul Ross and will bring him to justice," reported Secretary Porter, "Representative Song. We need to deescalate tensions amongst the Nuclear Powers and allow the United States to present the evidence to the World at the United Nations General Assembly."

"Madam Secretary, as we speak. Your proxies have launched a missile strike against Pyongyang, my Capital. The DPRK will shred your incoming missiles and prepare a counterstrike at a time of our choosing. Good Day! Madam Secretary," reported Song angrily. Kim Song stormed out of the UN conference room to rejoin the DPRK delegation.

"What just happened?" exclaimed Secretary Porter, "What missile strike? What is Song talking about, another attack?"

"Madam Secretary, During the meeting with Song, DPRK air defenses detected incoming missiles into Pyongyang. Cheyanne Mountain reports the incoming missiles are a false-flag on the DPRK radar systems. Someone faked the strike. South Korean air defenses did not detect a missile launch. DPRK believed it was real and targeted the fake incoming strike," reported a member of Porter's security detail.

"MR. PRESIDENT. THE Indian and Pakistani Ambassadors have arrived. General Roberts is greeting the Indian Ambassador. Secretary Cooke is greeting the Pakistani Ambassador. Both will make their way to the Oval Office," reported Ms. Pat.

"Ms. Pat?" opened the President, "Inform Dr. Greene that I may need to move this meeting to the Situation Room. Please, have her plan to address the inclusion of the Ambassadors attendance and NOFORN, with my approval." Ms. Pat's eyes widened as she thought, *the President is exempting the no foreigner requirement of Top-Secret intelligence, though Ambassadors, but still. The President's request signaled a critical concern. The President, General Roberts, and Dr. Greene need to make the point. Pointedly, the Ambassadors need to believe the trio. Or we are all going to live Armageddon. Xander is right to withhold RUBICON. 'Unbridled Power...,' as Xander says, '...needs to be restrained.'*

THE PRESIDENT STOOD as his distinguished guests arrived. Dr. Greene orchestrated the entrance, so both Ambassadors entered the Oval Office simultaneously with equal distance from the President. Diplomacy is knowing you have a rock in one hand, humility in the other, and knowing when to use either.

"Ambassadors, welcome to the White House, my friends. Thank you for accepting our invitation to discuss matters of state. Ambassador Khan, Ambassador Rameshwar, welcome," opened the President.

"Mr. President, Ambassador Rameshwar, General Roberts, Dr. Greene, and Ms. Pat, thank you for the invitation to the White House. I hope we can reach a peaceful settlement to the Indian aggressions in this climate of cyberattacks," returned Ambassador Mehdi Hamid Khan, the Pakistani Ambassador to the United States.

"Mr. President, Ambassador Khan, General Roberts, Dr. Greene, and Ms. Pat, the people of India, thank you for the invitations to discuss a peaceful path forward in these troubling times and fear of terrorism in Kashmir," returned Ambassador Ranij Rameshwar, the Indian Ambassador to the United States.

> "Gentlemen, please be seated. I have asked the Director of National Intelligence, General Roberts, and Dr. Malik Greene, Special Counselor the President, to join our discussion," began President Hammond, "Gentlemen, the cyberattacks wreaking global havoc are the work of the

> Ministry of Intelligence of the Islamic Republic of Iran (MOIS), the Qud Force of the Islamic Revolutionary Guard Force (IRGC), and a criminal sought by the United States, Paul Ross, an American. Gentlemen, the intelligence that both Pakistan and India are responding to is a false-flag created by Ross. The United States Government is actively hunting both Americans. And regrettably, we believe another American is assisting. We will bring both to justice and share the evidence with the world as soon as we can capture these criminals. However, I cannot allow Pakistan and India to fall victim to this depravity and deception. You may have conditions now driving the escalation. But for the sake of humanity, I am asking you to de-escalate the tensions and withdraw your troops and preparations for war between your two great countries."

> "Two Americans participated in the world's worst cyber-attacks. The United States attacked Iran and may invade with ground forces in days and weeks. I appreciate the discussion of peace. But the irony is poetic to me that the nation that developed the atomic bomb, the nation to use the atomic bomb, and the nation to use military force against another nuclear power is the very country lecturing us on the ethos, logos, and pathos of not defending ourselves against the naked aggression of tyranny and terrorism on our borders," noted Ambassador Khan.

"Today's discussion is ladened thick with irony. I agree with my distinguished colleague, Ambassador Khan. India has a right to protect our nation and citizens in the Kashmir region," affirmed

Ambassador Ranj Rameshwar, the Indian Ambassador to the United States.

"Gentleman, let me be clear. The United States will not allow the current crisis between India and Pakistan to escalate to a shooting war or, worse, to a nuclear exchange. The intelligence pushing both great nations to such ends is false," noted President Hammond.

> "Gentleman, if I may, the intelligence driving your current readiness and the resulting engagements is false," opened General Roberts, Director of National Intelligence, "The intelligence is a false-flag created to draw Pakistan and India into a shooting war in Kashmir. The United States asks you to stand down and withdraw offensive forces back to the 1972 Line of Control. The United States will hunt down the criminal responsible for the cyberattacks and false-flag intelligence and bring the evidence to the United Nations General Assembly. Gentlemen, your points about the United States' development and use of nuclear weapons are true. It is a burden that I must carry as an American. Gentleman, it is out of the pain of the burden that I speak from my heart to spare you a like burden, should you use nuclear weapons. Today, the United States and Japan are allies. Ambassadors, my life's work is collecting and analyzing intelligence. I am here imploring reason that the intelligence driving you to war is a false-flag with a sinister purpose."

"We, too, have intelligence capabilities, General Roberts. The Director of Research and Analysis Wing (RAW) shared that you, General, are a commendable person and an excellent officer. I do respect your many years of service and sacrifice for your country. Your counsel gives me pause to consider. I will pass to Prime Minister your concerns," noted Ambassador Rameshwar.

"The basis of the false-flag intelligence began with reports that Pakistan planned an attack beyond the 1972 Line of Control. As DNI for the United States, I know this is a false-flag. Ambassador Khan? Do you refute our assessment? Are you telling us here, in the Oval Office, that Pakistan intends to escalate and the intelligence of imminent attack in the region is true?" pulsed General Roberts.

"Of course not, General Roberts. Pakistan did not start or escalate. Pakistan has a sovereign right to defend its borders and its citizens, and I should not have to make such a case to the nation that just attacked a sovereign nation based on the same argument," pressed Ambassador Khan.

"Sir, if you agree that Pakistan did not plan an attack, why are India and Pakistan running to war. Eventually, and I fear sooner, one of you will trip into a shooting war," pressed General Roberts.

> "Ambassadors, I am prepared to escort you to the Situation Room to hear directly from Colonel Xander Ridge, Retired and CEO of Shepherd Defense Systems. Colonel Ridge is helping undo the damage from the cyberattacks, has supplied support to both of your governments, and is hunting down those responsible. He has suffered personal losses, and his wife still is missing. He is standing by on secure communications to walk you through the false-flag intelligence," offered the President.

"Ambassador Khan, would you walk with me to the Situation Room and learn a little more about what the Americans have to share?" pulsed Ambassador Rameshwar.

"Yes, I will walk with you in the hope we can stave off a shooting war," noted Ambassador Khan.

WRIGHT LISTENED TO the meeting in the Oval Office. He took a risk on real-time listening. He left behind a covert micro-sized transmitter used by the NSA. Since the downsized NSC and Daily Brief, he set the device to record and then send a microburst once a day to listen to the President.

The NSA is a formidable foe. The Secret Service frequently checked for eavesdropping and technical surveillance in the White House compound. However, Wright proved Xander correct. Wright or Ross would let their ego drive decisions and make a mistake. Wright just made one.

"Mr. President, the Secret Service detected a signal anomaly from the White House, specifically the Oval Office," reported General Roberts.

"WRIGHT!" exclaimed the President, "Did the Service find a device?"

"Yes, Sir," responded General Roberts, "It is an NSA device. Quite a challenge to find."

"He will exploit our meeting with the Ambassadors," noted the President, "Advise Ridge, he may be able to use this to lock on Wright and Ross."

"Tess wants to leave the device in play," relayed General Roberts.

"Yes," approved the President.

"AMBASSADOR RAMESHWAR. Ambassador Khan. Welcome to the White House Situation Room. Can the Steward offer a refreshment?" welcomed Dr. Greene. The President and General Roberts followed the group into the Situation Room, closing the door.

"Ambassadors, please allow me to introduce Colonel Xander Ridge, United States Army Retired, Founder and CEO of Shepherd Defense Systems," opened the President.

"Colonel Ridge, please, accept the prayers and wishes for a speedy and safe return of your lovely wife, Gabriella. Gabriella's humanitarian works are well known throughout my government," offered Ambassador Rameshwar.

"As do the people and government of Pakistan, offer you our prayers and wishes for a safe return. Please, know that our ISI stands at the ready to support the hunt for these criminals," added Ambassador Khan.

"Thank you, Ambassador Rameshwar and Ambassador Khan. I appreciate the prayers and well wishes of both your nations. I am honored and humbled by your kindness," added Xander.

"Colonel Ridge, the President, and General Roberts shared with us the basis of the intelligence pressing my country and Pakistan toward war is false. Created by these same cybercriminals?" pulsed Ambassador Rameshwar.

"Yes, Sir," replied Xander, "Paul Ross is using a tool developed by my company and used by the cybersecurity industry to attack Zero-Day vulnerabilities and use payloads to attack critical infrastructure. Ross uses the same tool to distribute false-flags across the world's intelligence communities. He is using the false-flags to agitate mistrust between allies and foes. In this case, he is using the Kashmir dispute to put India and Pakistan on a war footing. I need just a little more time to collect the evidence for the President and General Roberts."

"We have your word that the intelligence is a false-flag?" pulsed Ambassador Khan.

"You do, Sir," offered Xander, "Gabby is still missing and held captive. My family's lives are at risk, gentlemen."

"Mr. President," offered Ambassador Khan, "I will share this with President Sadr and the government of Pakistan. Pakistan will withdraw as requested."

"Mr. President, Ambassador Kahn, I will share the same with the Prime Minister. India will withdraw, matching Pakistan's de-escalation."

"Gentleman, thank you," noted the President.

# CHAPTER TWENTY-FOUR — GODMOTHER'S REVENGE

"Pakistan and India are a dry hole. Focus your efforts on North Korea. I am leaving DC. Ridge and Hammond are on to me," texted Wright to Ross. Paul sat back and read the text, mulling over his next move. Ridge is a formidable foe and plays five moves ahead when he is in the zone. Holding Gabby is a risk. But he will not risk losing Gabby.

Ross checked the dark web email for a reply from Chechen Separatists to support his efforts to destabilize Russia. Paul started working with Aum Shinrikyo, a Japanese cult aiming to overthrow the Japanese government. AUM wants to disrupt Japan's domestic terrorism unit by destroying the Public Security Intelligence Agency (PSIA), the Japanese DHS, the capability to collect intelligence. Paul had success contracting with the Abu Sayyaf group in the Philippines, which, along with the capability to disrupt the Japanese government, provides bona fides with China's Ministry of State Security (MSS). Paul's planning with MSS overnight worked out well. Paul expected a response shortly on a plan to exfil from the United States and dispose of Gabby. MSS is considering the options for Gabby. MSS wants RUBICON. Paul planned to duplicate the capability of RUBICON. To succeed, he needs the resources of a Nation-State. China meets this need exceptionally well. Paul was unsure whether Wright had developed a backup or exfil plan, but Paul learned a few tricks from Daniyah. MSS smartly sent a female case officer to the states to work with Paul.

Paul finished up the false-flag intelligence leak for North Korea. He set up RAVEN to work independently to harass the DPRK air defenses for 24 hours. DPRK would pick up intermittent radar contact approaching North Korea, specifically the missile sites. The radar blips would mimic B2 Stealth Bombers pre-stationed out of Guam, Okinawa, and the Philippines, which they are not. In reality, the DPRK would never see a blip from the B2s. But North Korea believes they can, so Paul created the illusion to fit the expectation. This would keep the DPRK on edge and force a strike from Kim Jong-un.

"TESS?" PULSED XANDER, "I have General Wright on RUBICON. I have him locked on his devices, all of them." Danny and Tess leaped from their positions in the SDS Situation Room with this news. Tess and Danny fixated on Xander's screens as he tossed up data and images linking General Shawn Wright to Paul Ross, the Foreign Intelligence Service of the Russian Federation (SVR), which explains why Paul had not hit Russia hard. It seems just a token attack. As Xander collected the intelligence, he found that Wright had bugged the Oval Office from the beginning of Hammond's Presidency but had only collected the audio files in microburst when in the room, which increased the challenge for the Secret Service to detect.

The evidence painted a dark picture of General Shawn Wright, Director of the National Security Agency. General Wright was a deep-cover Russian operative, using Paul to disrupt, degrade, and outright destroy the world's intelligence collection capabilities in Asia, Europe, and the Middle East. All areas that Russia wanted to increase their influence.

"Gabby," checked Danny, "Do you have a location on Gabby?"

"I am closing in on Ross," answered Xander, "Ross is in the United States. Kelly, Reyes, If Ross is in the U.S., can the FBI get Gabby back?"

"Hell, Yes, we can!" Kelly and Reyes exclaimed, "Danny, you are coming with us!"

"Hell, yes, I am," confirmed Danny, "I have SEAL Team 2 ready for hostage rescue east of the Mississippi and Seal Team 5 for west of the Mississippi."

"The FBI has HRT ready to deploy within CONUS," noted Reyes, "Danny, we are working with JSOC on a joint operation. I received word that POTUS reactivated your status in the Navy. You are now on active duty."

"Excellent!" replied Danny.

"Do you have Wright's location?" questioned Tess in a calm, quiet tone.

"Yes," replied Xander, "Tess, I can't let you..." Xander paused as Tess politely raised her hand.

"Xander," began Tess, "I am what I am. I need to go, do what I do."

"Tess, the FBI will issue an arrest warrant for General Wright within a few hours. We are already working on the search warrants," shared Special Agent Kelly. Tess pulled a sealed envelope with the Seal of the President of the United States from her bag. Danny motioned for Special Agents Kelly and Reyes to follow. Tess and Xander glanced at each other with a knowing look. Reyes was not sure what to make of what was happening.

"Tess," quivered Xander, "I have already lost Gabby. I may be losing Amelia. You cannot do this. I can't lose you."

> "Xander," quivered Tess, "I Love You like you are my own. But Shawn Wright is a traitor to the United States. He costs me more than I can ever tell you. The President and I

> have hunted ISCARIOT our entire careers. We suspected soon after Inauguration that Wright was ISCARIOT, JUDAS ISCARIOT. But we did not know who he was until today. The President and I are the last remaining CIA Officers to know of the case, searching for the deepest Russian operatives within the United States. Xander, there can be no trial."

"Let me go," pleaded Xander.

"No, Xander. You are a good soul. Amelia is my Goddaughter. I love Gabby as my own. I love you, like my own. Wright killed dozens of young Case Officers over the decades and burned dozens more in Russia. It is time for the Devil's dance to end. It is time for me to finish what I started forty years ago —I need to be the one," assured Tess.

Xander stood and embraced Tess in a deep hug as if he hugged his mother in Heaven. Tess placed her hands upon Xander's face in a gently motherly embrace and wiped the tear starting to fall. She kissed his forehead and whispered, "Finish the job, Son. Bring Gabby home. It is time for the Devil and his demon to return to the chasms of Hell."

SPECIAL AGENTS PATRICK Kelly and Mark Reyes continued to document the criminal and treason charges against General Shawn Wright. The FBI cannot stop the pursuit of justice. Knowing the Agents' intentions, Tess hurried to the SDS airstrip to board the government plane. Tess boarded the plane and settled in as the single passenger. In the opposite seat facing Tess rested a black canvas bag. Tess rose from her seat, found the refreshment bar, and fixed a drink. Knob Creek, 15-year-old Kentucky Bourbon, neat, settles the mind and steadies the aging capable hands. Shawn was arrogant and would overestimate the time to discover and find him. Tess hunted ISCARIOT for forty years. But the 90-minute flight from South Carolina to Maryland would feel like an eternity.

PAUL WAS SITTING AT his station, prepping RAVEN to execute the B2 Stealth simulation across the Yellow Sea and the Sea of Japan (East Sea) to force North Korea to force a nuclear strike against South Korea and Japan. Secretary Porter did not convince Kim Song, North Korea's United Nations Representative, that the intelligence was a false-flag. Tempting the world's intelligence community was like fishing, Paul mused. The more lures in the water, the more bites.

Paul heard a thud followed by another. He grabbed his radio to check on the security detail. Wright downsized Paul's security after he suspected that the Secret Service burned his Oval Office device and connected the dots to him. If the Secret Service had not, Ridge had. Xander would not take long to find Paul, so Paul sped up the DPRK timeline. Paul moved to check the surveillance cameras. Still no reply on the radio from the three-man detail. Paul felt the cold barrel at the base of his neck and froze.

"Your benefactor is on the run. Give me the USB Drive, and keep your hands out and visible. Slow moves only when I tell you, understood," the masked intruder said softly.

"Wright is our Guy, and you were his. I do not have orders to kill you. Your Chinese friends are not far behind. I am here for RAVEN, the payloads, your laptop, and the woman, Gabby. She is our insurance policy now," instructed the masked intruder. Paul followed the instructions. He had backups for RAVEN, the payloads, and set a remote destruct for the laptop.

"No problem, all the items you need are right here," replied Paul.

"Did you execute RAVEN against the DPRK?" pulsed the masked intruder.

"No, you pressed a gun barrel to the back of my neck," replied Paul, "You still do."

"Execute RAVEN. You have this set to run autonomously?" checked the masked intruder.

"Yes," replied Paul.

"Do it now," ordered the masked intruder. Paul followed the instruction executing RAVEN once more. North Korea would launch against Japan and South Korea.

"BOSS, WE HAVE PAUL Ross!" exclaimed Trinity. Xander swung his chair to Trinity's station.

"Activate the laptop's camera," requested Xander, "may I?" Trinity slid to the side, allowing Xander to drive RUBICON. Xander activated the laptop's camera. Xander's familiarity with the design allowed him to move quickly and undetected.

"Paul Ross is alive!" exclaimed Xander, "Wait, it looks like someone is behind Paul." Xander worked the settings and lightened the background.

"Yes, see. There are three people in black with masks behind Paul, and one has a gun to Paul's head," reported Xander.

"Maybe they will do us a favor," quipped Julius, "Xander do you have a location. I will get it to Danny and the boys."

"Yes, I have him. Northern Idaho, just on the north edge or Priest Lake! Julius, please have Danny get Gabby!"

"Yes, SIR," beamed Julius. Julius sent the location and satellite links to Danny and the teams. SEAL Team Five, FBI Hostage Rescue Team, and Danny would hit the Idaho area as soon as the jet could get the team in the area.

"Trinity, start collecting and sorting the metadata we are snatching on General Wright and Paul. The President needs a complete package," requested Xander.

PAUL CLOSED HIS EYES expecting the masked intruder to fire his weapon into the base of his skull. But after a few moments, Paul realized he was alone in the office. Paul recovered his backup laptop and RAVEN USBs. Paul was not in a hurry to burn the stolen laptop. He was unsure if the intruders were gone or the mode of transportation, so best not to tempt the Devil. The Chinese team would arrive and exfil Paul out of the United States within an hour.

GENERAL WRIGHT HUSTLED about his Maryland estate, collecting his things before meeting his Case Officer to leave the United States forever. Wright had completed a fifty-year mission as the deepest covert Russian operative in the United States Government. Russia would welcome him home to a hero's welcome. Though he had been in the United States for a long time, he struggled to remember Russian life. His American wife died last year of COVID-19 complications. He and DeAnna never had children. So, Wright had no ties to leave behind. He finished collecting his personal effects, a few clothes, and a sidearm. Looking around the familiar home one last time, Wright opened the back door and stepped into the damp cold darkness. He walked down the drive noting the loudness of his shoes. Wright slowed his pace and stepped softer to lessen the noise. The Moon cast an eerily light across the estate's grounds, trees, and shrubs.

Tess held tightly but expertly to her handgun. She fastened the silencer and waited for Wright to continue approaching her position. The Moon's glow created deep dark shadows and allowed her to remain unseen by the approaching Wright. Tess stepped out into the paved drive.

"I thought it might be you," noted Wright.

"JUDAS ISCARIOT, it has been a long hard forty years hunting you down," replied Tess.

"I have ten million in cash in the car. You are welcome to the car. I can toss you the keys? Or you can join me? —like old times. You know I still love you —regret our divorce," tested Wright.

"Keep your hands right where they are, Shawn," ordered Tess. The Moonlight backlit Tess, blinding Wright to the subtle movements. Wright could not see the silenced 9 mm aimed at his chest.

"So, now what?" pressed Wright, "I still love you, Tess. I always have —does he know? I don't think you have it in yo..."

Tess's finger pressed the trigger, resetting, and pressing five rounds downrange, with a skill that betrayed her true CIA skills. The rounds found a tight grouping in Wright's chest, knocking him slightly backward and to his knees. Tess found the clinking of the spent brass dancing on the pavement soothing. The steam broiling from Wright's chest against the frosty night air released forty years of anger for the honored dead at ISCARIOT's hand. Wright leaned back, gasping for a breath. Tess stepped forward and pressed the trigger once more. The round found the intended mark between the eyes of a traitorous soul, forcing the head backward at a violent angle, recoiling forward, eyes wide open. Wright, expressionless, fell to the pavement. Tess collected the spent shells and walked back to her rental.

# CHAPTER TWENTY-FIVE – IDAHO

The Chinese Ministry of State Security (MSS) assigned Li Chang as the Case Officer to manage Paul Ross. Li was an experienced Case Officer with matching military experience. Li's petite frame belied a powerhouse of Sanda, the Chinese military martial arts. Li was beautiful and studied the GOI Case Operative Daniyah Rahman's ingratiation methods and wore a diamond tennis bracelet and anklet as a subtle way to touch Paul.

Li Chang rode across the Canadian border on an electric all-terrain snowmobile to snatch Paul Ross from under the Americans. Li rushed to the mountain lodge to grab Paul before the American helicopters arrived. Paul donned the mylar outer clothing, covering head to toe, that camouflaged their movement from the SDS and U.S. Military satellites surveilling the area. The Chinese Military was training with the Canadian Military for extreme cold-weather exercises. The electric snowmobile and mylar outer clothing shielded the escape. The satellites could still see the three mercenaries killed by the Russian Operatives. Li snatched Paul from the driveway and doubled back on her snowmobile tracks. The tracks made the trek back to Canada and the waiting Chinese forces, training nearby, difficult. Li towed a bundle of evergreen branches to help hide the snowmobile tracks. Li had Paul place all his electronics in a Faraday bag to shield him from the satellites and SDS. The escape across the border was a twenty-mile trek through the rocky and wooded terrain.

Danny, SEAL Team Five, and the FBI Hostage Rescue Team (HRT) pulled over the ridge in five USAF Special Warfare CV-22 Ospreys separating smartly to surround the mountain lodge leaving Danny with HRT and a SEAL Chief Warrant Officer with three shooters to infil direct on the lodge with the four Ospreys dropping the remaining SEALs for perimeter security.

The team quickly breached the lodge and searched for Ross, three tangos, Gabby Ross, and computer and communications equipment.

"Danny, this is a DRY HOLE!" shouted the FBI HRT Leader.

"Damn IT! Whiskey Tango Foxtrot!" shouted Danny, "Who are the three tangos outside?"

"KIA, no gear left," reported Senior Chief, "Danny, HRT found drugs in the bathroom. Suspect the Tango drugged the Package. This is nasty stuff! Pass to HQ to get our Medics a protocol."

"Danny, this is SDS Operations; we detected four heat signatures ten miles from your current POS, due East. One appears down," reported Scout.

"EXFIL, new target ten miles due east, uploading TANGO POS and SAT Intel to team leaders," reported Senior Chief.

"WE NEED TO DUMP THE woman here. The Americans are on their way in CV-22s. We have only minutes," shared Kovalenko, "The Russian Embassy RSO confirms that ISCARIOT is dead. CIA shot him, leaving his home. We have the computer equipment that we need."

"With the woman, we have leverage over Ridge and the Americans!" pressed Koval.

"No, we have SEAL Team Five, FBI HRT, and an incredibly angry SDS SEAL en route to our POS. They will smoke us and take the woman. If we leave her here, alive and well, we can make our escape with the equipment. Our mission is RUBICON and the RAVEN payloads, which we have," recounted Kovalenko. Marina Kovalenko was JUDAS ISCARIOT's General Shawn Wright, Case Officer. The Russian team realizing their predicament, followed Kovalenko's orders. The youngest team member, Sacha, unbound Gabby and left a bottle of water and the rest of an MRE, peanut butter, and crackers. He was disgusted with how the Iranians had treated Gabby. He was not a fan of American foreign policy but found that most Americans were generous and mostly kind. He left the car's engine running with the heat on to keep Gabby warm and to flag the infrared satellite watching above and the inevitable drone. Marchenko noted Sacha's efforts, left his jacket to cover Gabby, cleared the snow away from the tailpipe, and turned the hazard lights on.

"We need to exfil, NOW," ordered Kovalenko. The team switched to the backup car and sped from the scene.

BOUNDARY COUNTY SHERIFF Deputy Kyle Harris spotted a car with the hazards on, the engine running, and a female sitting behind the wheel. Deputy Harris turned on his emergency lights and pulled behind the vehicle.

"Dispatch, 316. Found a car parked alongside Westside Road just outside Port Hill. Engine running, hazards on, and partially blocking the roadway. Suspect drunk driver; the plate is California BPC 0725," reported Deputy Harris.

"316, the car is reported stolen from Spokane, a rental car. Proceed with caution. Sending backup 20 minutes," reported Dispatch.

"316, Roger," replied Deputy Harris.

Deputy Harris approached Gabby and rapped on the driver's window.

"Ma'am, please shut the engine off and roll down the window," ordered Deputy Harris.

"Ma'am?" ordered Harris again. Harris tried the driver's door, which opened. He checked Gabby's pulse and breathing rate, finding both rapid and shallow breathing. *Yeah, she is high on something*, he thought. Harris reached and lifted Gabby out of the vehicle to her feet, noting that she could barely stand and swayed back and forth. Harris felt a little sorry for her, as she looked so helpless dressed in a torn men's dress shirt and barefoot. He sat her down and ran back to his cruiser for his workout sweats and tennis shoes. He returned to slide the sweatpants on Gabby, getting shoes and socks on her bare feet, and then lifted Gabby back to a standing position.

"Dispatch, 316. Female subject partially clothed, no shoes, shallow breath, rapid pulse, pupils dilated, sitting behind the wheel, engine on, in park, hazards, and lights on... I need you to roll a medical unit at once. Be advised there are loud aircraft sounds in the area, a lot of rotor noise," reported Deputy Harris. Gabby started to take a few steps after the frigid air began to wake her up from the drugged state.

"Ma'am, I need you to stand here and keep your hands away from me," ordered Deputy Harris. Gabby started to push the Deputy away and speak unintelligibly. Deputy Harris feared for Gabby's safety if she grabbed one of his weapons, so he placed Gabby in protective custody. As he started to walk Gabby back to his cruiser, he suddenly noticed he was not alone. He began to draw his weapon and move Gabby to cover. Dozens of armed men stood at the edge of the darkness, encircling his position.

"FBI! FBI! FBI! DO NOT MOVE! FBI! DO NOT MOVE!" shouted the FBI HRT Team Leader. Suddenly, the aircraft lit up Deputy Harris and Gabby, and lights turned night into day from all directions. Dozens of armed men pressed in on Deputy Harris and Gabby. Harris moved to shield Gabby as best he could before he finally heard the FBI HRT Team Leader.

"FBI?" pulsed Deputy Harris.

"Yes, Son," replied the FBI HRT Team Leader, "Yes, FBI. Respectable job, trying to get her and you to cover. But keep your hands off your weapons till we confirm you are a Deputy, Clear!"

"What in the Hell is going on?" pressed Deputy Harris.

"Well, you just found the hostage that the entire world wanted to find. You just found Gabby Ridge. And just missed getting smoked by a Russian Specs Op Team," shared the FBI HRT Team Leader. Suddenly a thick black roped dropped next to Deputy Harris, and a massive man in dark military clothing with large black weapons dropped on his position.

"Hello, Deputy Harris! I am Danny Bell, SEAL Team Leader. This is well, let's say, Bob, FBI Hostage Rescue Team Leader. Thank you, let me have Gabby, and you take a step back, young man. And keep your hands where we can see them. You have about forty guns aimed at you, so don't be a dumbass," said Danny.

"Get the medical CV-22 on the ground; we need to get Gabby the hell out of here!" ordered Danny.

"Sirs, Deputy Harris checks out, though he just called in Gabby's arrest," reported a member of the FBI HRT Team.

"Yeah, you want your cuffs back?" asked Danny, "I suggest you lose that paperwork and take these handcuffs off quick, Son."

"No problem, she was behind the wheel. I just called a squad and got her dressed so she would not get frostbite. She is in bad shape, with shallow breath, rapid pulse, eyes dilated, freezing, and out of it and grabbing at all my gear. She is high," reported a shaking Deputy Harris.

"Drugged, Son. Thanks for the ambulance. The bastards drugged her and damned near killed her. But we got a medical team right here," shared Danny, "You likely saved her life getting her up and moving."

"Son, you might get a couple of phone calls later this morning, and I suggest you take both. You just made several people incredibly happy," offered Danny, "Thank you, Deputy Kyle Harris."

"No problem, Sir," said Harris, still taken aback.

"Let's go! SEALs on me, Exfil! 'Bob' is FBI processing the lodge and car?" pulsed Danny.

"Yes, we will stay here with Deputy Harris, check the area, and wait for an FBI Evidence Team. Leave two CV-22s, one for cover and one to move the team, okay?" replied Bob.

"Yes, Sir. 'Bob,' thank you! Damn fine team. I gotta go," replied Danny.

"SDS ST5. We have the package and are exfiling to medical," reported Danny.

# CHAPTER TWENTY-SIX – THIRTY SECONDS TO MIDNIGHT

Dr. Greene and the NSA watched North Korean military traffic through the night with increasing alarm. DPRK reported intermittent radar contacts crossing the Yellow Sea and the Sea of Japan (East Sea), suspecting B2 Stealth Bombers. DPRK scrambled fighters to confirm, but the fighters did not see the same radar contacts once airborne and found no inbound planes. Kim Jong-un placed the DPRK on the highest alert level threatening a nuclear strike if any nation approached DPRK airspace or if they detected a missile. The false-flag intelligence, radar blips, and the refinery explosion primed the DPRK to launch an attack at the slightest provocation. Dr. Greene prepped the Situation Room to update the President and the SDS Team. Tess had returned to South Carolina and would join the briefing.

"Dr. Greene," opened Lt. Craig, Situation Room NSC Support Staff, "A commercial airliner is wandering off course near the DPRK. The plane is squawking 'ALPHA WHISKEY.' The pilots have lost control of the plane. We suspect that the airline failed to patch the software in time, and RAVEN is driving the plane to provoke North Korea."

*My God*, thought Malik, *They will launch*! Malik grabbed the emergency phone and requested the President to the Situation Room at once. Malik opened the secure video conference, adding the whole briefing staff. Today, the briefing centered on the disappearance of General Wright, the FBI arrest warrant for Wright,

North Korea, and of course, the successful rescue of Gabby Ridge. But the day just turned dark.

MALIK ENTERED THE SITUATION Room just before President Hammond arrived, checking communications and attendance.

"Mr. President, a commercial airliner declared Alpha Whiskey. Sir, the airliner did not upgrade all their planes after the false news of Paul Ross's death. Sir, RAVEN, has control of the plane and is flying the plane into DPRK airspace. RAVEN turned off the transponder, increased the speed, and changed the altitude. The analysis suggests RAVEN is making the plane look like a drone attack," reported Malik.

"Secretary Cooke, what do you have in the area if Jong-un launches on South Korea and or Japan?" pulsed the President.

"Sir, we have conventional anti-missile resources. The probability is low of downing the missile in time," reported Secretary Cooke.

"Mr. President, Mr. Secretary," opened Xander, "SDS has assets in the Pacific Region. SDS has a testing site with hypersonic missiles loaded and ready for our drones. We have the resources and capability. I am launching the drones as we speak," reported Xander.

"How soon until the drones can hit a missile," checked Secretary Cooke.

"Checking with Dr. Wilson," reported Xander.

"Xander, get your assets prepared. Secretary Porter work the phones with North Korea and convince them this is a false-flag and that it is a civilian commercial airliner," ordered the President.

DR. LAUREN HOLMES HAD not left Amelia's bedside since the attack and death of Dr. Stone. This morning's scans noted a decrease in the swelling around the brain stem, and the tumor did shrink post-TEMPLAR. If Amelia kept on this pace, Lauren hoped to bring her out of the medically induced coma. Lauren expanded SDS hospital staff to support Anne coming home to SDS and Gabby's expected arrival within a day or two. If Amelia could be awake for her mother's homecoming, it would be a welcomed blessing against the backdrop of Armageddon.

"MR. PRESIDENT! CHEYANNE Mountain detects a missile launch from the DPRK targeting the commercial airliner!" reported Malik, relayed by the NSA. Xander spun around and opened RUBICON to the full potential against the DPRK. He would not allow RAVEN to take another life or to the paranoia of a closed regime.

"Mr. President! Cheyanne Mountain detected a missile launch off the coast of Southern California. Submarine-based!" exclaimed Malik, "Time to impact in Los Angeles is fifteen minutes!"

"Sir, they crossed the RUBICON! Permission to engage," requested Xander.

"Granted," replied the President, "ENGAGE!"

Xander and the SDS Team leaped into action with RUBICON and pressed SDS defense systems into action. Xander diverted one hypersonic drone to launch against the two submarine missiles. The submarines fired surface-to-surface missiles that traveled on a lower trajectory than an intercontinental ballistic missile reducing the time to intercept. SDS designed next-generation weapons systems for the United States and tested new kinetic kill vehicles launched from multiple platforms. Xander pressed the drones into service, rapidly closing the distance to the inbound missiles. He had a solid lock and fired the hypersonic missile. The hypersonic missile burned through the atmosphere at 35,000 miles per hour. The inbound missile traveled at 3,000 miles per hour. The first missile approached the coast of Southern California, threatening 24 million lives. The SDS hypersonic missile found the target with less than thirty seconds to spare. The massive explosion and shockwave shattered windows for hundreds of miles.

The second SDS hypersonic missile found the last inbound missile with seconds to spare. Resulting in a massive explosion and shockwave that pummeled the area again, knocking a few structures down and people off their feet, but no lives were lost.

Xander was not going to allow the submarines to slip away. He locked on as soon as the missiles had launched. Xander pressed into service the hypersonic missiles launched from the satellite platform and fired. The missiles would take 15 minutes to hit the submarine traveling at 75,000 miles per hour. So Xander centered on disabling the submarine's ability to communicate and maneuver.

Trinity focused on the inbound missile targeting the airliner. The anti-aircraft missile was speeding toward the innocent passengers at close to 700 miles per hour. The intercept would be close and likely to damage the airplane, given the distance. Xander spun around and used RUBICON on the RAVEN attack to return control of the plane to the pilots. Xander and Trinity had less than two minutes to save 300 lives.

"Trinity," checked Xander, "Does anyone have communication with the Pilots?"

"No," replied Xander.

"Dr. Greene can the Air Force or Cheyenne Mountain contact the airliner?" pressed Xander.

"Yes," replied Malik.

"Advise the pilots to try to fly the plane. The attempt should stop RAVEN!" hurried Xander.

"Yes, Cheyenne Mountain relayed the message, and the pilots have control!" shouted an excited Malik.

"Great! Tell the pilots to turn southeast, dive to 5,000 feet, and expect significant turbulence. We are going to hit the inbound missile in 30 seconds. They need to create as much space as possible, turn and dive!" ordered Xander. The pilots executed the instructions turning hard and diving faster than Xander wanted. The SDS hypersonic missile struck the anti-aircraft missile, creating a massive explosion and shockwave that rocked the airliner, causing injuries onboard. But no lives were lost, and the pilots had control.

"Mr. President, we detected a silo door opening, expect a launch in 15 minutes!" reported Malik. Xander locked on the missile and fired again from the space platform. The timing would mean the missile would strike nose to nose, potentially releasing nuclear material but not a nuclear explosion. Xander unleashed the full fury of RUBICON. The DPRK simply went dark. All systems just stopped, civilian and military. North Korea was dark.

XANDER TURNED TO THE submarines just as the hypersonic missiles found their mark. One private military contractor has launched the first hypersonic weapons from drones and space, targeting air targets and two submarines. The eruption of displaced ocean water rivaled post-World War II nuclear testing, sending tons of seawater 12 miles high. The second hypersonic missile hit and created a massive shockwave felt hundreds of miles away and sent an enormous seawater plume skyward. The NSC watching this unfold, sat in shock. Within moments, he plunged a nuclear-powered nation station into the stone age with the stroke of a few keys.

"Mr. President, I have targeted all of the DPRK ICMB locations and am prepared to fire," reported Xander, "Awaiting your instructions."

"Madam Secretary, please advise the DPRK to step back from hostilities, or I will blow them back to throwing rocks and sticks," ordered the President, "Xander, hold for the moment, continue on the active silo."

"Sir, the submarines are, sorry were, Iranian," reported Xander, "Permission to engage remaining element in Iran," requested Xander.

"Secretary Cooke! Execute Phase IV! Xander, engage," ordered the President.

"Done," reported Xander, "RUBICON is dismantling the Iranian military and civilian systems. Thirty seconds to total blackout."

WITH THE DPRK AND IRAN in a total blackout state, Xander used the opportunity to collect intelligence and evidence of General Wright's betrayal and hunt Paul Ross. North Korea did not appear involved in the cyberattacks or aware of Paul Ross. It was a critical concern that the DPRK possessed nuclear missiles with a degree of sophistication not previously known. The DPRK planned to strike Honolulu, Hawaii, with the now-stalled missile sitting in the silo. The inbound SDS hypersonic missile would destroy the silo beyond DPRK's capability to repair.

The analysis of the Iranian intelligence metadata captured by RUBICON pointed to a Russian Operative known only as JUDAS ISCARIOT. The review confirmed that Iscariot told Iranian intelligence about the probability of weaponizing cybersecurity testing tools with custom payloads. Iscariot named Paul Ross to GOI as an exploitable target easily compromised with money and sex, thus Daniyah. The data suggests the Iranians did not know the identity of Iscariot. SDS analysis was correct that RAVEN, HERON, and CHAOS had not compromised the United States, Russia, or China's encryption. But the lower-level compromise was greater than assessed, and Iran could not sort the metadata of the compromise. The evidence suggests that Iscariot used Iran to exploit the cybersecurity vulnerabilities to weaken the world's economy by attacking power generation and refineries.

Of critical concern, the revelation that neither the IRGC nor MOIS was behind the SDS attack and abduction of Gabby Ridge. MOIS recognized that Daniyah, Yuriko, a small team, and Paul Ross disappeared at once following the attack on the SDS Charleston flight. The revelation suggests that it was the Russian Operative Iscariot and not Iran directing the attack. However, forensic evidence from Daniyah Rahman's laptop and cellphone shows coordination with Iscariot and Minister Abbas. Both strategic allies, Russia and Iran, wanted RUBICON.

In the broader metadata, SDS found a significant break in the French DGSE intelligence services. DGSE surveilled Daniyah, Paul, and an unidentified subject suspected to be JUDAS ISCARIOT before the attacks began. After Daniyah, Paul, and others fled the infighting between the IRGC and MOIS.

"MR. PRESIDENT. THE SDS strike was a direct hit," reported Malik, "The battle damage assessment, BDA, notes total devastation post-impact at the DPRK launch site."

"Well done! Xander," admired the President, "Secretary Cooke, General Robinson, what is the status of enemy offensive action?"

"Sir, the DPRK is offline. RUBICON effectively shut down the capabilities of Kim Jong-un. He can use a pen and paper, and that is about it. The two Iranian subs are down. Captain Amy Bauernschmidt of the USS Lincoln Battle Group reports a wide-area debris field but no added enemy contacts," reported General Lori Robinson.

"Sir, adding to the Chairwoman's report," suggested Secretary Cooke, "I recommend added strikes to take out Kim Jong-un's nuclear capability. Additionally, a joint strike with Israel to take out the Iranian nuclear capabilities. It is now or never. We have evidence linking Russians to the cyberattacks and attacks on American soil, two missile attacks by Iranian submarines, and an attempt to take out the President of the United States."

"Room?" pressed the President.

"Sir, reduce the number of nuclear states by two," replied Secretary Porter, "with the hypersonic SDS weapons system, we can do so ethically without using nuclear weapons."

"Xander, execute," ordered the President.

"Sir, the weapons systems have transitioned over to DOD," shared Xander, "SDS built the hypersonic systems for DARPA and DOD. The Air Force just completed the training this week. But have not deployed the assets since they just received them. I used the research and development assets."

"Appreciate the information Xander," pulsed the President, "Do you have the capability to carry out Secretary Cooke's request?"

"Yes, Sir," replied Xander.

"Execute," ordered the President.

"Roger," replied Xander, "Targets are pre-loaded, sending now, estimated time of strike 15 minutes."

"Martin," pressed the President, "Where are you on capturing General Shawn Wright?"

"Sir, the Department of Justice obtained the search and arrest warrants for General Wright within the hour. The FBI is en route to the Maryland residence to arrest and search."

"Very well, keep me informed," directed the President while looking at Tess on the video monitor.

"General Robinson take us to DEFCON 3," ordered the President.

"Xander, where is Gabby?" pulsed the President, "How is she, and of course, how is Amelia?"

"Sir, Danny reports that Gabby is in bad shape but improving. He is working on getting Gabby home to SDS Medical as soon as responsible. The medical team at Travis Air Force Base is doing a phenomenal job flushing her system and addressing her injuries. I miss her terribly. But if I leave Amelia, Gabby will kill me," reported Xander.

"Amelia?" followed the President.

"Yes, Sir, thank you," replied Xander, "Amelia is responding to the experimental TEMPLAR treatment. Targeting the atoms of the cancer cells is groundbreaking research and is shrinking the tumor. The swelling from the blast is slowing her recovery. Dr. Holmes plans to bring Amelia out of the medically induced coma soon."

"Xander, go spend some time with your family," ordered the President, "Tess, see to it."

"Yes, Mr. President," replied Tess and Xander.

# CHAPTER TWENTY-SEVEN – REUNION

"Daddy?" said Amelia, "Daddy..."

"Yes, Baby," replied Xander softly, "I Love You."

"Where is Mommy?" quivered Amelia.

"Sweetheart, there was a horrible accident. Mommy is in the hospital. She is okay and will be here soon," shared Xander. Amelia started to cry as she became aware and remembered the attack.

"Daddy, Katy is dead. I am so sorry," cried Amelia.

"Honey, I am sorry," quaked Xander, "I was not fast enough to get home."

"Is Mommy dead?" checked Amelia.

"No, Baby," he said through streaming tears. Dr. Holmes stepped out of the room to regain her composure. She and Dr. Stone were close friends. Lauren returned to the room, showing a strong face for Amelia.

"Hey, sweet girl!" opened Lauren, "You are awake, and you are getting better! Anne will stop by to visit soon. She is not feeling well. But leaped from her bed once learning you were awake, something about earrings and diamonds." Amelia held out her hands to embrace Lauren. Amelia knew she and Katy were dear friends and wanted to console Lauren.

"You are such a sweet girl. Katy loved you very much. You know that right," choked up Lauren.

"She loved you too," quaked Amelia.

"Your Mom is going to be okay. She should be here soon. I will confer with the Doctors this morning and work to get your Mom home to you, your Daddy, and your siblings," shared Lauren wiping tears from Amelia's tired face and hers.

"It will be a Ridge reunion, right here!" quipped Lauren.

"WHERE AM I," STRAINED Gabby.

"Hey, there," replied Danny, "Welcome back!"

"Hey Medic, DOC!" shouted Danny out the door, "Gabby is awake! Get in here!" Danny had little patience and wanted to get Gabby back to SDS as soon as responsible.

"Good morning, Mrs. Ridge," said Captain Hall, "I am your lead doctor overseeing your care. You have been through an ordeal. We are flushing the drugs from your system. So, you should start feeling better quickly. Your injuries from the blast are superficial but will require follow on care. I am meeting with your doctor soon to discuss your transfer."

"Thank you, Captain," replied Gabby, "Danny, where is Anne? Why are you not with her? Where are we, Xander, Amelia, the kids, Katy?"

"Slow down there," smiled Danny, "Anne is at SDS recovering and is with Amelia. Amelia is getting better. The swelling is down, and she is awake. Xander is with Amelia, dying to get out here. Kids are great, safe, and secure. Here is Travis Air Force Base," shared Danny.

"Katy," pressed Gabby. Danny turned to the door as Jonathan Ridge and Emily Ridge entered the room.

"Mom!" beamed Emily, "How are you feeling?" Gabby held up her IV-laden arms to embrace her eldest two children. Emily worked at SDS as a senior cybersecurity engineer, and the Marine Corps commissioned Jonathan as a First Lieutenant upon graduation from the Naval Academy.

"Mom, I LOVE YOU," hugged Jonathan.

"Oh, it is good to see you both!" exclaimed Gabby tearing up.

"Mom, Katy," paused Emily, "Katy was killed in the attack protecting Amelia. I am sorry."

Gabby teared up and quivered, "Oh, I so wanted that image to be a bad, horrible dream. I have been in such of a fog."

"They had you on some pretty powerful drugs. You will have short-term memory loss for a year or two. But the foggy feeling should subside in a few hours as we continue the flush," summed Captain Hall.

"Mom, I have my iPad," paused Emily, "I am sure Dad would love to have a video call, as would Amelia."

"Please, please, please, can we?" begged Gabby.

"Doc, can we have everyone clear out?" pulsed Danny, "I will check in with the SDS pilots and finalize the arrangements."

THE IPAD RINGING STARTLED Xander. As talented and skilled as he is, basic device use befuddled him. Often, he needed Amelia or Emily to sort out how to make the devices work. He strolled over to Amelia, who smiled and said, "Daddy!"

"MOMMY!" exclaimed Amelia as the video chat opened, with Gabby's face framed by Jonathan and Emily.

"Oh, sweet girl!" replied Gabby, "I have missed you so, so, so much! I will be home soon! Uncle Danny is working on the arrangements."

"Mommy, my head does not hurt anymore! I can move my neck!" shared Amelia excitedly, "Katy would be so proud!"

"Baby, I am so sorry about Katy," consoled Gabby.

"I know, Mommy," cried Amelia, "I Love You!"

"I Love You, too, sweet girl!" replied Gabby.

"I miss you, Jon!" squeaked Amelia, "I LOVE YOU!"

"Oh, I miss you too!" replied Jonathan, "I got you a palm tree for your room garden. Well, I am not sure if it is a palm tree. But it looks cool!"

"I can't wait," replied Amelia.

"Baby, is Dad standing next to you avoiding the camera?" paused Gabby, "Because he is teared up, with us being together, and you getting stronger!"

"Yep, he is!" teased Amelia, "He is a mess without you, Mommy. Lauren tells me he has been busy trying to find you, get the bad guys, and save the world!"

"Xander?" pulsed Gabby, "May I see your face, Baby." Xander stepped around to join Amelia on the video chat, no longer hiding behind a veil of tears. He embraced the emotion fully and showed his love for Gabby, Amelia, Jonathan, and Emily. The events of the past two months taught Xander that managing emotions, post-traumatic stress, and feelings takes courage as well. It is not strength to suppress emotions. It takes great strength to manage, express, and live life.

"I love you so much, Gabby!" said Xander, "Jonathan, Emily, Amelia, I love you."

Gabby leading the Ridges present on the call, exclaimed, "To the Moon and Back!"

"As soon as I get home, we are getting everyone home for family time and a cookout!" reported Gabby.

# CHAPTER TWENTY-EIGHT – GANG OF EIGHT

The Gang of Eight requested a briefing on the cyberattacks, the wild rumors circulating in Washington about General Wright, Director of the National Security Agency, a series of powerful new weapons systems, and the cyberweapon used to attack the Democratic People's Republic of Korea and the Islamic Republic of Iran. Dr. Greene prepared the White House Situation Room briefing, daring not to take the intelligence from the White House Situation Room.

"Mr. President," opened Senate Majority Leader Malcolm McLeod, "I would like an update on the whereabouts of General Wright and about the rumors circulated the District."

"Attorney General Bell, can you provide an update on the FBI's investigation?" requested the President.

"Yes, Sir," opened Attorney General Bell, "This morning, the FBI under the command of Director Mills, executed a search warrant on the residential property of General Shawn Wright. The FBI also has an arrest warrant for the General on a litany of federal charges, including espionage. However, FBI Agents found General Wright shot dead in his driveway of multiple gunshot wounds."

"Was he a traitor?" asked the Speaker of the House Nettie Parks, "Is it true he was a spy for Russia?"

"Yes," addressed the President, "General Shawn Wright is also known as JUDAS ISCARIOT. A codename for a deep-cover Russian Operative."

"Oh My God," exclaimed the House Chair of the Select Committee on Intelligence, Congressman Anthony Silva.

"Yeah," quipped the President, "Yeah."

"Who killed him?" pressed the Senate Chair of the Select Committee on Intelligence, Senator Monroe Ramirez.

"We do not know," replied General Roberts, Direction of National Intelligence, "CIA analysts are reviewing the metadata collected by SDS using RUBICON. The analysts have centered on communications between Iscariot, Wright, and his minion, Paul Ross; also, a traitor and sought by the FBI."

"Have we accessed the damage caused by Wright, Iscariot?" pulsed Senator Webb, Vice-Chair of the Senate Committee on Intelligence.

"That will haunt the halls of the White House, Congress, the Pentagon, Fort Meade, and this Government for decades to come," replied the President, "I respect the question. But the damage metrics equates to dozens and dozens of lives over Wright's career."

"What are you planning to make public?" pressed the Speaker of the House Parks.

"Nettie, specific to Wright, nothing," decided the President, "I am classifying the entire JUDAS ISCARIOT affair Top Secret. The Russians do not know what we know or how we know, and telling the world serves only to tip our hand. However, they know Wright is dead and the asset burned. The Russians do not know how much we know. I intend to play the hand dealt."

"Retribution against the Russians?" pressed Congressman Moore, House Minority Leader.

"None," replied General Robinson, Chairwoman of the Joint Chiefs of Staff, "We decimated the Iranian proxy, degrading the military capabilities to rocks and sticks. We degraded the nuclear powers by one based on solid intelligence and evidence. Russia used Iran as a proxy in this war. We won. There is no need to press the issue. We risk snatching defeat from the jaws of victory. We won. There is nothing to pursue on the battlefield."

"I disagree," argued Senate Minority Leader Senator Colter Stinton, "We cannot allow a fifty-year breach of our national security measured in lives, and the attacks go unanswered."

"Yes, we can," directed the President, "I will not risk burning our asset. How do you think the CIA knew of JUDAS ISCARIOT, Senator? We all play the same deadly game of cat-n-mouse. We dealt with the aggressor with the hand on the chess pieces."

"What of the relationship with Xander Ridge and Shepherd Defense Systems?" pressed Senate Majority Leader McLeod, "Is he a traitor as well? There was pretty damning evidence in the media."

"No," addressed the President, "CIA confirmed the news feeds are deep-fake and false-flag intelligence. Wright and Ross created and leaked the false-flags to throw us off the trail of Iscariot. Dr. Greene, please show the team the false-flag intelligence and deep-fake videos. Specifically, how you analyzed the evidence bit by digital bit, forensically?"

Dr. Greene walked the Gang of Eight through a deep-fake concept, how she and the Intelligence Community analyzed and reviewed each of the deep-fakes used during the CHAOS and RAVEN attacks. The deep-fake purporting Paul Ross's death caused the world to breathe easier and slow the security patching against RAVEN. A vulnerability sinisterly exploited by Ross that nearly plunged the world into Armageddon. The deep fakes of Gabby and Xander intended to tear apart their credibility and ruin their lives. Malik walked through each element and ended her briefing uncharacteristically for a seasoned analyst, "Majority Leader McLeod, Madam Speaker. Do something about this. Congress allowed a bill criminalizing the creation of deep fakes used for illegal intent to die in committee. The Intelligence Community and Law Enforcement need that bill. Please. When your time comes, I will sort out the truth and the facts. But I will not be able to prosecute the creators of deep fakes. This will cost lives, elections, and immeasurable harmful consequences."

"Dr. Greene," commended Majority Leader McLeod, "That was an incredible briefing. Message received."

"Malcolm," offered Madam Speaker, "I think we can find common ground on Dr. Greene's wise counsel."

"Nettie," replied Majority Leader McLeod, "We will. Despite party politics. You and I are Americans serving Americans. Though we often disagree politically, I respect you. And I sure as hell don't want to star in one of those deep fakes."

"What about this RUBICON," pressed House Minority Leader Moore, "The United States cannot allow a private military contractor to wield such power. I appreciate the evidence presented by Dr. Greene. Xander Ridge is not guilty of the allegations. However, how can we trust him to hold such power."

> "Because we will, Kevin," replied the President, "Xander is a true patriot and servant leader guided by an ethos, logos, and pathos the envy of humanity. Each of us watched Iscariot test Ridge and pressed him against the wall and into the grinder. He never faulted. He acted when he needed to act, driven by justice. He controlled his anger and focused on the mission, the protection of the United States of America."

"I appreciate the Captain America perspective," disparaged the Minority Leader, "But RUBICON is unlimited power in the hands of a private military contractor."

> "Because Xander is not a politician," delineated the President, "The day I stopped serving the CIA and caved to ambition to sit in the White House, I became a

politician. Kevin, the day you decided to serve the United States as a Representative. You became a politician. You and I battled the political spectrum for the best course for our Nation, the American People. That cannot work if one of us can know everything. That cannot work if I know everything. Everything you write, text, say. Know every Internet search, see every photo taken, every conversation, and then one step further – manipulation of it all. RUBICON leaps past firewalls, password encryption, and hides from intrusion detection systems. RUBICON is a Zero-Day generator and the first of its kind to crawl the Earth. We do not know. But I do know the creator and how he reacted under extreme duress. Will every occupant of this Office do the same? Have we not seen the risk of threatened power from both ends of Pennsylvania Avenue? Like a new virus appearing from the jungle, the virus needs a treatment plan or a vaccine for the world to survive." The President paused, and the room stayed quiet and still.

"I told each of you when we started this briefing," said the President as he leaned forward, "I will not compromise our Nation's greatest source. RUBICON will eventually lay everything, every secret, every encrypted secret naked before the world. Xander will keep RUBICON until he designs the defensive system."

"If we needed it," pressed the Minority Leader.

"Then he will be there," ended the President.

# CHAPTER TWENTY-NINE – DEVIL'S DANCE CARD

Paul settled into the new resort in the South China Sea, just off mainland China's coast. Li fulfilled every request for Paul's comfort and work requirements. The equipment, servers, satellite communications, and layered encryption are top-shelf. Paul's bedroom overlooked the South China Sea. The Chinese Ministry of State Security (MSS) equipped the resort-like mansion for Paul's and Li's enjoyment and intended to keep Paul working in isolation. MSS assigned Li, Paul's Case Officer, to keep Paul focused and address any need. The mission was to steal or develop RUBICON. Li even took the step to recreate Paul's favorite bar, Bar Hemingway. She recovered Paul's favorite Hemingway fountain pen and recreated Hemingway's Cuban Cabana's look to help keep Paul creative.

Paul's research and work area took on a more serious and modern appeal, mirroring the SDS War Room's spherical shape with floor-to-ceiling fiber-optic monitors. Paul was pleased with the resort mansion and committed to begin working at once. However, evening approached, and Paul requested the staff prepare dinner for the beach for Li and him. After a romantic dinner, Paul hoped for an evening stroll and a view of the mansion's yacht. The MSS supplied the crew, so Paul had no opportunity to escape. The Chinese Army managed the security detail to keep trespassers at bay. However, none were likely, but Paul and Li faced a critical threat from nation-states seeking RUBICON. The entire world sought the RUBICON technology, and many would cross the seas and endure tremendous hardships to steal and kill to obtain it.

Li preferred for Paul not to use RAVEN. Russia, the Americans, and now the FIVE EYE nations scoured the Earth for signs of RAVEN. However, Paul knew that the private sectors and some governments trailed behind patching the Zero-Day vulnerabilities. RAVEN is still an effective weapon for Paul and now for MSS. Li listened, acknowledging Paul's reasoning, but stayed firm that Paul would not use RAVEN absent direction for the Ministry of State Security. President Xjang would not tolerate attribution to China. The priority was RUBICON.

Paul awoke early in the morning, rolling over to caress Li's back in the early morning light. The new setting pleased Paul and was much warmer than Daniyah's or Wright's setups. Li woke and embraced Paul. Li was beautiful, perfect in all the ideal ways and talents. Paul rose and strolled to the shower with Li, waiting was coffee and a light breakfast, and then the lab to start work.

Li watched Paul walk down to the laboratory. Li, an experienced MSS Case Officer with a storied record of success finding and turning assets, worried Paul was more dangerous than assessed by MSS. Paul intrigued, worried, and frightened her. Paul showed no remorse for the murder of his family, the deaths resulting from HERON, CHAOS, and RAVEN, and certainly did not mourn Daniyah. The ways he tortured Gabby troubled Li. Paul drugged and raped Gabby repeatedly, most of the time, unconscious. Paul showed no empathy. Li wondered if she was dancing with the Devil. How long would the dance last, and who would consume whom? Was Li just the next pawn in Paul's and Xander's deadly chess game?

MSS had stolen pieces of RUBICON and supplied the brightest minds in China to help Paul and Li. Paul assessed the probability of success as high that China and Paul would have RUBICON within the next six months. Then Paul would return to his priority, the destruction of SDS and Xander Ridge.

# CHAPTER THIRTY – RED FLAG RISES

"Danny!" shouted Xander, "God, it is good to see you! Thank you, Danny!"

"No Worries, Brother!" shouted Danny, "There are some folks on this plane that would like to see you, Brother!" Xander scooped up Amelia and hurried down the gangway of the SDS Air Operations Center to the plane. Xander sent the company's 747 to pick up the team from Travis Air Force Base. Xander and Amelia rounded the corner from the hallway into the large entertainment area, where Gabby was resting. Gabby looked up at the right moment and met Xander's gaze. Xander glowed, she thought, much like the night the young Army Officer had introduced himself. Gabby loved him so. How could she ever tell, Xander, all that Paul had done to her? Much she still could not sort out from the fog of the drugs. But for the moment, she drank in every bit of his gaze as he held tightly to a beaming Amelia. Xander gently set Amelia down. Amelia looked small in Xander's arms comparatively. Amelia ran to Jonathan, Emily, Sophia, and Charles to embrace her siblings. Xander caught sight of the children, and he could not help but tear up. As Amelia said earlier, Daddy is Daddy. Gabby's touch brought Xander back to focus on Gabby. She caressed his beard and the back of his head, gently kissing him. Xander pulled Gabby close in a tight embrace, almost breathing her entirely into his soul.

Xander realized at this moment that a new context of warfare had emerged. Paul pressed the world to the edge of Armageddon, crossing a metaphorical Rubicon, a point of no return. Like the emergence of the Nuclear Age, the world entered a new age of warfare. The connectivity of the world through social media brought the asymmetrical battlefield to the doorsteps of every American. Disinformation and coercion campaigns aimed to control the truth's heart and soul. Holding Gabby deeply, Xander confronted these new vulnerabilities and struggled to balance his principles and patriotism. Xander looked at Gabby, bandaged and bruised, realizing that evil will exploit every vulnerability to challenge a principle, be it faith, love, honor, and duty. Paul would come again as an agent of evil, seeking to distort the truth to gain power. True patriotism is allegiance to founding principles of democracy, human rights, civil rights, liberty, opportunity, and equality. That these principles apply to everyone is absolute. Xander cannot allow a power structure to have RUBICON until he develops the countermeasure. The risk of a power-driven political patriot is too great. RUBICON's creation drove the technology that may save Amelia but set the stage for the battle between principle-centered and power-driven. How might today's world look and live had Oppenheimer weighed the same risks of trusting false patriots? Xander tightened his circle of trust. Patriots like Anne, Katy, Gabby, Webb, Rasulov, and Agent Brown paid the price for Xander's faith in Paul. Xander read the cover of Paul and missed the heart and soul of Paul's betrayal.

"Gabby, I am so sorry," quivered Xander, "How can you ever forgive me?"

"Sweetheart," cried Gabby, "Sweetheart, you saved Amelia, saved the World, and found me and brought me home. What have you done that needs forgiveness?"

"I was not there," choked Xander, "I should have been there."

"Xander. None of this is your fault. The fault lies with Wright, Ross, and that evil woman, Daniyah," replied Gabby.

"I am back with you. We have our family, our friends, and our home. We have our freedom. We have time to enjoy and love each other, anew," shared Gabby. Xander pulled Gabby in close once more.

DANNY AND ANNE REUNITED, embracing gently. Danny worried he might break Anne or disturb her wounds. SEAL Team Five sent a special gift to Anne for her bravery. The GOI attackers shot Anne, but Anne remained in the fight to take out a terrorist.

"Sweetheart, hold out your hand, please," asked Danny, "SEAL Team Five asked that I give something to you for your years of service as a SEAL wife and your heroism in battle." Anne held out her hand with a puzzled look. Danny gently placed a golden Trident in her hand as Anne gasped.

"Honey, this is your Trident. I can't...," Anne stopped as Danny held his hand.

"No, this is your Trident, as ordered by Admiral McRaven U.S. Special Operations Command and the Secretary of the Navy," beamed Danny, "Baby, I Love You!"

DANNY WALKED OVER TO Xander, who retreated a few paces to watch Anne, Gabby, and the kids enjoy each other and life. Tess joined the group, sat with Gabby, and hugged her Goddaughter, Amelia.

"God, it is a miracle to see Amelia looking so good and strong," exclaimed Danny.

"Danny, I misplaced my trust in the uniform and oath. Did my pollyannish perspective blind me to Wright and Ross?" pondered Xander.

"Sir, Wright was a Russian deep cover operative that eluded the CIA for decades. Paul is a disgruntled, greedy, and evil bastard. You are a good man who sees the best in his fellow Americans. Sir, not everyone who wears the uniform or swears an oath of service is a good person who intends to fulfill the oath with your passion," shared Danny.

"I think we all underestimated the effect of the Russian, Chinese, and Iranian disinformation campaigns," concluded Danny, "We need to look deeper at possible collusion and a broader attack strategy. I think we are in danger."

"Danny, let's tighten the circle of trust," reflected Xander, "I am not making this mistake again. No one gets RUBICON."

"Let's take the plane and the whole crew out to the Pacific, South Pacific, for a week or two. Let's take one of the big boats for a spin and log some R&R," prompted Danny.

"That sounds good. We should," said Xander quietly. Danny knew Xander as only a battle brother does.

"You have bad guys on your mind," observed Danny.

"Yes," replied Xander, "Paul is still out there. He will come again. The disinformation and active measures campaigns are leading domestic violent extremists to attack the Country. Paul will use our societal weaknesses to attack. Our dance is not over."

"Yes," considered Danny, "But you have something he does not."

"What is that?" quipped Xander.

"ME!" joked Danny, "And this Xander. In all seriousness, Paul will never know the love of a family, of a wife and best friend, or the loyalty of brothers. Remember that."

"I do," replied Xander looking up at Danny, "how long can I dance with the Devil before he consumes my soul?"

"In a dance between you and the Devil, my money is on you," replied Danny, "We will find Paul Ross and deal with him, soon enough."

THE END

# About the Author

A thirty-plus-year career with an insider's perspective motivated Barry to write RUBICON. The failure of imagination blinds thought leaders to the adversary's ingenuity and motivation to attack with terrifying methods. Civilians and critical infrastructure are within reach of threat actors with little more than a keyboard. The 'across-the-pond' defense mentality faded to obscurity at the dawn of the cyberweapon.

Read more at https://www.rubiconthenovel.com/.

CPSIA information can be obtained
at www.ICGtesting.com
Printed in the USA
JSHW021939080722
27722JS00001B/44

9 780578 395807